A COMMON LOSS

Kirsten Tranter grew up in Sydney, and lived in New York from 1998 to 2006, where she completed a PhD in English on Renaissance poetry at Rutgers University. She has published poetry, fiction, literary criticism and articles on contemporary fiction. This is her second novel. She lives in Sydney with her husband and son.

Also by Kirsten Tranter

The Legacy

KIRSTEN
TRANTER

A COMMON
LOSS

Quercus

First published in 2012 by Washington Square Press,
a division of Simon & Schuster, Inc.

First published in Great Britain in 2012 by
Quercus
55 Baker Street
7th Floor, South Block
London
W1U 8EW

A CIP catalogue record for this book is available
from the British Library

ISBN 978 0 85738 275 7

10 9 8 7 6 5 4 3 2 1

Typeset by Ellipsis Digital Limited, Glasgow

Printed and bound in Great Britain by Clays Ltd, St Ives plc

For Danny

One writes, that 'Other friends remain,'
That 'Loss is common to the race' –
And common is the commonplace,
And vacant chaff well meant for grain.
That loss is common would not make
My own less bitter, rather more:
Too common! Never morning wore
To evening, but some heart did break.

ALFRED, LORD TENNYSON, *In Memoriam*

I

The surprising weight of the animal is the thing that strikes me most. My shoulders, neck, arms, all strain with the effort of trying to lift it even an inch or two off the road, enough to get any traction. I exhale, loosen my hold, and try again, but it won't budge. Patches of its fur are bright in the surrounding darkness as though spotlit, as though the car headlights are still on and bearing down on it, but that can't be right. A sense of panic edges in as I contemplate the impossibility of the task. It is too heavy. But if we leave it here, someone else will crash into it. We have to move it. This might be a conversation that actually happens with one of the others, or an exchange of reason and reluctance inside my own head.

Another set of hands takes the deer, helping me, and suddenly it feels lighter by a tremendous degree. We lift it together, with effort, but nothing like the impossible, body-breaking strain of before. I feel a surge of gratitude and relief. Its neck hangs down at a lifeless angle, pale and spotted. We carry it off the road, dragging it up the low embankment and a few feet farther than we probably need to, just to the line of trees, and let it down slowly: haunch, torso, shoulder, curve of neck, head, and the legs and hooves, and a scattering of leaves and pine needles cushions it against the ground. The other hands brush against each other as though rinsing it off. They're Dylan's, of course, olive-skinned and finely shaped, and I find myself wondering at the strength contained in his slim body, the strength that helped me lift the deer, which is still strangely luminescent. I look up to thank him and that's when I notice the blood on his hands – his own or the deer's, I can't be sure – and the trickle of it on his face from his temple to his jawline, and meet his expectant gaze.

I'm aware of the crunch of feet on dry leaves – a heavy tread, uneven, stumbling – and then the sound of the car horn wakes me and I realize it's the blare of the alarm clock, and I open my eyes to find my room silent, the clock showing an hour or two earlier than I need to be awake.

I think the others struggled with dreams about the accident, too. Every night for the first week afterwards, several times I'd be hurled awake by the sensation of the car turning over and crashing to a stop: the last second or two that I couldn't consciously recall when I was awake. All the rest I remembered in maddeningly complete detail: the pale flash of the deer's body and face on the dark, empty road, my relief that Cameron was braking, not swerving, as the driving instructors had always said to do; panic as Cameron's instinct to avoid the animal kicked in and the car began to turn, his hands on the wheel trying to correct; and then the long moment when the car left the road, travelling fast, launched into the air, and rolled – once, twice. It landed upside down. That's the part I don't remember, the landing, but I do remember having to climb through from the back seat and out the open front passenger window with a sense of it being strange to do so with everything pointing wrong way up.

Shock does that, activates some part of the brain that records every minute detail of experience and sensation, and at the same time shuts down others. The contrast has always seemed bizarre to me, the way that a complete blank is immediately preceded by that acute sense of detailed recall where time is slowed down, virtually reshaped, so that the passage of two seconds takes five times as long to move through in memory as it did in life. Hyperconsciousness followed straight away by something like loss of consciousness.

I didn't lose consciousness in any literal sense. I don't think any of us did, except perhaps Cameron, who might have been out for a moment after the impact. But by the time I pulled myself out of the car, the others were all out as well, or in the process of getting out. I followed Brian, who had been sitting in the back with me, with Tallis in the middle seat between us. Brian waited for me, and we walked over to the others a few feet away, Cameron sitting with his head in his hands, Tallis lying down with his knees bent and feet on the ground, and Dylan standing, swaying slightly, with that trickle of blood down his face.

We'd come to a stop in a small clearing, surrounded by tall, old pines that we had somehow, miraculously, avoided crashing into. I stared at every one of those trees, imagining the car crumpled headfirst against the trunk and all of us trapped and injured inside; but we weren't and I wasn't. I was out of the car, not trapped. I was numb with adrenaline, in no pain.

The dreams about the actual impact – if I could call them that, since they weren't accompanied by images, and consisted solely of those one or two seconds of bodily sensation – stopped coming with such regularity after the first week. The dream about the deer didn't come until weeks, or maybe even months, later. The weird thing is that I don't actually remember carrying the deer away like that.

My recall of what happened after I pulled myself out of the car is patchy and unclear – the other, more predictable aspect of shock once the trauma is over. I remember sitting and trying to figure out exactly how much my neck hurt, and looking at the others to make sure they all had use of their limbs and were conscious. I don't know if any of us spoke.

Cameron made it to the road and a car stopped for him. The driver, an older guy with long, thin hair pulled back in a ponytail, happened to be a nurse. We wanted a ride – I think that's what Cameron tried to explain to him – but he looked us over and pulled out his phone and called an ambulance for us. I lay down. Cameron lay down next to me after the nurse guy told him to.

I don't remember there being a dead deer by the side of the road when we went over to meet the ambulance, but that could just be memory omission. Sometimes I think back and picture a dark, formless mass where the tarmac ended and the dirt began. Maybe I did move the deer with Dylan's help. Maybe we never actually hit the deer at all; maybe Cameron's swerve that nearly killed all of us actually saved the life of the deer. Sometimes in my memory of climbing out of the car there's a massive crack in the windshield, a spiderweb of fractures, but that could have been made, I suppose, by Cameron's head, or Dylan's; I don't like to think about it.

I thought about asking them, Dylan or one of the others, whether we had hit the deer, whether we'd moved it, whether it was lying there when the ambulance came, but it was harder to do that than you might expect. We didn't talk about the accident, although there were times during the first two weeks afterwards when each of us said something about how it was hard to stop thinking about it, and how much we wanted to forget it. I mentioned the body-hurled-through-space dream to Tallis and Brian when we were walking together one night through campus, and they both nodded as though they knew what I was talking about. But apart from that, it wasn't a common topic of conversation. The question of the deer didn't seem all that important.

At some point much later I started to think that whether or not it was based on any actual event, the dream showed something about my relationship with Dylan and his signal ability to provide thoughtful forms of assistance, my dependence on him. It seemed to encapsulate all this in such a perfect, crystalline form that I became unwilling to mention it to anyone else, afraid that it exposed too much.

The flashlit form of the deer in the dream is, most of the time, exactly consonant with how I remember seeing it from the car, its head turned to face us in the frosty New England night. I call it a deer but it should properly be called a doe; a female, perfect as a statue, beautifully coloured in tones of greyish brown and fawn and white. It's so still, and its expression so blank and calm, that it radiates diffuse symbolic potential: innocence, nobility, iconic femininity, something virtuous, something wild and sacred and out of bounds.

I felt that even at the time of the crash, and I remember swinging in and out of a state of superstitious paranoia as we waited for the ambulance, as though we had all been involved in a crime that would require ritual forms of punishment or atonement. We were driving a Saturn, or was it a Mercury? Cars with the names of gods and planets. A sickle moon hung above the trees; it looked cold and malevolent and I thought of Diana, the huntress, the goddess associated with the moon (I must have been reading Elizabethan poems or plays in my literature course at the time), unable to shake the idea that we had violated some arcane taboo.

We had all been drinking that night, more or less, and I must have been processing the fact that it was a bad thing for Cameron to have wrecked his car in those circumstances. Dylan had drunk the least. He was on antibiotics for a chest infection, a ragged cough that he'd been joking about for a week or so, saying that it made him feel like John Keats and then reciting lines from the ode about being half in love with easeful death – melodramatic, self-mocking. So he wasn't supposed to drink, and he'd stuck to ginger ale or Diet Coke for most of the night.

I didn't think about any of this while we were sitting there. But when the ambulance arrived and Dylan staggered over to the doctors or EMTs or whatever they were and said, 'I'm the driver,' his voice firm and edged with guilt, I understood what he was doing after only a brief second of wondering whether my memory was even more screwed up than I suspected. It didn't shake me out of my superstitious state of fear, though; instead it seemed only to drive it further in.

I dimly registered that people in uniform were asking him to breathe into a machine that tested the alcohol in his blood, and I looked away. One of the ambulance people made a comment about how lucky it was that we were wearing seatbelts. A sense of what could have happened started to dawn on me then, and nausea slowly rose. It was difficult to adjust to the idea that we were all alive, that this wasn't a trick of some kind, that we hadn't landed in an uncanny sort of afterlife that looked a lot like life but felt like something else altogether, numb and surreal.

And then we were in the ambulance, with Cameron laid out on the stretcher, his head supported by bright blue foam blocks, smiling wearily and saying that he was fine, just his neck and head were aching, and his arm, maybe . . . The sickle moon was gone from sight and all the mysterious significance of the night evaporated, leaving me with just a sickening hope that Cameron really was OK. We drove away, and soon all I could think about was the growing ache that radiated out from between my shoulder blades as the immediate anaesthetic of the shock wore off.

I never thought of myself as the centre of the group; does anyone ever think that? I don't know. I wasn't. As an outsider you can sometimes judge fairly quickly where the centre of gravity is in any given group of friends, the person who provides the glue that keeps everyone else stuck to one another, the leader. I don't think it would have been that easy to pick the leader from among our five. Tallis, maybe, would have stood out as a contender, with his height, his breadth, his sunny, easygoing arrogance, but that wouldn't have been quite right.

An onlooker might have picked Dylan. He was the most charming, and good with people. He didn't fit the profile of a leader exactly; he didn't hold us together by setting an example we wanted to follow or being someone we had to impress, but he did perform a kind of mediating role. That was part of his charm, I suppose, the ability to defuse a situation, to turn a conversation away from a direction of conflict and back towards amiability without anyone even noticing. It was only later, when you tried to remember who had won the argument, that you realized it had never been resolved at all, but had been replaced by a conversation about something else, something tangential that had seemed relevant — essential — at the time.

If any one of us had gone like that, died suddenly the way that Dylan did, it might have had a similarly disruptive impact on the shape of what was left of the group. Each of us played a different role, and the disappearance of any one of us would have made its own pattern of explosion, dissolution, fracture.

It happened ten years after we graduated, another accident involving a car, this time on a city street. A city expressway, slick with January rain; the standard case of a big car travelling fast and not seeing the bicycle in its blind spot before it speeds up to change lanes or make an exit . . .

By March, we were all still dealing with the aftershocks of grief, its strange and unpredictable stages and effects. That's how I explained to myself the difficulties of dealing with my friends as we prepared for our annual visit to Las Vegas in spring break. We'd been making this trip every year since leaving college, a reunion of sorts, and none of us had raised the possibility of cancelling it this time. If anything, it seemed more important than ever to go. But as the intended time grew closer, tensions between us worsened. Arguments over dates, hotels, petty details. I dreaded the phone calls, the emails; I dreaded the visit itself.

Natasha was the first person who seemed to understand something about why Dylan's death had the effect that it did, of pulling us apart at the seams. At the time I knew her only as a friend of Elizabeth's, who had been hired as a junior professor the previous year, like me, and had an office on the floor below mine, in the Art History wing of the building. Natasha was Russian, with dark hair and long bangs that were always falling into her eyes. She knew Elizabeth through some connection with Elizabeth's long-distance lover, a recent PhD on a fellowship at a university in California. We were all eating lunch at the café on the ground floor of my building, the humanities block where I teach in the English faculty. I was complaining about how impossible it was becoming to organize the trip, how exhausting it was to handle my friends and their increasingly annoying issues, venting all my resentment, being petulant and self-pitying about it.

'I thought something like that would bring you closer together,' Elizabeth said. 'With some of them at least. How many of you are there? Five?'

'Four,' I said. 'Now, that is. There's four of us.'

'Of course,' she said. 'Sorry.'

Natasha shrugged. 'I get it,' she said. 'It all falls apart.'

'I wouldn't say it's fallen apart,' I said, alarmed at the idea. Losing one of us had made me dwell more often on what it would be like to lose anyone, everyone.

Natasha twisted her mouth regretfully, a small movement, and shared a look with Elizabeth. She irritated me; it was impossible that she could even really see out of her right eye, the way her bangs fell over it. I was even more irritated by the desire I was fighting, a desire to brush her hair away, a gesture that seemed to hover disturbingly halfway between a shove and a caress. My hands felt heavy and strange. One rested on my thigh and the other held on to my plastic fork.

'It's early days,' Elizabeth said. 'You're still grieving. It could still work out between all of you.'

She brushed some crumbs off her folder of slides with a delicate hand. She studied Renaissance gardens, and the walls of her office were filled with beautiful architectural drawings. But no plants or pictures of plants, I'd noticed.

She'd assumed a sort of maternal attitude toward me after Dylan's death, always offering to have conversations about him if I wanted to talk, inviting me to lunch and drinks with other people every week as though it was her responsibility to make sure I wasn't withdrawing into a cave of isolation and grief. I found myself willing to accept the attention although I never wanted to talk with her about Dylan.

It was too hard to explain the weird coherence of the group, the way it seemed to exist properly only as a collective of five and just didn't make sense in the same way when there were fewer. I couldn't help wondering what it would have been like if it had been me who died. What would have happened then? Perhaps my disappearance would not cleave the group apart, but would leave a gap that simply sealed up with time like skin closing up after a minor wound, leaving only a tiny scar and, eventually, no real sign at all.

I suppose I saw myself as marginal to the group, never quite knitted into it in the same way, or as intensely and uncritically, as the others. This was probably part of a desire to see myself always as the detached, intelligent observer. I had grown into being comfortable with that position, especially as time moved on and I made other friends after college. But when I thought about what this distance meant, finishing my meal with Elizabeth and Natasha that day, it bothered me. If I was less knitted in, I could be more easily, more painlessly, excerpted than any of the others.

It wasn't a comforting idea. My first response was a rush of fear. I felt myself to be, for a moment, invisible, immaterial; for one irrational second, my companions at the table, the whole small café, the building, the campus, seemed impossibly dense and solid, and I was impossibly not, as though I had become my own ghost.

The feeling passed. Natasha kicked me under the table, accidentally it seemed, although I wondered. A desire overcame me to talk with my friends, with Brian or Cameron or Tallis, to prove to myself that I meant something to them, and they meant something to me, after all.

I pushed my plate away. A sad quarter of a sandwich and a wilting slice of tomato and parsley garnish were left.

Elizabeth said, 'Elliot, you need to eat. You know that,' appealing to Natasha to support her. But Natasha narrowed her eyes at me and didn't respond.

'I want a cigarette,' I said. Since the funeral I'd taken up smoking again in a half-hearted way.

Natasha surprised me. 'I'll join you,' she said, and rose. 'I need a refill first.'

She topped up a battered thermos with coffee from the stale-smelling urns behind us. Elizabeth said goodbye and stopped to talk to one of her students who greeted her anxiously.

Natasha and I sat on a stone bench outside in front of the café windows. It was a cold spring and the bench had been in shade all day. She pulled her black coat tight around her body. I was suspicious of her – that look she had given me a minute before made me think I couldn't trust her at all – and didn't offer anything to say. We smoked for a minute in silence.

'I lost a friend, once,' she said.

I waited for her to continue. 'A close friend?' I asked, eventually.

She nodded. She lifted a hand, the one holding the cigarette, to her face and rubbed a spot above her eye, just on her eyebrow. It didn't do anything to dislodge the weight of dark hair that fell back into place.

I wondered how it had happened. A variety of scenarios went through my mind – train wrecks full of people screaming, a surfer caught in a freak tide out at sea, a muted hospital ward with nurses soundlessly patrolling. A terrible car crash. Overblown, exaggerated scenes.

'Stabbing,' Natasha said, simply. 'That was back in Ukraine.' She smiled at me, a wry smile with half her mouth. She had an accent, but I had never noticed it so strongly before.

I hadn't smoked much of my cigarette and it had half burned down into ash. Natasha took a drink from her coffee thermos. My mouth felt dry and I wanted to drink some too.

I felt sure that Natasha's stabbed friend had been really close, a friend of hers, belonging to her, not like Dylan was to me – one of a group of friends that had been close in college and since then had been going through the motions, keeping an idea alive beyond its proper expiration date. That's what I thought, with a sense of the group as being dead and purposeless as keen as I had ever felt. The feeling of loss that came over me a second later was a complete surprise.

'Dylan died in a car accident,' I said, and corrected myself: 'Well, a bike accident – he was riding a bike, he was hit by a car . . .' I had to stop, because my voice got stuck.

Natasha sighed, a small breath that barely moved her body, and gave a faint nod. It was nothing like the earnest sympathy Elizabeth had offered me over the past weeks.

We sat in silence for a moment, and I watched her cigarette burn down as she held it between her fingers with their glossy black nail polish. Words began to form in my mind, phrases ready in response to the questions I expected, the routine questions about where it happened, how long we'd been friends, how old Dylan was, but she didn't ask for more details. The responses I'd been planning all dropped away. I wanted to tell her more, but wasn't sure what, exactly, only that it wasn't like whatever I'd just been thinking about.

Two students approached the table close to our bench, dragging the metal chairs with a scrape across the ground as they sat down, and the moment was broken. One of them I recognized from a class I'd taught the previous semester, but she was too absorbed in conversation with her friend, or boyfriend probably, to notice me.

Natasha ground her cigarette under her heel on the concrete slab under the bench, brusque and detached. I was left with the sense that she had extracted a kind of confession from me without even trying.

But it wasn't a confession that would have meant anything much to her. She stood and pulled the belt of her coat neatly closed, and gave me an affectionate smile – it was almost patronizing, and my awe turned slightly to indignant outrage. She raised her hand in farewell. 'Bye, Elliot. Take care.'

I nodded and returned her wave. She strode away in her high-heeled boots, shoulders tightly lifted.

I went back inside and upstairs to my office. It was my second year at the college, but it still felt at times as though I was on probation and the place didn't really belong to me yet. I closed the door, against the unspoken department policy that everyone's door was always left ajar, and glanced at the stack of library committee reports and minutes in a folder on my desk.

I'd been sitting on the committee since the beginning of semester, and had walked into a deeply factionalized argument over funding for various collections that had begun long before my arrival at the university. Lately those discussions had been pushed down the agenda, to my relief, by emergency talks over the fire-safety issues revealed by a recent report, which had recommended closing the research stacks to students altogether until major building work had taken place. No one wanted to close the stacks, or at least no one wanted to be responsible for closing them. Everyone wanted to keep the report as quiet as possible.

The report had given me a whole new, disturbing perspective on the shelves of books that lined the room. Since reading about the vivid scenarios proposed in the report (fire on the top floor that spread rapidly down, trapping students towards the back of the building with no exits; flames jumping from shelf to shelf as all that stacked and bound paper ignited), every time I sat at my desk I confronted a vision of the whole wall bursting into flame. Sometimes it was frightening or simply depressing; today was one of those days where the prospect was strangely exhilarating.

I picked up the phone intending to make the call I'd thought of making earlier, to one of my college friends. But my mind went blank and I couldn't think which one of them I wanted to talk to. The receiver was in my hand as I turned the question around in my mind – which one, what time was it where they were, where were their numbers? I placed the receiver back against the telephone.

There was a picture of the five of us in a frame on one of the bookshelves. It was maybe three or four years old, shot somewhere in Vegas, by the pool at the Mirage, I seemed to remember, but wasn't sure who had taken it – had Brian set the camera to shoot automatically? We were sitting all in a row on a bench. The sky was pale and bright behind us, a white blink of sunlight in the corner of the picture. Dylan was in the centre, wearing a sweet, knowing smile, brown hair grown long and pushed back from his face. High cheekbones, dark eyes, his features almost feminine from one perspective. You would have called him beautiful as well as handsome. The camera caught some aspect of his looks perfectly, crystallized it so that there never seemed to be a bad picture of him. For a while he had worked as a model, in his last year of high school. He'd found it demoralizing, he told me, and boring, and had recounted the strangeness of once sitting on the bus opposite a schoolgirl carrying a bulky homework folder that was covered in pictures of himself, cut out from magazines.

Dylan had always been attractive to men as well as to women. I'd never known him to be interested in that direction, but here in this picture I could see it more clearly than ever, the somehow universal aspect of his attraction, the absolutely seductive quality of his gaze, as though the camera were a secret lover.

Brian was on his left, one arm around Dylan's shoulder, looking as if he was about to speak to someone outside the frame, mouth halfway open, face in profile. He looked relaxed, earnest as usual, but happy, too, his face lit up with energy; there was an easy swing to his legs, one crossed over the other, ankle on knee, and with his arm thrown casually over Dylan's shoulder he looked almost athletic. On Dylan's other side was Cameron, tired around the eyes, his smile close-lipped and ironic. It must have been the year the twins were born. He sat a little forward, elbows resting on his knees, hands loosely clasped. Tallis was at the end of the row next to Cameron, the tallest one, fair hair turned to gold in the sun, his face open in a wide, exuberant grin, almost blurred with motion. One hand was raised holding a can of something, beer or soda. I was at the other end next to Brian, arms folded, the only one with glasses. They were my old pair, round lenses with thin tortoiseshell rims that appeared childish to me now. I'd bought a new pair when I got the new job: squarish, dark frames.

The ring of the phone startled me. I answered it. 'Elliot West.'

'Hey, Elliot. It's Brian.'

My heart lifted. We had a connection, after all, it wasn't a dead effort at friendship – somehow it seemed as though my desire to talk with him (with one of them) had reached him and been answered. This feeling sank just as quickly as our conversation progressed. Brian's tense voice held virtually nothing in common with the relaxed person in the photograph on the shelf. He was complaining about the choice of dates for the trip, trying to enlist my support in talking Tallis into changing them, yet again. Dylan had been a good mediator. I was crap at it, and yet somehow the task had fallen to me in these particular negotiations.

Brian had fallen out with Cameron two years previously, and now neither of them spoke to the other much beyond the simple necessities. It seemed as though neither wanted to be responsible for breaking the whole thing up, and neither wanted to be the one who withdrew. Pride, denial, attachment to the rest of us. They kept it civil most of the time, but it caused problems when we were organizing the details of the Vegas trips, which happened mostly by email. Brian would reply to the group but leave Cameron out every now and again, and the rest of us wouldn't notice until it was too late and a whole round of negotiating about dates and details had already happened – then we would have to bring Cameron back into the loop, and he'd be irritated and argue over the dates just for the sake of it, and so on. Something like that had happened now.

'I don't know, Brian,' I said. 'Why are you asking me? I can't do the Wednesday, I told you. The Thursday and Friday are better. Or the next week.'

'Why not? Remind me,' he said, impatiently.

'It's the dates of the break. I have a faculty meeting. I can't miss it. I can't get away until Thursday. Even that's pushing it.'

'Right, right. OK. It's just such a hassle, you know? Cameron's being so rigid about it as usual –'

'Just talk to Tallis. I've given him my dates.'

'And let's hope he doesn't put us in some place like that fucking medieval theme park he got for us last time.'

I tried to be patient. I looked out the window as we talked, at the bicycle racks and trash cans down below at the entrance to the building, and across the narrow road at the scaffolded Musicology building, which was undergoing a seemingly endless renovation.

Brian complained about Cameron and Tallis for a while more and then seemed to lose steam. We exchanged comments about how good it would be to see each other. I waited for him to let me go. There was a long pause, and then he spoke. 'There's something else, something I need to tell you, and Tallis. For the booking and everything.' He paused again.

'What?' I asked.

'I'm bringing someone,' he said, apologetically. 'I'm bringing Cynthia.'

'Whoa.' My attention snapped back from the window, where I'd been counting the railings on the bicycle rack, noticing the bent ones. 'Cynthia?'

'You know, this girl I've been seeing for a while. We're moving in together at the end of the summer, it's serious. She's coming. She wants to meet all you guys, she's interested in Vegas . . . I said it was OK.'

'But we have the rule.'

It was more like an understanding than a rule – there weren't rules, exactly, but after all this time there were customs that felt like ancient law. We didn't bring girlfriends. It was something to do with wanting the freedom to flirt with other women, but there was something else, too, the more intangible sense that the time we spent together there was about us, about the friendships, focused on one another rather than on the other significant relationships in our lives. It was a sure sign of ageing when relationships got serious enough that the partner would have to be included in every social activity. We had all felt the pressure of these distant-seeming things since Cameron had got married and had children and made it all seem scarily closer and more possible, but for him there had been no question of bringing Marie and the girls. If anything, he'd become more enthusiastic about the trip, despite his conflict with Brian, for the element of escape it offered from his overburdened life.

'I know,' Brian said. 'But it's all changed now, isn't it? Now that Dylan won't be there. Nothing about the whole trip will be the same. It'll be a totally different thing.'

'But it's the first time without Dylan,' I said, hating the feeling of saying it, acknowledging it. 'I thought that would make it even more important for it to be just the four of us.'

'Come on, Elliot.'

I reflected on it, on my knee-jerk resistance to the idea, and wondered hazily where it was coming from, dismissed it. Wasn't I the one who had been chafing against the annoying conventionality of the whole thing for so long now, complaining about the unchanging choice of venue, feeling myself detached and disinvested from the group, the experience, the relationships?

'You're right,' I said. 'It will be different, but that's OK. Part of the whole moving-on experience.'

'Thanks, man.' Brian sighed with relief. 'I knew you'd be the toughest to convince.'

'What are you talking about?' I asked. How would Tallis feel, I wondered, about a female witness to his endless chase of the cocktail waitresses of Vegas? And I realized that he probably wouldn't care at all.

'Cynthia's great, you'll love her,' Brian said, ignoring my question.

'She's interested in Vegas?' I asked, remembering his earlier remark.

'Oh, yeah. She's a grad student. You'll relate to that.'

I wanted to remind him, forcefully, that I was in fact no longer a student, despite having been one for more years than I liked to admit.

'Cultural studies, something like that. She's doing some kind of research on imitation versus authenticity. I think that's it. Anyway, she's been wanting to visit Vegas – she wants to write a paper about it, or a chapter.' He chuckled. 'She wants me to make a documentary about the place. I told her, it's been done. But seriously, you know, I can't stop her coming if she wants to. She won't hang around all that much. She wants to see those fake Eiffel Tower buildings and the Venice canals and all that stuff.'

'OK. I said it's OK.'

'Well, good, that's great.'

'Where's she studying?' I asked.

'Boston U.'

'Can't wait to meet her.'

'Great. Awesome. She's gonna love you. The two of you can

sit down and compare notes. Looking forward to seeing you, man.'

As I hung up the phone I looked back out the window and noticed a familiar figure walking along one of the paths that crossed the lawn outside. It was Natasha, returning from the direction she'd taken when we parted earlier. There was a man in a dark overcoat coming towards her on one of the other paths; he caught up with her and they stood for a moment, talking, animated, before walking off together.

It was hard at first to identify the feeling of resentment I had, watching them make their way up the low hill toward the other side of campus, where she worked in the Physics department on a research grant. He swept his greying hair back from his forehead, and gestured with one hand in an unmistakably European way as he walked. She turned her face toward him and slowed for a moment and looked as though she was about to kiss him. I knew the feeling then. It was jealousy, of course.

2

This isn't going to be one of those stories about a suburban boy seduced into a picturesque world of wealth and charm by a group of high-class eccentrics. I loved those stories, and in many ways that experience was what I wished for at college. But by the time of Dylan's death, the group was out of tune with everything else that seemed important to my life, everything I aspired to. I told myself I didn't like any of them much any more. Their shortcomings and irritating habits were much more present in my mind than any positive feeling. I suppose I liked the idea of having friends from college more than I really liked the friends themselves. Having them, the whole group of them, seemed to confirm something to me about myself. That I was a likeable person, I suppose; that I was part of something enviable, something that looked from the outside like a deep bond, even though I felt that it was shallow and contrived, or had grown to be that way.

Much of the tension between us stemmed from the fact that it was our eighteen-, nineteen-, twenty-year-old selves that had connected so strongly with one another, and the people we had become held less in common. Some groups of friends manage this passage of time with more success. I've seen it happen, over and over again, people staying friends with the people they met and befriended in high school, college, sometimes even elementary school, though the farther back you go the smaller and more divided the group usually becomes. It's not that uncommon to find people who have friends they have known for ten, fifteen years; it's rarer to find a whole group – five, in our case – that's maintained a lasting unity.

The group came into being as a kind of aggregate of friendships. I met Brian in my first week at college at a coffee shop just around the corner from campus. I'd sat down to begin reading *Clarissa*, a set text that I'd just bought for a class in English, horrified at how long it was, unable to believe that it was, as it claimed, the abridged version. There weren't any other tables, and when Brian glanced around, looking for somewhere to sit down, he caught my eye and asked if I minded, and I said no, go ahead. He hauled out a massive stack of photocopied pages bound together into a reader and set it on his lap, unable to fit it onto the little table along with the coffee cups and my overlarge novel, and we started talking. He was short by thirty-five cents for his second cup of coffee and I gave it to him from the change I had in my pocket, in dimes and pennies; he made a fuss about needing to go to the ATM but eventually just shrugged and accepted it. I'd known him for months before I figured out how wealthy his family was and that he hadn't wanted to refuse my money out of shame at being broke, as I'd assumed, but from being uncomfortable about how much money he actually had. He counted up the coins in little towers on the table and gave a grin when they added up to a dollar.

I ended up reading in that coffee shop a lot that first semester and so did Brian, and we often shared a table. I remember being embarrassed that four weeks later I was still reading *Clarissa*, until we worked out that it had more pages than his entire course reader for Intro to Film Studies, and wound up in a conversation about whether it was harder to read Richardson or the article on Eisenstein that he was supposed to be reading.

'But it's just a novel,' he kept saying. 'Really, it's just fiction. Even if it's old-fashioned language, it's still just a story.'

He wanted to know if there was a movie of it. He was unmoved when I made him read a few paragraphs, although he was both intrigued and suspicious when I explained that the whole thing was in the form of letters. This seemed to make it even easier to his way of thinking but decidedly less like an actual novel.

'I know it doesn't seem that bad,' I said. 'But it goes on. It goes on forever.'

That's when he noticed it was abridged, and I didn't feel as though I could keep complaining after that.

Brian met Tallis and Dylan at a Roman Polanski marathon one night; Tallis knew Cameron from high school; Dylan met Tallis and Cameron somehow, and seemed to know just about everyone anyway. Dylan was in my Introduction to the Novel class; I'd seen him once or twice in the lectures and then he showed up in my section meeting for the first time three or four weeks into the semester with his copy of *Clarissa* (unabridged), complete with notes in the margins. He was the only other guy in the section. I watched as all the girls realigned themselves subtly the moment he sat down with his long legs stretched out in front of him, crossed at the ankles, jeans torn at the knees and in a spot just below his front pocket, showing a dime-size glimpse of his thigh.

The first time I remember feeling as though I belonged to a recognizable group, a distinct unit, was when all five of us got drunk together on a bottle of good brandy that Dylan managed to find in the back cupboard in the kitchen at a debauched Halloween party. Dylan was the only one of us with a costume, if you could call it that: a threadbare, beautifully tailored tuxedo and a red-and-black plastic pitchfork that never left his side. I think at some point during the night he borrowed a set of vampire teeth; I have a memory of him grinning wickedly, brandishing the pitchfork and raising a glass, or a can, in a toast. There was a perfectly shaped kiss in red lipstick on his neck that seemed to be part of the whole effect; it smudged and migrated to his collar over the course of the night.

By sophomore year Brian and I were living in the same dorm, across the hall from each other, and the group began to have real cohesion. We coordinated our weekend activities, wound up at the same parties, ate hungover greasy breakfasts with one another. At exam time or when papers were due we sometimes wound up studying in the library together at one of the big tables in the common rooms downstairs, Cameron and Tallis with their impenetrable economics texts and laptops, Dylan with his novels in French and history journals. That was the year I tried to learn Old Norse, and Dylan would laugh at my struggles with the syntax, and then help me figure it out, with a maddening ability to quickly master grammatical forms.

It's hard to remember what we had in common, exactly, before the accident; it's not something you think about at the time. The rest of them watched games together, but that was something I couldn't get enthusiastic about, having gone from being always bad at athletics (glasses, uncoordinated, bookish) to being stubbornly uncaring about any game except tennis, which I watch with my father when I visit my parents around the time of any major match. Tallis used to say that my apathy about sport was impressively 'un-American'. He had grown up in England, and the games he cared about were all alien to us – cricket, soccer (or *football* as he called it) – except for basketball and any game that involved women players. Our college had an exceptionally good women's basketball team and Tallis loved to attend their games, and even convinced me to go with him once when no one else could make it. I agreed because he was so aggressively persuasive, and spent a strange couple of hours watching him alternately shout and sulk, seemingly oblivious to my presence except when our college team scored the winning point and he slapped me on the back with a broad, relieved grin.

Dylan didn't follow any sport with a passion but seemed able to talk about any kind of game with a conventional level of knowledge and enthusiasm, although I convinced myself that it was just a show, and that in reality he had more in common with my intellectual and academic interests. After college he wound up working in publishing, securing a job with a company in New York after years of internships at various presses and small magazines. I was envious of his career and grew more so the longer I stayed in graduate school, amassing debt in student loans and spending all my time in the library while he moved ever upwards in the literary world of the city, inviting me to parties every now and again where he would introduce me to intimidating authors and editors.

'It's not too late, you know, Elliot,' he would say whenever I complained about the endless labour of coursework, dissertation research, and working as an underpaid teaching assistant. 'There are plenty of people in publishing with PhDs. You could always get a job like that when you're done.' But after years in graduate school there was no way I could afford to spend several more interning simply for the value of the experience, as he had.

If I kept grumbling he knew how to placate me, evincing interest in whatever research project or class I was taking or teaching, surprising me with little pieces of specialized knowledge: the reception of Thomas Middleton on the continent, the significance of hotly contested aspects of Lutheran doctrine in late-Elizabethan court literature, the role of Philip Sidney's sister in his literary career. He always talked with a sense of admiration for the rigour of academic thinking and a touch of regret that he hadn't taken that path himself, and I would wind up encouraging him to apply to graduate school for a programme in Renaissance studies or French literature, and he would shake his head modestly and tell me that I was the clever one, that he didn't have the dedication to stick it out.

Dylan carried with him from LA a subdued West Coast aura (probably just an effect of his year-round discreet tan) and looked like someone famous: no one in particular, just the suggestion of possible low-grade celebrity. People often gave him a second glance as though they were trying to place him. I did it myself the first time I saw him, heading into class on a rainy morning, leaning his bicycle casually against a space on the wall, shaking the water out of his soaked hair, wearing a yellow raincoat that should have looked absurd but on him appeared deliberately stylish in an offbeat way. I found myself thinking he looked like a marginal character from a sophisticated teen TV show but I couldn't quite decide which one.

The first time I heard him describe his background I felt sure it was a lie, at least to some degree – it seemed so improbably glamorous, despite his modesty in the way he talked about it. His father, Leo, worked in the movie business as a film editor; this didn't have the flashiness of a producer or executive, but somehow had more dignity, more sense of artistic precision and seriousness. He had won an Oscar at some point in the early eighties, and it sat on a shelf in his cluttered office, surrounded by other statuettes and trophies I was less familiar with. Dylan's mother, Greta, was a psychotherapist and a writer who had made a bit of money with a series of self-help books about using colour to change your life – paint your room purple for prosperity, wear yellow for wisdom, that kind of thing. They lived near Laurel Canyon – one of the only LA neighbourhoods whose name I was familiar with – only not quite in it, but in the hills above it, which sounded even more discreetly fashionable.

Dylan came from relative wealth: his clothes and belongings and easy attitude to money, his lack of interest in it, showed that. But I couldn't help thinking that his background must be a cover story for some much less interesting reality: a banker and a housewife, or an accountant and a librarian or university administrator, something like that. I'm not sure why I doubted him. It's easy to think that I picked up on the secret he was hiding about his real origins, but that would be overestimating my powers of intuition or observation. I probably wanted to believe that he was more like me than he really was. It wasn't surprising that such charisma and style could be produced by money and Hollywood, but it was more comforting to think that it could equally have come from a background as mediocre as my own.

Dylan didn't act as though his background was impressive. Instead he almost deprecated it all. 'It's not Laurel Canyon,' he'd explain apologetically; 'He's an editor, not a "producer" or whatever, though he's pretty senior, gets to work on some good things'; 'The books are, you know, lowbrow. It's not Freudian theory or anything like that. Although she does write more serious stuff – like, in journals. She keeps writing the colour books because they do well.' Once when he got really drunk he admitted that the books had spawned a line of merchandise: coloured desk accessories, candles, scarves.

I asked Dylan once if he was named after the singer and he nodded patiently, not embarrassed as I would have been in his place. Like my own parents, his were old hippies. Unlike my parents, or my mother at least, his had grown out of it.

'What about you?' he'd asked a moment later.

'What about me?'

'Your name. Your parents poetry fans?'

'Oh, that. No. I mean, they are poetry fans. But that's nothing to do with my name. And it's spelled differently.'

'Of course. My mistake.'

It was a long while after that evening, a year or two later, that I watched him tell a different story about his name. It was the last class we took together, Autobiography and Memoir, in our junior year. I passed by him as everyone was leaving at the end of class and overheard a conversation with a girl he'd been flirting with all semester.

'No, the poet,' he said, readjusting the books under his arm. 'Dylan Thomas.'

'Oh, OK.' The girl nodded. 'That's so cool.'

Her name was Tyler, or Riley, I could never remember. Maybe they were discussing what it was like to have a gender-neutral name.

'I guess my parents were big poetry fans,' he said, and shrugged.

It didn't even occur to me to think that Dylan had been lying to me and telling the truth to Tyler, or Riley. I just assumed that he'd said whatever he thought would impress her the most, that he'd made it up, a line. Those words – *lie, truth* – seem too heavy somehow to even apply to something as minor as whether you were named after a singer or a poet. It was a small, meaningless thing. It was only later, that last time in Vegas, that I remembered that afternoon and his conversation with the girl and wondered with growing discomfort whether he'd been spinning me a line, not her; or whether neither of those things was true, and there was no romantic origin for his name at all.

There was no reason I could think of that he'd choose one famous Dylan over the other when it came to fitting a line to me and my prejudices; I didn't care either way. Or maybe I did, in a way that I wasn't even aware of and that Dylan intuited with his instinct for understanding what it was that people wanted to hear, conforming to tacit expectations, crafting subtle and elegant fictions and half-truths. Even at the very end I couldn't bring myself to resent him for that, exactly, even when I began to understand something of the extent to which I'd been taken in. I admired it; I envied it, probably.

After the crash, in the late fall of our sophomore year, that was the most obvious thing we had in common, but if we hadn't already been knitted together somehow I don't know whether it would have had the bonding effect that it did. At times afterwards I wondered why it didn't have the opposite effect, especially at moments when I found myself thinking about it when I didn't want to, and I found it harder to forget when any of them were around.

Cameron turned out to be fine in the end, as did the rest of us, although we all had whiplash from the impact and his seemed to be the worst, along with a fracture to his wrist. We were all complaining of sore necks by the time we arrived at the emergency room, and one by one we were wheeled into the X-ray room and zapped and then given instant coffee and Advil. After an hour or so my neck stopped hurting, or rather the pain became less distinguishable from the generalized ache that had started humming in my whole body.

The doctor looking after me and Tallis, a young intern with a row of colored pens in her coat pocket, said we could both go home, and wandered off with her clipboard. Dylan was over the other side of the room with Brian, having his face cleaned up by a serious young nurse. She seemed to be taking an unreasonable length of time about it.

I looked down and noticed that there was still a needle sticking out of my forearm attached to a short, hard plastic tube that had been used for an IV, although I wasn't sure what the IV had been for (generic 'fluids'?) or when it had been detached from the needle. On my wrist, below the needle, was the stamp from the bar we'd been at that night, showing I'd paid my entry fee and had ID. Brian knew the guys in one of the bands playing there, a punkish rock-and-roll group with four guitarists, none of whom could really sing. He'd played with them in high school. The stamp was a graphic that looked like a sharp-angled maze. The greenish ink had bled into my skin, collecting in the tracery of fine wrinkles at my wrist.

Tallis stood by my bed, where I was still sitting, staring at my arm. 'What is it?' he asked, his voice slow and tired. 'Let's find Cameron and get out of here.'

'Did you have one of these?' I asked him, indicating the needle.

'God, I don't know. I think they took mine out.'

We looked around for someone to remove the needle, but the place was busy. There was a child vomiting a couple of beds over, doctors and nurses walking busily by with hands full of papers and bottles of medication and kidney-shaped bowls. The attendants behind the central desk were all on the phone or talking to doctors. I'd caught sight once or twice of the guy who had stopped his car for us on the road, the long-haired nurse, but he ignored me and the rest of us, as though he'd never seen us before.

Tallis shrugged. 'Come here,' he said. 'Shut your eyes.'

I did as he said, and there was a swift, tearing pain, and then a small clatter as the needle and its plastic attachment landed on the metal stand by the bed. He took a square of cotton wool from a pile on the stand and handed it to me, and I pressed it against the wound. It didn't bleed much.

'Thanks,' I said.

'Anytime,' he said in a voice that I would normally have put together with a smile, but it seemed that, like me, he was too exhausted.

We couldn't find Cameron, and we eventually got hold of a doctor who explained to us that he was still complaining of pain in his neck. He led us over to a curtained bed where Cameron was lying down. We stood there and exchanged hellos.

'The X-ray hasn't shown as much as we'd like to see about his vertebrae,' the doctor said, blinking at us from behind round spectacles. They wanted to do a CAT scan and were waiting for the machine to become available.

When we asked how long the wait would be, he shrugged and said, 'Oh, around forty-five minutes,' and I could tell from the way he glanced over my shoulder and his vision glazed that it was just what he said in response to any question related to waiting times.

Dylan appeared next to us with Brian at his side. Brian folded his arms tight, as though he were cold. Dylan managed to look rakish with his row of stitches half hidden by his hair. 'You guys go home,' he said to me and Tallis. 'I'll stay with Cameron.'

Cameron couldn't take his eyes off him, staring guiltily at Dylan's injury.

Tallis seemed ready to argue, but changed his mind. Brian stayed quiet, as though he'd already agreed with Dylan to leave with us.

'It's really late,' Dylan said. He sat down in the one chair next to the bed, a green vinyl seat too low to the ground.

'OK,' Tallis said, and I said it, too, and we left.

My arm still hurt where the needle had been, and Tallis handed me some of the prescription codeine the nurse had given him. When we left the building I was shocked to find that it was already morning, dawn breaking fast on one side of the sky, cloudless and pale blue.

Tallis called someone to collect us, a girl he had gone out with a couple of nights before, Daphne. Her face was sleepy and smudged with eyeliner when she showed up in her blue Datsun, still dressed in pyjamas with a duffel coat over them. She looked us over critically, gave Tallis a tentative hug and a long kiss on the mouth. We all stared at the car.

'I'll ride in the back,' I said at last.

Tallis and Brian shared a look, and Tallis opened the other back door and climbed in, giving me a nod before he clipped his seatbelt. Brian sat next to Daphne and folded his arms again. Daphne didn't try to engage us in a conversation about what had happened, and I was grateful. For some reason, I discovered later, people tended to want to do that, to know the details of speed and time and impact. The size of the deer. Eventually I came up with a one-sentence description of the whole accident that conveyed that necessary information, and once I'd delivered it twice or three times I stopped even hearing the words as I said them.

I guessed Tallis had told Daphne everything she needed to know on the phone. She repeated variations on how lucky we all were, her voice hoarse with lack of sleep, and shared around a large cup of black coffee she'd picked up on the way. She wound her window down a couple of inches but still the car filled with smoke from her cigarettes, which Tallis expertly rolled from a pouch of tobacco and handed to her. I envied Tallis, imagining him going back to her place and falling into bed with her.

She dropped Brian and me off at our dorm, a three-storey white-painted old house called Derwent, and we headed upstairs. The whole place was still and quiet in that early Saturday morning way. A girl's sleepy voice carried through from a room on the first floor as we climbed the stairs, a stream of curses that broke into a smothered laugh. Neither of us spoke as we each unlocked our door. I turned to say goodbye before I closed mine, but Brian had slipped inside his own room already.

I woke in the mid-afternoon with a pain between my shoulders as though someone had struck me hard in the back with a club. I took another codeine pill and went back to sleep, and Tallis woke me up not long afterwards, banging on my door.

'Brian's not there,' he said. 'Cameron's still not out.'

We went back to the hospital in his 1970s Volkswagen. I didn't own a car. There had been a long wait for the CAT scan machine, and then some kind of problem with it, we discovered when we got there, and they were fixing it and had no idea how long it would take. In the meantime Cameron had to lie on his back. They had moved him into a room upstairs, which he shared with one other patient, invisible through the closed curtains around their bed. Cameron was furious and inarticulate after hours of frustrated attempts to find a doctor to talk to. Dylan was still there, eyes dark with exhaustion.

Something about the way Tallis carried himself, how he looked at Cameron, or didn't look at him, told me that he was angry with him, and that was the first time I allowed myself to consider that feeling. I thought about his hands on the wheel, my clear view of them, the way my heart sank and sped up when he turned, the hopeless attempt to correct once the car had swerved . . . It hadn't seemed to me that we had been travelling all that fast. Now I wondered. But the anger wouldn't stick; the effect of the shock was still too strong for any feeling to persist or develop. It faded away. I think it did for Tallis as well.

'Can you give me a cigarette, Elliot?' Dylan asked, yawning and stretching. I didn't have any on me, offered to buy a pack. 'OK, whatever,' he said. 'I just want to get out of here for a minute.'

I agreed, eager to be away from the harsh fluorescent lights, and the three of us made our way outside, stopping to buy cigarettes on the way.

'Have you slept at all?' I asked him.

He shrugged and gave a half-hearted smile. 'I lay down for a while. There was a spare bed next to where Cameron was. Everyone's being nice to us in there.' He stared at the cigarette in his hand and then raised his eyes to look at us both. 'I was driving,' he said. 'I just want to make sure you both remember that.'

Tallis reached over for Dylan's cigarette and took a long drag from it. He nodded, and tried to give back the cigarette. Dylan shook his head.

'I can't remember anything much,' I said. 'But sure, I remember that.'

Dylan smiled, his face glowing. 'Amnesia,' he said warmly. 'It's a wonderful thing.'

'You should go home,' I said. 'You should get some rest. One of us can stay. Or both of us. I don't mind.'

'No, no,' he said. 'I don't think it'll be long now.' He stretched again, raising his arms above his head, graceful as a dancer. 'Cameron feels badly about the whole thing, you know. But I told him, it could have happened to any one of us, right?'

I agreed.

'I'm glad you're all OK,' he said. 'You're all like family to me.'

It wasn't like him to be so openly sentimental, but I understood the impulse. It occurred to me that I ought to call Brian and see how he was doing.

'You know, you can't choose your family, but you can choose your friends,' Dylan said. 'I heard someone say that once. Or I read it. It's true.'

'Should we call Cameron's parents?' I asked.

I'd been so wrapped up in being glad that we were all OK that it hadn't occurred to me to contact them; it hadn't fully occurred to me that perhaps it wasn't all OK, and that they might want to know. And the whole thing had a guilty aura, like the kind of unlucky accident or mistake you would want to keep from your parents. The kind of thing that could get you in trouble.

'I talked to them already,' Dylan said.

We started walking towards the doors, back inside. I was still in the fuzzy state of aftershock and codeine so I didn't think too hard about what Dylan had said about us being like family, but I kept going back to his words later on. What he said was strange to me mainly because his family seemed so desirable to me. If you *could* choose a family, wouldn't you have chosen his? All that wealth and good taste; his easygoing, award-winning, well-connected father; his intelligent, poised mother; even his sister, Sally, was smart and beautiful. They were the family I would have chosen.

And us, his friends: why had he chosen us? Why had any of us chosen any of the others? I knew the answers were there, but they remained as diffuse feelings of warmth and attachment, resolutely not amenable to analysis. I decided that I liked it that way. It was a mystery. All I knew was that I was glad Dylan had chosen me.

When he sat back down in the chair next to Cameron's bed, identical to the green vinyl one downstairs, I saw him in a slightly different way, just aslant. I knew how he must appear to the nurses and doctors – the devoted friend struggling with his feelings of responsibility for Cameron's injuries. I wondered whether he thought of Cameron as a brother, whether it was as specific as that. He looked the part, sitting there patiently, if I imagined a version of sibling feeling that included only the positive strains of affection and shared experience and excluded all the petty resentments and irritations that coloured my relationship with my own sister. Maybe it was different for brothers.

The machine was eventually fixed, just before five on that second day, and Cameron and Dylan said later that the whole thing was so absurdly fast, it showed that nothing was broken or fractured, and he could go home.

About a month after the crash I made the mistake of going on a date with a girl, Thalia, to see an action film and had to leave the cinema about five minutes into the first scene, which was basically an extended, epic car crash sequence. I sat down on a sagging lounge in the hall just outside the exit, not exactly having a panic attack but breathing too hard and stuck for words, and ashamed. She patted my shoulder and drank from her bucket-size diet soda. We could hear the sounds of screeching metal from inside the cinema, and someone shouting orders, someone screaming.

Thalia was patient about it, but I didn't want to see the other movie that was showing, something about the trials of a teenage nanny. When I explained what had happened to Tallis and Cameron a couple of days later, they understood immediately.

'It's fucked,' Tallis said. 'I couldn't even sit through *Charade* on TV the other night. The most pathetic car chase ever.'

There was an opening. I felt some need to take advantage of it, and asked Cameron how he'd felt about driving since the crash. He'd bought another car, a secondhand Oldsmobile, a week later with a determined kind of insistence on driving again as soon as possible, and had taken to using the car even to do the smallest errands, as though proving to himself that he was capable. Four or five blocks to the general store, short distances to the library, to the coffee shop and the bar. None of us had been in the car with him.

He cleared his throat and frowned. 'I'm OK with driving,' he said. 'Surprising. But I can't handle anyone else in the driver's seat. That's when I start, you know, replaying it.'

'That makes sense,' I said, wondering whether it really did.

'Except Dylan,' he said. 'I'm OK with that.'

Tallis nodded. 'Dylan's a good driver,' he said.

I agreed. The two of them were heading over to his place to watch a game; it must have been basketball. I decided to go home and call Thalia, but by the time I got there the impulse had passed.

I'd agreed with the others about Dylan being a good driver more out of habit than anything else, and I tried to remember whether it was true. He didn't own a car, and only drove when he was home in LA. Recalling the hot, smoggy streets there, the one time I'd visited, and Dylan's relaxed air of possession and belonging as he negotiated the endless freeways, did something to chase away the beginnings of depression that had followed me home. But then the memory got mixed up with that other one, the swerving car, and as I closed my eyes against the image, it was Dylan's hands I saw on the wheel.

3

When I think back to the last time we all went to Vegas together, the five of us, it seems like the best trip of them all. Before Dylan died, it had seemed just the same as the previous trips: the occasional win, the occasional big loss; watching Tallis hit on every second woman that crossed our path and become fixated on whichever one turned him down the most harshly; all of us drinking more and more to chase that pitch of happiness and good company that came with the third drink and faded rapidly; awkward silences, when the background noise of the casinos would rise as though a volume switch were being slowly turned. The percussive slap of the cards. The hiss behind the music. The talk, talk of groups of women; the thick quiet of the serious tables.

Why did we choose Vegas? Dylan and Cameron went there in senior year for spring break, and then the year after we graduated we all met up there together. By then we had all moved to our different places around the country and around the world; it became the one time of the year when we were all reliably in one place. It was relatively inexpensive and easy to get flights there at any time of year; the weather was always good.

The choice of our destination was the most obvious demonstration of my always-existing distance from the group, my outsider status, the way it represented something at odds with who I wanted to be. I remember being against Vegas from the start, but that's probably just back projection. For the last few years I had put up more of a fight against the place – it was trashy, kitsch, the worst example of cultural emptiness and decay in the nation – and tried to get us to choose someplace else. The North Carolina beaches – Cameron had recently acquired in-laws with a house there. The Berkshires. New York or Chicago – somewhere with something to offer beyond drinking and gambling.

Tallis complained the most at any mention of change. 'Beaches? Fuck that. You know I can't tan, I burn to a crisp as soon as I go out in the sun. I want somewhere I can stay inside, be comfortable, be easily supplied with drink and amusement.' Or, 'I don't need to make this a fucking cultural event.' He lived in London by then, working for the UK office of a German bank. 'I'm coming to see you guys, not a museum or a lake. If you're that concerned about making it an enriching experience then let's stay at that hotel that has all the million-dollar paintings. Van Gogh or whatever.'

Sometimes Brian joined me in complaining, but never very seriously. It was too difficult to find an alternative option that was an acceptable compromise for everyone. I gave in, always, in the end, and Dylan always called me afterwards to offer reassurances.

Of course, that last trip seems special now because it was the last time we were together with Dylan. But there was one night that stood out, surely for all of us. And right after Dylan died it was good to have this one positive moment to hang on to. It became too hard to think back on the awkward silences and the haze of dislike that would start to show itself at odd times – early in the morning before breakfast was finished, in an argument over who would buy the first round of drinks, or late at night when we became bored with one another's company.

The exception on that last trip was the soccer game on TV. When we first arrived at the hotel there was a problem with Dylan's room: the previous guests had left late, or one of the faucets was broken, or something like that. The guy behind the

desk upgraded him with an apology and put him in a luxury
suite on one of the high floors of the building, way up from our
standard rooms on the sixth floor. It had a huge TV that took up
half the wall, and a kitchenette with a big fridge that we filled
with beer and vodka. We ended up spending more time in Dylan's
room than we did out of it. Two of us, at least, stayed on the
enormous couches on each of the three nights we were there.

The TV had a list of cable stations so long that we couldn't
scan through them all in a sitting, but Tallis cared only for the
one that showed the World Cup. We all thought of soccer as a
sort of girlish game that our sisters were getting really good at.
At English football finals time in college Tallis had always hung
out with another group of friends, the soccer fans, and we never
saw much of him for a couple of weeks. During this trip, he
watched every game and replay, talking about it without pause
whenever he came down to join us at the tables or to eat.

He was skilled at getting his way, employing a range of persuasive
strategies from cajoling to whining and sheer argumentative
bullying, aided by his height and plain intimidating bulk. And so it
was that when it came close to the time for the deciding game, on
the afternoon of our last day, we all gathered in Dylan's room. We
sat through replays of the semi-final games, and into the early
morning for the final, finishing just before dawn.

Dylan was at his best that day. He had played the game in
middle school for a couple of years, and while we watched he
explained the rules, telling us about the yellow card/red card,
the offside rule, the penalty kick.

'Tallis, why didn't you tell us that?' Brian asked over and over
again.

Dylan scrunched up a couple of sheets of newspaper – the
Las Vegas Tribune, delivered pointlessly to the room every
morning – and demonstrated the proper way to head a ball; and

played goalkeeper as each of us kicked and tossed the ball at him, making improbable, balletic saves almost every time, throwing his body lengthwise across the room, reaching out impossibly fast.

Tallis was more pleased than he would admit that we were all joining him for once in watching the sport he loved, but I noticed, too, that he was now and again suffused with a kind of envy as Dylan used his infectious enthusiasm to convince us to pay attention to a game that none of us had cared about for all the years we'd been friends with Tallis. It was a whim on Dylan's part: he could just as easily have persuaded us to watch the marathon of hit singles from the 1980s that was playing on MTV if he'd felt like it.

It was the second year that Brian and Cameron were quietly ignoring each other, but there were moments in our World Cup marathon when they seemed almost back to normal. Cameron passed Brian a beer and he took it. Brian sat down in the chair next to where Cameron was sitting on the end of the couch, and Cameron didn't get up within five seconds and change seats like he normally would have.

I remember seeing Cameron's hand rest on Brian's shoulder for a moment. It hangs there in my memory as a golden thing, lit with the warm light from the lamps and the cold light of the television, the green of the football pitch on the screen in the background. I can't remember the context for the gesture. It might have been that time of the early hours of the a.m. when we were all embracing and slapping at every save, every rare goal, but this doesn't feel exactly right.

I don't quite trust the memory; it seems like the kind of thing I would make up in looking back and constructing something good from the aura of that whole, longer moment of the night and day we spent in front of the TV. If it had really happened I imagine that the others would have noticed; I would have caught Tallis's eye and acknowledged – quick and quiet, careful not to show we had seen it – that a tiny rapprochement had happened, but I don't remember that.

I don't think any of us could pin down exactly when it was that it stopped being fun. I suppose it would be different for each of us. Maybe it never stopped being fun for Tallis. For me, I sometimes thought it was as early as the third trip. I was growing apart from Brian and Cameron, but I was still in touch with Tallis by email, and I saw Dylan every couple of months for a drink or coffee in New York.

The frostiness between Brian and Cameron followed an argument they had at a bar in New York one night. I was there, and Tallis was as well, in the city for a meeting with the New York branch of the bank he worked for. I was in the final stages of my dissertation at grad school at NYU, a bit scattered from just having handed in a chapter to my advisor, who was sure to hand it back to me in a month or two, as he had done with two previous chapters, with three or four brief and devastating comments in his almost indecipherable scrawl, in red ink. Three or four doesn't sound like many, but he made them count.

Cameron was in the city to see his family in Queens; Brian was there to talk to a rich couple, patrons of the arts, who might want to give money to the film he was trying to get off the ground. He had just started work for a small documentary production company based in Boston, and while he claimed to be happy with the job I had the feeling that he'd been holding out for something better.

The argument between him and Cameron was one they'd had before, but it was worse this time because of the new job Cameron had just taken on, a position at a big law firm in

Chicago that represented other big businesses. He would be mainly representing companies defending themselves against insurance claims. Cameron was undoubtedly the smartest of us all, and had done well at Chicago Law School. Even I thought it was a pity that he was putting his talent to use in the service of a company like Bridgewater Black.

In college the differences between the two of them were all there in the making: Brian always leaning toward the left, Cameron becoming more conservative as the years passed. Cameron, lower-middle-class, first-generation college student; Brian, trust-fund child, rebelling against the conservative certainties of his family. Watching them argue in those early years was often enjoyable, like watching a dance that had been performed so many times it was a struggle and an art to find new steps; and they were dancing over a connection so solid that the argument was just part of it, not a danger to it.

We had ended up at some awful bar in Midtown where Tallis had dragged us after drinking with his banker friends; it had an Irish theme, with shamrocks scattered around the walls, all reddish wood and brass and fake brown leather.

'Even you would admit that everyone deserves a defence,' Cameron said to Brian across the glossy table. 'Everyone deserves a fair trial. Or do you think they shouldn't be allowed to have defence attorneys at all? Do you think we should just hang them for being corporations?' His face had started to redden with anger and the effects of alcohol.

'They are entitled to lawyers. I admit that. But why do *you* have to be their lawyer?' Brian asked, jabbing his finger toward Cameron.

Cameron took a handful of peanuts from the bowl on the table and chewed them, talking through a mouthful. He accused Brian of being unfairly judgemental, and made some disparaging remark about his T-shirt, which had a slogan on it that I couldn't quite make out, under his black blazer. It seemed to be related to the documentary Brian was pushing, something to do with oil consumption.

Cameron would be defending the most powerful elements in society against the interests of the most powerless, Brian said – the families of people poisoned by unsafe chemical leaks; kids killed by improperly constructed cribs and car seats; people injured by medical malpractice.

It was true that the firm had recently fought a high-profile case on behalf of a manufacturer of children's products and did some legal work for a big tobacco company.

Cameron blustered furiously. 'Are you going to ask me how I sleep at night?'

'Yes. Wait – no. I don't want to know.'

I went to sit at the bar with Tallis, who had started chatting to some girl, and then I caught sight of Brian's girlfriend at the time, Bianca, who had been stuck at the table between Brian and Cameron. She smiled at me wearily and took the last sip from her glass, set it on the bar. I bought her another. We could hear them indistinctly, and I knew the argument had turned to Brian's parents.

They were well off, old Boston money, in antiques and the law. Brian was sensitive about it and, for a while, had refused their help. He spent two years at the end of college being as broke as I was, working at the library, checking people's bags as they left, and cutting bagels at the all-night sandwich shop near campus. Cameron's family had struggled to send him to college. In a strange way it had always seemed to me that Brian was envious of Cameron's background, rather than the other way around. Brian was self-conscious about the way his progressive politics looked from one perspective as if they were simply a reaction to his privileged status, a form of rebellion, less than fully authentic. It looked that way to Cameron, who used to tease him about his involvement in student politics, meetings and rallies and political campaigns.

He and Brian were the only ones among us responsible enough to actually vote in elections once we were old enough, but Cameron would never tell us who he was voting for. This at first enraged Brian, who spent every election day handing out campaign materials for the local Democratic candidate, and then I think Cameron must have confessed to him at some point that he didn't vote Republican, because Brian stopped harassing him about it and just seemed disappointed in him rather than actively disapproving.

Bianca rolled her eyes in the direction of the argument. She and Brian had been going out for a couple of months, and she'd come with him to New York to hang out and have a vacation, she said. 'I wanted to meet his friends. That was a great idea.'

I gave her my best smile. 'Not entirely a bad idea.'

'Not entirely. It's Elliot, right?'

Tallis reappeared at my side, towering and blond and smelling strongly of whisky and smoke. He had an unlit cigarette in his hand.

'Bianca!' he shouted, raising his voice more than he needed to over the noise of the crowd around us. 'Do you have a light? Would you like a cigarette? A drink? Hey!' He gestured to one of the guys behind the bar. 'Another for her. And – Elliot, what are you drinking? Stella? A Stella! Two!'

I'm not tall – not short either, about average height – but being around Tallis always makes me feel slightly smaller than I am. He knows how to carry his height, and women seem to be universally impressed with his English accent. Next to him I end up coming across as the bookish, sensitive one, or that's the way I try to think about it.

Bianca handed him a book of matches from a box on the bar. 'Are they arguing about the car accident?' she asked. 'I mean, do they fight like this because of that?'

'The car accident?' I asked. 'You mean the one in college?'

She nodded. 'Brian talked about it once or twice,' she said. 'He still has a bad neck.'

'It was an accident,' I said. 'And none of us was really hurt. In fact, Cameron was hurt the most. He's the one who wound up in hospital for days.'

Tallis leaned in. 'Brian might still carry a grudge about it,' he said. He looked away, and then back with a sigh. 'What I think is that Brian probably blames himself in a way for it. I know, I know,' he said when I started to protest. 'But it was Brian's friend's band we were out seeing that night, you know, it was all his idea, and we stayed so late because he wanted to keep drinking with that stupid fucking singer, or the guitarist, whatever. He said something about it once. If only we'd never gone, et cetera. I think he was more fucked up by it than any of us. You know he's never owned a car since.'

That was true. Brian had always claimed it was an environmental statement, but now I wondered.

'That's crazy,' I said. 'It was just an accident.' But something about what Tallis had said, that weird oscillation of blame and guilt and trauma, made sense.

Cameron and Brian were on their own at the table now, and we could still overhear scraps of the argument as it continued. It had moved on to the subject of Cameron's hypocrisy; his family were Catholics, and he'd been married in an extravagant Catholic ceremony, although he didn't go to church apart from Christmas and sometimes Easter. Brian had things to say about all of this.

After an hour or so I decided to leave and went over to the table to say goodbye. Brian's face softened for a moment when he saw me. 'Hey, man. You have to leave? Now? Sorry we didn't get to catch up . . . Tomorrow night . . .'

'Call me,' I said. 'Bianca's great.'

Cameron nodded and said goodnight but his face remained dark and serious.

Tallis called me the next day. 'I'm flying back this afternoon, just wanted to say goodbye. I was so fucking wasted last night I can't remember you going.'

I asked how long he had stayed. A while, he said. Cameron had left at some point without saying goodbye – I got the impression he'd had enough of the fight and had stormed out in some fashion – and Brian had been completely drunk by the end of the night.

'He was a mess,' Tallis said. 'It was a waste sending Bianca home with him.'

We talked for a while about how much we liked her. Brian wasn't the best-looking of the five of us but he managed to go out with girls that we all envied him for – not the beautiful ones that Tallis picked up all over the place, or the neurotic poetess types that I found myself with, but girls who seemed to have it all: looks, brains, sense of humour, passion. His relationships with them never seemed to last long, which was mollifying to the jealous part of me.

Tallis thought the argument had turned so poisonous this time because of Cameron's own feelings of reluctance about taking the job, which he'd mentioned to Tallis before Brian had arrived. He'd had other offers, apparently, including ones from less evil but worse-paying firms. Marie had pressured him, he claimed, although Tallis thought it was equally likely that Cameron wanted the money and status himself, although he'd never admit it.

'He's playing golf now, you know,' Tallis said. 'Anyway, he couldn't say any of that to Brian.'

'Why not?' I wanted to know. 'It would have been better if he did.'

'No way,' Tallis said with a laugh, 'it would have been worse.'

I decided he was probably right, and gave in to a sense of anger at them both. The feeling dissipated so rapidly it took me by surprise, leaving only something apathetic and resigned in its wake.

Brian was an earnest guy, in a way that managed to be attractive rather than off-putting. He wanted to do some good in the world. He played guitar badly, with feeling. His secret vice in college had been hard-core pornography, though in public he said that pornography exploited women and went through a phase of calling himself a feminist.

I discovered the pornography by accident, the year we lived across the hall from each other in Derwent. I went into his room to retrieve a notebook he'd borrowed from me – I knew he was in class, and noticed that the door was unlocked, and we were close enough that it wasn't so unusual to let myself in. Anyway, there was the magazine on the bed, and some poking out from under the mattress. I sat down at his desk to look through them. They were curiously unexciting to me, a lot of close-ups of shaved body parts and various instruments of pleasure, or torture, it wasn't always clear. The baldness of the women's genitals destroyed some of the more important distinctions between inside and outside, sex and not-sex, so that there were only endless folds and expanses of skin, flash-lit and garishly coloured. The few faces in the pictures were blurred or cropped, at the very edges of the frame or half-glimpsed behind other parts of the body – breasts, a taut back, a grasping hand. They looked shocked, eyes wide open and thickly lashed, or glazed.

The picture with the taut, arching back was the only one I wanted to look at again. It was too brightly lit, but the woman's hair made a beautiful mess of asymmetrical curls against her skin. Her thighs were spread wide open by another woman's hands, red-painted nails with the polish chipped. It could have been a preparation for some kind of penetration – another of the pictures seemed to be from the same series and seemed to show exactly that, the red-nailed hands again manipulating body parts to show a particular angle – but it was more compelling as sheer display, a preparation for nothing but the photograph itself. The pressure of the woman's hands on the other woman's body was the most erotic thing about it to me; that and the coiling, dark hair, a compensation for the lack of hair down below. I was looking at it when Brian appeared at the door.

'Oh my God,' he said, mortified, his whole body deflating in front of me.

'Brian,' I said to him. 'Under your mattress? What are you so worried about?'

He sat on the bed, elbows resting on his knees, and shook his head. Then one of us started laughing – him, I think, from pure awkwardness – and it was OK.

'Can I borrow this?' I asked, half joking.

'Take it – it's yours – don't give it back.'

'No, it's OK,' I said. 'I'll just come in and browse when I feel like it.'

He gave me a pleading stare and made me promise not to tell the others about it.

'It's at odds with your anti-sexist image, isn't it,' I teased him.

'Yeah,' he said and rolled his eyes. 'There was one girl – do you remember Diane? She found it – she was really into it, in fact. But it freaked me out.' He shrugged.

Diane was a hippie-ish girl Brian had met in a film studies class, with wispy light brown hair that came down past her waist. I was surprised to hear that about her; she seemed more like the type to be hanging out in the Women's Room in the Student Centre.

Being friends for as long as we were, I imagined that we all knew secrets about one another – some that were shared with and known only to the group, like the fact that Cameron had crashed the car, not Dylan, and some known only by one or two of us.

The secrets of mine held by the others were mostly ordinary, personal and embarrassing. The more serious thing, the one with potentially devastating consequences, was known only to Dylan.

I'd taken a class on Victorian literature in the first semester of senior year, against my better instincts. My schedule was more complicated than I'd wanted it to be that semester and my choices in English were Victorian literature, a class in Old Norse for which I wasn't qualified, or a contemporary drama course cross-listed with performance studies that required actual acting in front of other students, a nauseating prospect.

The Victorian lit course had a whole unit on poetry. Poetry has always been hard for me, which I suppose is odd considering that I went on to study early modern drama, which is pretty much all in verse of some sort. I wrote some poetry of my own when I was an angsty teenager (I didn't read any, so I'm not sure what my models were for the sad, banal expressions of alienation in free verse that I came up with). But poetry as such has a repellent opacity for me, and did even before the Victorian literature class: something about its dependence on metaphor and ambiguity of one kind or another; the idea that there are meanings always beyond my comprehension that I'll never be quite smart or educated enough to see for myself.

The final assignment in Victorian lit was a paper on one of three topics: *The Wings of the Dove* by Henry James, which I couldn't choose because I'd written on it for the previous assignment; George Eliot's *The Mill on the Floss*, which I hadn't read because I'd been too busy reading *The Wings of the Dove*, and *Hamlet* for another class; or Tennyson's elegy for his dead friend Arthur Hallam, *In Memoriam*. After skimming the poem enough to get through the class on it I put off actually reading it until the last possible moment, days before the paper was due, and found it impenetrable. The poet's tortured reflections on his inability to find words to express his grief only seemed to mirror my own excruciating inability to understand the significance of the whole thing.

It's a long poem, comprising dozens of smaller poems made of little, maddening, claustrophobic rhyming stanzas. By the time I got around to writing the paper I was worn out with finishing other papers due at the same time; I'd put it off too long and couldn't find the energy. The professor took pity on me and granted me a week's extension, but it was no good. I spent the time in a daze, checking dozens of books out of the library on the elegy, on Victorian poetry, Victorian literature, Tennyson, Tennyson's friends and rivals, fictional biographies of Tennyson, the phenomenon of death at sea, Victorian graveyards . . . At the end of the week my room smelled like a library stack, its floor crowded with pillars of books, faded towers of red and green and blue cloth covers, but I was no closer to producing any writing.

Dylan dropped over a few days before my official new due date. I could tell from the way he regarded me, his cheery greeting turning quickly to subdued concern, that I wasn't looking good.

'We haven't heard from you for so long,' he said. 'Tallis thought you might have been spending the week in bed with Katie, but I didn't think so.'

'Katie? Oh, Katie. No. I went out with her that one time. No.'

The idea of spending a week in someone's bed seemed like heaven to me at that moment, although it wasn't delirious sex I was thinking about, but simply the prospect of being somewhere else, in someone else's bed, someone else's place, any life other than the one I was in. I pictured a large bed with a billowing down quilt, a cocoon from the world.

'Elliot?'

'What?'

'I asked if you were still finishing a paper? Mine are all handed in by now.'

'Oh, yeah. I got an extension.'

I told him about the paper, stammering. He glanced around and took in the teetering piles of books. He sat at my desk and I sat on the bed and he opened a small bottle of bourbon that he seemed to conjure out of thin air. He poured a glass for each of us, a solid two or three inches of liquor.

'Drink that,' he said. 'Now. Don't be so stressed out about this. It's not a problem.' And he told me how to solve it, and offered to look into it for me. It was easy to find someone to write a paper for you if you needed to, he said. He knew someone really good.

I had never contemplated the idea of cheating before – unless I count the time in fifth grade when I looked up from an important test in class and found that I had a clear line of sight to the answers of the student sitting ahead of me to my left. She wasn't the brightest student and I guessed that my own calculations were probably just as likely to be right as hers, and I looked away. I think the week alone with Tennyson and the library books had distorted my perception of reality; I hadn't been anywhere except the library, my room, and the campus general store the whole time, and hadn't been answering the phone.

I hated Tennyson by that point, and was overcome with a sense that I didn't owe him anything. It was a stubborn feeling that my brain put up like a screen in front of my normal way of thinking. It wasn't logical. Tennyson wasn't asking me to do anything, after all, and didn't care what I thought about his poem, but all I could think of was how badly I wanted to not think about him or the poem again, how good it would be to get those hypnotic four-beat lines out of my head, and how much I wanted my room to not smell like the library any more. For years afterwards, whenever thoughts of the essay slipped into my mind through all the barriers of repression, they would always be accompanied by that feeling of personal animosity, that deluded sense that all I'd done was refuse an unreasonable request from a man I disliked intensely.

Dylan lit one of the French cigarettes he sometimes smoked – red Gauloises, impossible to buy in town – and passed one to me. I lifted my glass of bourbon, inhaled the sweet, smoky smell of it. By the time I was halfway through my drink I felt as though I had to say yes just to please Dylan, as though he would feel that he'd failed me as a friend if I didn't accept his assistance. I didn't want to hurt his feelings. He made it seem almost like a favour to him that I agreed to let him 'look into it'.

We found the sheet with the paper topics on it, surprisingly clean and unworn, at the very bottom of a pile of books and CDs on my desk that I thought had been there like that for at least three months. He folded it up into a neat origami square and put it in his pocket. And that's how it happened.

When Dylan left I rearranged the piles of books into several neater stacks by the door. He showed up two days later with the ghostwritten paper and accompanied me to turn it in, and we got drunk together, celebrating.

Cameron offered me a ride in his car one day soon after, and

I made several trips up and down the dorm stairs, carrying as many books as I could hold in my arms. They filled the back seat. I pushed them one by one through the slot in the metal return bin in front of the library, conscious of each heavy thud as they fell.

The smell in my room lingered even though I opened the windows as wide as they could go, letting in all the chill, sharp winter air. The next morning I woke up shivering and shut the windows, deliberately lit a cigarette, and chain-smoked for the rest of the day to restore the room to its proper, non-Tennysonian state. It wasn't anything like a conscious decision, but every part of me colluded in a resolution that I wouldn't think about the paper again. For a week I'd been in another world, which I'd fallen into through some strange, book-lined tunnel, and now I'd followed a thread back to reality. There was no way to reconcile what I'd let Dylan do (I found it hard to think about it as something I'd actually done) with how I thought of myself. A pocket of willed amnesia formed around my decision, the dark matter of denial. I determined never to study poetry again if I could avoid it, and a lifelong aversion hardened into place.

It's probably significant that in my other English class that semester, Renaissance Drama, I discovered the field of study that became my academic passion. I excelled in the course and became obsessed with the complicated politics of Elizabethan England, the scandal of the Spanish match, Charles I's abortive courtship with a Spanish princess, and the role of the theatre in the public outcry around the incident. The teacher nominated my paper on Middleton's obscure play *A Game at Chess* (meticulously referenced and cross-checked) for some kind of department award, and it won an 'honourable mention'. She wrote letters of recommendation to graduate school for me, and off I went to write a dissertation about the politics of English drama in the years 1601 to 1640. I chose to fully embrace and expand the version of myself that performed so well in that particular class, as though by doing so I could blot out the disastrous failure in that other course. I discovered that it was possible to avoid the entire nineteenth century even with the period requirements in graduate coursework. I didn't have to think seriously about Victorian literature again.

I had a few nightmares about the paper, dreaming that someone in my department would discover the truth about it when I was up for promotion or tenure or publication and undo my career. It was more than potentially embarrassing, but I never let myself think in any detail about what the consequences would be if it were discovered, and the pocket of forgetfulness around the whole event stayed in place most of the time. In my first year at graduate school a group of tipsy students at a party decided to play a version of 'I've Never', or 'Truth or Dare' – some appalling adolescent truth-telling drinking game – and I hurried away, despite how long the odds were that it would ever come up. Odd things would bring it to mind every once in a while: a certain arrangement of books of various coloured bindings on a library shelf; the smell of bourbon and fresh tobacco smoke; the sight of old, tall trees with complicated roots that matched my imaginary sense of what a yew tree might look like – one of the images from *In Memoriam* that had lodged itself in my memory.

Occasionally I wound up in conversations with other graduate students about the insecurity many of us held in common: the idea that underneath our veneer of wide knowledge and showy, articulate powers of clever analysis we were frauds, and that one day we would be unmasked. It surprised me when I first learned that so many others shared that feeling, but my wonder lasted only for a moment and then it seemed somehow a natural and inevitable form of neurosis for people who did what we did, attempting to master fields of knowledge that only seemed to grow exponentially and become more impossible to grasp the further you explored and the more you learned.

I experienced the sympathy that comes with sharing a common fear, and at the same time felt irrevocably isolated from the rest of them by my secret. For them, this anxiety was merely a phantasm they could laugh about even if it was genuinely painful and sometimes – momentarily – crippling. But mine had tangible form, an actual basis. Again, stupidly, I felt angry at Tennyson. Because of him – because of my own failure to come to terms with his writing, and the choice I made to deal with that, I reminded myself – I was vulnerable to exposure in a way that my peers were not. I compensated furiously and became obsessed with academic rigour as though it were a fetish, trying hard to complete the insanely long and difficult reading lists for class, researching thoroughly every essay, every presentation, every conference paper. I was a conscientious student. By the time my qualifying exams were over I felt as though I'd proven something to myself.

At my first MLA conference, my doctorate freshly conferred, I wound up on the edges of a hushed after-dinner conversation about some history student at an Ivy League school who had just been stripped of his PhD after another student who had read his work tried to visit the archive in Greece on which some of this ex-PhD's dissertation was based, only to discover that the whole thing was a fabrication. From my seat at the far end of the table I strained to hear the details, consumed with ambivalence about whether I wanted to know the whole story, or block it all out. I tried to figure out whether there was even a library or document repository in the obscure village in question, or just no file or cache of documents that mattered, as had been claimed; either way . . .

'Can you imagine?' said one of my friends at the table. 'A whole archive?'

The archive forger had just landed a job at another Ivy League school and had been forced to turn it down. It looked bad for the school; it looked bad for the field, for everyone. A whole archive – *that* was shocking, and an insult to scholarship, and indicated a contempt for the field as well as a neurotic desire to be exposed. My transgression was so little in comparison. I quelled the incipient anxiety, the desire to leave the table.

I wondered how the student had felt, the one who had discovered the absence of the archive: the shock, the moments of self-doubt, wondering if she had the wrong address, or had gone to the wrong village, or had been mistaken about the name of the files . . . and then the dawning, unbelieving comprehension, and the decision to tell someone, and the question of what to say, the burden of knowing that her evidence would have such devastating consequences even if it was true and right to bring it forward.

So that was my big secret, and, as far as I was aware, only Dylan knew about it. Somehow it didn't occur to me that there would be darker, more potentially damaging secrets buried within the group, secrets that I was excluded from. I was naive, all the while thinking of myself as the knowing, insightful one.

4

It was exactly a week after that lunch with Elizabeth that Natasha walked into the bar where I was sitting and drinking with two colleagues from my department, Marcus and Felix. They were both stressed to the point of physical illness by anxiety over whether they would get tenure this year. We had come for a drink following a talk by a visiting academic, who had been taken out to dinner with the chair and other colleagues more senior or more interesting than us. More in the visitor's field. We sat at the end of the bar, and graduate students and other junior faculty members drank around us, and the occasional undergraduate. I recognized a couple of seniors from one of my classes the previous semester, serious young guys talking intensely over their beers. Everything was doubled and blurred in the stained mirror along the wall: strings of lights, bottles, faces, faded celebration banners from somebody's birthday months earlier.

Marcus and Felix had spent a while discussing their ailments – chronic sinus infection for one, or both, perhaps, and incipient ulcers. I nodded sympathetically and tried not to think about the burning feeling I sometimes experienced in my own stomach. Not an ulcer, surely. Marcus seemed to have lost some hair in the last year or so, but he'd grown it longer as well, a decision that was probably made with the idea that it would disguise the balding issue but unfortunately worked the other way. They started talking about baseball, which was less dismal than the talk about ulcers but just as alienating to me, and I lost my hold on the thread of conversation when one of them started telling the other about a website where you could order team stickers for your car, for your bike . . .

Natasha appeared by my side; I looked and saw her pale profile; she was trying to catch the bartender's eye. She turned and smiled at me. 'Hello there.' She brushed her fringe of hair aside, performing exactly what I had wished to do, and my own fingers tingled. For once her hair stayed where it was and I looked into her eyes, gleaming brown.

'Hi, Natasha. Have you been here for a while? I didn't see you.'

She shrugged, looked away from me to the bartender, who had finally approached us. He asked her what she wanted. She ordered a beer.

'Do you want one, Elliot?' she asked. 'What are you drinking?'

I blinked down at my beer, three-quarters finished. 'Whisky,' I said, on impulse. 'On the rocks. Johnnie Walker.'

'A whisky on the rocks. Johnnie Walker,' she repeated. I opened my wallet. 'No,' she said. 'I'll buy you a drink.'

I started to protest and she shook her head, smiling.

'OK. Thanks,' I said. 'Are you here with someone?'

She shrugged again. 'I was with some people. Over there.' She nodded toward the other room, the one with booths and tables. 'They just left. I saw you here and thought I would say hello.'

'Well. Hello.'

The drinks arrived. I raised my glass and she clinked hers against it with some force. 'Cheers.' The music that had been coming from the jukebox stopped, and the gap it left felt long and awkward. When another song eventually began it was disappointing, with too-fast, electronic beats.

I asked how her work was going.

'It's going well, actually,' she said. 'I like it here. It's nice to have no students.'

Her research fellowship included no teaching for the first two years.

'I'm envious.'

She smiled. 'Are your students that bad?'

'No.'

'You are just weary.'

'Yes, that's it,' I said, enjoying the poetic possibilities of the word.

My colleagues were now arguing with passion about a game that had taken place two weeks ago, or two seasons.

'Do you want to see if there's a table?' I asked Natasha.

She shrugged again. It seemed to come with a kind of nod. I wondered whether there were different kinds of shrug for yes and no and maybe, and for not caring. I decided I was going to work it out.

She glanced over into the adjoining room. 'I see one.' She led the way.

I've heard it said that when you fall in love with someone, you're really just falling in love with a mirror, the ideal version of yourself that you see reflected in the eyes of the other person. This rang true to me in some ways. Falling in love came with a need to present the best, most attractive version of myself; and then, if the feeling was returned, a short-lived period of triumph while I basked in the sense of achievement and forgot that the version of myself was just that, a limited version that hid all the things that I didn't consider interesting or attractive – a kind of fiction. Then the less interesting and less attractive parts of myself would naturally assert themselves, and I'd spend a while feeling like a fraud.

With Natasha I'd had this sense from the start – from the conversation about Dylan's death – that all my normal efforts at presenting a more attractive self would be transparent. But I didn't know how to act any differently. I concentrated all my efforts on impressing her in the most invisible, least obvious way possible.

Her main discernible attitude towards me seemed to be pity. This in itself wasn't without potential. Pity could go hand in hand with sympathy, concern, a desire to comfort that could shade into desire. I'd probably played that hand a little with Elizabeth, who seemed to find me more attractive after Dylan's death than she had before, her hand lingering on my shoulder when she said goodbye, or on my forearm when she was pressing home a point or trying to convince me that talking about Dylan would help me 'process' the experience. But pity could also go the other way, into colder territory where you just felt sorry for the other person: the other pathetic, undesirable person.

Pity that blended into desire was something I associated with women who liked to be needed. But Natasha wasn't like that. The sense of self-sufficiency she presented was impressively solid. It was hard to imagine her needing anyone – although I tried, and the conjured picture was disturbingly beautiful: all her strength turned to liquid distress, and me able to be of service. But this image quickly dissolved; it wasn't her. So: pity, shading probably away from desire, and an unnerving kind of psychological X-ray vision. That's what I thought Natasha had for me.

As I followed her through the bar towards an empty table I found that I badly wanted to convince her. That's how I thought about it, as though my own self was an argument I could win by some rhetorical sleight of hand, a performance of emotional *sprezzatura* – the art of doing everything brilliantly while looking as though you aren't really trying.

We found a table, its surface covered with crumbs from chips and popcorn and wet rings left by glasses. Natasha swept her hand across it, knocking most of the crumbs to the floor, and brushed her fingers against her jeans as she sat down on one of the red vinyl-covered chairs. I'd been concentrating so hard on my thoughts about being convincing and her self-sufficiency that I'd stopped noticing everything else, and as I watched her sit, it all came back – the noise and chatter of the people around us, the oppressive warmth of the air in the place, the sickly yellow of the light from the fake antique wall sconces, the music. The song finished. Another one started. It was familiar, but I couldn't place it. It sounded right. If I could have chosen it as a soundtrack I would have. A guitar's heavy chords, a catchy melody in the bass.

Natasha looked up at me. She was sitting almost on her hands, thumbs tucked under her thighs, her arms straight. 'Are you going to sit down?'

I sat. Her arms relaxed and she put one hand to her drink. 'I like this song,' she said.

'Really?' A glance over toward the jukebox. 'I programmed it. I thought it was never going to come on.'

'Hmm. That was thoughtful of you.'

I smiled and leaned forward, crossing my arms, elbows on the table. 'OK, I confess, I didn't put it on. But I wish I had. I was going to.'

The trace of pity was still there in her face. Right then I decided to do my best to get her drunk, with some idea that I would be more likeable if she were more intoxicated, or that at least I wouldn't feel so much under scrutiny from her gaze if it was less focused.

It might seem weird that in the throes of grief – not the noisy extremes of tears and terrible pain, but the less noticeable phases, the ones that are all about numbness and lack of awareness – I became riveted by this person who was so obviously not warm and sympathetic at all, who wasn't looking at me kindly and waiting for me to pour my heart out. It's not right to say that she wasn't sympathetic at all, but her form of sympathy felt entirely different from other people's. In those minutes we had spent together smoking on the bench outside the café after lunch that day, in the way she had so briefly and drily shared her own experience of loss, I had felt understood in some generous way that went strangely hand in hand with the feeling of being analyzed.

'How is it going with your friends?' she asked. 'Are you still going to Las Vegas?'

In the last couple of days I had been through yet another round of conversations with the other three, trying to finalize some more details, mediating a disagreement about which restaurant to reserve for our first night, or whether to make a reservation at all. Tallis had tried to engage me in a lengthy complaint about the tension between Brian and Cameron, and his opinion about how exactly each of them was at fault. It was a conversation I was more used to having with him when we'd both had several drinks and the repetitions of grievances didn't feel so annoying but instead had a therapeutic aspect, a kind of bonding ritual. But this time he had been sober – he had called me at home, when it was early morning for him in London – and his complaints had had a hectoring, almost hysterical tone. I had invented an excuse to hang up, and depressed myself afterward by watching hours of forensic crime shows on TV, one of them set in Vegas. The casino interiors looked remarkably authentic, as they always did when I saw Vegas represented on television, only a little cleaner.

In any case, I found it hard to answer Natasha's questions simply, to put her off and change the subject, as it seemed proper to do. 'We're still going,' I said. 'My friends are all still at each other's throats.'

'Including you?' Her left eyebrow seemed to be almost

permanently raised, or about to be lifted.

'Not me,' I replied. 'I'm, you know, trying to smooth things over.'

'Why are you doing that?' she asked, as though I'd told her I was trying to talk them all into something ridiculous, like a trip to Australia, or group therapy.

'To make things easier, I guess.'

How was it possible to explain it, I wondered, this thing that seemed to me a basic role of a friend: to deal with conflict, to try to resolve it.

'But it is making things hard for yourself.'

'I mean, easier once we all get there.'

'You can't make any difference,' she pronounced with an air of great authority, and it seemed as though she wasn't talking about me specifically, in this situation, but about anybody, anytime, making a difference to anything. It didn't sound bleak, like that might suggest; it sounded comforting. 'It's making things hard for you right now,' she repeated, with her drawn-out inflection on the long vowels. 'Forget it. Have they always relied on you to, what did you say, smooth things over?'

I began to wonder if I had overstated my role as essential mediator in the petty conflicts and minor irritations that were going on.

'Dylan was so good at that,' I said. 'We left it all to him.'

'The one who's gone now.'

I nodded.

'You'll all be there without him,' she observed after a pause. 'What will that be like? You're expecting fighting the whole time?'

I laughed, imagining Brian and Cameron fighting it out with their fists on the boulevard or on the gaming floor. 'I really don't know,' I said. 'I don't know what to expect.'

'How many years?'

'This is the tenth.'

'Oh. Every year, you go?'

'Every year.'

'You must be such good friends.'

The pity element in how Natasha looked at me was still there. I was probably making it worse, and I was overcome with aversion at the idea of days with my friends, without Dylan, in those Vegas spaces that managed to be both overwhelmingly large – rooms the size of three football fields – and entirely claustrophobic, crowded with machines and people.

Natasha reached for her purse. 'I'm going to have a cigarette,' she said. I followed her outside.

'We're not such good friends,' I said to her once she had lit up. 'I like the idea of having friends from college, I guess, more than I like them.'

'It's a nice idea. So you don't like each other –'

'It's not quite like that,' I interrupted her. 'It's me – I'm the one. I've just grown apart from it. From them. They still like each other – well, not Brian and Cameron, that's a long story – but what I mean is that they don't feel like I do. They still like me. I think they do.'

She offered me a drag of her cigarette; I realized I had been gazing at it with longing, at her fingers holding it and her mouth drawing on it. I took it, our fingers touching as she passed it over, and drew in a satisfying, poisonous-feeling lungful.

It was exaggerating to say I didn't like them any more. It wasn't strictly true. I wasn't sure. It was possible to outgrow friendships, after all. But that hadn't happened with Dylan. It was impossible not to like him – he was so sure of himself, with none of the insecurity that I imagined being so unattractive about myself.

We went back inside to our table and drinks. I asked her about the man I'd seen her walking with on campus that day after we had parted outside the café. Her face hardened, not against me exactly but around the idea of the guy, whose name turned out to be Eamonn. He was Irish, and married although separated and not in a great hurry to get divorced.

'It's complicated, in a deeply boring and predictable way,' she said.

He was in her department but worked in some very different field – I couldn't keep straight in my head the differences among astrophysics, particle physics and biological physics, which was her area of research; apparently these fields were very competitive with one another.

'I don't think he likes being seen with someone as junior as me,' she said. 'His wife is a full professor at some Ivy League.'

'He's crazy,' I said. 'He must be an idiot.' I meant it.

'OK, very funny,' she said. 'Stop now.'

I uncrossed my legs and my knee came to rest against her chair. I could feel the way that the weight of her body held the chair in place against the pressure. I left it there, and knew she was aware of it; it came close to the intensity of direct physical contact but with its own erotic charge, all the more precise for being mediated.

'Your turn,' she said. 'I'll have what you are having.'

I don't know how I came to tell her about the Tennyson essay, Dylan's great favour to me, but I did, later on, when something finally came unstuck that had been steadily loosening since his death. I had tried to turn the conversation away from myself – maybe they weren't huge or adequate efforts – asking her about her life before she came to the States, what it had been like to move here, how she came to choose physics. She resisted my interest in the details, but she did tell me some of it, in her particular kind of personal shorthand – brief sentences punctuated with shrugs and tilts of the head. It wasn't quite the childhood of poverty that I had imagined – her parents had both been engineers, and had emigrated to the United States when she was fifteen.

I did my best to be a good listener, but I was haunted that night by thoughts of my friends, by Dylan especially, by the essay. I had pulled it out of its drawer a few days earlier. One day the paper would yellow with age; I kept waiting for that to happen, for the physical object itself to show me how much time had gone by, how much it was a relic of an ancient past that was barely relevant to who I now was. But it stayed stubbornly pristine-looking, bright white, printed out in sharp, expensive-looking laser ink. The staple in the top left corner looked old, at least; it was starting to rust and mark the paper.

I'd never told anyone about it. That's how efficiently the amnesia pocket had worked, or how hard I'd worked to preserve it. As I started talking, I knew I could never have told her if Dylan had been alive. There was some vestigial sense of loyalty to him, a sense that it was his secret, too, and not fully mine to share, but I felt it falling away from me, leaving me lighter and emptier than before.

'Dylan helped me out once with a really big problem.' That's how I put it. 'I was taking this class. I shouldn't have taken it. I couldn't do it.'

The rest came easily, in a few sentences, so short in the end that the event felt diminished by its telling.

Talking about Dylan's role in it was one of those moments when I realized all over again that he was gone. That realization seemed to come in various forms with sickening regularity from day to day, week to week. It wasn't exactly as though I forgot he was dead and then was struck with the fact as though for the first time; it was more like different pieces of loss falling into place, or falling away, leaving new spaces, new perspectives on a future that didn't include him.

I didn't expect her to absolve me or to tell me it wasn't a big deal. I think I expected the opposite. After all those years I probably craved some measure of blame or criticism being levelled at me from outside myself so that I could either properly defend myself or, as I more strongly wanted to do, admit my fault.

She listened and nodded slowly and asked me the occasional question, but didn't pronounce the judgement I desired. The closest she came was something like a wince when I admitted it had been senior year, in the subject that became my field. She was an academic, too; she knew how serious an infraction it had been. It wasn't the stupid error of a freshman.

She asked me what grade I got for the paper. (An A minus, which I remember finding completely annoying for a second before I couldn't bear thinking about it.) It's at that point, towards the end of the conversation, or confession, or whatever it was, that my memory of the evening blurs. Some part of me tuned in with a measure of clarity just before the phase of serious drunkenness set in, and observed that it looked from the outside as though I were falling apart after my friend's death. That's what it looked like, and maybe that was actually happening, but the thought turned to static before it could resolve.

My head hurt a lot when I woke up in Natasha's bed the next morning. Fierce lines of sunlight marked the wall next to me where they had made it around the corners of the window blinds. They were large windows, out of proportion with the wall they were set in. I found that I couldn't look at them for long.

It was a surprise to find myself there. I must have drunk more than I had realized. The walls were tobacco-smoke yellow. I hoped it was the intended color and not actually the effect of

years of accumulated smoke. The thought was sickening. I tried
to sit up; changed my mind, lay back down. There was a desk
against the wall opposite, the kind with a shelf built into the top
of it, lined with fat books. A closed laptop, cords snaking down
to the floor. There was no sign of Natasha. I wanted a glass of
water. My mouth felt dry and sour, and my T-shirt smelled stale.

I felt around for my glasses, relieved to find them quickly
beside the bed. It was then that I noticed the face at the door
across the room; a small, olive-skinned face with a pointed chin,
level with the door handle; wide, assessing brown eyes.

My mental image of Natasha underwent a rapid, nauseating
shift. Somehow the idea of a child wasn't too hard to accommodate;
after all, I didn't know her very well. How brave she was, I thought,
imagining her as a self-sacrificing single mother struggling on
with her studies, her research, her work. Then came a sense of
dread and vague responsibility – how was I supposed to act
around a child, I wondered; would the child be confused by a
strange man in the house, scarred, traumatized? – which shifted
to an indulgent kind of compassion. There was something else as
well, a sneaky gratification of whatever confused desire for
maternal sympathy I had been harbouring the previous night.

The little face kept on looking, not blinking, one small hand
holding the door. A smile grew very slowly there, a not entirely
friendly smile, but not traumatized either. It looked like a boy
rather than a girl. Children's ages were impossible for me to
guess. Four? Three?

Natasha's face appeared above the boy's for a second, and she
came into the room. 'Good morning,' she said. Her bare feet
were slim and brown against the scratched-up polished floor. I
sat up and tried to focus. She sat at the chair by the desk.

'Piotr!' she called to the little boy.

He came running over and stood there between her legs,

facing me, his hands resting casually on her knees. She put up a hand to ruffle his hair. Their stance, her caress, the shape of his small head against her blue shirt, made her for a moment into a dark-haired madonna cradling a fiery-eyed, impetuous little god. The boy ran out as quickly as he had come in.

'Natasha,' I said. 'I had no idea . . .'

She frowned and looked unsure for a moment, and then she laughed, a deep chuckle. 'He's not mine. Is that what you thought?'

'I . . .' The word drew out but the thought didn't finish.

'My cousin's visiting. She came over for breakfast this morning. We'd arranged it already . . . He's hers.' She thought for a second. 'I guess that makes him . . . do you say second cousin? I don't know.'

A lazy, gurgling child's voice drifted in from another room.

'Coffee?' Natasha asked.

I nodded.

'How's your head?'

I smiled. 'Not great.'

'I have Advil.' She put her hand over her mouth to stifle a yawn, eyes squeezed shut, vulnerable and tired-looking for a second before she stood and left the room.

Her voice and another woman's echoed down the hallway, exchanging rapid phrases in Russian. Peals of laughter from both of them.

I pulled on my jeans, moving slowly, and ventured out. The kitchen was dimly familiar from the night before, all clean surfaces and pale morning colours. The same over-proportioned windows as the bedroom, wide-slatted blinds pulled halfway down. A carton of eggs rested on the counter next to the sink. I looked away, queasy at the thought of food. A coffee maker croaked gently. Natasha's cousin was sitting at the table with

Piotr on her knee. She was peroxide blonde and very young-looking. I nodded at her, wondering whether she spoke English.

'Hi,' she said, in a perfect New Jersey intonation. 'Nice to meet you.'

I shuffled over to the table and sat down by her.

'Hi,' I said. 'Elliot.' My voice sounded creaky. I wasn't sure how my presence had been explained to her.

'I'm Elena,' she said, and turned back to Natasha, picking up whatever conversation they'd been having when I walked in, a stream of words in Russian that ended in a big smile. Natasha made a short reply and they both started laughing again. The cousin's laugh ran down a scale, over and over again, five notes, four. It hurt my head, though at any other time I probably would have thought it was pretty.

Just as I was on the point of becoming paranoid about being the subject of the joke, whatever it was, they stopped and became businesslike, setting cups on the table, offering sugar, pouring milk, switching back to English.

I kept my coffee black and held the mug in my hands, hot and comforting. Natasha sat down and pushed the hair out of her eyes, resting her hand against her temple with her elbow on the table, her gaze clear and open. There was a bottle of pills beside her cup and she pushed it toward me, letting her hair fall back.

'You met Piotr?' the cousin asked.

'Hi, Piotr,' I said.

The little boy had stayed impassive through all the laughter and talking. Now he stepped away from his mother's knee and around the corner of the table to stand by my side. He couldn't be older than four, I thought, and I wondered if he was shy. Then, without warning, he sank his teeth into my arm, just below the shoulder. His teeth were sharp and he was strong. I howled briefly, a shock of pain in my flesh, and pulled my arm away. The boy stood there, looking at me for a moment and then at his mother, his expression unreadable, hands by his sides. There was one second of silence and I had a horrible feeling that they were going to start laughing again – but instead Elena started talking angrily to the boy in a mix of English and Russian, holding him firmly by his upper arms. I glanced down and saw a mark on my shirt from his wet teeth. The place where he'd bitten me throbbed.

'Elliot –' Natasha said. She reached out, touching my arm lightly before dropping her hand back to her knee.

'Ouch,' I said, and smiled weakly. 'I should go.'

I put my mug down on the table, trying to brush away a creeping sense of humiliation. Natasha came with me back to her room, where I looked for my shoes and socks. It took a while to find them: awkward, silent seconds, searching under the bed and in corners. I got to see all the tiny pieces of dust gathered in the corners and odd places as I looked. Eventually she picked up the second sock from a space behind her desk and handed it to me with a smile of relief. How had it made its way there, I wondered; had I thrown it over there?

'I'm so sorry,' she said in a rush, and I realized that we were both suffering equally from embarrassment.

'No, it's OK, I'm sorry,' I said, knowing there was something to apologize for – drinking and talking too much, passing out – but unable to put it into specific words.

She gave a little shrug, and I felt absolved. 'Don't worry, Elliot,' she said.

Memories from the night before flashed in and out, frustratingly partial. Sitting cross-legged on the bed, on the yellow-patterned bedspread; watching her arm rise in the dark to loosen the cord of the window blinds and bring them down; the curve of her hip as I brushed against it; her hands gently taking my own from where they had covered my face. Above all, my own maudlin voice, though I couldn't remember the words. Just the tone.

We hadn't slept together; we hadn't even kissed, I was sure of it, and now, looking at her mouth, I regretted it fiercely. I tried again to remember the previous night, sure that there must have been a moment I could have taken advantage of, that I could have seized, and worried that it had passed irrevocably. But then I met her eyes – patient, sardonic – and began to doubt that such a moment could have existed. It was the certainty in her face, the way she looked, like she always looked, as though whatever I thought about her didn't matter as much to her as her own thoughts mattered to me.

Recover, I told myself. Be amused, not wounded.

'Can I see you again?' I asked.

She raised her hand to my shoulder and started toward the door, walking me out with her. 'Sure,' she said. It was her same voice, the intonation somehow flat and musical and ironic all at the same time, the way it seemed to curl luxuriously around the *rrr*, but there was something else in there, a glimmer of intimacy. My headache grew, surged. I hadn't finished my coffee or taken the Advil.

As we stood in the hallway, Natasha opening the front door, Piotr appeared, marched out of the kitchen by his mother. He stood in front of me. 'Sorry,' he said, grudgingly.

'OK,' I said, and made myself appear cheerful, tolerant. You little bastard, I thought.

Elena patted Piotr's cheek and nodded goodbye. There was a glint of triumph in the boy's eyes. Whatever obscure test had been set, I had failed dismally.

5

I started to understand that there were things I didn't know about Dylan when I visited home for the first time after his funeral, just a couple of weeks before the trip to Vegas. I resented the visit, having already been home for Thanksgiving and Christmas. It was my father's birthday, which wasn't something I was always there for, but it was his fifty-ninth and somehow this had assumed an importance almost equal to the birthday that would come next, or that was how my mother had made me feel when she'd talked to me on the phone about it.

'It's the last birthday of his fifties,' she'd said to me, a few times.

'I get it that sixty is important,' I said. 'I just don't see why fifty-nine is.'

'You don't need to see. You just need to be here.'

'I've just been there.'

'It's been a while since Christmas. And in any case, we need to start planning for next year. For the big six-oh.'

I sighed.

'Elliot. After Dylan passing — I think it's really important for your father for you to be here.'

Somehow my parents had managed to turn Dylan's death into a tragedy that affected them more than me. They remarked often on how terrible it was for parents to lose a child, the reversal of the natural order, and at those moments they would look away from me and stare fixedly at some other object, shaking their heads, or take a couple of seconds of intense silence if we were talking on the phone. It made them think about losing me, about what that would be like. That was the unspoken thing.

I agreed to go.

My parents live in a town near the Jersey Shore, not far from Atlantic City, a couple of hours from New York. 'There are some really nice parts of Jersey,' people liked to say when I mentioned it, as if consoling me, or trying to impress me with their open mind. Sometimes followed by, 'The woods around Princeton are so lovely.'

My father, a lawyer, works in his own small office above a storefront downtown that he shares with a partner, Lawrence, and Lois, their secretary. His name, Nathan West, was on the window in gold and black, blockish capitals that had started to peel and speckle over time. For as long as I could remember, Lois and Lawrence had been having a secret affair that my father ignored. Lawrence had turned sixty the year before, and my mother had told me all about his party, dismayed at the poor quality of the wine, full of ideas about how we should do things differently for my father.

The sun was a weak orange haze in the far-off horizon when I arrived at my parents' home after hours on mind-numbing miles of expressways and turnpikes. The familiar sound of the piano came from the house as I turned into the drive, and the front of the car scraped on the curb as it always did, no matter what kind of car I drove. It seemed to be worse with this recent one, a newish Volkswagen. Somehow my father managed to negotiate the drive smoothly every time, while my mother had given up trying years ago and accepted the dent in the front of her old red Honda.

The scratch of concrete against metal; a flamboyant trill on the piano keys in a high register; quiet as the engine switched off; a resonating final chord; home. It sounded like Mozart. An aggressively cheerful sonata.

My mother had been a music teacher at the local high school ever since I'd started kindergarten, attached to the pupils who showed real talent, resigned to the lack of musicality in her own children. When I poked my head around the door to the music room, she was there at the piano, straight-backed, hands still touching the keys, arms relaxed. The notes still sounded in the air. She reached up to close the book of music, and I saw SCHUBERT in green capitals on the familiar yellowed paper cover.

She came and kissed me, and said, 'That sounded like a terrible scrape!'

'You have to get that driveway fixed.'

She sighed. Every visit began with the same exchange.

I followed her to the kitchen, where she picked up an apron that was hanging over the back of a chair. A large joint of beef sat fatly in a baking dish, bristling with rosemary. She started peeling potatoes, letting the spirals inch down into the sink.

I rinsed out the coffee maker and opened the cupboard. 'Where's the coffee?' I asked.

'Right there.'

'It's decaf.'

A half-full packet sat on the shelf next to innumerable boxes of herbal teas: Tension Tamer, Blueberry Hill, Peppermint Patty, Green Peach, White Peach, Peach Mango. The cupboard smelled of peach flavour and stale coffee.

'Oh, we're all drinking decaf now.'

'Is Lily here yet?' I couldn't picture my sister joining in the decaf drinking.

'She's upstairs. There's instant if you want, you know, the real thing.'

Behind the teas was a small glass jar with some brown sediment along the bottom.

'Lily!' I called upstairs.

A door slammed somewhere. Lily called back down to me. 'Elliot! Can you go get some coffee?'

'Sure.' I picked up my keys from where I'd tossed them on the dining table. Its surface shone, giving off the scent of lemon.

Lily thumped down the stairs. Brown sheepskin boots came into view, then jeans, a draped black sweater. The glassy smell of shampoo surrounded her, and her hair was still wet.

My sister carried herself at home as though she were fighting a return to a teenage way of being in her body, awkward and tense and confrontational and insecure all at once, with a permanent pout and more of a glare than usual. Away from here, in New York, in Brooklyn where she lived, she grew up by years. I kept my eye on it once – the subtle transformation seemed to begin and end a few steps from the door, halfway between the porch and the sidewalk.

It was probably the same for me, I knew with gloomy certainty. This was one of the reasons it was so anxiety-making to think about bringing women home to my parents' house: they would see for themselves a version of my adolescent self, more embarrassing and beyond my conscious control than any set of old photographs my parents could dig up and display.

'Oh, Elliot,' my mother said. 'If you're going to the store can I get you to pick up a few things?'

I left with a list; once it got to be more than four things my mother decided it ought to be written down, since they were all important things, and then it stretched to ten. Forty-five minutes later I returned, dazed from too much driving and the overbright supermarket lights, the trunk full of groceries and alcohol in plastic bags. I'd remembered coffee while standing in the checkout line, and had pushed the shopping cart tiredly back through the aisles, then back to the line again. By the time I carried the bags into the kitchen it felt like time for a drink rather than coffee, but I spooned some into the machine in any case.

My father turned his key in the lock at the moment the coffee started to release its aroma to mix with the other ones filling the kitchen — that peachy tea, the roasting meat, plus a kind of chemical burning smell the oven always seemed to give off, as though some non-essential part was slowly melting. I recognized the sound, the way he opened the door, his unique signature. There was the sound of his briefcase being placed onto the floor, his coat being hung on its hook, and the sigh he gave when he had completed those two actions and loosened his tie.

'Elliot,' he said when he saw me, and smiled. 'Are you making actual coffee?'

'Hi, Dad,' I said. 'Yes, it's the real thing. Happy birthday.'

He laughed and embraced me.

My parents retired for the night by ten. I heard the sound of the television in their room, the static blips as the channels flipped. Lily and I finished tidying the kitchen, stepping around each other in familiar ways, passing plates, drying glasses, stacking and clearing. We drank the last of the red wine and I felt the dull blade of the inevitable headache begin to edge its way around the inside of my skull. I poured a glass for each of us from one of my father's birthday presents, a well-aged single malt, and we sat out on the steps of the back porch in the cold night while Lily smoked.

'So, are you going to see Dylan's, you know, "real" family while you're in Vegas?' Lily asked. 'Do some reminiscing, or whatever?' She dragged on her cigarette and looked at me sideways.

I didn't know what she meant. 'What?'

'I guess it would be weird. You didn't ever mention seeing them before.'

'What are you talking about?' My glass felt heavy in my hand. 'Dylan doesn't have any family in Vegas. They're all in LA.'

Lily's eyes gleamed with satisfaction. 'Well,' she said, drawing out the word, and turned so that she was facing more towards me. 'You know Dylan and I had a kind of thing, right?' She batted her eyelashes.

'Don't flatter yourself,' I said. 'Yeah, I know you made out with him once. Whose party was it?'

'It wasn't just that once,' she replied. 'But that party – you remember, it was that one in Brooklyn, you came as well and spent the whole night arguing with my friend Mitchell – we took acid together. It was amazing. And he told me a whole bunch of stuff about himself. Stuff that maybe you don't know.'

'How do you know he wasn't just spinning you a line? Especially if he was on drugs?'

'Well,' she said, 'I thought of that. But the thing is, he was worried about it. Not worried exactly, just . . . concerned maybe? Next time we got together – he took me out for a drink – he wanted to talk about it, as if his memory of that night was kind of fuzzy. He said' – she looked at me from under her eyelashes and mimicked Dylan's voice, the hushed, intimate tone he used when he was trying to be especially convincing, or seductive – '"I hope I didn't totally embarrass myself. What terrible secrets did I tell you?"'

'And what did you say?'

She smiled and shook her head. 'Oh, I didn't say anything. I don't like to go over those times with people afterwards in that kind of detail. It spoils the magic. And anyway, I kind of enjoyed the situation, seeing him squirm a little, wanting to know exactly what he'd told me. I just told him he'd been a regular cliché, you know, seeing the music and all that, hours absorbed in the patterns in the driveway gravel. And there was plenty of that, too, let me tell you.'

'OK. And the rest?'

'His real family, you mean?' She exhaled slowly, her lips pursed, a thin stream of smoke. 'He was adopted. You know that, right?'

This was news to me and I still only half-believed her. I wasn't sure how much to let on to her about what I did and didn't know. It was embarrassing to not know. 'No,' I said eventually. 'I didn't know that. He never mentioned it.'

'Really.'

'I didn't know,' I said again, letting her relish my ignorance. 'But I'm still not sure whether I believe this or not.'

'It happened.'

'OK, something happened, but, you know, you were both high. Are you sure you remember right?'

'I'm sure. It's the kind of thing you don't forget.' She shrugged. 'It made me feel, well, sorry for him.'

'Sorry for him?'

'You remember what he was like – this sense that there were old secrets and wounds simmering away there under the surface . . .'

I started to say that no, I didn't remember that about him, but then thought that he must have seemed different to girls.

She continued. 'He had this other life – another family, at least, that wasn't part of his regular life. I couldn't tell why – I couldn't tell why he didn't tell you or anyone else. Why it was a secret.'

'Why did he tell you?'

'I don't know. The drugs must have been stronger than he realized.'

'So tell me about it. This family.'

'It was his brother that he mentioned. Colin. A younger brother.'

'In Vegas?'

'Yeah, in Vegas. He lives there. "I have a sister," he said to me – we'd been talking about you, what it's like for me being your sister – "she's a little bitch, but I love her," and he laughed. "But I have a brother too," he said, "I bet you didn't know that," and then he went on about how he and I both had brothers, but his was a younger brother, and you're my older brother, and how different that must be . . . I asked him when was the last time he saw this brother of his, and he said it was the last time you were all there, in Vegas. "I go to see him once or twice a year," he said. And he said that his brother looked just like him. Same mother. But she's dead. That's what he told me. He didn't seem that sad about it. I asked him what her name was, but he gave me a weird look as though he'd suddenly woken up and realized what he was saying. That was what made me think he really was telling the truth. I wasn't sure up until then. Like you said, I thought it could have been the drugs, something in his imagination. A hallucination. But it's a weird thing to hallucinate, isn't it – that you have a brother?'

'And a dead mother,' I said, after a pause.

She was quiet for a moment. 'The only other thing he said about it – he gave me that look, and then he turned away from me and said, "I did OK." I asked him if he meant he did OK with his family, with the family he ended up with. He said, "Yeah. They're OK. It's better than winding up in Vegas for life," and we both started laughing then, we couldn't stop.'

She gave a small, secretive smile. I guessed that the kissing part of their evening together, or whatever it had included, had started after that.

She ground out her cigarette on the bricks next to where we were sitting, and picked up her glass. Then she said just what I had been thinking. 'I wonder if his brother even knows he's dead.' Her smile was gone. 'I don't know how often they were in touch, if they talked on the phone or anything. He must know, though, right?'

I shook my head. 'I don't know. Someone might have told him – Dylan's parents? Greta and Leo, I mean.'

'Yeah,' she said. 'They would have to know that Dylan had been seeing him. They would have found a way to tell him.'

I nodded, but I wasn't sure at all. The more I thought about it, the more likely it seemed that Dylan wouldn't have told his parents – his adoptive parents (now I would forever have a kind of stammer in my brain when I thought of them as his parents) – that he was in contact with his brother. It seemed to me that it was the kind of secret he would have enjoyed keeping. This was back before I really understood just how much he loved secrets, and how many he carried around, but I knew something about it.

I thought back to the funeral. There had been some unfamiliar faces there, but I hadn't paid any attention to them. The whole event had been so surreal that every face had an unfamiliar cast. Had there been a young guy who looked like Dylan? I could remember someone in a dark blue suit, towards the back, as we came in. Shorter than Dylan. I didn't know why he was standing out in my mind now. All I could recall was a back turned towards me, a stiff, athletic stance, half a profile, a sharp line of cheek and jaw. The image faded into the bright sunlight that had pierced the room for a short while, angling in through the high windows, before the service had started. It could have been anyone.'

'He would have told Sally,' I said, meaning his sister.

Lily nodded. 'Probably. And she couldn't have cared less about telling this brother of his when he died.'

Girls tended to hate Sally. Lily was no exception.

'I'll ask her,' I said.

Lily raised one eyebrow artfully. 'You do that,' she said out of the corner of her mouth as she lit another cigarette.

I was unsteady on my feet as I stood, legs stiff and numb. My cell phone was inside the house, in the pocket of my jacket, slung over a chair. Sally's number was in there. I thought about calling her, and then it seemed like such a complicated task to go in, retrieve the phone, scroll through the names until I found hers . . . It wasn't that late but I was suddenly as exhausted as though it were the early hours of the morning.

This was what it was like, being around my family, worn out after only half a day in their company.

The glass sliding door stuck when I tried to open it, and eventually gave way with a thud.

When I did find Sally's number in my phone it went straight to voice mail. She sounded young and old at the same time, girlish and rough and Californian, like a twelve year old who has been smoking a packet of cigarettes a day for years. 'It's Sally.' Other voices sounded in the background, a muted shriek. 'Leave a message.' And it ended abruptly, cutting off the end of the last word. There was a long beep.

I hadn't thought it through – I probably should have hung up, but some kind of politeness training took over. 'Sally, hi, it's Elliot. Dylan's friend.' Lily gave me a withering stare over her shoulder. I paused. 'Give me a call when you get a chance. OK, bye.'

I picked up the bottle of whisky to take it out to Lily. Sitting there on the porch, she reminded me strongly of Sally for a moment, with her straight hair tied back like that in a long ponytail. I wondered whether Lily was thinking about Dylan. She had been so quietly triumphant just then, with her revelations about him, pleased to be able to claim an intimacy that I couldn't. I wondered about this 'thing' they'd had, but it seemed to amount to just that time at the party on drugs and a drink another time, probably a night together. I found that I wasn't that interested.

There didn't seem to be any reason to doubt her story. When I tried to remember who had originally come up with Las Vegas as the place for our first post-college get-together, it wouldn't come clear. It could have been Dylan, but I couldn't remember him making a concrete suggestion. It would have been like him to guide the conversation in that direction in a subtle way, so that it felt as though it had been someone else's idea, or an idea that just suggested itself naturally. Dylan had never shown any strong feelings about it one way or another. He hadn't seemed too upset the one year we had gone somewhere else; we had ended up in California that time, convenient to his family – his adoptive family; the unconscious correction again. He could have paid a visit to Vegas himself easily from there in any case. And he hadn't seemed overjoyed when we decided to go back to Vegas the following year – or had that been his idea, as well?

Lily stood and stretched her arms out wide, showing her yoga-trained poise, then raised them above her head and swung them down again. I'd been standing there, lost in thought, and hadn't taken the bottle out to her as I had intended to do. She turned around to face me and smiled, then yawned.

'TV for me,' she said. When she came through the door, she stepped over to me and stood close. I thought she was going to put her hand on my arm, but she didn't. 'I know you miss him,' she said, meaning to be kind.

I thought of Dylan, sitting in the bar at the Flamingo with his gin martini in front of him, and tried to picture this brother there next to him, a younger twin. It didn't work. I couldn't imagine that he'd hang out with him at the hotels on the Strip. Somewhere downtown, maybe. Somewhere out of the way.

Where did people live in Vegas, in a city whose population was made up mostly of visitors? From the plane, flying in and out of the city, you could see the uniform blocks of residential neighbourhoods that spread out into the desert, apartment buildings, houses with backyards, houses where families would live. Imagine growing up in Las Vegas; imagine going to school there, I thought; and reminded myself that it was probably a lot like growing up and going to school anywhere.

And there were other places. Driving to and from the airport, you passed plenty of sad motels where people obviously lived on a more or less permanent basis, problem gamblers who went broke and couldn't leave. That life was a mystery to me.

Somewhere out there, in some part of the city I'd never visited, was someone who looked just like Dylan. It didn't occur to me then that I would ever meet this person, that he would ever be part of my life.

Lily poured herself another drink and switched on the television. She turned the sound down low, and slouched down in the couch so that she was practically horizontal. I sat next to her. She raised the remote control and started flicking through the channels. On a shopping channel a woman was displaying her hands proudly for the camera, showing the rings and bracelets loaded onto her fingers and wrists. Lily kept going. Cops getting into their car, a recent episode of *Law & Order* or some other police show. A space shuttle hurtling into the sky. The silent face of the moon, black and white. Blips of sound. A submarine movie.

'Stop,' I said.

'No,' she said. 'No submarines.'

She continued to press the button and eventually came to rest on a repeat episode of *ER*, old enough that it had George Clooney in his green doctor's outfit, smiling and then switching into serious hospital mode as the ambulance crew came crashing into the room, pushing a patient on a trolley, shouting commands and statistics. 'Intubate!'

I felt suddenly cold. 'Turn it off,' I said.

'I want to see this.'

'I don't want to watch it.'

'So fuck off and go to bed,' she said, genially enough, and shifted her position, lifting her feet up to sit cross-legged. She looked toward me a little as she moved. 'Shit,' she said. 'Sorry.' She pressed the button. A different submarine movie appeared, dark interiors and steady red lights, and Lily let it be.

It must have shown on my face. The medical crew, the emergency room, the desperate, rushing urgency of the actors' voices and movements – all I could see was Dylan there on the trolley, as I'd imagined him to be after the accident, surrounded by hopeless activity, the life already knocked out of him.

It had happened in LA, a work trip; he'd been staying with his parents. Sally had been the one to call me, early the next morning. It sounded as though she were reading from a script; she'd probably called several other people before me. It was instantaneous, she said, he was dead by the time he reached the hospital, there was nothing anyone could have done.

'What about the driver?' I asked.

It took her a second or two to figure out that I was talking about the driver of the car that had hit him. It was a girl, she told me, driving her parents' SUV. 'She's from Santa Barbara, that's all I know. She's fine. The car's fine. I guess she'll be totally screwed up for life.' She started crying then, small, choking sobs.

I offered to call Tallis and the others. Sally stopped crying and slipped back into script mode. She'd already called Brian. She wanted to call the rest of them herself. I didn't argue. I called Brian right away, but his phone didn't pick up and we didn't talk until later that night.

'It's OK,' I said to Lily, 'I'm going to bed anyway.'

But instead I sat on the couch, my body seemingly glued there, and stared at the screen without seeing it. I kept thinking about the others – Cameron, Tallis, Brian – and wondering whether they knew about the brother. A strange sensation a little like vertigo crept up on me, as though the mysterious force of gravity had suddenly shifted sideways, altering my balance, my sense of relationship to all other objects and people.

Dylan wasn't exactly who I thought he was. Lily knew something about him that had been a secret from me. This changed my idea of her relationship with Dylan, which was evidently more intimate than I had known, and my idea of her as well. And I wondered about the others. Did they know? There it was again, the vertigo, the ground tilting under me.

I raised my glass to drink and saw that it was empty. I put the weird tilting thing down to being a little drunk, and suddenly relaxed. I thought about calling one of them, but didn't, unsure whether I wanted to reveal my ignorance.

Next to me on the couch Lily fidgeted and drank. 'Can I change it now?' she asked. 'You know how claustrophobic I get with these submarine movies.'

'Change away,' I said, and leaned my head back and shut my eyes, shutting out the sounds of the movie Lily eventually settled on.

Cameron, Dylan and I had younger sisters, while Tallis and Brian had no siblings; Cameron was the only one among us with a brother, an older brother, and we probably all envied him that a little. My thoughts travelled back to the hospital after the car crash in college, the afternoon I'd visited with Tallis. Just as we were about to go, leaving Dylan sitting next to Cameron, who was sleeping, Cameron's brother, Sean, had arrived. I guessed that Dylan had called him and he'd driven up from the city. It was the first time I'd met him. Sean was a carpenter of some kind, tall and broad, several years older than the rest of us. Dylan introduced us and we all shook hands like adults, and I immediately felt less grown-up than usual, and as though in some way it was impolite of us to be up and walking around while Cameron was still on his back.

Just before Dylan stood up to greet Sean I saw something flash across his face, before the solemn, welcoming smile; something swift and immediately concealed. I didn't quite know how to read it: resentment, hostility, a mysterious angst? I couldn't think of any reason for it to do with Sean personally, and it didn't seem directed at him anyway. At the time I had wondered whether Dylan was upset on some level about being displaced from his position as surrogate brother by the bedside, a role he'd taken to so well. Now I looked back on it and imagined that expression endlessly complicated by the idea of his adoption, his distant Vegas brother.

I saw Dylan not only giving up his place by the bed to Sean, but I also wondered what he saw of himself there, the lost chances he might have perceived to do with himself as an older brother to be looked up to, to act as protector or guide. I didn't know when Dylan had found out about his adoption, whether he'd always known, or when he'd found out about the extra detail of the younger brother, but when I thought about the way he'd looked at Sean I felt sure that he must have known then, and that he was watching a tableau that he felt excluded from in so many ways. It was a role he played with all of us in his own way, the collection of friends that he'd chosen, the surrogate brothers he'd constructed for himself.

When my phone rang I was asleep, lying on the couch. My neck gave a twinge when I pulled myself up to a sitting position, echoes of that whack between the shoulder blades years earlier, some muscles and bones that had got pulled out of place and still complained from time to time. The phone bleeped and quivered on the corner of the coffee table, inching its way over toward the edge with the force of its vibrations. Sally's name and number were illuminated on the little screen.

'Hello?' I said. 'Sally?'

'Hey, Elliot.' The rough, smoky voice. 'You called me. Are you in town?'

'What? No.'

'Were you asleep?' she asked in disbelief. I looked over at the clock in the kitchen. It was 12:30. 'Elliot? You called me.'

'Yep.' I stretched, tried to wake up, tried to put a question together for her.

Her voice was muffled for a moment, as though she was talking to someone else with her hand over the receiver, then it came clear. 'Where are you?'

'I'm at home for the weekend.'

'OK. What's up, Elliot?' I could hear the sound of her lips pinched around a cigarette, then the smoke as it was released.

'I'm good. How are you?'

'I'm just fine.'

'Sally.'

'Is this about Dylan?' she asked.

'Yes – sort of. No, not sort of. Yes. It's about Dylan.'

'OK, fire away.' Her breezy tone slipped and I could hear an edge of sadness in her voice, or maybe I just wanted to hear it. She coughed, a terrible rattle that belonged to a much older body.

'Look, I was just talking to Lily tonight.'

'Lily?'

'You know, my sister.'

'Oh, OK. Go on.'

'Did you know Dylan had a brother?' A beat of silence. 'Did you know he was adopted?'

'Lily told you that?'

'Yeah.'

She sighed. 'I didn't know he talked about that with her. That is bizarre. Never mind. OK. To answer your question, yes, I knew about it. And yes, he was at the funeral, he knows about Dylan being dead.'

'I had no idea.'

'No, I know. I can't believe he told Lily.'

'I can't believe he didn't tell me.'

'He didn't like to talk about it.'

'Are you adopted, too?'

She sighed again. 'What, are you drunk? No, I'm not adopted. Just Dylan. Why are you interested?'

'I'm just . . . surprised, I guess.'

'Dylan was full of surprises.'

'I'm sorry, Sally.'

'I know I woke you up just now. Go back to bed.'

'Can I give you a call in the morning?'

I could hear her smiling. 'Oh, sure. Take care, Elliot. Goodnight.' A singsong pitch to the last word, dragging *night* out over two notes. She spoke again to someone with her – 'OK, OK, I'm coming!' – and the phone went dead.

Sally was short for Semele, a name she hated. It was Dylan's custom to introduce her as Semele, and she would always say 'Sally', correcting him, blinking and smiling brightly while he watched her, amused. He called her Sally the rest of the time just like everyone else.

Semele was the name of a nymph in a Greek myth. Greta, their mother, explained it to me when I first visited the house, telling me how she'd come across it while reading Ovid for the first time, and always knew that it would be the name of her daughter.

'And she grew into it, don't you think – look how she owns it. She could be a nymph. She's so beautiful.'

Their house was a sprawling, modernist piece of 1950s architecture, low slung with plenty of glass that made me feel always slightly exposed to outside view. We were in the kitchen looking out over the terrace at the swimming pool. It was late afternoon heading toward evening, blue leaching out of the sky, paint-like streaks of cloud reflected in the glass walls. The place was like a mirror and a fishbowl at once, all display and reflection.

As we were talking Sally swam across the pool with an elegant breaststroke. She climbed out, wearing an orange swimsuit with holes cut out to show the sides of her body, long hair streaming water down her back and her high, sharp cheekbones glowing in the harsh final rays of sunlight.

'A water nymph,' Greta said, admiring her.

I had to agree. Greta seemed to watch me to make sure I was also appreciating her daughter to the proper extent, willing to offer whatever worship was due to unnaturally beautiful nymphs. She smiled, content and statuesque, a little like a goddess herself, and seemed to be satisfied by whatever I said and however I looked as I watched Sally wrap herself in a midnight-blue shirt and walk up the terrace from the pool to the house.

From what I remembered about Ovid, nymphs that got a mention in his stories usually met bad ends: got raped or cursed, metamorphosed into trees or birds or plants. Sally stepped inside, making wet footprints on the floor, just as I was about to ask Greta what had happened to Ovid's Semele.

'I was just saying to Elliot what a beautiful water nymph you are,' Greta said.

Sally opened the fridge and pulled out a can of soda.

'Oh, Mom,' she said. 'Give me a break.' Her wet swimsuit and skin had soaked through her shirt, darkening the fabric. She opened the can with a loud crack, handed it to me, and took another for herself. She took a long drink and wiped her hand across her mouth. 'The water's nice, Elliot. Are you going to swim?'

'Ah, no.'

She went back outside and unwrapped herself, and lay down on her stomach on the tiles by the side of the pool, reading a Penguin paperback whose cover matched her swimsuit. It was Camus, or Sartre, something serious and French. The sunset that came on was fiery orange – everything in LA was edged with that colour, it seemed.

Greta had a similar kind of powerful affection for Dylan, a fierce pride that was potent in everything she said to him, every touch. She loved to be around him, but never harangued him into spending time with her, or at home, or complained that he wasn't staying for dinner or calling often enough.

My own parents' pride in my achievements often left a sour taste in my mouth. Without meaning to I had managed to fall into a career that matched with their sense of what was valuable and significant. 'He's a professor,' my mother loved to say, and would use the word *literature* as much as she could in connection with my work, never the more prosaic *English*. She and my father both pronounced my work 'wonderful' on the few occasions I gave them samples of it. One of these was my first published article, an overly long piece on an obscure collection of plays that appeared in a decent journal the year I graduated. The journal had sent me ten copies of the piece, beautifully typeset on small sheets of paper, and in a moment of happiness and generosity I had sent one to my mother. 'Wonderful.'

They had insisted on receiving a copy of my dissertation, bound in its ugly green cover. It was now gathering dust on their bookshelf, causing me some revulsion whenever I visited and caught sight of it, taller and fatter than anything else around it apart from the ancient encyclopedia set with which it was placed.

My sense of how Greta felt about Dylan was coloured by my own desires, my fantasy of what it would be like to have her and Leo as parents. Greta's way of being proud and admiring of Dylan had always struck me as having a kind of integrity, not contaminated and overdetermined by her own priorities. She asked him questions about his studies, about his work, that seemed to stem from actual interest in what was important to him, never peppered with the 'Haven't you thought about . . .' and 'Wouldn't it make more sense to . . .' that characterized my parents' conversations with me. You could tell that she was always aware of Dylan's place in the room, her ear tuned to the sound of his voice, even when she took part in other conversations. She loved Sally as well, but although I never saw them argue, there was a simmering tension between them that was less evident with Dylan.

I marvelled at the way Greta never seemed to become overbearing. Dylan felt differently about it. If I ever expressed anything of my admiration for his parents and their relationship with him, particularly his mother, he quickly became dismissive.

'Oh, she knows how to perform. The perfect mother.'

'I'm not saying she's perfect,' I would protest, at the same time wondering, guiltily, what imperfections there could possibly be.

'All I'm saying is, you see her in public. And she's very good at reading people. She wants to be liked. She wants you to like her,' he said once.

This was surprising, because she always seemed so confident, so sure of herself. It was also absurdly flattering.

'See, she has everyone all figured out. She . . .' He sighed. 'She calculates. She thinks everything through. She's always busy being perfect. And she expects us all to be equally busy being perfect for her benefit.'

This was confusing to me.

'It's lucky I'm so perfect, isn't it?' he said, with a rare dose of sarcasm. 'It reflects well on her. She's very pleased with how I turned out.' The bitterness in his voice surprised me.

Knowing about the adoption now, I struggled with new interpretations of all those dynamics. Dylan, the adopted one, the child who was chosen and definitely wanted – although perhaps only on terms that Greta established. I couldn't help reflecting on whether his charm, his charisma, was something he had worked at in order to compensate for having been given away in the first place, or to earn his parents' love. It hadn't occurred to me that Greta's love would be conditional like that – it seemed so fixed and complete – but now I wondered. What if he hadn't turned out good-looking and good with people – so evidently perfect? And what if Sally hadn't turned out like a nymph; how would she have worn her name then?

As I tried to fall asleep in my old bed later I made another effort to remember the funeral in more detail, to see if I could put a face to the Vegas brother with more confidence, but the scene was as hazy as it had been earlier. I'd taken the red-eye to LA and the plane had been late. In a way the delay was probably not a bad thing: I spent hours waiting at the airport, on the plane, in the taxi in bad traffic from the airport worrying about being late to the funeral or, worse, missing it entirely, and this anxiety overshadowed all the nervousness and difficult feelings that went along with the event. If I had started thinking about what it would be like to see Greta or Leo in person, or Sally, I would have been overwhelmed with concern that maybe I wouldn't get to them at all. At the same time, a small, treacherous part of me sat calmly throughout the whole journey, quietly thinking that maybe it wouldn't be the biggest disaster, the worst thing ever, to miss the funeral, to miss seeing all those people and going through the whole thing, especially through no fault of my own ... That voice grew quieter as I grew closer, and by the time it became evident that I was going to make it after all, the feeling of relief worked in its own way to drown out the other worries.

Another taxi pulled into the drive outside the small chapel at the same time, and Cameron stepped out seconds after I had closed the car door. He turned and saw me, and I walked toward him.

He gave a long sigh. 'I thought I was going to be late.'

'Me too.'

He searched my face, so intensely that it unnerved me, and I looked away.

He put his hand on my shoulder, and then pulled me into an embrace, his arms tightening around me before letting go, and we passed through the tall arch of the doorway into the chapel, where Tallis was already waiting with Brian close to the front. I caught sight of Caroline, Dylan's girlfriend of half a year or so, her face set and blank, sitting with one of Dylan's work colleagues, an editor from the publishing house.

Sally had approached me just as I'd been deciding whether or not to go over to talk to Caroline. I'd called her a couple of times over the past week without success.

'Cremation?' I asked. Cameron had mentioned it to me on the phone a few days earlier.

Sally glanced over at the coffin at the front of the room. I couldn't bring myself to look at it. She nodded.

'What are they going to do with the ashes?'

'There's a place we used to go on vacation, further north, in Washington ... You know the San Juans?' Her voice was more ragged than ever, soft and thin sounding. 'I mean, he didn't leave instructions or anything.' She squinted at me. 'I mentioned to Mom and Dad that he might like, you know, you guys to take them to Vegas.'

'Really?'

She shrugged.

A girl her age in a black dress came up and stood next to her, waiting to talk to her, ignoring me.

'It doesn't matter,' Sally said, and the girl led her away. The room was filled with people, but the faces of my friends were the only ones I focused on, the only ones I remembered with any clarity.

The day before my flight to Vegas there was a knock on my door sometime in the late morning while I was trying to get through a pile of grading that was supposed to be finished before I left. The night before, I'd sabotaged the effort with a fourth glass of wine and wound up watching old movies on TV until I fell asleep on the couch. I lived on the third floor of a house that had been converted into apartments, and the downstairs buzzers had been broken for as long as anyone could remember. When I opened the door Natasha was there in her black coat, cheeks flushed with cold, mouth shiny with red lipstick. She smiled with her lips closed.

'Hi. You left this at my house,' she said, and handed me a button-down shirt I'd been wearing over my T-shirt that night.

I almost said 'Great,' wanting to say that it was great to see her, and managed to welcome her inside.

'I was on my way to campus,' she said, 'so I thought I'd bring it over to you. I called but your phone was busy.'

I'd made one brief call that morning, to a student who had left me a message the day before, wanting another extension on the due date for a paper.

'Well, thanks. Would you like some coffee? Or tea?' I gathered a pile of papers strewn across the coffee table and put them on my desk on top of other papers. 'I was grading,' I said.

'I don't want to interrupt.'

'No, you're not. Sorry, it's a mess. But let me make you tea or something,' I offered, trying to keep her there.

I went into the kitchen, which was just a small corner crammed with sink, fridge and stove through an archway from the living room, and filled the kettle. The gas flame lit with a whoosh.

'Take off your coat,' I said, adjusting the flame. 'It's hot in here. The heat's broken.'

The radiators had been making loud banging noises all night and all morning, as though someone in the building were hitting the pipes with a heavy wrench, and it felt like about eighty degrees. Turning the knobs never seemed to make any difference to how much heat came out; they twirled around uselessly in endless circles.

'Or I can make coffee,' I said.

Her coat made whispery sounds as she shrugged it off and set it down. 'Tea would be nice. Thank you. Milk and sugar.'

She was sitting on the couch when I came back in, and I sat at the other end, handing her a mug of tea. I'd made mine the same as hers although I didn't normally take sugar, and the sweetness hit my mouth hard when I tasted it.

'There's your shirt.'

She'd laid it over the back of the armchair by the couch. It had been next to my body, and handled by her. The shape of my arms was still there faintly in the way the sleeves lay, creased around the elbow and soft at the shoulders. It had a deflated, empty look about it, like a dent in a mattress that shows the imprint of a body, or rumpled sheets that tell you exactly the gesture the person used when they pushed them out of the way.

'Thanks,' I said. 'Sorry about that.'

'It's not a problem,' she said.

I set down my mug on the table. It was one I rarely used, a gift from my mother with musical notes printed on it. Something famous, something she'd decided was my favourite piece of classical music. It was the only other clean mug available.

'Aren't you going to Vegas soon?' she asked.

'Yes. Tomorrow, actually.'

'Tomorrow?'

'Yes,' I said, and was on the verge of asking her if she wanted to go out with me that night, to get a drink or dinner.

'I'm going down to New Jersey this afternoon,' she said.

'Seeing your cousin?'

She nodded.

I thought about telling her about my own Jersey origins but decided it could wait for another time.

She stood and stepped over to examine my bookshelf, mug in her hands. 'You have a lot of books,' she said.

It could have been a compliment or a criticism. It didn't seem to require a response although it made me defensive for a moment. It didn't seem like a lot to me; they barely filled the built-in shelves on either side of the fireplace. Most of my books were in my office.

'You like Russian literature?' Natasha asked me with a smile.

She'd been looking at the three Dostoyevsky novels on a lower shelf, holding her hair away from her face with her free hand. I'd started *Crime and Punishment* years before with some idea that it was essential reading for anyone in my profession and couldn't get through it. It was starting to feel as though everything she said or asked was some kind of trick question.

'What you see there is the extent of my Russian literature collection,' I said. She had moved on already.

I found myself rehearsing in my mind the conversation I would have had with Dylan about her. He was the only one of them I actually talked to about women, about heartbreak and loss, and the times when things worked out, as they sometimes did. He would have listened attentively and then convinced me in only a few words that she was waiting for me to make the first move. I got that far with it before I remembered. At that moment he appeared in my peripheral vision, leaning against one of the bookshelves with his ankles crossed and arms folded, smiling apologetically, and then was gone.

'Elliot?'

Natasha was looking right at me and I guessed from her expression that I was acting like a person preoccupied with loss. Even at moments like those, when I could see that my behavior was coincident with documented symptoms of grief, my actions weren't quite convincing to myself; I somehow doubted their authenticity. Because I wasn't preoccupied, not in a constant way. Sadness was not an ever-present foreground hum; it faded in and out and took its place alongside all the other usual anxieties and desires. Days went by when I wouldn't think about him at all, and then I would, and the sadness would slink out from the background mix and envelop me.

I know it looks like grief, I wanted to confess, *but it's something else.*

Something else – what? Less deep, or more? Something more shallow, or more complicated, or just somehow lacking? I was probably resistant to the idea that my own emotional processes could conform to any conventional diagram, any predetermined structure of feeling. I wanted to believe I was exceptional, that I had individual elements of interesting unpredictability that meant what I felt wasn't like what everybody else felt. But at some level there was also the suspicion that I was missing some fundamental psychological piece, the idea that other people, who were better adjusted, or better friends, or simply better people, would feel the proper, authentic stages of grief.

'Sorry,' I said. 'How's Eamonn?'

'Oh.' She rolled her eyes and turned to the shelf again. 'Forget it.'

I couldn't tell whether she meant that I should avoid the topic, or that it was a hopeless situation, or that she ought to forget him. All of the above.

When she turned back to me I could see pity vying with other feelings. She frowned, as though I was a problem she was trying to solve. I wondered whether her brain, with its scientifically trained ways of thinking, travelled entirely different paths in its approach to problems than mine did. I felt strangely paralyzed in that way that you feel in dreams sometimes, wanting to move and yet unable to take a step. Was this another symptom of grief, I wondered, catalogued and tagged somewhere? Or just my own typical inability to act on impulse?

'Good luck with this trip of yours to Vegas,' she said. 'I hope your friends behave themselves.'

I walked her to the door and she buttoned her coat and pulled on a hat, a loose black beret. Her skin was pale against all the dark clothes, faintly luminous in the dim light of the hall. She reached her face up to mine when she was right at the door, standing close to me, and kissed my cheek briefly, her hand on my shoulder. When she stepped back I gave into one impulse – I smoothed the pieces of hair away from her eye, and her brow was warm under my fingers for a second. Her eyes closed and opened in a long blink. She smiled and said goodbye.

I closed the door and took the shirt from the armchair, reluctant for a moment to wash away whatever imprint of herself she'd left on it.

6

We stayed at a different hotel each year in an attempt to inject some kind of variety into the experience. They were always decent ones on the Strip after the time Cameron screwed up and put us in a really bad hotel at the wrong end of downtown and we all had to arrange somewhere else to stay after we found bedbugs in every room. There were only two real requirements: the hotel had to have at least four stars and we had to have rooms that didn't look out on an air shaft. Tallis was a little more precise in his personal requirements and routinely complained his way into an upgraded room (farther from the elevators, a better view, a higher floor).

We followed a routine, of sorts, that never varied: each night of our visit we would all meet at 7 p.m. at the bar in the centre of the gaming room at the Flamingo. In the mornings if we were up by eleven then we met at the buffet of whatever hotel we were staying in, but this was a looser arrangement. The rest of the time we usually ended up spending together in any case, more or less, but the rendezvous at the Flamingo was the one place and time we were guaranteed to meet at least once a day.

It started out that way because the Flamingo was the first hotel we stayed at, our first visit in the mid-nineties. Back in those days there was a nervous edge around the place; other old-school Vegas classics, like the Sands, had been demolished to make way for newer, flashier casinos, and no one expected the Flamingo to hold on the way it did. It had never been the classiest or the cheesiest or the biggest or the best, but it managed to hang on anyway, flying somehow under the demolition radar, with its cast of loyal, unstylish gamblers. The nervous edge gave way to laid-back confidence.

When I walked up the shallow steps in the hot, tired air of the evenings, the giant lotus flower suspended over the entrance never failed to make me think of an enormous electric vagina, with its rows of pulsating light globes in shades of pink turning on and off in a carefully timed pattern to create the effect of undulating waves. If you stared at them for long enough the effect of wavelike motion stopped, and you saw only a collection of single globes, alight, then not alight. On, and then off.

It had crossed my mind that it might be somehow appropriate for us to stay at the Flamingo again this time, to commemorate that first visit when we were all together. I mentioned it to Tallis when he was in the first stages of organizing the trip but he hadn't been enthusiastic.

'I looked into it,' he told me. 'They're renovating. The old rooms are shit. The new ones won't all be ready yet, they won't be able to guarantee it, and we'll get stuck somewhere with a crap bathroom and stains on the couch.'

I didn't tell him that my rooms in Vegas over the years had almost invariably had problems of exactly the kind he'd mentioned; it seemed to be part of the deal if you didn't book the more expensive suites.

Tallis hadn't been in charge of organizing for a long time, and he was determined to do a good job. 'It won't be all over the place like it was last year, when Brian totally fucked it up.'

Brian had left it until the last minute – he never should have been put in charge of arranging anything for the group, since he still wasn't talking to Cameron and resented having to include him at all – and we ended up not being able to all stay in the same place. Brian and Dylan were parked up at the Venetian, in rooms full of velvet cushions and tassels, and Cameron, Tallis and I had rooms miles away at the Luxor. We could have got rooms together at the Excalibur, Brian explained, but no one wanted that, not after the previous year when we had all stayed there and hated it.

On this trip, we were staying at the MGM Grand, a place we hadn't been to before. Tallis had spent hours online comparing the various kinds of available deals and had ended up booking us one that included free entry to one of the hotel nightclubs and a discount on a poolside cabana. On our last trip Tallis and Dylan had split the ridiculously high cost of renting one of these little tents for a day, and Tallis liked the experience so much that he was determined never to go to the pool without one again. It was true, what he said, that it was impressive to girls. And provided necessary shade.

The airport was the usual nightmare of crowds and endless waiting for luggage, the walk from the gate to the exits impossibly long, filled with rows of slot machines that nobody played. I stepped out into the dusty heat, and two giant men in matching Elvis costumes – one black with clear crystal rhinestones, the other white with ruby-coloured stones in an identical pattern – pushed past me with their Ray-Bans and sideburns, unsmiling. The line for a taxi was long and the afternoon was hot and glary. Already my jeans were sticking to my skin. I bought a ticket for a shuttle and climbed on board to wait while it filled up. A bride-to-be and her family, flat Midwestern vowels all around, were already on board, each of them on cell phones to a different member of the bridal party. An elderly Indian woman in an olive-and-gold sari climbed on, followed by a young girl who might have been her granddaughter, solemn-faced in T-shirt and jeans too short for her long, thin legs. They sat in front of me. I shut my eyes and leaned my head against the window. The bus filled up within ten minutes and drove away.

The bride-to-be and her entourage got off at the Excalibur. I'd heard Marcia, the bride, explaining to someone on the phone how the place was really family-friendly, that the kids would be hanging out at the pool all day. The low point of our stay at the Excalibur last year had been the short time we spent at the pool one afternoon, which was crowded with a gang of undergrads who were smoking, drinking, practically fucking, and vomiting both into the potted palms and the water at one end of the pool. I wondered whether I should have warned her but couldn't think what I would have actually said. It was all booked by now, and they had a bargain, as I'd heard her and her uncle and aunt discussing on the way there. Her gown was medieval style. It had a medieval veil. I knew far more than I wanted to about her wedding outfit and everything to do with her wedding after fifteen minutes on the bus with them.

It always amazed me that people actually came to Vegas with the intention of getting married – it wasn't just drunk people being impulsive and going on down to the chapel with their boyfriend or girlfriend or someone they'd picked up the night before; it was actual engaged people who planned it all and came here for the entire package with their extended families. I suppose it wasn't that weird – they came for much the same reasons that I and my friends did: it was accessible, inexpensive.

The shuttle arrived at Hooters Casino Hotel, across from the MGM. The Indian woman and the little girl with her rose from their seats and went slowly down the steps. I followed them. They collected three large suitcases from the baggage compartment of the bus, each one held together with pieces of knotted rope. I offered to help them but the woman just shook her head, her face a mask of contempt and disbelief as she looked at the hotel. The little girl's eyes were wide as she glanced around, gripping the handle on one huge wheeled suitcase.

I crossed the busy road to the MGM and entered the lobby. The smell wasn't too strong just inside the entrance. That smell was my strongest sensory memory of Vegas, the thing that told me I had really arrived: old smoke and sweat and stale air-conditioned air recycled a thousand times. I never got used to it, no matter how many days I stayed. The farther I moved inside the hotel, the stronger it became.

The lobby was a massive expanse of golden polished granite with a disproportionately low ceiling. Each check-in counter had a line of at least twenty people snaking away from it. I made my way over to the shortest one and recognized Brian in the line next to me, his arm around a woman with light brown hair cropped close to her head. She was small, slim, boyish-looking, wearing a short denim skirt. So this was Cynthia.

'Brian,' I called.

He turned around. 'Hey, man! Good to see you. Come on over here.'

I wheeled my suitcase over and joined them in the line. The overweight couple behind us, dressed identically in orange T-shirts and beige shorts, sun visors and sunglasses, shifted noisily. She said something to him in a language that sounded like German, or possibly Dutch. He repeated the same four or five words back to her, but with a different intonation. I gave them an apologetic smile.

Brian released Cynthia in order to give me a hug, a quick embrace that finished with a short, hard pat on the back. I'd never quite gotten the hang of it myself.

'This is Cynthia,' he said.

She shook my hand with a light grip. 'It's great to meet you,' she said, smiling and showing her perfect teeth. 'It's great to be here.'

She looked too clean for someone who had just come off an airplane. Everyone else in the lobby was wrinkled and tired and dazed, apart from the impeccably dressed Japanese guy directly in front of us whose jeans had knife-sharp creases down the front.

Brian put his hands into his pockets, nervous.

'It's great that you could make it,' I said, and saw his shoulders relax. 'I hope you won't be too bored.'

Cynthia looped her arm through Brian's and smiled again. Her eyes were deep-set under straight brows, a washed-out denim blue. 'Oh, no. I've been looking forward to this. You know, it's all research for me.'

'That's right. Brian mentioned that.'

'I won't be in your way. I'll be wandering around, looking at all the casinos. All the sights.'

'You're in cultural studies, is that right?'

'Yes. I'm working on my dissertation proposal now.' I could hear the crisp, graduate-student professionalism in her voice, the voice she used for talking about herself to her superiors. 'And Brian tells me you're at Riverford, that's wonderful.'

We had made it to the front of the line. 'Here we are,' Brian said, and hauled his duffel bag over to the counter. Cynthia had a suitcase on wheels with a hard, shiny black shell like an insect carapace, all new-looking apart from two long scratches on one side as though it had been dragged over something sharp. Brian took over the job of dealing with the clerk, a young woman with heavy pink lipstick and hair lacquered close to her head. 'I'm checking in . . . two bookings . . .' I heard him say, and let him go ahead.

'Well, it's a job.' I smiled at Cynthia. 'It's my second year there.'

'Oh, it's wonderful,' she repeated.

I wanted to agree with her – I was new enough in the profession, close enough to the agonizing experience of being on the job market and the sense that any job would indeed be wonderful if only it would bring the process of the search to an end. And it *was* a good job – that was how everyone had described it. It was the sort of job that just about anyone would be happy with. The school was respectable, it was on the East Coast, the classes weren't too big, there were sabbaticals and fellowships, they even occasionally tenured people. But I didn't want to let on that I would have been happy with just about any job; or that by the time I'd got the call for my job interview I'd already started sending out my résumé to publishers and testing companies and private schools and other places that seemed as though they might be interested in hiring someone with a PhD on an obscure aspect of Renaissance drama.

'You're in English, right?' she asked.

I nodded, and before I had a chance to say more Brian was passing her a room key, a slim, white plastic card, and it was my turn to hand over to the clerk my ID and a credit card.

Brian tried to take Cynthia's suitcase in some show of chivalrous behaviour. They wrestled over it for a moment while I was issued with my own key, and she offered to let him carry her purse, which was large and heavy-looking in brown leather. Brian wasn't interested in that. He pretended it was something to do with already carrying his own bag over his shoulder.

'OK, take it,' Cynthia said, finally. 'My feet are killing me. Let's go.'

I looked down and realized she was wearing high heels, almost stilettos. Even with them on she barely came up to my shoulder.

Figuring out how to get to our rooms was a complicated process. The clerk had handed Brian a couple of maps of the hotel grounds and we studied them; there were several towers, some of them at the other end of the huge hotel complex. We turned out to be staying in the most central one, which the clerk had marked with a red circle, and only had to walk through one room of slot machines and a mazelike set of corridors, a convenience store and a gift shop to reach the elevators. Every corner we turned was emblazoned with several signs and arrows giving directions to attractions such as the pool and restaurants.

'Where are the lions?' Cynthia wanted to know. 'Where's the spa?'

The MGM was famous for its lion habitat, with animals they claimed were descended from 'the original' MGM lion, the one that roared on the studio logo above their motto, Ars Gratia Artis. Art for Art's Sake.

Brian glanced over at the list of signs near the elevators. 'Lion Habitat' was there at the bottom. 'We'll see the lions later,' he said. 'They're over there somewhere. You'll have to call the desk to find out where the spa is. I think there might be more than one.'

I asked whether the spa was part of her research, only half joking.

'Very funny.' She smiled. 'Well, I have to look my best for all this clubbing we're doing tonight, right, Brian? I guess it is all in the name of research. Pedicures for research.'

'You're researching nightclubs?'

'No. I'm working on –'

Whatever she said was drowned out by screams of 'Yahoo!' from a group of people behind us. There weren't any machines in that direction – not that I'd seen, unless there were machines in the convenience store, which seemed possible but unlikely.

'I'm sorry?' I asked.

'Replicas,' she said. 'Authenticity.'

The 'Yahoo!' scream started up again, more people joining in this time.

'Are there machines over there?' Brian asked.

'I don't know,' I said. 'But it sounds as though someone just won something.'

There were ten elevators, a crowd of people waiting for each one. I got out at the sixth floor. Brian and Cynthia were up on twelve.

'See you at seven,' Brian said.

My room was at the far end of the corridor, away from the elevators. I pulled my suitcase over the soundless carpeted floor. The walls were lined with black-and-white portraits of stars from Hollywood's golden age, larger than life, in heavy gilt frames, in keeping with the theme of the hotel: Old Hollywood glamour. Cary Grant grinned at me. I'd always hated his self-satisfied smile.

The room was all tones of dark beige and brown, like a sepia photograph. An ugly armoire faced the bed, and opened to reveal a television inside. The windows gave me a view of a dirty hotel rooftop and Hooters across the road, and the false skyscrapers of the New York, New York casino. The windows didn't open. They barely even had frames, were basically large, thick plates of glass stuck into the walls. It was hard to tell whether they were tinted or dirty, coated with a fine layer of brown desert dust that darkened and condensed around the edges. The air-conditioning hummed and whirred.

It was 5 p.m., the clock beside the bed told me. The sun was still high in the sky. I showered and dressed, paced the floor for a while, and looked inside the fridge at the obscenely expensive little bottles of wine, tiny bottles of vodka. It was tempting. My shirt itched. Television, I thought, and looked for the remote control. It took a while; by the time I found it, in a corner of the armoire, the effort it would have taken to turn on the set and figure out how to watch anything didn't seem worth it. I looked through the stack of brochures and papers on the desk.

When I looked back at the clock it still said 5:00, the red digital numbers unblinking. I tried to find the switch to change the time, but all I could succeed in doing was getting the numbers to flash 00:00 a couple of times before they went straight back to 5:00. The colon between the numbers started blinking on and off, although it seemed too fast to be counting down actual seconds.

I could have called one of the others. Instead I decided to go down to the hotel bar alone and get a drink. I started to look forward to it, imagining the soft sound of a piano in a high-ceilinged space, the sight of women's legs in skirts and high-heeled shoes, the taste of alcohol. By the time I reached the elevator my mood had lifted already in anticipation. Vegas was like that for me. I never failed to expect that atmosphere, even though I never discovered it.

The piano sounded just as I had expected, although the ceiling was low and dark. The tone was muted and soothing, the player hidden from my view by large potted palms. I ordered a Manhattan and thought of the imitation skyline across the road, the fake Empire State Building, and the real one, my most common view of it, seen from one of those blocks at the intersection of Greenwich Village and the East Village around the NYU campus. Low cloud sat across it in my memory. I couldn't imagine clouds coming near this Vegas version. The weather was one big thing they couldn't imitate or manipulate. What was the Empire State Building without the clouds obscuring its top, the tower reaching into the sky? Or the Eiffel Tower without the miles of green park around it, and mist; Venice without the humidity and ever-present stink of wet decay?

I thought of Natasha and imagined sharing my clouds-across-the-Empire-State observation with her. I was quickly overwhelmed by a desire to be there in the city with her, to be with her in a place that mattered to me. I couldn't imagine her being very impressed with my remarks about the Empire State Building, although I did want to share the actual view with her.

I had first started drinking Manhattans in Manhattan, and the taste of the drink reminded me even more strongly of the place. I missed the sight of the Empire State Building – not pretty, like its glamorous friend the Chrysler, but just massive, just tall, not making you think anything except how big this building is. At night, when those clouds went across it, the coloured lights on its spire would shine and gleam through, making it beautiful. I'd caught sight of it once on a winter's night from outside Penn Station, the first snow of the season driving across the sky in a hard, cold wind, and it was lovely then, but in a harsh way, like a diamond. Pure icon.

The campus where I taught was high up on a hill, and in the colder months was often covered in mist, sometimes for the whole day, everything shrouded in white, wet cloud. Just the week before there had been a cold, foggy morning, mist across the entire campus transforming the place into a silent wonderland. On the walk across the mall from my building to the library, other people on the pathways were grayish blurs until they were just a couple of feet away. I wanted to be there now, in my office, looking out at the bicycle rack and the trash cans and the enmeshed Musicology building across the way, and not here, where it was permanent, dry summer outside and unchanging no-time-of-day inside. The bike rack would have been virtually empty, the campus blissfully devoid of students.

The drink worked fast on my empty stomach, producing a melancholy haze. The night ahead seemed long and it wasn't even six yet. The music coming from the piano was impossible to place, no recognizable theme or structure, bits and pieces of vaguely familiar sounding tunes strung together. I turned on my stool and looked around, and that's when I saw Brian at a table on the far side of the room in a quiet corner.

He was hunched over, sitting with his elbows on his knees, leaning in so that the table pressed against his arms. An empty glass stood in front of him, and another one half-filled with what looked like vodka and ice. Tallis was there beside him, leaning back in his chair as though wanting to put distance between himself and Brian. He reached over and put a hand on Brian's shoulder, a tentative gesture of comfort, then dropped it to the table and grasped his tall glass of beer.

I took my drink and headed over. Tallis met my eyes, his face grave. Brian continued to stare at his glass. There was a letter-size manila envelope on the table in front of him.

'Hey,' I said. 'What's up?'

I looked at Brian, and he raised his eyes to meet mine. Dark-lashed eyes, hazel that looked green when he wore brown. He had on a wrinkled, sandy-coloured T-shirt, the same thing he had been wearing when we'd run into each other in the lobby. He smelled of sweat and the sweet chemical fragrance of hair product or some kind of deodorant. There was fear in his eyes, and guilt. I thought of that ridiculous moment years before when I had stumbled on his pornography collection. This was a distant, older relative of that expression. I took a chair.

Tallis cleared his throat. 'We've got trouble,' he said, regretfully.

'Did you get one of these?' Brian asked me, words fast and urgent.

'One of what?'

They both looked from me to each other, to the envelope. Brian's name was written on it in a plain, upright hand. A waitress walked by and collected Brian's empty glass. She smiled brightly at us all.

'Can I get you anything more to drink, gentlemen?'

Tallis looked up at her and shook his head mutely, letting his gaze rest on her waist for an extra few seconds. She was young, with dark hair pulled up into a complicated construction of curls.

Brian raised his hand. 'I'll have another. Put it on the tab.'

'Yes, sir.' She smiled again and walked away.

'What is it?' I asked again when she was gone. 'Did you get some bad news?'

'Sort of,' Brian said. 'It's not exactly news. Well, it's old news.'

'So? Did you get one?' Tallis asked, repeating Brian's question.

'I don't know what you're talking about,' I said. 'I don't know what that is.'

Brian glanced at Tallis. 'Should have known.' He put his hands to his glass and turned it around and around. 'I told you he might come down. You called him, didn't you? You texted him. Why did you bring him into it, anyway?'

Tallis leaned farther back. 'Calm down,' he said. 'I didn't call Elliot.'

He sounded worried. I was starting to worry too. Brian was handling the envelope, holding it as though it had something really heavy inside.

'It's a nightmare,' he said. Then he looked up at me, challenging. 'It's not your problem though, Elliot.' He started to rise. 'I'll take off now, take a shower, see you later at the Flamingo.'

Tallis stopped him with a hand on his arm. 'Sit down. It won't hurt to tell Elliot.'

Brian paused and then sat. He took the envelope onto his knees, hiding it under the table as he pulled his chair in.

I looked to Brian for a sign: a desire for help, a desire for me to leave. But whatever was in his eyes was unintelligible. They hadn't meant to include me. As I found myself on the verge of being excluded, I looked for a reason to make them trust me. It was a strange sensation; these were the people I trusted probably most in the world, in an unthinking, ingrained kind of way. A deep emotional structure inside me began to creak complainingly as it was forced to shift into unfamiliar shapes.

'Why did you ask me if I'd got one? Did you?' I asked Tallis.

'No. I was just curious. And just out of curiosity, what did Dylan have on you?' he asked.

'Dylan?'

He nodded.

'What did he have on me? Do you mean, did he know something about me?'

I hadn't thought about it like that before. There had been no need. I had thought of the secret we'd shared about the essay as one of those things that bind people a little closer. *What did he have on you?*

'Well, I wouldn't say he "had" something,' I said. 'Although there is something. From the past. Something only Dylan knew about. Just something embarrassing.'

'Embarrassing,' Tallis repeated, raising his eyebrows a notch.

'It was a long time ago,' I said.

'From a galaxy far, far away?'

It felt as though all the whisky and sugar in my drink had already started to sweat out through my skin.

'Something embarrassing that I did, something Dylan was involved with as well.' That's all it was, I reminded myself; an embarrassing secret.

'How embarrassing?' Tallis asked carefully.

I shrugged. 'Embarrassing enough.'

My drink was finished. I lifted it to my mouth in any case and got a trickle of water from the melted ice, stale and terrible-tasting.

'But *you* don't look embarrassed,' I said to Brian. His hands were clenched into nervous fists. 'You look scared.'

He laughed then, and almost relaxed for a second.

Tallis studied him, pity and impatience in his eyes. 'Don't joke,' he said. 'He fucking well should be.'

The waitress came back and placed Brian's drink in front of him. She had another Manhattan for me as well. She smiled at me.

Tallis gave me an encouraging wink. 'Thought you might be ready for another.'

I frowned at him and put some dollars on the waitress's little tray. Brian rested his head in his hands.

'Are you going to tell me what this is all about?' I asked.

Tallis and Brian looked at each other, that conspiratorial glance again. Had they ever acted like this before? I didn't remember noticing any kind of special intimacy between them. This in itself, the indication of a shared knowledge, a closer relationship than had previously been revealed, was as unsettling as the worry about what secrets – clearly more than embarrassing – were contained in Brian's envelope.

The envelope had gone from being a mundane object, the kind of thing I saw all the time in my mailbox at the department, ten a day, to being something else. Brian's reaction made it into a sinister thing, and I began to suspect that it was what it looked like in his hands: the icon of blackmail.

'What did you do, kill someone?' I asked, impatient now.

For a horrible moment as the words left my mouth I wondered if they might have hit on the truth.

Tallis gave me a withering look. 'Don't be a moron. No.'

'OK, OK. But I'm in the dark here. Are you going to let me in or not?'

'Yes,' Brian said. 'Of course, Elliot.'

He seemed to gather resolve, and it looked as though he was trying to find the right words to start with. But his composure unravelled as he handled the envelope. Seconds passed.

Tallis stepped in. 'If I may.' Brian nodded. 'Well. This concerns some . . . events that took place in Brian's freshman year.'

'Jodie White,' Brian said suddenly, raising his head, his resolve returned. 'I raped her.'

I stared at him, incredulous.

'Oh, shit,' Tallis said, very softly. 'Brian, tell the whole fucking Strip, why don't you.'

'You raped a girl?' I asked.

'No,' Tallis said, before Brian could answer. 'That's not what happened. That's not what happened,' he repeated, more firmly, when Brian started to protest. Brian sank back into his chair, defeated. Tallis fixed me with a serious look. 'It was a complicated situation.'

This is the voice he uses to persuade people, I remember thinking, the voice he uses to sell someone something, to get someone to do something, think something, anything he wants.

'Date rape,' Brian said.

Tallis silenced him with a glare. 'I'm telling Elliot what Dylan told me' – he glanced at Brian – 'what you yourself told me, Brian, at the time, not long afterwards. There was a party, there was plenty of drinking, there were drugs – you remember what it's like at those college parties, the fraternity houses. This girl, Jodie, she was drunk and high, probably didn't quite know what she was doing, woke up the next day and felt regretful about it.'

'Jodie White,' I said. Faces passed through my mind, girls from college, the memory of a party, or of several similar parties all clumped together in my head: girls talking, girls huddled together, giggling in a corner on a couple of couches. Adrenaline, anxiety like the smell of cordite in the close air. A redheaded girl getting up and separating herself from the group and stepping carefully across the room, picking her way past people sitting on the floor and dancing and leaning over the stereo, smiling at me briefly as she went into the next room to get a drink. I remembered stained and patterned carpet underfoot; looking back at the huddle of girls; one face among them, quick dark eyes, long legs, a plastic cup in her hands, a broad smile. Not the redhead. Her.

The jingle of a slot machine, its brief little burbling song, cut through the sound of the piano. I looked over and saw that the piano stool was empty, the bar's sound system having taken over without any obvious change.

'Did you know her?' Tallis asked, alarmed, seeing the recognition in my face.

'No. I remember her, though – I must have met her at a party.'

Brian had shrunk back into his chair, looking remorseful, holding his glass.

'Did she go to the police?' I asked.

Brian closed his eyes, squeezed them shut and opened them again, fixing his gaze on a far corner of the room where neon-striped fish swam around a huge tank set into the wall. He had decided to let Tallis tell the story.

'She didn't end up pressing charges,' Tallis explained. 'But she was going to. She named Brian to some of her friends. And then to the police.'

She had ended up in a room upstairs with a guy called Glen who was friendly with Brian. After she and Glen had 'spent some time together', Tallis said, Glen had called Brian in.

Brian roused himself at this point. 'I'd been flirting with her all night,' he said defensively. 'She'd kissed me. Right near where everyone was dancing. So when Glen came and said, you know, Jodie's upstairs, go on up, I had some stupid idea that she'd asked to see me. I don't know. I flattered myself. I don't know what I was thinking. When I got up there she was really out of it. We, uh, we made out for a while.' He started tapping his foot up and down, a nervous tic. 'We had sex. I was totally fucking drunk myself.' His defensive tone returned. 'I should have charged *her*. She could have forced *me* into it. I didn't know what I was doing.'

'Keep telling yourself that,' Tallis said, quietly. He cleared his throat and continued. 'One of Jodie's friends walked in. She was in bad shape by then. Her friend came back with some other girls and they took her home.'

'Tell him how you came to be involved,' Brian said, meanly.

Tallis rolled his eyes. 'Since you mention it. It happened to be my room. The party happened to be at the house I was living in. But I didn't know anything about it. And you know that's true, Brian,' he said, as though Brian had been about to speak. But Brian just sat there looking contemptuous. 'Jodie never included me in her account of that night. I was downstairs the whole time. My room was empty and they took it. I moved out the semester after that.'

I knew Tallis had been a fraternity guy at some point, but by the time I met him he was living in an apartment off campus in what had seemed like a very grown-up style: his own place, a one-bedroom with newish furniture that matched, except for the couch — long, faded, yellow-gold, showing a couple of cigarette burn marks on the arms. I had slept on it a few times.

Jodie remembered bits and pieces the next day, Tallis said; at first she was just embarrassed and shaken up, and then she talked to another girl who'd had the same thing happen to her at a party the week before, and she got angry. There was a kind of crack-down happening at the time, the college coming down hard on the excesses of fraternity nightlife, and she went to the police.

'That's when Dylan got involved,' Tallis explained. Dylan knew Jodie, had dated one of her friends for a while. He heard that Jodie was starting to talk about bringing charges and tried to convince her not to do it.

'How did he do that?' I asked.

Tallis looked uncomfortable. 'He tried to appeal to her, you know, her better nature. Brian apologized' – Brian nodded vigorously – 'while still maintaining, as he does now, that he thought she had consented to the whole thing. She wouldn't listen. Unfortunately, her memory was quite sharp where Brian was concerned, more so than for the other guys.'

'Other guys? I thought you said it was only Glen.'

'Did I? There might have been one other guy involved. Like I said, her memory wasn't very good. Anyway. Dylan could be persuasive, you know.'

'Yes,' I said.

Watching him persuade others had always been a compelling spectacle. Once he'd made up his mind to convince someone to do something – or, as in this case, not to do something – he almost always seemed to achieve it, never by openly pressing the point, but usually by using his charm, or piece by piece through careful, well-timed tactics. Flattery or pressure that stopped short of blackmail. From what I had seen.

Dylan had slept with Jodie, Tallis told me, gone out with her a couple of times, got close to her, got her drunk, found out just about everyone else she had ever slept with or made out with, complete with details about what she'd done with them, and tracked down people who had sold her drugs or taken them with her.

'He put together a whole dossier for her,' Tallis said, sounding almost admiring. 'He persuaded her that not only would her case be, uh, compromised by some of the details he'd come up with but that it would also be pretty embarrassing for her – pretty damaging – if everything that he'd found out were to come out.' Jodie had not only bought drugs for herself but also for her friends, and had sold them once or twice to other people, too. 'That looked bad for her. That and the fact that one of her ex-boyfriends swore that he'd had a threesome with her, and that it had been her idea. He was making it up to impress Dylan, I think. Or maybe coming on to him? Well. It's unfair, isn't it,' Tallis said. 'But there it is.'

I couldn't come up with any other memories of Jodie apart from that one indistinct party scene with her glazed eyes and plastic cup. Now I was having trouble not thinking about her in some of the positions Tallis had just described – it was disturbing, and arousing in a distant, awful way. She was raped, I reminded myself. My instinctive horror at the word competed with other feelings – a threesome? With another man or a woman, I wondered. Remembering Brian's words – *date rape* – I wondered why it was called that, when the whole situation seemed so ludicrously, pathetically far away from what you might call a date, a mockery of it.

'Jodie dropped out,' Tallis said. 'Transferred. Nebraska.' I nodded. 'Did you ever sleep with her?' he asked.

I shook my head and wondered if he'd been reading my thoughts. 'I said before – I didn't know her, just met her at some of those parties.'

'Oh, yeah,' he said, with a thin smile. 'But it sounds like quite a few guys met her at those parties and got to know her pretty well, pretty fast.'

I remembered her long, coltish legs. 'No,' I said. 'I didn't have much luck at those parties.'

'I hate having sex with drunk girls,' Tallis said thoughtfully. 'No energy. Or too much, all in the wrong direction. Tipsy, happy, yes. Drunk, falling down, no.'

'So if Jodie dropped the charges, or whatever she did, then what's the problem?' I asked.

'She did file charges, then she dropped them and took it all back, saying she couldn't remember well enough. But it turns out that Dylan was very thorough not only in his research but also in his record keeping. There's a copy of her original statement to the police in there. God knows how he got hold of that. There's also a transcript of a conversation she must have had with Dylan . . . it looks like he taped it. We don't have the tape, but from the transcript the conversation includes a lot of detail about Brian and that night. It wouldn't look good.'

'But the police wouldn't get involved now, would they?'

'No, I don't think so,' Tallis said. 'Unless she changed her mind, and I can't think why she'd do that. I think it's more the personal repercussions for Brian . . . Obviously he doesn't want this to be in the public domain. We worked hard to keep it from getting out at the time.'

Brian sat there quietly, humiliated, and, I realized, angry. He stared at the envelope in his hands. 'That fucking cunt,' he said.

I thought for a second that he was talking about Jodie. But something about his expression told me that he wasn't. He was talking about Dylan.

'Yep,' Tallis said. 'I need another drink.'

I found myself short of breath, tensed as though preparing to absorb a physical blow. I wondered whether Dylan had been equally thorough in keeping such detailed records about my own secret mistake. I wondered if there was an envelope sitting right now in my mailbox in the department, or at home, with a copy of the essay inside it.

I looked down a long, telescopic tunnel at my younger self, my undergrad self on the verge of a breakdown over a Tennyson poem and an English essay. A nervous wreck. And remembered how pleased and relieved I had been when Dylan had the idea, when he set it all up so quickly and easily, how he solved the problem. I was a lonely, stressed-out figure in this memory, dressed in my blue-black jeans that never got washed, clutching a stack of folders, shaky from the effects of too much caffeine. A mess. And then the relief of Dylan's reassurances.

The image didn't fade away down the telescope like memories usually do. Uncomfortably, it seemed instead to zoom towards me, moving against the rules of time and motion, and dissolved only when it was right in front of me, too close to focus on, a blur of pixels that slipped right inside my skin like a malevolent spirit. Instead of feeling the distance from that old version of myself I felt only the closeness.

This sensation wasn't helped by being in the presence of people who had known me then, who still saw me essentially as that person, or so I suspected. Neither of them knew about the Tennyson essay. As far as I knew.

I wondered what Tallis's hypothetical envelope held. Or Cameron's. It hadn't occurred to me that the others would have had secrets like my own, or worse, held only by Dylan; I just hadn't thought about it. Now it seemed obvious. And Dylan had guarded those secrets so carefully and, it seemed, with such potentially malicious intent. He had never indicated to me that he would ever wield the power that his knowledge about me gave him, but looking at Brian now, it seemed possible that Dylan had held this kind of power over him, and maybe used it harshly.

But it wasn't Dylan who had sent the envelope. He had collected the information, but it wasn't him now bringing it to light. He must have shared it with someone else.

'Who sent it?' I asked Tallis. 'Is it signed?'

'Someone called Colin Andrews,' Tallis said. 'There's a note with it: *Looking forward to meeting with you all.*'

The name rang a distant bell; I reached for it; it faded, obscured by the fear I felt at the inclusive form of address. *You all*. It seemed to be a terrible warning.

'What does he mean, "you all"?' I asked.

'If he knows this, he could know anything,' Tallis said. 'He could know everything about us. We have to be prepared for that. He obviously knew Dylan.'

I understood now why they thought it was possible I might have received an envelope as well.

'Whoever he is,' Brian said, 'he knows exactly where we are.' He indicated his name on the envelope. 'Hand-delivered. It was waiting for me at reception when I checked in.'

I tried to remember him collecting it, but I'd been busy talking to Cynthia.

Tallis glanced at his watch. 'We'll have to go to meet Cameron soon,' he said. 'What about Cynthia – she's joining us when?'

Brian shrugged. 'I said I'd call her. She'll be hours in that spa.'

'OK,' Tallis said. 'What about Cameron?' Brian looked mutinous. 'Brian,' Tallis said firmly, 'I told you before. We have a better chance of getting to the bottom of this if we work together. And I've had it with you two. You have to stop being such children. Think of this as an opportunity to just get the fuck over it.'

Brian nodded, a quick, jerky movement. He didn't look happy, but his tension over the mention of Cameron seemed to quickly fade and give way to something else. It looked as though he was thinking about Dylan, as we all were. His face was filled with sadness and hatred in equal measure, disappointment and resentment.

I had expected to sit around with my friends over drinks, thinking about Dylan, remembering him fondly, keeping my own thoughts about my cheating past to myself. This was impossibly far away from anything I had imagined – constructing an image of the dead man as master manipulator, the fucking cunt, that was clearly as familiar to the two of them as it was utterly strange to me. A world of unease opened in front of me as I prepared myself to re-examine so many things that my head hurt: Dylan's character, the nature of friendships that I had so long taken for granted. Everything had changed beyond recognition, and the two of them were still sitting there right in front of me, just as they had countless times before.

Tallis laughed. 'We'd better make a toast to the old bugger. I didn't think he'd go this far. Fucking us up from beyond the grave.'

He drank cheerfully. I recognized this attitude in him, exaggerated bonhomie that disguised anxiety.

He checked his watch again. 'We should call Cameron. Get him down here and go over this before Cynthia joins us.' He said her name with an irritated, false American inflection.

'Don't start in on Cynthia,' Brian said. 'I agree, it was a bad idea. But she's here now.'

Tallis had pulled out his phone and was dialling Cameron's room.

'So,' I said to Brian, wanting desperately to change the subject, to fill the silent space between us. 'How's it going with Cynthia?'

He shook his head. 'Good.' He started chewing his fingernails. 'How's it going with Elizabeth?'

I'd mentioned her once, soon after I started in the job, and he had it in his head that I was pining away for love of her.

'You know we're just friends.'

'Did she open your envelope by mistake?' he asked, with an unkind smile.

'No. I told you, I didn't get one.' I gave up the small talk.

Tallis closed his phone. His conversation with Cameron had been brief and upbeat.

'Should we be talking about this in here?' I asked. The tables directly around us were empty, but the bar was starting to fill with people as the evening progressed.

'It's OK for now,' Tallis said. 'See how it goes. Brian, stop biting your nails.'

I was struck again by the dynamic between them, so unlike the way they had always acted around me, and yet it was a relation that seemed deeply habitual to them both. It wasn't strange to see Tallis in this position of authority – he liked to order all of us around, and was comfortable issuing commands and insults – but it was strange to see him assuming it so completely and humourlessly with Brian, and to see Brian accept it, for the most part, so passively. The Brian–Tallis link had always seemed a fairly weak one in comparison with the others in our circle, but the reemergence of this event from their shared past seemed to bring to light a previously hidden way of being with each other.

I tried to think back. Had Tallis always been this way with Brian, at least a little? Had Brian always been like this with Tallis? I retrieved small, silent glimpses of memory: Brian and Tallis arguing, a seemingly minor point, and Tallis growing impatient and shutting the conversation down with a harsh word, eliciting a blank, set face from Brian. That had been years back; there seemed to be a roulette wheel behind them in my memory of the moment; it must have been in Vegas, one of our first visits. The effort was exhausting. I realized with a nauseated lurch that this was only the beginning, this new reckoning of the past, and it would be Dylan's role, his words and gestures and expressions, that I would be forced to re-evaluate the most seriously, and in relation to all of us, not just myself.

The two of them had fallen quiet. Brian looked at Tallis with a defensive stare, hostile and yet pleading at the same time.

'I remember it all very well,' Tallis said. 'I've never held it over you – have I? Come on. Don't start trying out your arguments for your innocence with me.' He looked over at me. 'Save it for Elliot here. He'll want to think the best of you. As we all do, my friend.'

I did want to think the best of Brian. I put aside how much he had exasperated me over the years, my frustration with his judgemental brand of politics, his childish feud with Cameron. He looked so forlorn in his wrinkled, sweaty shirt, as if the victim of a dreadful injustice. A thread had come loose in the stitching on the edge of his sleeve, a pale twist of cotton; I pictured it unravelling, the whole thing, and him with it, a thread that would lead me to a different version of Brian, a stranger.

'You know I'd never really do anything like that, Elliot, you have to believe me,' Brian said. 'Tallis wasn't there when it happened, no one was. He's probably heard all of Jodie's version of it, which can't be trusted, obviously.'

I nodded. 'Right.'

My sympathy was with him. But then I remembered Jodie, her face that stood out from that group of girls, her wide smile. I wondered what justice might possibly look like for her, and Brian's victimized stance was harder to stomach.

There were no clocks in the bar; there were no clocks inside anywhere in any of the Vegas casinos. The interiors were all designed to stop you noticing the passage of time, to create a suspended reality that didn't match with any actual recognizable time of day. My watch said it was 9:37 p.m. Still on East Coast time. I tried to pull out the little wheel on the side to change it to Nevada time but it wouldn't budge. My fingernails weren't long enough to lever it out. I gave up. Tallis rose and wandered off in search of a bathroom.

'I need to take a shower,' Brian said.

I thought back to my recent conversation with Lily, her revelations about Dylan's adoption story. The name snapped into place.

'Did you know that Dylan had a brother?' I asked.

Brian looked at me with something like the expression I must have worn when Lily told me about it. 'What are you talking about?'

'He had a brother.'

'He didn't have a brother. What − do you mean he had a brother that died?'

'What? No. No one died.'

Two seconds of silence followed, filled with both of us thinking the same thing, that Dylan had died.

'What brother?'

'He was adopted.'

Brian leaned closer. 'Dylan was adopted?'

'That's right.'

'How do you know?' He asked it in a genuinely curious way, not exactly challenging the truth of the information, or how I in particular would come to have it, both things I had expected. 'How did you find out?'

'Lily,' I said. 'He told Lily. On drugs one night.'

'On drugs.' Brian's eyebrows lifted, sceptical.

'On acid.'

'Oh . . .' He was thoughtful now, eyes narrowed. 'Did you ever take acid with Dylan?'

'No. You know I hate acid.'

'It was like a truth serum for him. He always avoided it because of that. Why was he taking acid with Lily?'

'I don't know. It was at a party.'

'When?'

'Last year. In New York. Oh, you know what? I think it was in the punch.'

Someone had mentioned it to me – a woman in the kitchen, stepping up on her tiptoes to whisper it into my ear, as though it would delight me, her breath hot and sweet from fruit-flavoured lip gloss.

Brian nodded slowly, convinced.

Tallis came back to the table. 'The waitress likes you, Elliot.' He flipped a matchbook case toward me. There was a phone number written inside it.

'I don't need you to do that,' I said.

'Do what?'

'Fix me up. I'm not that desperate.'

'Don't be so sure. Well, the night is young.' He laid both hands flat on the table and looked back and forth between the two of us. 'What did I interrupt?'

I ran through it again for him. He hadn't known. He asked the same questions as Brian, only with more scepticism about the reliability of Lily.

'She always had a bit of a crush on him, your sister,' he said.

'According to her they made out for hours. In the driveway.' I'd started to sound like Lily, bolstering the idea that there had been something between them, in order to increase the validity of her story. 'Who knows? She did have a crush on him. But – this is the thing. She said that he asked her about it afterwards. He couldn't remember exactly what he'd said to her, but he knew it was something he wouldn't have normally said. Something he wouldn't have wanted to tell her.'

'It's completely believable for some reason,' Tallis said.

'I know,' said Brian. 'I'm not surprised.'

'Aren't you surprised that he never mentioned it?' I asked.

'Yeah. In a way,' Tallis said. 'But he looked like them, didn't he? His parents, I mean. Leo and Greta. So it wasn't something that came up automatically. And some people don't even look like their real parents.'

'Their biological parents,' I said automatically.

'What, are you going to get fucking politically correct about it?'

'Maybe he was embarrassed about it,' Brian offered.

'Why would he be embarrassed about it?' I asked.

'Maybe not embarrassed exactly. It's just very . . . personal.'

'But we were his friends.'

'It's typical of him,' Tallis said. 'It was, I mean, it was typical.'

We were all quiet for a moment then, aware of how much we had to do this to the way we talked about him, convert everything all the time in our minds, our speech, from present to past tense.

'There's something more I need to tell you about Dylan's brother,' I said.

'The dead one?' Tallis asked, frowning, as if struggling to focus on my face.

'No, there's no dead brother, I told you. He's alive. As far as I know, he's alive. The thing is, he's living here, in Vegas.'

'In Vegas,' Tallis said slowly.

'His name is Colin. Lily told me. I knew it was familiar.'

'Fuck. It's him, isn't it,' said Brian.

I shrugged. 'It could be. Why not?' I remembered my conversation with Sally that night at my parents' house. 'I could call Sally,' I said.

'Does she know about the brother?' Tallis asked. I nodded. 'So call her. Get his number.'

I pulled out my phone. 'What should I tell her? I mean, why do we want his number?'

Brian looked at me. 'We're here, aren't we? We'd love to meet him.'

'We'd love to meet him,' Tallis echoed.

Sally didn't answer, as I'd expected, and I left a brief message asking her to call me.

'I didn't understand this thing of his,' I said. 'This thing with secrets. I didn't realize how . . . well, how secretive he was.'

They both stayed quiet for another moment.

'No, I know,' Tallis said.

7

It hadn't worked out quite like I had expected, being able to tell them something about Dylan that they hadn't known. Part of me had assumed that they did know, ever since Sally had confirmed Lily's story. They had been closer to him than I had, or so I thought. And so I'd been a little afraid of looking like the odd one out when I brought it up, of being the only one not in on the secret, who didn't have the information. But I had also imagined scenes a bit like this one, where it wasn't me who was the excluded one, but the other way around: I was the one who had the information the others didn't have, and in my imaginings of the revelation it made them see me differently. It gave me something. But instead, the way it was, it didn't seem to give me anything.

'Where's Cameron?' Brian asked.

Tallis shook his head. 'We should get going if we're going to get there by seven.'

'What's the point?' Brian asked. 'Let's skip it. We're all going to be here anyway. If he ever actually makes it down here.'

It made sense. But it didn't feel right. I'd been dreading this trip, all of it, looking forward with tired reluctance to especially, exactly, our rendezvous at the Flamingo. But without it the whole thing felt like even more of a pointless waste of time and energy.

Tallis was scrutinizing me. 'We couldn't do that to the traditionalist over here,' he said to Brian.

'Is that what I am?' I asked, laughing. 'The traditionalist?'

Tallis shrugged. 'Of course. Don't worry. We'll go. I have my own sentimental attachments to the old place.'

'The traditionalist?' I asked again, wounded, realizing it hadn't been a joke.

Tallis and Brian both reached out at the same time to pat me on the shoulder. I shrugged them off.

'I don't know what you're talking about,' I said. 'I'm not the one who insists on coming here, coming back here year after year.'

They had both tuned out. Again, I had a strange sense of seeing them differently, acting in concert in an unfamiliar way, this time from a shared, unspoken assumption about me. I did want to go to the Flamingo, I found. As a kind of show of respect for Dylan's memory if nothing else, although that was turning out to be a complicated prospect now. Maybe I *was* the traditionalist, after all.

They were getting ready to leave, putting money on the table.

'Go and have a shower, Brian,' Tallis said. Brian rolled his eyes but appeared to be compliant all the same. 'Get dressed properly. Hurry up. We'll see you over there.' He adjusted his shirt cuffs, pulling them down so that they sat right with the sleeves of his suit jacket. 'Elliot? Ready?'

'See you there, Brian,' I said. 'Hang in there.'

He walked off without saying goodbye, one hand in his pocket, one holding the envelope close to his side.

'Feel like a walk?' Tallis asked with a smile. He picked up the matchbook with the waitress's number on it and tucked it into his top pocket.

'Sure,' I said.

I hated walking in Las Vegas, but Tallis loved it, especially on nights like this when it stayed unseasonably warm way into the evening. We stepped out onto the Strip: car exhaust, cigarettes, perfume and men's bad cologne. And something else, something like dust and baking bitumen.

'We can't walk all the way to the Flamingo from here,' I said. 'It's miles away.'

'I know the hotel is kind of shit,' he said, ignoring my remark. 'But the deal I got us is good.'

'You told us that already,' I said. 'And yeah, it's kind of shit.'

'Oh, come on,' he said, getting defensive. 'What's wrong with your room?'

'You're the one ... Forget it. My room is fine. It's just too big.'

'Your room?'

'No. My room is probably too small. It's fine. The hotel is too big.'

'It's Vegas,' he responded. 'It's all big.'

'It's too big.'

'The nightclub is supposed to be good.'

There had been a flyer for the hotel's various nightclubs among the stacks of brochures and leaflets in my room. The image for one of them showed a man's hand placing a tiny disco mirror ball, the size of a golf ball, into a woman's open mouth. I suppose it was meant to be erotic but the mirror-ball idea ruined it for me; it was cold and fractured and metallic, the opposite of flesh.

We were approaching a stop for the Deuce, the bus that went up and down the Strip. 'Can we take the bus?' I suggested. 'Or a cab? It's too far to walk.'

'No way. We can slow down if you like.' He slowed his pace a little.

The twilight was just starting to fall, a dirty purple sky fading into pink and orange, low, thin banks of clouds settling on the horizon. We walked on.

'All that feminist posturing, eh?' Tallis said after a time.

I nodded. 'We've all done things we regret.'

'That's a cliché and you know it.' He smiled as though he was pleased with me. 'What is it they say? That there's truth in all clichés?'

'I don't know,' I said. 'Who says that?'

'I don't know.' He threw the burning end of his cigarette into the gutter. 'I've heard it said.' He gazed straight ahead as he walked, in an unseeing, preoccupied way. 'But I remember college. Women. Parties. How fucking confusing it could all be. How you were meant to behave. It's not as if there were guidelines to consult.'

I agreed in some kind of noncommittal way. It had been confusing; it still was confusing. 'But all the same,' I said, 'it wasn't *that* confusing. I don't know if Brian was exactly confused. I don't know if that's the word for it. It's easy for him to say that now.'

He didn't seem to hear me. 'It's all a darkness, right?' He winked.

His smile this time was less pleased, but he seemed to regard the topic as being closed. It sounded as though he was quoting something, a phrase I should have known, but I couldn't place it.

By the time we arrived at the Flamingo it was close to seven. Or so I thought, checking my watch and adjusting from East Coast time. The little wheel on the side still wouldn't budge. Tallis noticed me tinkering with it as we walked up the steps. I'd fallen a step behind him, concentrating on the watch.

'Haven't set your watch yet? I always do that on the plane, as soon as it takes off.'

'No – that's a good idea, yes, but I forgot, and now it's stuck.'

He glanced back at me. 'Stuck?' he asked. 'Let me have a look.'

He stood close and waited while I undid the strap and handed it to him. The wheel wouldn't budge for him either. His hands were large but his fingers moved with a surprising dexterity as he pushed and pulled at the mechanism. 'Hmm,' he murmured, and turned the thing over, inspecting the back of it as if he expected it to have some kind of written instruction, or explanation of this peculiar mechanical deficiency. Eventually he gave it back to me. 'Never mind. Just add four hours, or take them away, whatever it is.'

'I can never keep track of it.'

'What do you need a watch for? Relax.'

The pink lights on the giant flower over the entrance glimmered and undulated obscenely. We passed under them and into a large gaming room with red-and-pink carpet in a fractal, distorted paisley pattern. The Vegas smell was sweatier and staler here, with an artificial note in it, some kind of chemical fragrance that made me think of hibiscus flowers, although when I tried to think what a hibiscus flower actually smelled like, nothing came to mind. I couldn't think of the last time I had seen one; here in Vegas, probably, in the tropical rainforest at the Mirage.

Tallis had stopped outside the serious poker area of the gaming floor, a large corner filled with several long tables. The players were all men, almost all of them over fifty. One player was wearing a cowboy hat so large it was impossible to see his face, his head tilted down toward his chest, but he seemed younger than the rest of them. A balding, heavyset player turned and glared at me with an unnerving, unblinking stare. He wore glasses with lenses so thick that his eyes were magnified to twice their normal size.

'Come on, Tallis,' I said. 'This is a bad idea.'

He sighed. 'I know, I know.'

The one time Tallis had fallen into a bad gambling spree had been at the Flamingo, at one of these poker tables three years back.

Poker was in fashion. He'd been playing every week or so with some friends in London and his confidence had grown. He was the best player among them, won a bit of money over several months, and made a big deal when he arrived in Vegas about how he was going to play with his 'winnings'. The winnings turned out to be quite substantial, in my terms at least, seven thousand dollars or so – the friends he played with were all corporate types like himself who could afford to lose that much over a few months in a friendly game. Tallis hit a winning streak on the first evening, right after our 7 p.m. drink, and bought us all an expensive lunch with bottles of French champagne the next day. But he went straight back to the poker room afterwards, and the money was gone in a matter of hours. He withdrew enormous amounts from his savings account and lost it all, and soon turned into a mess. I'd seen his addictive tendencies with drugs and alcohol, but they had never seemed very serious – tendencies rather than actual problems. In the poker room it turned into something else. Grey-faced under the fluorescent lights, chain-smoking, dull-eyed, desperate. On our last day there we all began to worry that he would both ruin himself and miss his flight; he was booked to leave at the same time we all were, early that evening.

Dylan had been the one to talk him down in the end, of course. He convinced him to take just one quick break – just five minutes, he said, just two minutes, just come across the road to the veranda café at Caesars for a minute, they were mixing these incredible milkshakes and smoothies, Kahlua and coffee, caramel, one with Midori and real melon.

Dylan had consulted with me briefly before going in to him. 'I think he'll go for it,' he said. He'd remembered Tallis's sweet tooth and ultimately childish tastes, and judged correctly that an alcoholic milkshake would be the thing to convince him to get up and leave.

I had been sceptical, but thought it was the best chance we had. I'd already tried what I'd regarded as a sure bet, promising that a girl Tallis had tried chatting up had run into us again that afternoon and asked for his number, asked where we were going that night, tried to set up a date. He hadn't been interested.

'Once we get him there,' Dylan said to me, 'what should we do? I've got some Ativan – should I put some in his milkshake? Two or three? You can't taste it once it's crushed up. And the alcohol will mask it. And the ice cream and whatever.'

'Ativan? I don't know,' I'd said. 'That seems a bit harsh.'

'No,' Dylan had said, '*this* is harsh. He's going to feel like shit if we don't get him out of here.'

'It's his choice,' I heard myself saying.

'It's not his choice,' Dylan corrected me. 'He's not capable of making a sensible choice right now. That's what I'm talking about.'

I hadn't liked the idea of drugging Tallis, but it said something about the worrying nature of his rapid transformation, and Dylan's persuasive abilities, that it didn't seem as bad to me as it might have done otherwise.

'Why don't we just see how it goes?' I suggested. 'If you can get him out of here, if he wants to go back in afterwards, see how it goes.'

'They don't work right away, you know.'

'They'll be mixed with Kahlua,' I reminded him.

'True,' he said thoughtfully. 'You're right. Do you want one?'

'No, thanks.'

'Suit yourself,' he said mildly, and walked with his slouchy walk, hands in pockets, over to the poker table. I watched him – low voice in Tallis's ear, hand on his shoulder, keeping up the smile – and I saw the moment when it worked, when Tallis nodded and lifted his eyes to scan the room in a way that told me he'd decided to leave.

When we crossed the road to the veranda bar, Cameron and Brian were both there, Brian talking conspicuously on his cell phone, Cameron drinking something fluorescent blue in a large, round glass with a chunk of pineapple wedged onto the side. There was a small, plastic tropical fish floating inside – an angel fish, with its delicately arched fins. I looked closer and saw that the glass had a double wall, filled with glitter and other tiny fish, like an outsized version of a child's toy cup.

'Pretty, aren't they?' Cameron said, raising the glass to drink from a long, bendy straw.

Dylan ordered for us all, and I wound up drinking something in a tall, cool metal cup that tasted a lot like the malt shakes of my childhood, only not quite as sweet, and thicker, with an oddly medicinal aftertaste that grew stronger the more I drank.

'What's in this?' I asked Dylan.

'Vanilla,' he said, kindly.

'And what else?'

'Vodka.'

We all laughed, in an exhausted, hysterical kind of way.

Tallis didn't need the Ativan after all. Or Dylan decided to dose him anyway, without my knowing. He was shamefaced and quiet until he finished the first drink, a shake similar to mine in a metal cup. A waiter came by to clear the table and Tallis straightened up, pulled his shoulders back, and smiled. 'I'll have a Coke, thanks.'

'One Coke coming up, sir. Anything else?'

'I'll have another of whatever that was,' Dylan said.

Tallis grinned, a little sloppily. He ordered more things, a hamburger, a sundae. It must have been a while since he had eaten.

★

The guy with the thick lenses and homicidal stare was still glaring at me. 'Let's go,' I said.

We headed over through the forest of noisy machines to the bar. It wasn't very different from the one we'd just come from back at our hotel. If you sat up at the bar you could play slots or other games at the consoles embedded in the countertop. We had done that once, but I found the blinking lights distracting and preferred to sit elsewhere. If one was free, we sat in a spacious corner booth, with seats of pinkish-red leather. One was empty now, and we squeezed in behind the table. They had redone the ceiling since we had last been here, and now it was covered in little squares of gold with a pinkish tinge, not smoothly stuck on but hanging in a glittering, uneven expanse, patches of darkness showing where some had fallen off.

Tallis had a cigarette in his mouth. 'Do you want one? Or are you still being virtuous?'

'No, thanks,' I said.

I'd given up, more or less, a couple of years earlier, and hadn't bought any since the packet I'd shared with Natasha on campus that day. My first visit to Vegas as a nonsmoker had been difficult, the constant stink of smoke an ever-present temptation, and I'd find myself standing in the middle of the gaming floor at the hotel breathing in the passive fumes in a helpless, unthinking fog of desire. The following year had been different; I'd managed to really stop, only three or four cigarettes in eight months prior to the trip. When I caught the scent on people's clothes, in their hair, it made me recoil. The hangover I'd had the first day of that visit had been of historically bad proportions, or had seemed that way purely because I'd forgotten how much worse it was after cigarettes, and I'd broken down and smoked half a pack on the very first night. After four drinks – I could calibrate it exactly now, the amount of alcohol it took – three if they were strong, the cigarette smell went from acrid to beautiful, chemical burn to desirable toast, nostalgia in physical, evanescent, available form.

Tallis exhaled. The smell of fresh, close-up smoke joined the fog of stale fumes around us. It was only a matter of time before I accepted a cigarette, or asked for one, but it seemed worth waiting until later, when that alcohol-induced turning point arrived. Until we got Cameron and Brian together, at least; cigarettes would be needed then, I realized, and thought about buying a pack – two packs, I wondered, would that be necessary? – with a sickening need to think of anything that would ease the situation we were about to find ourselves in.

Tallis summoned a waitress and ordered fast for both of us – whisky, ice water – and looked at me, his eyes bloodshot. He'd flown straight from London.

'How's the jet lag?' I asked.

'It's a bastard,' he said wearily. 'Worse every fucking time. The vertigo – do you ever get that?' He didn't wait for a reply, took his drink gratefully as it was offered to him from a tray, giving the woman holding it only a cursory inspection.

Tallis was a special kind of hypochondriac, wanting not so much attention for his various ailments and weaknesses as admiration for his stoicism in dealing with them. He liked to be seen to be 'soldiering on', as he put it, against an array of bodily challenges that he only sketched, never elaborated in any real detail. The sketches could be dramatic. Migraines that blinded half his vision for days; flus that led to ear infections; versions of strep that caused his voice to virtually disappear, though he croaked on; old sporting injuries that flared up from time to time, necessitating vast amounts of prescription painkillers, invariably washed down with Guinness, as though the Guinness itself specially enhanced their effects.

He narrowed his eyes. 'Are you sure you didn't get an envelope? Didn't want to let on in front of Brian?' 'No,' I said. 'I didn't.'

You might as well tell him about the paper anyway, I thought, and put the idea away for later. No doubt it would spill out about the same time as I smoked my second or third cigarette. Fine.

'Cameron doesn't know anything about that thing with Brian, with Jodie, by the way,' Tallis said. 'I'm sure of it. He would have said something before now. That kind of thing would matter to him. You know, with his sister and everything.'

'Oh, right.'

I remembered. There was some issue with Cameron's elder sister, a suit she had brought against an uncle who ended up spending time in jail. It had happened while we were in college, one summer. Cameron had come back to school in the fall a lot quieter and somehow angrier and sadder than he had been. The thing with the uncle had happened when they were kids, when his sister was eight or nine. Cameron went through a lot of grief about the fact that he hadn't known.

'I knew something was wrong,' he said. 'Maybe I just didn't want to know exactly what it was.'

That fall he became especially sensitive to the kind of harassment that girls went through; he seemed to notice for the first time the way some guys treated women, especially when they were drinking – the pressure, the innuendo, the ass-grabbing. He didn't date anyone that semester.

'The worst thing,' he said to me once, at the end of a night drinking schnapps together in my dorm room, 'is how common it is. Did you know that?' He shook his head. 'It's, like, three in five, something like that.' Girls who were abused, he meant. 'It's, like, so many that you feel as though you have to start with the assumption that it probably happened, with any girl you know. It's more than likely.'

It was one of those statistics that I found impossible to reconcile with my own reality. I knew it was true; it was probably not even the whole truth when you took into account all the kids who never told anyone about it (this question was especially haunting for Cameron); but I didn't know what to do with it. What would it mean to start with that assumption, as Cameron thought about it? What did I know about what it meant, anyway?

'How do you deal with that?' Cameron had asked.

I'd suggested that he read a book about it. He'd laughed at that. 'Of course – check the library catalogue, you would say that, Elliot.' It didn't seem like such a stupid idea to me.

His sister had a boyfriend, a guy she'd known since middle school, who had been a good source of support. Lucas. He was a schoolteacher. I considered suggesting that Cameron get some advice from him, but thought better of it.

'Do you think it's a good idea to tell him about it?' I asked Tallis now. 'I mean, he won't like it. It won't make him like Brian any more than he already does.'

'You're right, but I don't fucking care.' Tallis ground out his cigarette with unnecessary force. 'He'll have a good idea of what to do to deal with the situation.'

'Can't we play it by ear, at least?' I asked. 'Why does he have to know the details?'

He gave it a moment's thought and shook his head, then focused on me, deliberate and alert. 'Now tell me what you know about this brother. The lost Las Vegas family.'

I told him. It wasn't much. That Dylan's biological mother had lived here, although she was now dead, and the brother, and Dylan had visited them, presumably while we were all here. A younger brother who looked like him.

'Was Dylan born here?' Tallis asked.

'I don't know. Maybe so, if his mom lived here.'

It made me think again about the town out there beyond the walls of the casinos; the streets and houses and schools and playgrounds and hospitals where people were born and lived and worked and had kids and died. My eyes came to rest on the two guys working behind the bar – early twenties, tired-looking, maybe just like Dylan's brother – and I wondered where they lived, how long it took them to get home.

Cameron arrived and we both stood to embrace him.

'Sorry,' he said to Tallis. 'Marie called just after I talked with you, and then the office, the usual crisis. It was easier to just meet you guys here.'

He was broader and heavier than I remembered. He'd explained to me once that it worked for him in his job to try to look older than he was, and that was the reason his haircut always looked as though it had grown out by about two months more than it should have. His boss had lectured him once when he turned up with it cut extra short; it would make the clients take him less seriously, he'd said. Otherwise, he looked just like he always did when we first arrived – tired, and relieved to be away from work and home.

'Never mind,' Tallis said. 'You're here now. Elliot – get the man a drink.'

'How's Marie?' I asked. 'How are the girls?'

'Oh, great,' he said. 'They're all good.'

I had the sense that Tallis wanted me out of the way while he brought Cameron up to speed before Brian arrived. Maybe I was already jumpy and resistant to the group dynamic. I took my time wandering over to the bar and back, and decided it was OK that Tallis got to tell the story of Dylan's secret brother this time around.

When I returned, Tallis and Cameron were positioned so that each mirrored the other, arms crossed on the table. They didn't move much when I sat down, just reached for their drinks, and drank them. Tallis lit a cigarette. I held out my hand for one and he offered me the pack. I turned away his offer of a light, preferring to just hold the cigarette in my fingers.

'Did Tallis tell you about Brian?' I asked.

Cameron nodded, his face blank.

'What about you? Any envelopes waiting for you at reception?'

He paused. Tallis stilled to attention.

'Someone contacted me just before I left. An envelope like that, yeah. It came to me at the office. Same as Brian's: *Looking forward to meeting you all*. What about you?'

'Me? No,' I said.

He nodded, and looked me in the eye. 'But there could be.'

I shrugged, looked away. 'I guess.' I studied the cigarette between my fingers. 'Brian says he didn't do it, you know,' I said, trying to sound reasonable.

'Huh.'

'He says —'

Tallis spoke over me. 'Light the bloody thing. Don't sit there and play with it.' He took the cigarette out of my hands, lit it from the one he was smoking, and handed it back.

'Brian can speak for himself,' Cameron said, ignoring Tallis like he would ignore a child making an annoying bid for attention. He had a lot of practice doing that at home. 'You don't need to defend him.'

That word *defend* reminded me of what it was that Cameron did for a living — defending people, organizations, most of whom Brian would say were indefensible. There was something ironic, if that was the word for it, about Brian now having to defend himself.

'Anyway,' Cameron said, 'it was a long time ago.'

I'd never taken sides in the Brian–Cameron feud, just wished that they would get over it and stop making life more difficult for the rest of us. I could always see both points of view, the reason why each was irritated or even sickened by the other, but had never really understood why it hadn't cooled off, except for a disheartening sense that neither of them wanted to be the one to make the first move towards talking again. Both too proud, too self-righteous.

I saw Brian approaching at the same moment as I remembered the time we'd all spent together watching the World Cup, and the signs I had seen (or imagined) between them of an ease in the standoff. The hand on the shoulder that I could picture so clearly, but not quite believe in.

Brian stood for a moment, beer in one hand, and looked us over, his eyes resting last on Cameron. He reached out a hand to him. It had a fresh bandage around it, a long piece of cloth wrapped around his palm and secured with a small metal fastener. They shook – more gently than usual, due to the bandage, just a bare version of the gesture – and he sat. He held up the injured hand for us in a kind of wave. There was a small bloodstain on one section of the bandage. 'Broke a glass. Bathroom sink. Just a small cut, nothing minor. I mean, nothing major.'

The mixed-up words got jumbled further in my head and I thought of major and minor keys, chords, Brian's bandaged hand playing guitar.

Tallis inspected him severely. 'Are you sure?'

Brian held his hand out, palm up, for Tallis to see.

'Hmm,' Tallis said. 'OK.'

Brian took a long drink. He had showered and changed, and his hair was still wet in places. I thought his hand, the one with the bandage, was shaking but couldn't be sure.

Seeing him and Cameron sitting at the same table together, I realized that I'd held out some hope that the gathering here would be one of reconciliation. The idea was that Dylan's death would help them put their petty feud in perspective; a catalyst for putting it behind them that didn't rely on either of them losing face by making the first move. The circumstances, the tragedy, just seemed to require it. The funeral hadn't been the place to expect any real shift in attitude: too soon, too raw. It had turned out to be easy for them to make it through the whole event and the wake that followed without having to speak to each other. I felt sure that they'd had some kind of encounter there, but imagined it being a silent one, composed of nodding heads and downcast eyes, with the implicit understanding that when they next saw each other, the next time in Vegas, things would be different.

With Dylan at the table it had been easier for them to stay out of each other's way. Something about the way a group of five people worked made it less complicated to negotiate the conversation; you could keep two patterns of conversation going, one of two, one of three, that switched around and around, Cameron and Brian never managing to end up as the two or two of the three. With four of us it was different, and sitting there together I remembered the odd uncomfortable moment on previous visits when that configuration had occurred. Now we were without our natural mediator.

Tallis wasted no time. 'You two,' he said, moving his eyes from one to the other. 'OK?'

They both nodded, casting their eyes briefly toward each other.

'I'll drink to that,' Tallis announced, raising his glass, and clinked it against each of ours in turn. There was silence as we all drank, a longer draft than the required toasting sip.

'So,' Tallis said expectantly, looking in Cameron's direction. It was obvious, then, how intently he'd been waiting for Cameron to relieve him of his self-appointed position as ringleader.

Cameron shifted uncomfortably. 'Like I said, I got an envelope, anonymous, whatever. The information in it was stuff I assumed only Dylan knew.' He paused and his lips tightened. 'And you, Tallis.'

Tallis kept his gaze steady and drew on his cigarette.

'It concerns someone I was involved with,' Cameron continued. 'A long time ago.'

'Malcolm,' Tallis said. It could have been a question or a statement.

Cameron looked at him sadly in assent.

'Where is he now?' Tallis asked.

'Wisconsin.'

'Is this a gay thing?' Brian asked.

'A gay thing?' I repeated in disbelief.

'It's ancient history,' said Cameron. 'But yeah, it was a gay thing, if you want to put it that way.'

'How can that be something that belongs in an anonymous envelope?' I asked. 'That's so . . . Victorian. It's not like you're a politician or something. How could that hurt you?'

'It would be a big deal for Marie,' Cameron said. 'She's . . .'

'She goes to church,' Tallis explained for him. Cameron shrugged and nodded.

'OK. I can see that she wouldn't like the fact that you'd made it a secret for so long,' I said. 'But you guys are married. How serious would it be?'

'She wouldn't like it,' Cameron said, and sighed. 'What can I say? I don't know. Anyway, it's ancient history, like I said, it's no longer an issue. Malcolm wouldn't confirm anything.'

'Hang on,' Tallis said. 'He might not, but you don't know what else Dylan had on him.'

'There's nothing to be had,' Cameron said. 'I talked to Dylan about it, like, once.'

'Photos?' Tallis tried.

'There were no photos,' Cameron replied. He sounded confident. 'No letters, whatever. Look, we weren't together for that long – it wasn't like we were dating; it was, I don't know, a couple of times.'

Tallis looked at him with a critical stare – not at the idea of the relationship, it seemed, but at Cameron's dismissal of it. 'So you say.'

'Did you know him?' I asked.

Tallis nodded. 'He was our TA.'

'It was an economics class I took with Tallis,' Cameron said. 'He was a grad student; he graduated. He ended up teaching somewhere else – Wisconsin.'

'When was this?' I asked.

'Senior year, OK? That's all I'm going to say about it.'

I tried to remember senior year, what had been going on with Cameron at the time. He'd started seeing Marie sometime in that final semester. I pictured her always with a pile of textbooks in her arms. She was pre-med, a serious student, and it was always hard to put together her calm, focused demeanour with the passionate fights that Cameron occasionally described.

I decided that it was entirely predictable for this to be the secret of the committed family man among us, but it was still hard to imagine Cameron embroiled in an illicit gay affair with a teacher.

'When?' I asked. 'I had no idea.'

'In the fall. It's not like I have some secret gay life.'

'He was gorgeous,' Tallis said. 'Even I will admit that. And he was a total genius. I didn't blame you. Every girl in that class wanted to fuck him.'

'Were there any girls?' Cameron asked, smiling. 'Oh yeah, a couple.'

I summoned a faint memory of meeting Cameron and Tallis one night at the bar in town we used to drink at, right before the break that semester, and being introduced to someone who was a TA. I hadn't paid much attention to him; he'd sat at a table that looked like it was mostly other grad students. We'd gone over to sit at the bar, and he'd joined us at some point to talk to Cameron and Tallis. All I could remember was a slow, easy smile.

'Did I meet him? At Roy's one night with you guys?'

Cameron frowned. 'Yeah. I think so. We didn't stay in touch.' He looked around at us in turn. 'You know, this is one of those times I really wish I smoked.'

'It's not too late to take it up,' Tallis said. 'Go ahead. No? All right. Stick to booze. Now tell us. What is in your envelope, if you didn't leave any evidence? Love notes from him on one of your exams? How did Dylan even get hold of anything?'

'I don't know how he got hold of them,' Cameron said. 'OK, there were a couple of notes, emails.' Tallis nodded, satisfied. 'They were on my computer. You know what Dylan was like, you couldn't leave him alone in your place for five seconds before he started noting every prescription in the bathroom cabinet or reading your diary. I guess he got a look at my email account.'

'Or Malcolm's,' Tallis said.

'What?'

'I just wouldn't have been surprised, that's all.'

Cameron shrugged.

'Jealous?' Tallis asked.

'What matters is that this stuff is no longer an issue for me.'
He sighed. 'Here's the thing. Malcolm's sick. But I don't think
Dylan knew about that – there's nothing to indicate that he
knew. He must have got slack about keeping tabs on all this
bullshit.'

'What do you mean, he's sick?' Brian asked.

Cameron didn't answer.

'He means he's got AIDS,' Tallis said. 'Is that what you mean?'

'He's got HIV,' Cameron answered.

'I thought you didn't keep in touch?' I asked.

'I heard,' he said. 'I know some other people on the faculty
there. Friends of his.'

'I'm sorry,' I said.

'Yeah. I don't know. I think he's doing OK so far.' He glanced
toward Brian, who was staring at him. 'And yes, I'm fine. Look,
it was a long time ago.'

'So what does this mean for us?' Tallis asked.

'You're on your own with this,' Cameron said. 'This is not my
problem.'

It wasn't very convincing. I wondered to what extent he was
trying to deny the potential seriousness of what was in his
envelope; how he really felt about the prospect of Marie
receiving an envelope of her own, and then asking him to deny
the allegation or the evidence or whatever was in there. I
wondered how he would feel about lying about it. He was a bad
liar. I didn't know Marie very well but had the sense that he was
even worse at lying to her than to most other people.

'Does Marie know about the accident?' Brian asked.

'Do you mean does she know I was driving the car?'

'Yes.'

'No. She knows it was Dylan.'

'How could you not tell her?' Brian asked.

'Why would I tell her?' Cameron said. 'I never talk about the accident. I never think about it. I think it came up maybe once.' He sighed heavily. 'And you know what it was like – you remember. The way we told the story. I started believing it myself sometimes.'

I knew what he meant. In all my versions of the story it was Dylan. Even when I told the story in the years after college, as I rarely did, it was always just 'a friend of mine was driving', but I thought of the friend as Dylan; it was his shadowed profile I saw in a fabricated memory of the event as I talked about it.

'Would that matter now?' I asked.

'Cameron's a lawyer,' Tallis said. 'It would look bad. Evading a drunk-driving charge.'

'There was nothing about that in the envelope,' Cameron said. 'There's no reason to think that's an issue.'

I could see that Tallis didn't agree. I wondered what he had to hide that was making him so nervous about the whole thing.

'You know what?' Brian said. 'That is fine with me. This is what I would have expected from you, Cameron.'

'Brian, leave it,' Tallis ordered, barely looking at him. 'Elliot,' he said, using the same commanding tone. 'Please take Brian away for a few minutes while I talk to Cameron. Go and play roulette or something.'

I was about to argue when Brian stood up. 'Let's get out of here,' he said, and started walking away.

'I'll call you,' Tallis said to me.

I looked for Brian in the crowd and found him easily. Sweat had formed tiny beads on his forehead, his upper lip, even in the frigid indoor climate. He fidgeted with the poorly tied bandage around his hand. I wanted to put my hand on his shoulder, to make some kind of comforting contact, but as usual the exact gesture escaped me.

'Hey, man,' he said.

'Hey.' I smiled as best I could.

'Fuck them. Let's get something to eat.'

An hour later we were sitting in a bad restaurant, finishing expensive hamburgers, and I was thoroughly tired of hearing Brian complain about Cameron: his lack of ethics; his weakness of character; his hypocrisy. Brian was distracting himself from thinking about his own problems, I knew, but that made it only marginally more bearable. I was still coming to terms with this idea of Cameron's closeted gay love affair in college, wondering how significant it was, whether he really was gay, and if the wife and kids were an elaborate, old-fashioned cover. It didn't seem that way.

'Brian, please,' I said eventually, while we were waiting for our plates to be cleared. 'Stop. Enough. Can we just not talk about Cameron? Give it a break.'

Brian had done better with his meal than I had: his plate showed only a faint swirl of ketchup, whereas mine still held a pile of uneaten french fries at the side and three slices of pickle. He slid down further into his seat and gave a half-hearted shrug in assent, and reached to take my leftover pickle when the waitress came to take the plates.

'Wait,' I said, speaking as the idea came to me. 'Did Cameron make a pass at you?' Suddenly the years of avoidance between the two of them took on a different cast. 'Is that it?'

'What?' Brian said. He shook his head and looked away. 'I have no idea where that is coming from. And you know, Cameron's not gay. It was just that one time with that professor, the TA, whatever. I'm pretty sure about that.'

'Right,' I said.

Brian kept staring over in the direction of the kitchen, where it was possible to watch a row of men in white paper hats flipping burgers and shaking baskets of fries, with the occasional hiss and faint roar of flames. He stayed quiet, preoccupied and wounded-looking, and I couldn't help feeling as though I'd touched a nerve, although maybe from the wrong direction. Had it been Brian, not Cameron, who had made a pass, or had feelings that weren't returned? I wondered whether the years of passionate bickering and then semi-obsessive avoidance and criticism were the other face of an unrequited crush, or love, or longing of some kind I couldn't guess at. Another potential secret there under the surface of things; or maybe I was slipping into paranoia, seeing conspiracies and lies where there were none.

'What about Cynthia?' I asked. 'Don't you have plans with her?'

He groaned. 'Oh, shit. We're supposed to be going out later on.'

He asked me to come along to the club they'd planned to visit, 'for moral support,' he said, and I agreed, feeling at once obscurely guilty and pleased to be able to do something, anything, that would earn me any kind of gratitude.

'Have you thought about telling her?' I asked. 'About Jodie? About what's going on here?'

His face was sad and resigned. 'No. I don't want to tell her, Elliot. I just want to deal with it ourselves, between us, if that's OK. I don't see what there is to be gained by telling her anything.' He drank the last of his Sprite and tipped the glass back and forth, making the ice in it clink. 'I really want this to work out, I'm serious about this thing with her. Fuck. I just . . . I don't want her to see me that way, you know? And if the people I work with found out about it . . .'

Brian was happy at the production company he was working for now, Ethos, and talked about it with pride. They had just won a couple of prestigious industry awards for their most recent film, and he'd emailed me a link to a series of photographs of the award night, which included several of him in suit and sneakers celebrating with some relatively famous names.

'You know Linda, my boss? She made her name with a student film about sexual assault. Following a case through the courts. That's what she's famous for.' He stared at the table. 'That's how I met Cynthia – some feminist film conference that she was helping to organize, and they invited Linda to be the keynote.' He shook his head. 'This would be such a disaster. A rumour went around about a guy I know, last year. A director's assistant. Some girl on set – she wasn't even part of the cast, really, she was an extra or something – she complained that he harassed her. She let it be known. Apparently it wasn't the first time someone had said that kind of thing about him.'

'Did he lose his job?' I asked.

Brian shrugged. 'It's not quite like that. The job finished. He got another job. But he applied for a job with us and Linda wouldn't even interview him. And that was nothing, really – I mean, maybe it was harassment and that's terrible, obviously, but in the scheme of things, you know . . . And in Boston, it's not like I'm working in Hollywood. It's a small world. It doesn't matter that Jodie didn't press charges, or that it was back in college. All it takes is a rumour. And there's been that big case recently, at Michigan or wherever, with that girl. There's a lot in the papers about Harvard, the fraternity houses there.'

I nodded, and thought uncomfortably about what he meant by 'the scheme of things'. I considered whether I wanted him to talk to me about Jodie, to give me a clearer picture of what had happened that night. Part of me was still angry with him: for whatever he had done in the first place; for allowing Dylan to manage it the way he had. I was angry with him and Tallis for excluding me, and at the same time grateful that I hadn't had to deal with it.

'I'm really sorry,' Brian said, leaning toward me. I backed away from the smell of the pickle he'd just eaten from my plate, the briny, oversweetness of it. 'I tried to tell that to Jodie at the time – I did what I could.'

I waited.

'You know what Dylan could be like. He just kind of . . . took over.'

'Brian,' I said. How to ask? Part of me needed to know just how bad it was – had she said no, was she unconscious, was there any kind of struggle – but there was no way of asking, no way of knowing, and I wondered why the details mattered. Was I hoping for information that exonerated Brian, or put further blame on him? I didn't trust him to tell me the truth about it, but I was still curious to see what he would say. 'I still don't get how it could have happened. How could you not have known? I mean, how was it possible to misread the situation that badly?'

He bit the inside of his lip. 'We'd both been drinking a lot.'

'I've been drunk. I've never raped anyone.'

He glanced away, studying the decor of the restaurant. Fifties kitsch. 'I admit, it was poor judgement.' He stared down at the table, and then looked up at me. 'What do you want me to say? I regret it. I'm sorry it ever happened, I wish I'd never gone to that party, I wish I'd never met her.'

It was easy to feel a sense of moral superiority, but I didn't really trust the sentiment. I couldn't help thinking back to a night I spent with a girl in college. Nadine. A narrow twin bed, sheets a candyland pink. A girlish diary with a tiny, elaborately edged lock on her desk alongside leaflets for the environmental action group and the black fishnet stockings that I'd peeled off her in a hurry. She hadn't wanted to have sex without a condom and we didn't have one, but we got carried away and kept going. It wasn't the only time that had happened, but it stuck in my head more clearly than the few others. I remembered too clearly the moments of reluctance on her part that I could have acknowledged and didn't: the held breath, the hesitation, the look of being about to speak that dissolved; my desire to ignore all those things and my very short moment of shame about that. There wasn't any forcing, there wasn't even any elegant or impassioned persuading; I got my way very easily and with no sense of victory.

I could have remembered all that and thought about how different it made me from Brian, how distinct it was: she never said no, after all, and we were both far from drunk if not exactly sober. And part of me did think that. I couldn't say that I understood, or that he'd acted on desires that I might have shared, or anything like that. But I couldn't judge him all that harshly when I recalled those moments, quick and deliberately unthinking, when I decided to follow the impulse to go ahead anyway, despite Nadine's ambivalence.

'And what about you?' Brian asked. 'When are you going to tell us what's in your yellow envelope?'

My head started to ache.

'I stole something,' I said. 'I mean, I bought something.'

'What? Did you steal something or buy something? What was it?'

'A paper,' I mumbled, and my phone started ringing.

'Paper?'

'Just a second.'

I answered the phone. It was Tallis, asking me and Brian to rejoin him and Cameron. They had been eating sushi at the Bellagio, he said. My mouth still tasted like overdone meat and fries and I envied them. We agreed to meet at the bar next to the sushi place.

I closed the phone and told Brian. He nodded and settled further into his seat while I signalled for the check.

'So you stole or bought some paper?'

'I bought a paper. *A* paper.'

'In college?'

'Yes.'

The check came. I put money down, overtipping, eager to leave.

'Dylan organized that for you?'

'Yeah.'

'That's it?'

'That's it.'

We wandered out of the air-conditioned building, back onto the warm street. I wasn't sure whether I wanted to impress on Brian the seriousness of what I'd done, the magnitude of it in relation to the career I had now, the potential damage it could do, or play it down. Playing it down meant that I met some of the expectations and ideas of his and Tallis's that I was beginning to become more familiar with: that I was the one least likely to fuck up, to take risks, to do the kind of thing that would have such catastrophic consequences that it required serious covering up.

'That would cause problems for you now, wouldn't it,' Brian said, saving me from further explanation.

'Yes.'

He laughed out loud. 'I can't believe you let Dylan do that for you,' he said, shaking his head. 'You're the smart one.'

The smile transformed his face, wiped out the anxiety for a moment. I let myself laugh along with him for a couple of seconds, to see what it felt like.

'I know,' I said.

'And he never mentioned it after that?'

'Never.'

'Amazing!'

'How did you stay friends with him?' I asked. 'I mean – it's hard for me to understand it now, seeing how you guys feel about him.'

'Dylan?' Brian asked, as though I might have been talking about someone else. 'It's hard to explain. He had this way of dealing with people that I couldn't stand. You wanted to stay on his good side, that's for sure. But in a really weird way I trusted him more than anyone, at the same time as I didn't. He would have done anything for me. Or for you – for any of us. You know?'

'I know,' I said.

Brian nodded. 'Of course, the things he did to help you ... they weren't always what you expected or what you would have asked for. It was always a risky bargain with him. He's one of those people who likes to be needed. He was . . . dependable. Strange as that sounds. I think he really meant it when he said that we were all like family to him.' He forgot the injured hand and tried again to put it into his pocket, swore, let it swing by his side.

'I don't have any brothers or sisters,' Brian said. 'I've got cousins, but that's different, I guess ... Anyway, I suppose he was a bit like family – you know: you love them and hate them at the same time, but you know they'll always be there. That's a good and a bad thing. You don't have a choice about it.'

I didn't doubt that Tallis would be able to talk Cameron into helping. His desire to enlist him seemed like something more complex than simply wanting the practical utility of Cameron's clever brain and expertise. There was some kind of loyalty at stake, a desire to know that Cameron would stick with him, as a friend. It didn't seem collective, about devotion to the group;

it was about Tallis and whatever history the two of them shared.

The fountains were dancing at the Bellagio as we approached: colourful, spectacular, surprisingly noisy as gallons of water leaped and splashed with absurd pneumatic force. We stood and watched for a minute before going inside, leaning on the sculpted bridge. One jet wasn't working properly and drew my gaze hypnotically, sending the water only half as high as the others, a half-second beat out of sync.

Tallis had that intense, stressed look he got when he was under a lot of pressure, when he could drink for hours without it seeming to have any effect until a certain point when it would hit him all at once and he would either pass out or throw up, or both. I reminded myself to watch for any signs that the moment was on the way.

Cameron appeared chastened. 'Let's talk about our problem,' he said, addressing us all as if we were clients. The word *problem* had a wonderfully decisive ring in his Queens accent – there was no question of calling it an 'issue' or a 'situation' or any other euphemism. It was a tremendous relief at that moment to be in his presence – the capable attorney, the advocate.

'I have to tell you,' Cameron continued, 'I know we all loved the guy, but part of me, when I heard he was dead, part of me breathed a sigh of relief.'

Tallis and Brian nodded to themselves. By this stage I suppose I was deep in shock; was I the only one that Dylan hadn't ever threatened while he was alive?

'The one thing he always said about this stuff was that he kept it to himself,' Brian said.

'When he wasn't threatening to, I'm sorry, *not* keep it to himself,' Tallis added.

'He said that?' I asked.

'Never directly,' Tallis said. 'But he never let us forget it.'

'Well, I guess he did keep it to himself,' I said. 'I mean, I had no idea – I had no idea about this thing with you, Brian, or any of you.'

'He always went easy on you, Elliot,' Brian said. He tried to lift his glass with his bandaged hand, forgetting about the injury again, and winced, laid his hand back on the table, and then gingerly on his leg.

'That's true,' added Cameron.

'He never held it over me – this thing he had, the thing he knew . . . I never felt, I don't know, intimidated by him about it.'

Cameron looked at me, not unkindly. 'You have a trusting nature.'

'He was one of my oldest friends,' I said.

Tallis gave one of his barking laughs.

'He was,' I insisted.

'I know,' Tallis said. 'But Cameron's right. And anyway, it's obvious that even if he kept everything locked up when he was alive, he's – what's the word – *bequeathed*? Made a bequest? Basically he's given a whole lot of information to someone else, who is now fucking with us.'

Brian half-straightened from where he had been slouched down in his seat, and blinked. 'Right. The Vegas brother.'

'I've given Cameron a brief rundown on what was in your envelope,' Tallis told Brian. 'And he's got his. I think we can assume that Elliot and I could get one any day. I think we can expect to hear from him soon. He knows where we're staying.'

'How does he know?' I wondered aloud.

'It wouldn't be hard to figure out,' Cameron said. 'We should check with the hotel desk tonight, in case there's any messages.'

Brian's pallor had returned and worsened. The freckles on his face stood out more than usual. 'I'll call,' he said, and opened his phone and dialled the hotel. He met Tallis's eye and nodded at him after he'd asked whether there had been any messages. His face stayed pale and set as he listened. 'OK. Can you read me the number? Thanks.' Cameron handed him a pen and he wrote on a napkin, phone squeezed against his shoulder. 'Thanks.' He closed the phone. 'So. A Mr Colin Andrews called to make sure I received the documents he'd left, and to call him on this number if I had any problems.'

'I hate the way he's spinning it out like this,' Tallis complained. 'All the mystery. The envelope, the cryptic phone message.'

'OK, Brian, call him back,' Cameron said.

Brian looked at him in disbelief. 'You call him.'

Tallis took Brian's phone and glanced at the napkin with the phone number written on it, punched in the numbers, tried to hand the phone back to Brian, who refused it. Tallis held it there against Brian's ear, blank-faced.

'Hello?' Brian said, and cleared his throat, took the phone. 'Yes, this is Brian.'

A pause while the other voice sounded, a faint murmur.

'Yes,' Brian said darkly. 'I think I know who you are.'

Another pause.

'Let me write that down.' He flipped the napkin over and wrote on it; an address. 'No problem.' He paused. 'Yes, the others will be there, too. See you then.' He closed the phone carefully with his injured hand.

'He wants to meet us tomorrow morning.'

8

A couple of hours later, after losing a game of blackjack with Cameron and Tallis and watching them play, I made my way over to the nightclub back at the MGM where I'd arranged to meet Brian and Cynthia. I waited at the bar, long enough to order a beer and think about what Cynthia would want to drink. I thought about ordering something else, a cocktail that might make me look more sophisticated. But was sophistication something that would impress Cynthia? She was, after all, writing a dissertation about Las Vegas. Or was it only a chapter?

There was a square, sunken dance floor in the centre of the room, with wide, shallow steps leading down to it. The steps were lit from beneath, glowing red rectangles of plastic that went on and off in a pattern that created a chequerboard effect. I watched it for a while and couldn't discern a rhythm to it, the on and off.

I couldn't help thinking that the steps would present a hazard for people who had been drinking and dancing all night, but they were shallow enough that you wouldn't have far to fall. It was the kind of thing I would be likely to do, even – especially – now that I'd seen the potential danger and tried to warn myself against it. A woman in spike heels walked down the steps, followed by a man. They showed no sign of tripping over.

A few other people were on the dance floor, under coloured overhead lights that swivelled in their own random set of motions. There were cages set up at the sides of the floor, four of them, elevated on fat black podiums, with girls dancing inside. This was the kind of thing I never saw outside of Vegas, and it had taken some getting used to the first time we visited. They were everywhere.

I saw Cynthia from the back, the only woman in the place with short hair. It was cut so close to her head at the back right near the nape of her neck that you could see the scalp through it; or should it be called skin at that point? I couldn't see it from where I was standing, several feet away, but knew that I would be able to up close. She was wearing a sleeveless dress with a low back that showed her spine all the way down to her waist. As I watched, she raised one hand to the back of her neck, to near the place I had just been looking at. She was talking to two men, and the hand on the neck looked like a coy gesture. Brian wasn't with her. I scanned the room once, twice, and couldn't see him.

She turned around then, while I was looking for Brian, and I was grateful that she hadn't turned and looked at me while I'd been watching her. I was able to raise my eyebrows and say 'Hey,' as though I hadn't been looking at her back and her neck for a while already. She came over to me with a smile and her confident walk, her incredibly high heels.

'Hi, Elliot,' she said.

'Hello. You look great.'

'Thanks. So do you.'

She was cheerful, upbeat, as she had been before, in the lobby. A couple of dimples formed when she smiled, small ones. There was a fine gold chain around her neck, of links so small that it clung to her skin, draped over her collarbone like a line painted on with a brush.

'Sorry —' I caught myself, stopped staring. 'Do you want a drink? What are you drinking?'

'A vodka martini, Grey Goose, dirty, two olives,' she said brightly. 'Thanks.'

Once she had her drink in hand, I thought about asking her whether Brian was coming. It was an unreasonably complicated question to construct. 'Where's Brian?' sounded wrong, petulant somehow. 'Is Brian with you?' was a possibility; 'Is Brian going to join us?' could work, but sounded overly formal. In my head, at least.

'Brian has a headache,' she offered, sparing me the question. I must have acted unsurprised. 'Did something happen earlier?' Her eyes narrowed. 'It seemed like something might have happened with you guys, you know, when you had that drink together.'

I was aware of gripping my glass too tightly and forced my hand to relax.

'What did Brian say?' I asked.

'So something did happen? Did you have a fight?'

'No – no one had a fight. Is that what he told you?'

'He didn't tell me anything.' She moved closer in. 'That's why I'm asking you. He seemed . . . unsettled.'

I decided to fall back on the grief argument. 'It's hard for all of us, you know, being here without Dylan. Maybe it's just hit Brian hard all of a sudden. I wouldn't be surprised.'

'Hmm,' she said.

The music grew louder. At the other end of the bar two women climbed onto it using a step stool that the bartender held for them. Their expressions changed from flat to glossy smiles once they stood up there in tight, black shorts and cowboy boots. They clapped their hands together as though they were going to start playing patty-cake, then turned and bumped their asses together, and started dancing. It was fairly restrained compared with the dancing going on inside the cages on the dance floor; they had to think harder about questions of balance. I saw them share a glance, and one of them rolled her eyes with an ironic smile, performing all her motions with a kind of amused detachment.

Cynthia stared at them thoughtfully. 'I guess regular women get up there to dance by the end of the night,' she said. 'This must be some kind of encouragement.'

I imagined that Dylan or Tallis would have known exactly how to handle this situation: standing at a bar with someone else's girlfriend while half-naked women were gyrating on it, and in cages a few feet away. For me it was impossibly awkward. I tried not to look at the women. I looked at Cynthia instead. Her short hair framed her face, falling onto her forehead just a little, not nearly long enough to cover her eyes. She didn't ever reach up to touch it. I thought of Natasha and felt a swift pang of longing from my hands to a place inside my chest, like a branching vein.

Cynthia gave me an appraising glance. 'I don't have any plans for getting up there myself, in case you're wondering.' I smiled. 'But who knows what might happen after a few more of these.' She stirred her drink with the toothpick, then picked it up and ate one of the olives, pulling it off with her teeth. 'I suppose it could be, you know, research,' she said when she'd swallowed it.

'Are you writing about tabletop dancing?'

'Not specifically. But it's Vegas. Naked girls will have to come into it somehow.'

'There's a few of those.'

'Do you ever go to the shows? You know, the naked girl shows?'

I shook my head. She had put the question to me casually, but at the same time as though I were an informant. It wasn't clear exactly what I would be informing on: she could have been curious about what Brian got up to normally when we were here, or it could have just been a question about Vegas. For her research.

'We're going to one tomorrow night,' she said. 'The one at the Paris casino. The cancan show.'

'I don't think they're completely naked. If that's what you're looking for.'

She smiled again, broadly. 'No, I'll be happy with some strategically placed feathers. Or sequins.'

It was hard to not think about Brian's pornography collection, his own interest in naked women, pictures of them at least, lacking in strategically placed anything. I wondered how much Cynthia knew about it. She seemed like a tolerant person. She seemed as though she might even take an academic interest, or be the kind of girl who was interested in porn. There was a graduate student in my department while I was finishing my PhD who'd claimed to be a 'sex-positive' feminist, which seemed to show mainly in her talking with unembarrassed enthusiasm about pornography in the student lounge and at department functions. From being on the edge of those conversations I had learned that there was such a thing as pornography produced by and for women. Apparently it avoided all the patriarchal power issues of regular pornography.

'She has great curves,' Cynthia said, indicating the dancer closest to us. The surface of the bar vibrated a little from their movements. Some kind of agreement seemed to be called for. I nodded.

'Oh, you're not even looking,' Cynthia scolded me. 'I've always been envious of women with bodies like that,' she said.

This seemed like the perfect example of a trap. 'They're probably envious of yours,' I tried.

'Small, but perfectly formed,' she said, with heavy irony. 'Do you want another drink? No, wait, let's dance.' She issued it as a sort of gentle command, rather than an invitation.

I followed her down the shallow steps, eyes on her revealed back, concentrating hard on keeping my footing. The dance floor was alternately slick and sticky in places, from spilled drinks and wear. Everyone in the club seemed to have the same idea at the same time we did and the space was suddenly crowded with bodies. I tried to pay attention to the music, to see if the song had changed, but it sounded just the same – monotonous, bass-heavy techno – as it had the whole time we had been there.

Cynthia reached one arm out behind her as we made our way, and turned her face toward me, smiling with her lips closed and dimple showing. Just as I reached forward to take her offered hand, the music changed, or the song stayed essentially the same but a faster, more insistent beat emerged. Her hand was small against mine, as I had expected; it was just our fingers touching, lightly. Skin warm and dry, fingers alive. She turned her face so that she was facing forward again and led me through the throng to a space near the centre of the floor. I wondered what she was up to; how to read this invitation to dance, this outstretched hand, the liveness of her slim fingers.

It was a relief to be away from the dancing girls on the bar. We were now closer to the ones in cages, but they were easier to ignore, raised up on their platforms and less in the line of sight. Cynthia moved with ease, all sinuous motion, arms lifted, hips twisting. She spun around slowly and shifted so that her dress crept lower and revealed the top of a tattoo low on her waist at the back, just below the line of fabric. I couldn't see the whole design; it could have been the curve of a dragon's tail or a bluebird's wing or a stroke of a Chinese character, anything. She moved again and it was gone from view.

She looked down at the floor; she looked up and arched her neck so that her throat showed, and tilted her head to the side; it felt like a performance designed solely for me, like a careful piece of persuasion, an argument, a deliberately laboured point. The point wasn't just that she was beautiful and that I was allowed to desire her, although that was part of it. I gave myself time to work it out, to allow myself to be persuaded of whatever it was. I had drunk enough that I was willing to dance, although it would take a couple more before I was really relaxed about it.

We stayed on the dance floor for what seemed like a long time. The songs changed. I caught another glimpse of the tattoo, and another, and was no closer to figuring out what it was. The straps of Cynthia's dress seemed always poised on the point of slipping off, but never actually did. She didn't adjust them, as some women around us were doing – pulling back sleeves, hitching fallen bra straps – just as she never touched her hair; she seemed to be so much all in place, and so unthinkingly sure about it. I pushed my glasses back up my face, sweating, and envied her.

The place where her dress shifted to reveal her tattoo began to obsess me, and I started to wonder whether this was part of the point of the dress. It began to seem obvious that it was, even though that seemed like an overly blunt device for Cynthia, with her subtly crafted beauty argument. But then I looked at it for long enough that it didn't seem blunt at all, but simply maddening, and more than anything I wanted to know how the fabric would feel if I touched my fingers to it, and pulled it down just enough to show the design of the tattoo more clearly. Texture – that was what I wanted to know more about – the silver-grey dress; the tanned, vulnerable-looking skin. Would the tattooed skin feel different from the skin around it?

A couple moved by on their way to another part of the dance floor and pushed us momentarily very close together so that we touched. 'What's that tattoo on your back?' I asked, trying not to shout to be heard over the music. As if in unconscious response to the words in my mouth, my right hand moved to touch her waist.

She moved in even closer and stretched up to speak into my ear, a word I couldn't make out.

'What?'

'A dandelion!' she repeated, and grinned up at me.

Self-consciousness overcame me then: my hand on her waist, her face upturned so close to mine, radiant, the sheen of sweat on her cheeks, and I let go.

'Come on,' she said, and took my hand again, just the fingers. 'Let's get another drink.'

I led the way this time.

'Do you want to go someplace else?' she asked, when we reached the top of the flashing red-lit steps.

'Sure,' I said.

'Is there some club you usually go to when you're in town? I should have asked you earlier.'

'No – I mean, nowhere in particular. There's a bar downtown I like. But it's quiet – no dancing. Another time, maybe.'

'Downtown.' She raised her eyebrows. 'Well, that's interesting. There's a place down there I want to visit. Let's go later. Do you mind if we go to the White Room first? At Caesars? It's one of the places on my list to check out.'

'Sounds good.'

'I'm trying to visit, you know, the places that are on TV a lot. For my research.' She smiled, apologetic. 'I'm going to text Brian.'

She pulled a phone out – the heavy-looking leather bag had been exchanged for a small purse in crackled silver leather – and started pressing buttons.

'Do you want to call him?' I asked.

'Maybe when we're on our way.'

'Sure.'

'Is Tallis coming along tonight? Or Cameron?'

'I don't know, I left them playing blackjack.'

'Well, let them know if you like. In case they want to come. But I know they probably don't want to hang out with the girlfriend.'

'Oh,' I started, about to protest, then stopped, feeling sure that she didn't need me to protect her feelings. 'I'll let them know anyway.'

Her phone buzzed. She read over the text. 'His head's still bad. Whatever.' She pressed a reply and flipped the phone shut. 'You're going to tell me what you all fought about.'

Her voice was sweet; she took my arm and pressed lightly against me, and didn't seem to want an answer right then and there.

We headed for the exit. I wondered how soon it would be before she found out. It didn't seem likely that Brian would be able to keep the secret from her for much longer, although her discovery of it seemed to be the thing he feared most. I'd seen the naked guilt in his face, the hopeless longing to confess in conflict with his desire to keep lying – to himself, to everyone. Cynthia seemed to have the kind of tenacious instinct that would keep going until she found out what was going on.

Our walk out through the maze of the hotel took us by the lion habitat.

'Look!' she said. 'Here it is.'

The glass enclosure was empty. A sign explained that the lions were there daily until 7 p.m. The waterfall was still running, pouring down thinly, silently, over the fake rocks. They looked fake, at least; with rock it was hard to tell. I looked for signs: what are the signs of real as opposed to fake rock? There was a lurid greenish stain all around the waterfall that could have been natural or synthetic, or a growth of something natural on top of something synthetic. The rocks didn't give the impression of mass and heaviness, somehow, that actual rocks gave. I couldn't tell whether their edges were smoother, or more rough, than real rock would be. My knowledge of actual rock was very limited; I'd seen a lot of it in the form of smoothly cut and polished stone on the facades of city buildings, but not in its natural state. But then I remembered the gorge just at the edge of campus at the college where I taught: the cold, gray harshness of it. I didn't pay attention to it whenever I had to walk by; looking down into that depth felt unsettling, even in summer when vines and other plants grew over and hid some of it. Every year at least one freshman died by jumping into the gorge, or falling into it while drunk. In spring, the vastness of the water rushing through it was a roar, all the surfaces of the gorge wet and slick with spray, and I always hurried over the bridge that spanned it. The bridge that, now I thought about it, was built of rough blocks that looked similar to these in the lion habitat – brownish-gray, not quite real.

Cynthia pressed her hands against the thick glass wall smeared with fingerprints. It showed a faint blurry reflection of the two of us standing there.

'What do you think about the rocks?' I asked. 'Real, or fake?'

She frowned. 'Of course they're not real,' she said, gently. 'They're fake.'

I expected her to follow up with the usual comment, 'Like everything in Vegas,' but she didn't.

She had said something earlier, by the elevators when we all arrived, about her work being about fakes and something else opposed – the real – authenticity, that was it.

'So where's the authentic stuff in Vegas?' I asked. 'Isn't it all fake?'

'Oh no,' she said, all serious now. 'You've been here so many times — you must know. It's so important that everything isn't fake. It's important that so many things are real, or authentic. Like these lions — they want you to know that they're all descended from the original MGM lion.'

'His name was Leo,' I offered. I'd learned about Leo that afternoon, when I was depressing myself in my room and reading the hotel literature.

'Right, Leo. And the lions here are all sired by him. Or related to him in some way.'

'Is that true?'

'I don't know. I don't see any reason to believe it or not believe it. But the point is that the lions matter — they have value — because they are the real thing. Or they claim to be.'

'They cycle them in and out, you know.'

'I know. There's forty of them or something out in the desert someplace nearby. They're all asleep now.'

'Or prowling,' I suggested.

'Or prowling, yes. That sounds good. Do you think there are facilities for prowling in a lion sanctuary?'

'Yes. Definitely.'

'Let's come and see them tomorrow.'

'OK.'

My phone buzzed. No number identified. I answered it.

'Elliot?' It was Brian, his voice an anxious squeak.

'You sound terrible.'

'Oh, yeah.' He cleared his throat. 'I'm fine, really. Elliot . . .'

Cynthia was looking at the lion enclosure again, reading one of the signs.

'Do you want to talk to —'

'No.' He cut me off.

'She's right here.' I tried to keep my voice down.

'No, look, I just can't do it, I can't go out with her tonight. Just ... you know, having some trouble dealing with ... all this.'

'What are you going to do?'

'Thinking it over, man. Tallis is here.'

'OK.'

'We're thinking it over, making a plan.' I could begin to hear how drunk he was already.

'Take it easy.'

'It's going to be fine, Elliot. Don't sweat it.'

'Just take it easy,' I repeated.

'Take care of Cynthia.'

I looked over towards where she stood with her back to me, arms loosely by her sides, the dress not showing the tattoo. The dandelion. 'Sure. She can take care of herself.'

'I know, I know, I'm just saying. Thanks for hanging out with her.'

'It's fine.'

'I know that, you know, you weren't crazy about the idea of her coming –'

'Look, it's OK. She's great.'

'Great. It's all good.' He sounded tired now.

'Is Cameron with you?'

A pause. 'Cameron's with us, yeah. We're sorting it out, Elliot. I know it's overdue.'

'OK, good,' I said, knowing the relief in my voice had to do with the fact that Cameron would be out of the way, that I'd have Cynthia to myself for the rest of the night. 'I'll check in with you later.'

'No problem.'

We said goodbye and I closed the phone, and looked up to

meet Cynthia's eyes, greenish-looking in the pale light from the lion enclosure. I felt sure she knew it had been Brian on the phone, but she didn't say a thing. Instead she took my arm again and we found our way to the exit.

Her silence took on a new quality in the taxi as we rode up the Strip toward Caesars Palace. She sat still, pressed up against the end of the seat, face staring intently out the window, her knees an inch or two apart. I tried not to look. There was something transgressive in what we were doing now. Drinking and dancing at the club in the hotel was one thing, with Brian upstairs somewhere in the building; this was something else.

They were moving in together, Brian had said. He'd lived with one girl before, a couple of years back, but somehow it hadn't seemed serious. She had just moved to Boston from somewhere else, Connecticut or Vermont, and was staying with friends and subletting until she found her own place; and moving in with Brian had seemed like just another step towards something else that didn't necessarily include him – or that was my impression when I'd stayed with them once while attending a small conference at Boston University. She had insisted on reading a draft of the paper I was presenting, and managed to spill red wine on it so that when I did read it at the conference the pages were stiff and warped and pink.

I found myself wondering now whether it was true that Cynthia was moving in with him, or something he'd invented, or exaggerated. There was no reason to think he was making it up except that it was hard to reconcile how I felt at this moment, being with her in the car, with the idea of her being so committed to Brian. I wondered what it was that she saw in him, as I always did with his girlfriends – not because it seemed so crazy for them to be attracted to him, but with that sense of wondering how he appeared to people who had known him only a short time compared with how long he and I had been friends.

In some ways Brian didn't seem to have changed that much in the years I'd known him. His display of sensitivity to women, his openness to feminism, had perhaps become more subtle over time but was still there, a carefully calibrated performance. It wasn't all for show, it was something he did seem to really believe in even as he appeared to perform it in a way designed to impress. The books from the college courses he'd taken on gender and sexuality in the English department and the politics of the gaze in film studies were still on his bookshelves at home, some of them fringed with old yellow Post-it notes. I wondered now whether he'd taken those courses out of guilt, or an acknowledged need of self-improvement or education in this direction, after what happened with Jodie White. It seemed more likely that he had managed to put that experience firmly away, in a compartment separated off from the rest of how he thought about himself.

I wondered again how I ought to judge him. I understood something about how it was possible to balance desires and feelings that should have been contradictory or mutually exclusive. Maybe it looked from the outside like hypocrisy or opportunism, but I knew it was more complicated than that, more deeply and strangely felt. All the same, I saw Brian differently now; and trying to see him as Cynthia perhaps saw him involved a lot more than the usual slight shift in focus. It was as though a vein of ruthlessness in him, of manic self-interest, had risen to the surface after being carefully suppressed for so long, and now, as I thought back, I could see it everywhere – not directly, but its shadow was apparent, an inescapable element in the peripheral vision of my memory.

It's hard to say how I would have felt about Cynthia if I

hadn't just been exposed to this new aspect of Brian, if I hadn't just learned that he'd done something that was impossible to justify. I don't think I would have normally indulged in this level of moral superiority, but it was difficult to resist for the way it made me feel less treacherous, for the way it seemed to give me some kind of exemption from whatever sense of obligation or taboo I would otherwise have felt. I could feel those strictures loosening as surely as the clean thread of a screw being turned, destabilizing a whole intricate framework of connections.

The driver accelerated to overtake another vehicle and I gave in to the way the speed of the car pressed our bodies back into the seat. I watched, transfixed, as Cynthia took a tube of lip gloss from her bag and drew it across her mouth once, twice, three times. She looked toward me then and smiled, her eyes gleaming, and her lips glittered and sparkled and shone.

A moment later the taxi stopped and let us out into the warm night. It was a brief few steps into the cold air of the casino. I suppose I should have expected it, but her next question took me by surprise.

'So what was he like, this Dylan?'

We were in the lobby of Caesars by then, had just passed by the fountain in the middle of the room. It splashed faintly, lit pink and yellow. I'd been here with Dylan, possibly right in the exact space that Cynthia and I now occupied. I glanced over at the counters where a few weary-looking tourists were still checking in or checking out and saw Dylan there, a spectral form for a moment, leaning his long, slim body in that way he had, positioning it in relation to the person he was addressing so that he seemed to be concentrating his entire energy on them, smiling beatifically and folding his arms, unfolding them. The spectre disappeared.

'Hasn't Brian talked about him?' I asked.

'Oh yeah, a little. He went through a lot in those weeks after he died.'

We kept walking toward the elevators.

'Brian didn't want to talk about him much, actually,' she went on. 'Once or twice he got drunk and said how much he missed him.'

'Hmmm.'

She reached out casually and snapped her hand on the elevator button. The arrow took a second to light up, and we waited.

'Once,' she said, 'he got really drunk and came over to my place – really late at night, like three in the morning – and said he was glad Dylan was dead. That was the last thing he said before he passed out.'

The elevator doors pinged open, disgorging a crowd of women and clouds of perfume. We let them pass. Cynthia looked over at me, eyebrows raised, once we were inside.

'It's not the kind of thing you want to bring up again the next morning over coffee,' she said.

'I guess not,' I replied. 'Did you ever bring it up again?'

She shook her head. 'He didn't either. He didn't mention him again after that.'

I nodded.

'So I'm sort of curious to hear more about him. From his other friends – from Brian's other friends. You guys were all so close.'

'We were.'

'I'm still in touch with some of my friends from college, from high school, even. But not in that kind of, I don't know, group sense that you all have.'

We were on familiar ground now and I began to relax. Most

people expressed admiration and envy at the way we had managed to stay friends and meet up together every year. The loyalty, the commitment, the affection for one another, the fact that we did what everyone else said they would like to but never got around to doing – whatever it was that people saw in us. But Cynthia didn't take it in that direction.

'Doesn't it ever feel . . . well, claustrophobic?'

'Claustrophobic?'

As the word left my mouth, I began to be conscious of the smallness of the space we were in. The elevator slowed and opened its doors just as I was beginning to stare at the red panic button. We stepped out not far from the entrance to the club. Twenty or more people were waiting in a ragged line behind a white velvet rope strung along silver posts.

Cynthia walked up to the door and handed a couple of cards to the woman controlling access. She towered over us both, dressed in white leather with skin like espresso and a mane of dark hair, her eyelids encrusted with silver glitter. The cards were line passes, I saw, supposed to get you past the rope and in the door; guys sometimes sold them or handed them out on the Strip. The woman glanced at the cards and looked carefully at us both before nodding approval and finally smiling, showing oddly pointed incisors, and motioning us through with a bored wave of her arm. The doors were heavy, thick glass and made me think of the lion enclosure. Through them the space was dark and blue-lit. I followed Cynthia inside, and recognized the place, roughly, from having seen it on TV.

'What show was this on?' I asked.

'What?'

A group of people next to us, shrieking and laughing, drowned out our voices.

'What show was this on?'

'What show did I see? Are you talking about the naked girls? The Paris show?'

'No, no, doesn't matter.' I decided to wait until we had drinks and a quieter place to stand or sit, or just to forget it.

The crowd cleared all of a sudden and I could see our way through to the doors that led to a large outdoor terrace overlooking the Strip.

'Do you want to go outside?' I asked.

'Yes! Oh, you know, I have to go to the bathroom. You go – I'll meet you out there.'

'Do you want a drink?'

'Thanks. I'll get the next one.'

I started to say no, don't worry about it, but she was gone.

There was a long, low white leather couch free at the end of the terrace, a candle glowing in a round glass holder on the table in front of it. I caught the eye of a waitress passing with a tray full of empty glasses and trashed paper umbrellas, and ordered our drinks. It was quieter outside than inside, but still loud with music coming from speakers set around the terrace.

I thought about what Cynthia had said in the elevators. *Claustrophobic.* It described pretty well what I'd felt earlier that evening when I'd sat with Brian and Tallis, that terrible yellow envelope on the table between us, all feeling trapped by the past, trapped by our knowledge of one another. Cynthia, I thought, you have no idea. But I liked her for saying it – for having something to say apart from the usual comments about how great it must be, and how good it was that we all had one another, that we could be there for one another after Dylan passed away.

I wondered whether she was going to ask about him again. What I had to say about him now was different from anything I would have said a day or so earlier, or so it seemed. I considered the things that were different, and the things that were the same. It was still true to say that he was likeable, and funny, and persuasive. And resourceful — the kind of person you could turn to in order to solve any kind of troublesome situation, no matter how impossible. I'd always had some sense of the more disturbing aspects of his problem-solving capacities but had never felt them so keenly. He convinced you that there was a solution for every difficulty; he could provide it, and he didn't ask you to look very carefully at the real cost of the answers he offered.

I remembered his seductive ease, how soothing he had been when he'd shown up with the Tennyson essay in a manila folder under his arm. I'd looked at it with uneasy caution once I'd figured out what it actually was, once he'd come in and explained and sat down on the floor in my dorm room the same way he always did, settling himself in one fluid movement, one long leg stretched out in front of him and one bent, a hand pulled loosely through his hair then rested, elbow to bent knee. The folder had looked so flimsy once I knew what was in it — so open, so prone to falling and spilling, I wanted to tell him to be more careful with it — then I realized at a certain point, with a rush of strangely mixed confidence and fear, that there was no need to worry about it falling and spilling. My name was on it, it was mine. In a matter of minutes I would be carrying it myself, over to the English department, my main concern that it not fall out onto the muddy pathways and get messed up.

And Dylan had smiled so happily, and passed me a cigarette, lit it. He'd brought coffee as well, a large paper cup with extra cream and sugar.

'You probably don't need the caffeine, I know you've been so stressed out,' he'd said, 'but here you are.'

He'd handed it to me carefully, resecuring the plastic lid with an air of indulgence, like giving a treat to a distressed child. It was hazelnut flavour, which Dylan liked and refused to believe that anyone couldn't. For once I didn't mind it.

There had been two copies of the paper in the folder and a disc with an electronic version, along with the two essays of mine that I'd given Dylan to show the writer, to give him a sense of my style. I glanced at the essay long enough to see that it was on the right topic and fit the length, but couldn't bring myself to actually read any of it.

'I've had a look over it,' Dylan said, drawing lazily on his cigarette. 'It's good, it's fine.' He met my eyes and spoke with his usual lightness of tone, but somehow more clearly and slowly than usual, making sure his words sunk in. 'At some point soon you should read it – just in case, you know – but don't worry about that right now.'

I nodded. Outside the window was another sunset starting to happen.

Dylan managed to rise with the same liquid grace he'd sat down with. 'OK,' he said. 'Let's go and turn this in. We don't want to miss Stanton's office hours.' That was something else he did when he went into full-on reassurance mode, assuming the collective plural in everything. 'We'll work it out.' 'We'll get it done.'

We walked over to the English department together, along the slushy pathways edged with muddy grass, as the day got darker and colder, the sky red by the time we arrived at the grey stone building. All around us were other students, shoulders hunched against the chill, alone and in talkative groups, their voices turned to brief clouds of mist in the air, sounds quietened by the damp cold. I had transferred the paper into an envelope by then, and it felt sharp and light in my hands.

Dylan pushed the door open for me and held it, followed me inside the building with his hand on my shoulder. We walked straight into the professor coming out of the mailroom holding a thick stack of papers and envelopes, his head down. We managed not to actually bump into him, but it almost happened.

'Elliot,' he said in greeting once he had stabilized the stack of things in his hands. He looked closer at Dylan as I mumbled hello. 'Dylan, how are you?'

'Hi, Professor Stanton. Great to see you.'

'You, too.'

'Elliot here has been telling me so much about your class. It sounds great.'

'Well, thanks. Dylan was in my Whitman seminar last spring,' he explained to me.

Dylan smiled graciously, as though accepting an extravagant compliment, which was in fact how Stanton had made his comment sound. Dylan knew how to stop short of obvious flattery. He didn't go on to say 'That class was so great' or 'I wish I could have taken this class this semester', though that would have been the obvious next step. I watched him, able to admire him even through my haze of anxiety and exhaustion. There was a compression to his movements when he flirted with men — it wasn't exactly flirting, but some more complex acknowledgment of his own attractive qualities, his sense of their admiration, an acceptance of it that was more subtle and challenging than the welcoming of it that flirting would have involved. He didn't slouch; he held himself not stiffly but with a feline tautness, relaxed as always, but stiller somehow.

Professor Stanton sighed. 'Well, Elliot. A paper for me, I hope?' He leaned forward, almost onto the tips of his toes, and tilted back again.

I handed it to him. 'Sorry again . . . thanks . . .'

'That's all right. Get yourself some rest. Goodnight.' He nodded to both of us.

Dylan raised his hand to my shoulder again – he was directing me, steering me, I realized – and we turned back towards the doors. I felt much lighter, as though the envelope had weighed pounds and pounds and I hadn't noticed until it was gone.

Outside the building, the few minutes of real twilight were still bringing a shimmer to the air.

'Come on,' Dylan said. 'Let's get you a drink.'

I loved him then unreservedly, with a rush of gratitude and affection, and thought about reaching out to embrace him, hesitated. He seemed to read my thoughts and leaned in to put his arms around me – swift, taut, completed with that elusive pat on the back. We released each other.

'I think I'll be buying you a drink,' I said. 'Several. And you'll have to tell me what I owe you.'

'It's a favour.'

'No way. I know these things don't come free. And you said this guy was good.'

'Oh, he's good. He's the best.' Dylan picked up a fast stride, hands in his pockets against the cold. 'But he's an old friend. I called in a favour with him. It's a favour for you.'

'I don't want –'

'Elliot.' He cut me off, smiling, warning. 'Shut the fuck up about it.' He laughed, a short, genuine laugh.

I shut up about it. I had a moment of being unsettled by the feeling of being in his debt, but I didn't think about it too much. It was a part of friendship, after all, and at that moment it was a part of friendship for which I was very grateful. I thought at the time only of how much he might have had to pay the writer – the ghostwriter, as I thought of him, the mysterious anonymous person who now knew my style and my name – or how big a favour he must have called in to get the paper. It didn't occur to me to wonder how Dylan knew the writer, or how he might have incurred such a balance of favours and debts – or rather these questions drifted into my mind for brief seconds, floated there, stretched out only slightly into imaginings. High school? Another class? His sister? LA? For all I knew the writer wasn't anywhere nearby at all but somewhere in another state, another country – I hoped he was. Then they evaporated. One of them stuck around, concretized itself enough to get me to ask Dylan, halfway through that long night of drinking, how he knew the writer.

'Oh, he's an old friend,' he said again, dismissive, relaxed.

'What's his name?' I asked, a gallery of faces passing through my mind.

'Seth.' Dylan met my eyes, smiled, looked back to his drink, signalled the bartender for another round. 'Just stop thinking about it, Elliot. It's all over now. So, tell me. How's Tallis? Where is he?'

Tallis arrived only seconds after Dylan had brought the conversation around to him, and I'd been drunk and tired enough to be superstitiously awed by it. Dylan seemed to have conjured him up, a vision of distraction to take my mind away from the question of the essay, the question of the writer.

'Yes, he did it,' Dylan had announced when Tallis asked how I'd gone with that final paper, and raised his glass in a general toast. 'With a little help from your friends, right, Elliot?'

I had raised my glass in turn.

'Now, where's that girl you said you were going to bring, Tallis?'

Tallis had started sleeping with some girl in one of his classes who also waitressed at the bagel shop in town. She seemed to be as interested in casual sex as he usually was, and her lack of clinging, the thing he hated in other girls, was driving him mad. He groaned. 'She's killing me, Dylan. She chucked me tonight – she's going out with a fucking junior, a comp lit major. Fuck.'

We commiserated. The congratulations were in, the subject was closed. I felt the remaining questions in the back of my mind fizzle and fade.

Our drinks arrived; I'd ordered a martini in Cynthia's two-olive style. It tasted salty and made me wish immediately for a glass of water. The dry air sucked moisture away from my skin busily. When Cynthia finally appeared I couldn't tell whether she'd taken a long time or no time at all.

'Well done,' she said. She sat down on the white couch and crossed her legs, lifted her glass and clinked it against mine. 'Cheers.'

'Cheers.'

There it was again, her clean smile. There was an electric tension in her body, a restlessness that hadn't been so obvious before. The lip gloss was still there, shiny like wet candy. Her eyes moved across the terrace, out to the balcony, the skyline. The mountains were out there somewhere beyond the glare of lights, dark and brutal and ancient.

'It's kind of beautiful, isn't it?' she said. 'In a monstrous kind of way.'

I nodded.

'So, Cynthia,' I began, ready with a set of questions about her research.

'Call me Cyn,' she said. She laughed. 'Everyone does. Now, Elliot – there's no nickname for that, is there? Just Elliot. One *l* or two?'

'Two,' I said.

She smiled. 'Oh, like in *E. T.* Now. I just bought some amazing coke from someone in the bathroom. Do you want some?'

'Cyn,' I repeated. 'Of course.' Her eyes glittered, and suddenly everything seemed to become clear.

'Of course – like, OK?'

'Sure. OK. I mean, thanks.'

She laughed again. 'Relax.'

I tensed at the word, hearing her say it in a way that made me think of Dylan. He would have been the one to acquire the good coke in the bathroom, if he'd been here. I considered whether this was a Dylan memory that would make sense to share with Cynthia.

'You would have liked Dylan.' Her eyes brightened. 'I mean, everyone liked him. But you would have related to him.'

'Oh, really?'

'He always had the good drugs.'

'Huh. Interesting.' She pressed her hand to mine, and in it was a small plastic bag. 'Don't take too long,' she breathed into my ear, and brought her mouth to her glass.

I tapped a small pinch of powder onto my hand in the bathroom stall, noticing the paleness of my skin in the sparkling overhead light. It was sharp and then numb in my nose, a bitter, glorious trace down the throat. I washed my hands and marvelled at the chill of the cold water, the brightness of it.

Time telescoped and collapsed after that as though strobe-lit, patches of illumination followed by blur. More dancing; more drinking. On the dance floor, arms raised above her head for a moment, Cynthia was caught by the white flash of a strobe and appeared to me like a goddess, all silver and powerful and divine. Her arms dropped, the lights changed pattern, and she was human again, a thin film of sweat visible on the skin of her face, eyeliner beginning to smudge.

More cocaine, both of us squeezed together in a stall in the men's bathroom, where I forgot about Brian and everything else. The world outside the small, white box stopped existing, and all I was aware of was Cynthia and her silvery dress with the straps that never fell down. I raised one finger, trying to be slow and deliberate about it, and pushed the strap down her shoulder so that it lay against her arm. She kept smiling, lips compressed. I put both my hands to her shoulders and turned her around. She pressed her hands to the wall, turned her face so that I could see her profile, her nostrils flaring slightly with each breath. I brought my thumb to the back of her dress and pulled it down to show the tattoo. There it was, like she had said: a dandelion, delicately drawn, tiny starlike pieces floating away across her hip. Her skin was smooth. She twisted back to face me.

The bubble around us burst as two people entered the bathroom; the scratch of high heels on the tiles and a woman's low-pitched laugh, accompanied by a man's heavy tread and voice, though I couldn't make out what he was saying to her; a suggestion that ended with ' ... don't you?'

I was painfully aware of how our two pairs of feet must be showing in the gap between the door and the floor. The same feeling arrived that had come upon me in the elevator, the walls breathing, and closing in.

'Don't worry,' Cynthia whispered in my ear. 'They'll just think we're fucking, or doing drugs.'

'I want to get out of here,' I hissed back.

It was impossible to escape unnoticed. I'd given up worrying about that and had my hand on the latch when we heard the unmistakeable sounds of the two people out there starting to have sex. She moaned; he said 'yeah' over and over again; there was a rhythmic sound of something metallic crashing against the tiles, though I couldn't work out what it might be.

Cynthia looked disbelieving, embarrassed on their behalf. She caught my eye and we both suppressed laughter.

'Let's go,' she said. 'They could be here all night.'

I nodded and pulled my shirt straight. She smoothed down

her dress. I touched her hair where it had been slightly squashed when she had pressed her face to the wall, and felt a real stir of desire as I passed my fingers through it. Short, soft. Her eyes widened.

The woman's moans from beyond the door grew louder. It was the opposite of arousing. Cynthia smiled and raised her chin a little, waiting for me. I opened the door and walked out, not glancing at the couple over against the washbasins in the corner except to register in my peripheral vision that the woman had a handbag slung over her shoulder festooned with metal buckles and chains that were responsible for the clanking noises.

Once we were out of the bathroom Cynthia took my arm and groaned.

'On the washbasin! Get a stall, at least.' She shook her head.

Why not get a room? I wondered to myself. The city was full of hotels; we were in one. It seemed easy enough.

The moment of tension between us had passed, the electric seconds when my fingers had touched her back, when the idea of sex in a bathroom hadn't seemed so crazy. It dissolved, and we kept drinking like old friends.

9

I wasn't sure what to call the part of Vegas where the diner was, where we were meant to meet Colin. Tallis had looked it up; he was good at maps and directions and had it all planned out. All he would say to me was that it was west. He'd arranged a hire car that could be collected from somewhere out the back of the hotel complex.

We all met for breakfast at the Hollywood Diner buffet at the hotel. I was surprised to see Cynthia there, sitting next to Brian and across from Cameron at a big white table. She looked clean and put-together as usual, her face freshly scrubbed, and she seemed to be in the middle of a conversation with Cameron. Small, empty plastic containers of grape jelly and butter were strewn across the table. I sat down with my cup of coffee and drank it, burning my tongue.

'Hi, Elliot,' she said, and kept eating her toast.

'Good morning,' I said. My tongue smarted from the burn.

'Cynthia's doing some sightseeing today,' Brian told me.

I wasn't sure what to say about what we were doing, in case she asked. She kept eating cheerfully, opening more tiny tubs of jelly and spreading it on pieces of toast. There was a pile of it on her plate.

'Go ahead. Have some,' she said. 'You look hungry.'

The thin gold necklace was still there around her neck. I tried not to think about her shoulders underneath her clothes, the way they had looked in the silver dress the night before, the dandelion on her back and the sensation of her skin under my fingers. I ate some toast and it did something to take away the sour taste in my throat, cocaine and alcohol hangover.

'What sights are you seeing?' I asked.

'The lions. Some of the other animal exhibits. I want to go over to the Paris later, the Venetian maybe.'

The Paris. It sounded wrong and right at the same time.

Brian and Cameron weren't talking, but it didn't have the same edge as it had before, when it took the form of explicit ignoring. This was more normal, early morning, too-early-for-conversation kind of behaviour. Brian pushed the cream towards Cameron without really looking at him. Cameron poured and pushed it back in the same way. Watching them sitting there on opposite sides of the table, drinking coffee, I couldn't see any of the flames of secret longing between them that I'd imagined were possible the day before.

Cameron straightened. 'You're just in time, Elliot,' he said, as though I'd only just sat down, or he'd only just noticed I was there. 'Tallis is meeting us outside with the car in . . .' He checked his watch, a heavy silver thing with several dials. 'Fifteen minutes.'

He seemed surprised to find that there was so much time to spare. Brian lifted his eyes to the ceiling in quiet disapproval.

'But I don't know if you have time to eat,' Cameron continued.

'That's OK,' I said. 'I'll just eat Cynthia's toast.'

She winked at me. I looked away.

'There's plenty of time,' Brian said.

He stood up with his plate and headed over to one of the buffets. A minute later he was back with a plate piled with sausages and bacon and scrambled eggs, another plate that he placed in front of me, and a fresh pile of toast that he deposited on Cynthia's plate. She accepted it silently. He slung one arm around her shoulders, like he had when I'd spotted them in the check-in line the day before. She leaned in just a fraction and smiled at him. He began to eat with dogged determination and little pleasure.

'Elliot. Go ahead. There's enough here for three of us. Go on,' he said, his mouth half full, when I shook my head. Eventually I took a piece of toast and some eggs and discovered that I was actually hungry.

Cynthia picked up her conversation with Cameron; it was all about the various law firms in Boston and Chicago. She had a couple of friends from college who had wound up in those places, and they gossiped about the bosses and the partners, and who had won a case against whom. She nodded at things Cameron said, and said, 'Mmmm!' in agreement, with her mouth full. I studied her face for signs of tiredness, awkwardness, any trace of consequence left by the night before, but couldn't find any.

Brian sank into a still, self-absorbed state that I recognized as his way of dealing with pressure and, often, anger. When we all rose to leave, he put a black messenger bag over his shoulder, slung over his neck and across his body. I caught a flash of yellow against the black interior where the flap closed over and left a small gap: the envelope, inside.

Cynthia kissed him hard on the cheek once we reached the door and gave us a wave before she walked away.

'I should check at the front desk,' I said once she was a fair distance from us.

We walked there in silence, through what seemed like miles of rooms of slot machines and games of poker, blackjack, roulette. Some players had evidently been there all night: stifled yawns, stiff bodies. Others were just starting out for the day, alert and shifting in their seats. With some it was hard to tell; a certain glazed expression could come over people's faces so quickly, and looked much the same after five minutes or several hours.

The clerk at the desk glanced up from his computer when we approached.

'Yes . . .' he said in answer to my request, typing in fast, sporadic bursts, and spun around, collecting an envelope from a shelf against the wall. It wasn't yellow, like Brian's, but a pale grey. For a moment I wondered if it might be something else altogether, not a packet of blackmail, something innocent. But then I saw the handwriting and knew what was inside.

Cameron spoke to the clerk. 'Can we see if there's anything for our friend to collect, also? Hyde, Tallis Hyde.'

That earned him a long stare. 'I'm sorry, sir, we can't do that without the guest's permission.' He went back to typing.

'If you look it up, you'll see we have a group booking,' Cameron tried. The clerk looked unconvinced. Cameron pulled out his phone. 'Here – I'll call him.'

The clerk raised his eyes, irritated, picked up the phone on the desk next to him and punched in a number he read from his computer screen.

'Mr Hyde? Good morning, Peter here from the MGM Grand, sorry to bother you, sir. We have someone here enquiring whether he is authorized to collect any documents that might have been left here for you?' He looked at me. 'A Mr Elliot West, sir?' A short pause. 'Thank you so much, Mr Hyde, and have a wonderful day.'

He replaced the phone and went to the shelf, returning with another grey envelope in his hands. 'Have a wonderful day and enjoy your stay at the MGM Grand,' he said, in the same smooth tone he had used on the phone.

The envelope was so light it might have been empty. I shook it a little and felt the weight of small things inside, pieces of paper or photographs.

Walking to meet Tallis with the envelopes under my arm was uncannily like that walk I'd made with Dylan all those years ago to the English department that evening, the essay in my hands, waiting for it to fall in a puddle. The heat hit me with its brutal, casual familiarity when we stepped outside, the contrast with that cold winter twilight somehow bringing it even closer in my memory.

Brian and Cameron kept glancing at the envelopes I was carrying.

'You know what's inside?' Cameron asked, eyes shielded behind sunglasses.

'I guess,' I said.

Brian started to smile.

Tallis pulled up in a long black sedan with a fresh-looking scratch all the way along the side ending in a small dent toward the tail-light.

'What's with the scratch?' Cameron asked when we all got in. He sat in the front passenger seat, and I sat behind him in the back, conscious that he and Brian had unthinkingly positioned themselves with maximum possible distance between them. Or maybe they had thought about it; habit and conscious decision might have become inseparable by now.

'The scratch was there already,' Tallis said. 'They gave me a discount.' He grinned, lifting his sunglasses to reveal bloodshot, bright blue eyes. His skin showed a faint flush of pink, already anticipating the sunburn he would have by the end of the day just from walking between the car and the door of whatever building he entered. 'Good morning, everyone. All in?' He tipped the glasses down again and pulled out into the traffic, too fast. 'What do you have for me from the desk of our esteemed hotel?' he asked.

Again, the cheery bonhomie. I felt myself beginning to sulk already, resistant.

'Just this.' I held up the envelope and he glanced at it in the rear-view mirror.

'Throw it over here,' he said when we pulled up at a red light moments later. I passed it to him. He opened the seal with some difficulty, shaking it a little like I had, to convince himself that there was actually something inside.

'Oh, fuck,' he said quietly. 'I knew it.' Then, louder, a stream of curses, increasing in vehemence and force, as he gripped the steering wheel with his large, pale hands.

Cameron shrank slightly over to his side of the car, alarmed. Brian was the calmest among us. I felt sure that he was enjoying the spectacle of all of us, one by one, being subjected to something like what he had felt the day before.

'The light's changed,' Brian said, leaning forward. 'Tallis. Green light.'

Tallis gave a final, definitive-sounding 'Fuck' and put the car into gear. He remained ominously silent for minutes, changing lanes recklessly, earning horn blasts from other drivers. At the next red light he lit a cigarette, his hands slipping on the lighter.

'Do you know where we're going?' I asked.

We had turned off the Strip a few blocks earlier, and were now heading west – I thought – down another busy boulevard. No one answered. Tallis always took it as an extreme of bad manners if one of us ever questioned his navigational ability, and I didn't want to press it.

Many possibilities passed through my mind. Mainly I pictured us driving west for miles along this road until we left the city and wound up on a dirt track fringed with trailers and shacks and dusty, half-derelict gas stations. It was hard to shake this idea I had of Colin as belonging to a vaguely imagined Vegas underclass. I thought of his dead mother having her other child adopted because of youth or poverty or both. He must be desperate, I thought, he must be poor; why else would he be motivated to do this, if not for money?

The question of money had preoccupied me that morning as I forced myself to consider the question we hadn't been able to address yet, collectively – what was it that he wanted? What was the goal, the aim?

I didn't have a lot of money, and had no obvious way of getting my hands on any, or not very much, in any case. For a single person, my salary was fine, but a lot of it went toward paying the massive student loans I had managed to accrue in graduate school. Tallis and Cameron each earned good money, but Cameron had a family to support. Brian didn't make anything much, but his family was rich.

I wondered whether Dylan had given money to his brother while he was alive. It seemed possible, even likely, although it couldn't have been much given his small salary in publishing and the crazily high rent he paid in Manhattan.

Blocks passed, shopping malls, supermarkets, bars.

'Should we talk about this?' I asked. 'Shouldn't we have some sort of, I don't know, a plan?'

Cameron glanced over at Tallis and then twisted around in his seat to talk to me. I knew then that they had talked about it in some detail the night before.

'I think we need to check him out, find out what his intentions are,' Cameron said. 'Let me do the talking.'

'OK.'

'Elliot?' Cameron asked.

'Yes?'

'What's in that envelope of yours?'

It sat on the seat beside me, already a little creased, still clean around the edges except for one faint fingerprint near one corner, probably my own.

'It's a paper,' I said. 'Once, in college, I didn't have time to finish a paper I was working on – I ran out of time. Dylan knew someone who could finish it for me.'

'He got someone to write it for you?' Cameron asked.

'That's right.'

'So it's like, plagiarism? Or would you call it fraud?'

I shrugged. The light hit his glasses so that I could see the darkened shape of his eyes behind them, but couldn't read their expression.

'Is that it? I mean, is that the only thing?'

'That's it.'

'I can see that something like that could be embarrassing for you.' He kept looking at me.

I stared hard out the windshield. The mountains were there, I knew, beyond the line of buildings, the same ones I'd seen from my window that morning. It was just concrete now before me, and neon struggling to show itself against the bright sunlight.

'But it wouldn't cost you your job, would it?'

'I don't think so,' I said, and hoped that I sounded convincing.

'But tenure can be so tricky, can't it?' Cameron mused, turning back to face the front, almost as though he were talking to himself and not to me. 'You never know what little thing is going to make a difference.'

'Yeah.'

'Unless, you know, your book changes the world and they'll do anything to keep you, right? If you win, what is it, a genius grant or a huge prize or something?'

'That's right.'

In the silence that followed I reflected – and I'm sure Cameron did too – on how unlikely it was that my work would have that kind of impact, that kind of value, or that I would be up to the task of engineering the kind of networks of admiration and influence that led to nominations and prizes. In recent months I had been procrastinating on the question of how to shape the thesis into a book manuscript, or whether to give up on that idea altogether (not a thought to mention to anyone with influence in my department). I pretended to be 'extending the argument' of one chapter by reading and taking copious notes on one of Middleton's even lesser known works, a probable collaboration with some other playwright.

It's not like I was hopeless at that stuff – I'd managed to get good fellowships going through graduate school, impressive publications, appeared on the right panels at a couple of conferences, got a good job. But Cameron was right: tenure was tricky, and any little thing could make a difference. The discovery of a fraudulent paper in college was exactly the sort of thing that could make a difference.

Plagiarism was a serious issue in our department, and the chair had recently encouraged the whole faculty to adopt a more rigorous and uniform approach to it. Since my days in college the internet had only made it easier to get access to papers, and easier to cover your tracks if you did. Felix, my colleague with the ulcer, had shown me a website one afternoon where you could not only pay good money for an A paper, but also for a B paper on the same topic, and a C plus if you didn't want to draw attention to any vast improvement in your writing skills. Felix's student had purchased the A minus option for his final paper (which Felix had actually graded as A, I noticed, glancing at the papers on his desk) and B plus for the previous assignment. The whole thing was horrifying to me, for the spectres it raised from my own past, and Felix mistook my dismay for genuine academic outrage.

'It's unbelievable, isn't it?' he said, rocking back in his ergonomic chair. 'They're so good. It's no wonder . . .' He seemed to be feeling bad for not having caught the faked B plus when it had been handed in.

'It's no wonder you didn't see it,' I reassured him.

The chair let out an alarming creak, as though something was about to snap. He didn't change position, eyes fixed on the screen.

'Do you want the password?' he asked me as I was about to leave his office. 'You need a password to log in to this website – the one that lets you put in the text, find the papers, all that.'

I froze. It would have looked strange to refuse. 'You know, I'm not too worried about my students this semester.'

He looked injured. 'Right. Good. You can never be too careful, though. I mean, look at this . . .'

He gestured hopelessly toward the B plus on his desk, the A minus beside it. It was covered with comments in blue pencil: *Good thesis!* next to the first paragraph; checks in the margins.

'Can you email it to me?' I asked, trying to save face.

He nodded. 'Yes.'

'I won't lose it that way. Be on the safe side.'

He turned back to the website, scrolling through samples of papers on topics in his field. He worked on twentieth-century fiction, Nabokov; I dreaded to think how many papers there would be available to buy addressed to topics close to those he would have spent time perfecting, analyzing those particular passages he would have carefully chosen as the most significant, the richest or least appreciated. Confronting our own lack of originality in the way we taught or thought was one of the worst aspects of the process of detecting faked or stolen work.

The prospect of confronting plagiarism in my own students' essays troubled me for obvious reasons, and I probably turned a blind eye to any suggestion of it apart from instances I couldn't help noticing: the stupid version of it, where pages of barely punctuated prose were suddenly interrupted by a perfect paragraph lifted directly from a website or copied in carefully from the pages of a reference book. Those cases aren't the ones that students fail for, or risk getting put on academic probation like they can expect if they fake a whole paper or copy another student's exam. In those minor cases I could get away with simply grading down a full grade and writing a cautionary letter advising them to consult the guidelines for correct citation of sources, or asking the student to resubmit. A few times I'd managed to do that and feel almost not haunted, almost righteous. I might have performed the most serious infraction – paying someone else to write a paper for me and pretending it was my own work – but at least when I did write my own work, as I had for every other assignment, it was all my own. I was scrupulous about obeying MLA citation for every source, giving credit to every critic whose ideas I used, making sure I got every quote exactly right.

The car slowed. We stopped at a light, waiting to turn. I didn't think about the accident these days much at all, but something now brought it back to me, travelling in the back of the car. It was a slight shimmer in the fabric of time and memory, as though the past was for a moment uncomfortably closer than usual. Each of us was in a different position in the car than we had been then. Brian was still huddled over in his seat, arms folded tightly.

'What about you, Tallis?' I asked. He hadn't spoken since the stream of invective. A muscle in the side of his jaw worked, tense and busy.

'I'll tell you,' he said, through teeth that didn't seem to want to open. 'Let me find the place first.'

It might have been my imagination, but I thought I heard his English accent slip, thought I heard a hardness around the end of the word *first* that shouldn't have been there. All the years he'd lived in the States it had seemed strange the way he spoke with no American inflection. His English accent always sounded exaggerated to me; I didn't ever get used to it, or not hear it. I noticed that he took up some American idioms, words and phrases – he liked to say 'awesome' and 'dude', for instance, always in a very self-conscious way – but the words never lost their distinctive, different sound.

He drove in silence the rest of the way, four or five blocks after the turn, and started backing into a space next to a hydrant.

'Tallis,' I said, looking out the window at the chipped yellow hunk of metal.

'Fuck it,' he said, glancing over his shoulder as he turned the wheel.

'They'll tow the car,' I said. 'Not just a ticket.'

'Elliot, calm down.' It seemed to help him relax, to be able to scold me in that familiar way. 'No one will tow the car. Christ.' He turned off the engine and let the key sit in place.

'So,' he said, and looked at me with tired eyes. 'It's about my father. This thing Colin has on me, that Dylan had. It's not about me, exactly. It's about him.'

Cameron knew about it, whatever it was. He slouched further down in his seat and sighed.

I'd met Tallis's father once, in our junior year when he'd paid a quick visit halfway through the spring semester and then taken Tallis away for a weekend in New York. He and Tallis's mother were settled back in England by then – they seemed to move every few years – but he travelled back and forth to the States for work. I'd stopped by Tallis's place that Thursday morning. His father had answered the door and greeted me with a lazy, utterly disarming smile and a beautifully pronounced 'Hello', as though I were the person in the world he most wanted to see at that moment. He was thin, with the emaciated face and slight stoop of the serious alcoholic, and a cigarette burned in his hand.

'Hi,' I said, and introduced myself. 'Is Tallis here?'

'Of course. Come in.'

He stood back from the door with a movement like a compressed, enervated flourish, like someone who used to be graceful and quick on his feet. I looked through into the apartment and Tallis stepped out of the kitchen, looking at once grave and boyish, preoccupied, hands busy drying a glass with a dishtowel.

'Elliot, there you are,' he said as I walked in. He gestured toward his father. 'This is my father, Richard Hyde. Richard: Elliot West.'

'It's delightful to meet you.' He shook my hand with an air of arch amusement. 'I so rarely get to know any of Tallis's friends. Are you named after the poet?'

He had unusual eyes, those David Bowie eyes, one blue and one brown, and I looked back and forth between them as he held my gaze. He must have been used to people staring.

'No,' I said, and felt an impulse that very rarely came, to lie about it and say yes, because it seemed like it would have pleased him. 'Two *l*s.'

'Ahh,' he said, as though this were equally interesting.

I waited for a cue from Tallis, not sure whether he was going to invite me to sit down. It wasn't that unusual for me to drop by on a Thursday when we both had mornings free. We would drink coffee together, and he'd sometimes talk to me about those English sports he was into, cricket and soccer – football. I liked those mornings. Tallis had a calmness and confidence at home in his own space. All the public bantering, the needling and strutting, was toned down and his manic energy seemed somehow contained and focused. It was knowing him in this way, this version of him, that made it possible to put up with his overbearing behaviour at other times.

The radio was often on, playing the classical station or the BBC World Service. This, and the sport obsession, were the only signs that he missed England, something he would never admit. He kept the place scrupulously clean, to a degree that seemed slightly obsessive. There was none of the mess and accumulated grime that characterized every other student dwelling I knew. I suspected that this was one of the reasons he'd found fraternity life difficult, dealing with other people's stuff in the communal spaces of the house.

That morning, the apartment displayed a few glaring spots of disorder. His father's jacket, a fine tweed blazer, had been thrown on the couch carelessly so that one sleeve hung down over the arm and the rest of the jacket was wrinkled as though it had been sat on. There was a crumpled soft pack of cigarettes and an ashtray on the coffee table next to a newspaper, folded loosely, with pages out of alignment. There was a glass there as well, half full of clear liquid that I felt sure was gin rather than water, judging from the faint smell of alcohol that permeated the room. As I glanced around, other things looked slightly wrong: chairs set at an unfamiliar angle; Tallis's unmade bed, covers spilling onto the floor, visible through the half-open door to his bedroom. The place itself felt ill at ease. It was possible that I had walked in on an argument. I felt an instinctive desire to close the bedroom door, to avert my eyes, to straighten the chairs.

Richard sat on the couch, crossed his legs, and dragged deeply on his cigarette, watching us patiently. Tallis didn't look at him, but that somehow only made it more obvious how much of his attention was absorbed there. When he offered me coffee, I refused, making up some story about reading I needed to catch up on for class later that day. It didn't seem as though he wanted me to stay.

When I'd caught up with Cameron later, he'd explained to me about Richard's drinking. Cameron had known Tallis longer than any of us. They'd gone to high school together for their senior year – Cameron had a scholarship to this wildly expensive prep school that Tallis got dropped into when his family moved to New York from the UK. The drinking was bad enough to cause serious problems for Tallis's father at work and at home, Cameron said – Tallis's parents had separated twice before and seemed to be permanently on the verge of divorce. His father lived part-time at the Four Seasons when he went on a binge and Tallis's mother threw him out.

'It's hard on Tallis,' Cameron had said. 'He's an only child. He used to think it was all up to him to solve the situation, to watch his dad's drinking, to hide it from his mother, et cetera.'

I didn't tell Cameron too much about what it had been like coming across Tallis and his father together. That glimpse of the unmade bed, all the rest of it, had felt like an unauthorized moment of intimacy. It was as though Tallis had exposed something to me unintentionally, a vulnerability that he would regret.

When Tallis showed up after that weekend with his father, he was exhausted, turning up to the bar to meet us already half drunk and drinking with a solid, troubling determination. He tried to pick fights with all of us. Cameron had treated him with patience, walked him home. I'd wondered about the drinking, the seeming irony of the way Tallis appeared to be driven to it in order to cope with the problems it caused in his own family. It made sad, complete sense.

Tallis was looking at Cameron in the car as though waiting for Cameron to reassure him, to indicate that he should tell us the story. Cameron didn't say anything, didn't seem to move, but something passed between them. Tallis turned around to face Brian and me more fully.

'I've met him,' I reminded him, trying to be encouraging. 'Richard.'

'That's right. I forgot about that. You met him that time he came to visit. Well, this is about something fairly recent. Cameron, do you have a cigarette?'

Cameron glanced at me with a worried frown. He was the only one of us who never smoked. I reached into my pocket. There were two cigarettes left in the pack and I gave one to Tallis. Cameron pressed the lighter in the dashboard, and handed it over. Tallis lit the cigarette carefully, first turning the key in the ignition enough so that the electronic windows worked; he wound one down, letting in a wave of heat, and blew smoke straight towards me. Brian coughed. I lowered my window as well. Tallis turned the engine off.

'My father's been trying to stop drinking for a while,' he said to us, sounding almost apologetic. 'Going to AA and all that. My mother's going to leave him if he doesn't stop. It's bad for him.' He turned to flick ash out the window, his forearm glowing bright white in the sun for a second. 'And it's bad for her,' he said, all casual understatement. 'Last time he visited the States he fell off the wagon pretty badly – this was just last year. I was in London, I couldn't get over here, and Dylan helped out when I got the call.'

'What did he do?' I asked.

'He got into an argument with someone,' Tallis said. 'I don't know exactly what happened. I think they were both pretty far gone. Drinking at the hotel bar. He ended up pushing this guy too hard – literally, he shoved him, and the guy fell over. Sprained his wrist, or his ankle. Broke a chair, a table, something else. The guy called the cops. Pressed charges. Assault.'

Something about the way Tallis spoke made me think that he wasn't telling us everything.

'Was your father OK?' I asked. 'Was he injured?'

Tallis shook his head. 'Not badly. He hurt his hand.'

'And the other guy broke his wrist?'

Tallis paused. 'Sprained.'

I let it go. 'Did Dylan get him a lawyer?' I asked.

'Yes,' Tallis said.

I looked at Cameron.

'I couldn't get through to Cameron,' Tallis said. Cameron kept watching him. 'It was an emergency,' Tallis continued. 'I called Dylan. I knew it was a bad idea, but, you know – I knew he'd be able to do something. He found someone who sorted it out. It was expensive, but the guy didn't take it to court. He agreed to drop the charges. So. My mother didn't have to know about it, and neither did the company.'

'And Colin knows about the lawyer?' Brian asked.

'He has his number.'

'But wouldn't the lawyer just deny it?'

'Colin's also got a record of the arrest.'

'Shit,' Cameron said.

'Obviously I'd prefer it if my mother didn't find out about this. Or anyone else connected with my father.'

I remembered what Cameron had said about Tallis's feeling of responsibility, the adult part he felt he'd had to play as a child. His fury on the drive over appeared potentially more complicated now; I wondered how much of it was anger at his father, for creating the situation in the first place.

'Here we are, anyway,' Tallis said, and replaced his mirrored glasses. 'Let's meet Colin.'

★

The place said simply DINER in red block letters against white-painted concrete over the entrance. There were long glass windows onto the street. It was either self-consciously retro or just old and relatively freshly painted. The interior presented the same ambiguity: a chrome counter, red vinyl-topped stools, red vinyl booths. It was empty apart from a woman reading a battered paperback at the end of the counter. It felt as though we had walked into an Edward Hopper painting at the wrong time of day. Somewhere a radio started up, static and crackle, then a song, someone rolling through the dial, through the sound of talk and more music and the unmistakable overenthusiasm of advertisements, until they settled on a station – still staticky, but not too bad – playing seventies rock. It sounded like the Eagles.

A tall, thin Asian man with long hair appeared behind the counter, a half-full bottle of ketchup in his hands, wearing a waiter's half-apron. He nodded at us.

That's when I noticed Colin. He was sitting in the booth at the very end of the room. There was a stunted-looking plant in a pot on the floor next to him, a sickly, miniature version of the palm trees that lined the street outside. Its trunk leaned over slightly towards him.

Somehow I'd been expecting him to look like almost a twin of Dylan's – it must have been the thing Lily had said, about Dylan mentioning that they looked alike. But the person at the end of the room wasn't a younger, slightly less good looking version of Dylan, as I had imagined. He was unmistakably Dylan's brother, but not in any way I could put my finger on at first. In the hour or so that we spent with him I eventually caught sharp glimpses of resemblance: his profile, as he looked down and away to the side; something in the shape of his hands, the attractive, loose way they held a cigarette, the long fingers; and, most disarmingly, a particular way of smiling that wasn't exactly about the shape of any distinct features but was a combination of things, the way they were put together – the angle of the head, the twist of the mouth, the look in the eyes. It was there for a moment, definitely Dylan, and then it was gone, something else. But for the seconds it was there it was so alike that I wondered whether he had actually learned this way of smiling from Dylan, seen it and emulated it and practised it. I could imagine Dylan noticing and encouraging him.

He was slim like Dylan, although a little shorter. That was noticeable when he stood to greet us, dragged on his cigarette, and stuck out his hand toward us. We all exchanged a nervous glance, except for Brian, who looked him right in the eye, walked over and sat down in the booth across from him, ignoring the proffered hand. Colin showed a brief second of discomfort and then lowered his hand, touched the table, and waited for us to take our seats.

The booths were wide and long but couldn't accommodate four people sitting in a row. I ended up next to Colin, in the corner, while he stayed on the outside, next to the drooping plant.

The waiter came over and stood silently, pen and notebook in hand. He wore a small name tag pinned to the right-hand side of his chest: ANTONY, it said, in red letters engraved into the white plastic.

'Coffee all round,' Tallis said, and reached up to remove his sunglasses. He blinked as though he were in direct sunlight although it was dim and cool inside. Hangover.

'Are you guys hungry?' Colin asked. Those were the first words he said.

'Just coffee,' said Cameron. 'That will be fine.'

'The tuna salad sandwich is great,' Colin said.

He met Antony's eyes, gave a half-hearted smile. The waiter smiled back, a look passed between them, and I wondered whether they were friends, and how often he came here. For a moment it seemed as though he was planning to order the sandwich and eat alone.

'Next time,' he said.

The waiter came back quickly with a handful of mugs, thick porcelain ones, and poured coffee for all of us from a jug. I was cautious this time, with my burned tongue, and sipped carefully. It was weak, but fresh.

'Great coffee,' said Colin.

He seemed to be the kind of person who wants to talk too much when he's nervous, and tries to keep a rein on it.

'I remember you,' Tallis said, accusation in his voice, 'from the funeral.'

Colin nodded. 'Semele gave me the news.'

Tallis looked confused.

'Sally,' I said. 'He means Sally.'

'Right, right,' Tallis muttered.

Colin's friendliness disarmed all of us; whatever else of Dylan we had been expecting to find in him, it hadn't been that – the instant, hypnotic charm that sought to put everyone at ease so smoothly. Colin had only a diluted version of it, but it was undeniably present. He must have been working very hard to project it. His nervousness showed only in pieces – the slightly compulsive talking, a certain tension in the smile.

Dylan's skin had an olive tone that deepened whenever he tanned; Colin instead had the kind of healthy glow that comes from just being outdoors, a look I never seemed quite able to achieve apart from a few days in the middle of summer, if it wasn't a summer spent entirely indoors trying to finish a paper or a chapter or a research assignment, as many of my summers were.

Whatever Colin was, he didn't seem to be a representative of the poor and desperate Vegas underclass I'd had in mind. He looked something like a young River Phoenix, with high cheekbones and that suggestion of vulnerability. His hair was short and neatly parted, a more golden colour than Dylan's dark brown, his shirt ironed and clean, a light bluish-grey that Dylan would have worn. It looked as though he had put himself together carefully for our meeting. He reminded me of a minor star of the forties, someone whose movies I might have watched on AMC in the daytime, whose photo might hang in one of the lesser corners of the MGM Grand. With a modest moustache he would have looked the part exactly.

I was the only one looking at him. Brian had fixed his eyes on some point in the middle distance outside the window, his mouth fixed into a compressed pout; Tallis kept glancing at his sunglasses and squinting, as if he wanted to put them back on; Cameron looked at his coffee, and eventually met my eyes.

'How did you get to know Dylan?' I asked. It was somewhere to start.

'You're Elliot, right?'

'Sorry, yes – I'm Elliot, this is Cameron –'

'It's OK,' he said. 'I recognize you. I've seen you all in photographs – I asked Dylan to show me once. So I know your faces, I put the names to the faces. You're Brian, Tallis, Cameron.' His eyes moved over them one by one, and drew their gaze at last.

'Dylan contacted Diedre, our mom, a few years ago. When was it – about ten years ago. I was really young, like twelve or thirteen. That's right. He'd found out, about the adoption thing, and got in touch with her. He came out here – came to our house.'

'Had you known?' I asked.

'No, I had no idea. Mom had never told me, she'd never talked about it. She didn't want to see him at first. She tried to close the door. But, you know, he convinced her.'

Something in the air changed — the others shifted slightly in their seats, and so did I. In that 'you know' there was something true. An acknowledgement; a point of connection, of recognition.

'Anyway, he said he wanted to get to know her a little, and he stayed and talked for a while. And then he came back a few months later, and then he visited about every year. Mom died three years back. It was a heart attack, kind of sudden, but she'd had problems, some health problems.'

I wanted to ask him what she had been like. No picture of her would come into my mind, no matter how hard I tried to imagine her, beyond a shadowy image of a young, thin woman, faceless. It was too difficult to separate the image of Greta from Dylan in connection with the idea of motherhood.

'What did your mother do?' Cameron asked.

'She worked for the city,' Colin said. 'She was a secretary. In the Office of Water Management.' He faced Cameron. 'You expected her to be a showgirl, right? You probably came here thinking I grew up in a trailer.' He kept up the smile and the friendly tone but there was something else under it now, more brittle.

'I don't particularly trust anything you have to say,' Tallis said.

Colin ignored him. 'She grew up in Vegas. She went to secretarial school here. When she had Dylan she was, like, sixteen or something, she'd just dropped out of high school. Her mom had worked in a casino; she was a waitress. There you go — teen mom, no job, no money. Is that more like what you had in mind?'

'It's OK,' I said. 'I'm sure there was a good reason for it.'

'Dylan did all right out of it, didn't he?' Colin said, with an affectionate smile but the same unsettling tension in his voice. 'He knew it. He never said a bad word about his parents, his new parents. He never blamed Mom. It wasn't like that.'

'Is your father alive?' I asked.

He glanced out the window. 'He's not around.' He looked back at me, smile in place. 'Dylan's either. That's obvious, I guess.'

I think everyone goes through fantasies of having been adopted when they're a little kid – the idea that your real parents must be kings and queens, fabulously powerful and rich, and one day they'll come to claim you and take you away to a world of power and prestige, a fairytale. What must it be like to find out that it's true – your parents aren't your real parents – and then discover that you don't come from Camelot or anything like it, but instead Las Vegas? And that you have a brother: the baby your mother decided to keep.

It was Dylan's adoptive parents, Greta and Leo, who were, in my eyes at least, close to the kind of royalty you'd dream about being descended from as a child, with their glass palace on the hill and Hollywood clout. Thinking about Greta, about the times I'd spent at their house, the soft, almost fascinated way she had of watching Dylan, reminded me now of how she had been in grief. Once that memory came it obliterated the others like a rapidly spreading dark stain. She had worn large sunglasses at the funeral, at the wake; her face was pale next to them and the indigo silk shirt she wore. I saw her eyes only once that day, when we were all filtering out of the building after the service and I'd come upon her standing outside, waiting for the car to arrive. She'd taken the glasses off – why, I didn't know, since the sun was a bright, uncompromising midday glare – and her eyes were red-rimmed, palest blue and naked without the heavy eyeliner she usually wore, the whites a spidery network of red.

I'd walked over to her and we embraced; she seemed smaller and thinner, weakened by it all. The car drove up, Sally, grim-faced, at the wheel, Leo in the back. She slipped her glasses back on, I opened the door for her, and she gripped my shoulder briefly, understated as ever, before sliding in with all her usual elegance and economy of movement.

'So, Colin,' Brian began, slowly, painfully. 'What is it that you want? If you just wanted to catch up, reminisce about old times with Dylan, you could have just called us. Obviously you know where we're staying. And obviously you know a lot about us.'

Colin smiled in an almost self-deprecating way. 'To tell you the truth, I wanted to make sure I had your attention. I didn't know how you'd feel if I just called you.'

'You have our attention,' Tallis said, his voice dangerously quiet.

'How *is* your father doing?' Colin asked him.

Tallis's face turned pale, then the colour started to come back in blotches of angry red.

'OK, sorry. Look, what I want is to get out of this town. I need help to do that. This was all really bad timing.'

'Timing?' Tallis asked.

'Dylan was going to help me. We had plans to talk about it this visit. He was going to get me to meet you guys, all of you, we were going to talk about college . . . it was all set up.'

'OK,' I said, trying to ignore how disturbed I was by the way he'd described Dylan's death as a matter of bad timing for his own plans. 'What do you do?' I asked. 'Do you have a job?'

'I have a job, yeah. I work as a croupier. And I'm in college. Freshman at the University of Nevada, right here.'

'What's wrong with that?' I asked. 'It's not a terrible school.'

'That place you teach,' he said. 'I'd like to go there.'

He said it calmly, as though I'd offered to buy him lunch and he had decided to order a sandwich. It didn't sound like a simple observation, nor was it quite a request. Was it a demand? It was hard to tell.

'Do you mean you would like Elliot to assist you with looking into the possibility of transferring?' Cameron asked, all business. 'I'm sure he could help you come up with a list of reputable colleges where you would be a good fit, a good match.'

Colin regarded him blankly.

'There's nothing we can do about your transcripts,' I said. 'It would depend a lot on that.'

'There's no problem with my transcripts,' he said. 'My grades are good.'

'The fees are expensive.'

'I could use some help with that, sure.'

'So that's it,' Tallis said with contempt. 'Money.'

'Elliot's right,' Colin replied. 'Fees are expensive where he teaches. And at the other places I'd be interested in going. But look, I can get financial aid. I could do it that way. I'm not asking for a million dollars.'

'Colin, we haven't made any decision about whether we're willing to, uh, help you, as you say, with your school fees or anything else,' Cameron said.

'There's not just fees to consider with college,' Colin went on, for all the world like an average student talking with a father or an uncle who's agreed to help pay for college. 'They're expensive, yeah, but I've got to get in there in the first place. That's the hard part. I'm talking about opportunities. College, and beyond. Tallis, you could really help me with opportunities in the business sector. And Brian – I have some great ideas for scripts. For films. I'd really like to get your feedback. I brought some outlines along with me, to give you, and a couple of scripts I've been working on.'

He reached into a bag by his feet and retrieved several spiral-bound documents, pushed them toward Brian. 'Dylan always talked about that – he always said how much you'd connect with my ideas, that you'd be able to put me in touch with producers, with people who could make that happen.'

'Make what happen?' Brian asked.

'You know – the green light, Hollywood production. Or maybe not Hollywood. He said you were right into the whole independent scene.'

'Did he?' Brian said.

'Yeah, he mentioned it. He was going to approach you about it, you know, he was going to come to you with these ideas, he was just waiting, uh, waiting until it was the right time.' He cleared his throat. 'He hadn't told his parents, his adoptive parents, he hadn't told them about me and Mom, about finding us again. He was waiting to tell them.'

'What was he waiting for?' Brian wanted to know.

Colin studied his coffee.

'Well?' Brian pressed.

'It's complicated,' Colin said.

'What's complicated?'

'It was hard, I guess – after all these years – he didn't want to hurt their feelings.'

'Did you see them?' I asked. 'At the funeral – did you talk to them?'

Colin shook his head. 'I talked to Semele.'

'Sally,' I corrected him automatically.

'Dylan always called her that. Semele. I talked to her. Dylan had told me that she knew – yeah, she told me about the funeral. She's the one . . . she called me. After he died. She pointed out Greta and Leo, her mom and dad.'

'They were his parents, too,' I said.

'Yeah, right. Right. Greta was hard to miss anyway. I didn't talk to them.'

'Maybe they would have liked to meet you,' I suggested.

He met my eyes with an almost hungry look. 'I thought that, for a second there, at the funeral. I wanted to talk to them. I thought, you know, it wouldn't be so bad – why would it be so upsetting for them? I'm, like, a part of Dylan's life. Maybe they would have liked to know I was there.' He shrugged. 'It was too hard. They were so . . . I just couldn't intrude.'

I thought about what it might have been like for Colin, coming to the funeral. There was something unbearably lonely about the idea. I remembered the dark-suited figure towards the back of the room and felt sure that it had been him.

'Were you wearing a dark suit?' I asked.

'Everyone was wearing a dark suit,' he said. 'Except Leo.'

Leo had turned up in one of the linen suits he favoured, a beautiful Italian one in a colour like old parchment. He never wore dark colours. It sounded strange to hear Colin using Dylan's father's name when they had never actually met.

'You could have said hello to us,' I said. 'To one of us.'

He would have recognized all of us – from the photograph, just as he'd said earlier.

'Like I said, I didn't want to intrude. You all weren't doing so great yourselves.'

It occurred to me that he could have been sitting there thinking about ways to apply pressure to us, weighing up whether to approach us individually or as a group, trying to assess the lines of loyalty.

'It didn't seem like the right time,' he continued.

Brian had started to drum his fingers on the table, a faint galloping sound. Tallis nudged him and he stopped. My sense of sympathy for Colin that had surfaced as I considered his lonely place on the margins of the funeral gathering, gave way to other feelings. I began to experience the start of real, tangible hatred for him – his carefully pressed clothes, his patronizing tone, his attempts at smug arrogance that didn't properly hide the fact that he was desperately nervous and uncertain. I hated the fact that he seemed to want us to like him – to actually like him, of all things.

All the feelings of resentment towards Dylan that had started to sharpen and coalesce since my talk with Tallis and Brian the previous afternoon now shifted direction and pointed at Colin. It was much more comfortable to hate him than it had been to resent Dylan. And he was, after all, the reason behind my having to so drastically reassess Dylan and my whole friendship with him, as well as the revelations about Brian that I still hadn't figured out what to do with. I forgot for a moment that it had been Brian who had done those stupid things and Dylan who had kept the records, and could only think that it was Colin who had made me aware that they existed at all, who was threatening us now.

Colin stayed motionless in his seat, but his stillness had an air of defiance about it, as though he was battling to keep from shifting nervously. He raised his chin and set his mouth firmly. I saw Dylan's features echoed there in his face through the movements and gestures that were nothing like his, and the sharpest point of my newly minted hatred deflated.

Maybe it was no surprise that Colin saw blackmail as the path to connection with us. I thought about Dylan, cementing his friendships with gestures that bound us to him not only in gratitude for his generosity, in debt to him for the potentially serious cost they incurred, but also in the way they gave him power over us. Colin was acting out with us an extremely crude version of Dylan's own tactics, just as you might expect a younger brother to emulate an older one, especially one who wasn't a very scrupulous teacher.

I tried to imagine the scene where Dylan had handed over the information he had on us, or talked with Colin about it. Picturing it showed me a Dylan who was disturbingly alien, a stranger in my friend's body. Had he handed over these envelopes on one of his recent visits, with a whispered conversation about the potential impact of what they contained? Had he left one big file with Colin, or sent it to him in the mail? Had it all been in a safety deposit box somewhere, a key with Colin, with instructions to open it after Dylan's death?

My imagination ran crazily down these noirish paths, each one more like a scene from a heavy-handed movie, but it was no wonder: the moment the envelope had arrived for Brian, all our lives had moved into strange territory that could not be negotiated through experience, for there was no comparable experience in life, for me at least. This could only be approached through the scripts of fiction.

Cameron asked the question in my mind. 'Did Dylan tell you to do this? Did he leave you all this in a secret will? How did you get it?'

Colin kept his hands on his mug of coffee. 'I went to New York, after the funeral. I wanted to see where he'd lived.'

'You'd never visited?' I asked.

He shook his head. 'It was always so hard to organize, you know? It's so hard to get the timing right with these things. I was going to come visit this summer – we'd talked about doing that.'

I glanced at Cameron, wondering whether he shared my sense of doubt about Dylan's promised plans. His eyes widened. He raised his eyebrows as he met my gaze for a second.

'Anyway,' Colin continued, 'the place was empty. Semele and Greta had been through by then.'

'You had keys?' I asked.

Colin smiled. 'He kept a whole huge set of keys at my place here in Vegas. That's the only thing he kept here – that and some photos, pictures of me and Mom. He never said exactly what they were for but I guessed that some of them were house keys. Apartment keys. I knew his address. I knew he had a storage unit. Semele didn't know – I told her about it after I went there. It was just a small unit, right out in Brooklyn somewhere in a big building. I went there on the subway.'

He said this as though it were an accomplishment we would respect, his navigation of the subway in New York. I did respect it, I found, remembering riding it my first few weeks in the city, bewildered by the labyrinthine tunnels of connection between lines, the fear that came when trains would stop for no apparent reason for long minutes underground, under the city, under the river . . .

'There was all the usual stuff – boxes of books, old videotapes, old toys, a couple of old cameras,' Colin said. 'There was a microscope – that was cool. I took that with me as well. And there was a file box there. I knew most of it.' He glanced at Cameron. 'He'd told me most of it. He told me about the accident.'

Cameron stayed quiet.

'So he didn't exactly leave it to me,' Colin said. 'But in a way, he did.'

'In what way?' Tallis asked.

'He left me the key,' Colin said. 'What else was it for? He left me the key. And I used it.'

'How much of this stuff was there?' Cameron asked. 'Is it just us – are there other people involved?'

Colin thought about it carefully, as though he was searching his memory for obscure information. 'You know,' he said eventually, 'that really doesn't matter.'

'It might matter to us,' Cameron said.

'I just can't see why it's important.'

Tallis intervened just as Cameron was readying himself for another comeback, lifting his hand in a gesture that said 'Stop'. I didn't see why it mattered, how many other people were involved; all I cared about was that we were involved, and I wished that we weren't. If there were other, richer, more willing people involved I supposed that would take the pressure off us a little, maybe. I was glad that Cameron was there, and Tallis, maintaining some kind of handle on all the possible permutations, or at least giving the illusion of doing that.

But the illusion of control started to crack as soon as I'd noticed it. Cameron's eyes, when I looked back at them, didn't appear hard any more, but tense and worried; Tallis remained pale and angry.

'Look,' he said, in his bullying, superior way. 'This is a shock and an insult. You must understand that.' I could see Colin harden at his tone. But Tallis continued. 'You seem to enjoy a very distorted view of our collective resources and abilities. I don't know what Dylan told you. He almost certainly exaggerated.' He paused and changed tack, and said almost apologetically, 'We loved Dylan. But he wasn't always the most realistic person. I mean, he wasn't always the most truthful person.'

'There's no ambiguity in the information Dylan left me,' Colin said.

'No – you're absolutely right, of course not.' Tallis's tone was almost intimate now. 'Of course not. But I don't know how you've come to believe that we could provide the sort of, uh, help you're imagining. Dylan may have exaggerated our . . . our influence . . . in the situations you're talking about.'

Brian leaned over. 'I'd love to be so powerful in Hollywood

or the Sundance universe or whatever that I could get any movie made that I like – but it's not like that. I'm not that guy. I work for a company that makes documentaries.'

Colin stared at him, unmoved. 'Dylan always said how talented you were,' he told Brian. 'He could never understand why you didn't just go into production yourself. You have the means to do it. You could finance it yourself.'

I could see Brian responding to the flattery almost involuntarily – eyes cast to the side for a second, mouth twisted in a shadow of a self-deprecating smile – even as he visibly winced at the open reference to his family fortune.

'It's not like that –' he started.

'I know you want to make it on your own terms, Dylan always said what fantastic integrity you have,' Colin cut in, warming to his topic, reverential on the subject of every opinion Dylan had imparted to him. 'He said that's why you'd make such a great artist.'

Cameron rolled his eyes and sat back heavily in his seat.

'We could make a fantastic partnership. I'd love to run some of my ideas by you,' Colin continued, gesturing toward his scripts.

'I don't know,' Brian murmured, visibly confused.

'Colin,' Tallis said sharply, 'Dylan exaggerated. Your brother was a bit of a liar.'

'I don't think that's true,' Colin responded. 'And in any case, it's irrelevant. I know more – Dylan knew more – about your finances than you're probably aware of.'

Tallis kept his face and body still.

'Why do you want to go to college?' I asked, thinking selfishly of my own role in his plans, and how it could be minimized. 'It sounds as though you're so passionate about the movie business.'

'I like the *idea* of college,' he said, meeting my eyes with an almost erotic gleam. 'You know? Not this – whatever this is, University of Nevada – I mean a real college, that whole experience. The whole Ivy League thing. I know,' he said, when I started to protest, 'this place you teach at isn't strictly Ivy, I know, but it has that same, I don't know, ambience. It has the kind of thing I'm looking for.'

The air-conditioning whirred around us, cool but not as frigid as the air inside the big casino hotels. A passing car sent a painful glint of reflected sunlight directly into my eyes, and I became suddenly conscious of just how hot it was outside and how much energy it took to maintain these comfortable interiors. The spacious, empty diner, the baking concrete block outside, the whole city extended and stretched out around us, relentlessly bright. I had never visited the campus of the University of Nevada. I imagined carefully manicured quads and buildings constructed in perfect imitation of Harvard and Princeton, gardens planted with just the right species of ivy. Maybe it wasn't like that; maybe it was all red-brick, square buildings. Either way, it could only be an imitation, an approximation, of the romanticized idea of the 'college experience', and being in Colin's hometown could never provide that crucial aspect: the experience of going away to school, to another, rarefied atmosphere, a better world.

'Nevada's a good school,' I repeated weakly.

'But you know what I mean,' Colin replied, and I did. It was a moment of understanding that included a small, wary grain of sympathy.

I remembered my final year of high school in New Jersey, the hours of work put into college application essays, driven and buoyed by the sense that escape was possible, that if I found the right words and got the right score I'd find myself somewhere that I would fit in, somewhere that matched my own fantasy: a glamorous idea of academic labour and decadent yet sophisticated campus life. But those hours of work and study and exams had been gruelling. My sense of sympathy with Colin evaporated fast when I faced up to the role he expected me to play in bringing his fantasy to fruition.

Colin checked his watch. 'Sorry, guys,' he said. 'I have to go to work. But thanks. It's great to meet you all. Can we talk again tomorrow?'

For a moment none of us responded, and then Cameron said, 'Sure.'

We made arrangements to meet the following morning, Cameron arguing over the precise time, trying to regain some measure of control over the conversation. Colin left, briefcase in hand, with a quick wave to Antony behind the counter as he walked to the door.

The four of us sat there in silence, trying not to look at the pile of screenplays on the table. Brian reached for them, and put a ten-dollar bill in their place.

10

There was a piece of paper stuck under the wiper on the windshield of the car as we approached. A ticket, I thought, and had a moment of feeling vindicated in my concern when we had parked there, followed by a sense of release: the ticket wasn't my problem. Tallis could deal with it. As we grew closer it became obvious that it wasn't a ticket at all, but a flyer advertising a strip joint, with a picture of a seminaked woman on it surrounded by dollar signs. Tallis reached for it and crumpled it in his hands, tossing it to the sidewalk.

He took the driver's seat again, Cameron next to him, while Brian and I swapped sides in the back. For a long few seconds we sat there in silence. Brian placed Colin's screenplays in the middle of the seat between us, where they started to slide towards me. He stared at the back of the headrest in front of him. Cameron gazed at Tallis with an expression of such tender concern that I wanted to look away when I saw it. They had walked close together side by side as we left the diner and made our way to the car, Tallis shaking his head now and again, and Cameron talking softly to him in a reassuring tone.

Brian broke the silence at last. 'There's no doubt that guy is Dylan's brother.'

Cameron nodded.

'Do you remember him at the funeral?' Brian asked.

'I think so,' I said. 'Do you think Dylan was ever really going to tell us?'

'To get us to meet Colin?' Cameron asked. 'Who knows.'

'I can't believe he could've kept it a secret forever,' I said.

Tallis sighed and shook his head; wondering at my naivety, or the inscrutability of Dylan's plans, or both.

'He's serious about this,' Brian said. 'He's fucking serious.'

'Did you think he wasn't serious?' I asked. But I understood Brian's incredulity in a way. It was one thing to get the envelope. It was another to be confronted by the person who had sent it.

'He's serious,' Cameron said. 'But it's totally bizarre. It's like he wants to be our friend.'

'I know,' I said. 'He wants some kind of relationship with us.'

'Why the fuck would he go about it like this?' Brian asked.

'It's just a version of something Dylan would do,' Tallis said, 'a very crude version. But that's what it is.'

He was answering Brian but he was talking to me, gauging whether I understood, evaluating how I was coming to terms with this new idea of Dylan. They'd all known this side of him – manipulative, opportunistic – a lot more intimately than I had; I'd been the naive one, the one he'd shown his good side to. I held Tallis's gaze for a second and then found that I couldn't, and closed my eyes, not wanting to see the trace of pity that was there. I didn't tell him that I'd already figured it out, the way Colin's scheme had something in common with how Dylan had operated. At that moment I wanted to be far away from all of them.

'Imagine what it was like for him,' Cameron said. 'Stuck here in Vegas – not in a trailer, right, like he said, but still. It would be hell to grow up here. Can you imagine? He's twelve, thirteen, he's just starting to realize what a shit hole it is that he lives in, and Dylan shows up. He's got an instant big brother from LA.'

'He would have idolized him,' I said.

'Yeah,' said Tallis. 'Yeah, he would have: a big brother who managed to get the fuck out of Vegas and land in fucking Laurel Canyon, and who leads you on forever about how he's going to introduce you to his friends and family and take you to Hollywood then never does.'

'It's never the right time,' Cameron said, quoting Colin, and shook his head.

'I feel sorry for him,' I said.

On some level I suppose I felt something in common with him: we'd both loved Dylan and wanted to see the best in him. Colin didn't want to let go of his illusions about his brother, even as he struggled with resentment about what he probably saw as Dylan's good fortune to be adopted out of the life he himself inhabited.

'He's deranged,' Brian said. 'And he doesn't just want to be our friend. He wants a lot more than that. What the fuck? What are we going to do?'

'Don't panic,' Cameron said. It was still hard to get used to them talking directly to each other without rancour. 'It's not bad that he wants to be our friend. That's something that could work to our advantage. I think he genuinely doesn't want to hurt us.'

'I don't think our feelings matter very much in this equation,' I said.

'He's willing to talk,' Cameron went on. 'It doesn't seem impossible, Brian, really. It doesn't.'

'OK,' Brian muttered, but he was shaking his head.

'That thing about wanting to be friends was weird,' Cameron said. 'But overall it's not that different from what I expected. It's really just a matter of money.'

'I don't know,' I said, but the rest of them seemed convinced. It seemed more complicated than that to me: it was the connections he wanted, the connection to Dylan through us, and the steps toward mobility that Dylan had promised him.

Tallis started the car and it came to life with a short sputter. A convertible cruised past as he started to pull out and the driver shouted, 'It's a hydrant, asshole!'

Tallis squinted and shook his head. 'Why does anyone give a fuck? There's other hydrants.'

I glanced back at the hydrant and saw that it was leaking: a dark circle of water around it on the concrete sidewalk, a trickle making a shiny path down its yellow-painted front.

The air-conditioning in the car grew cold at last. Brian sulked in his corner. Tallis drove calmly. I started to feel the shadow of the claustrophobia that had come over me in the elevator the night before, hating the sensation of being in a confined space.

I wondered again about Dylan's relationship with Colin, the ambiguous gift – if that was what it was – of the keys. Colin was the family Dylan hadn't chosen, the one he had discovered for himself; was that a kind of choice, I wondered. He could have decided not to go looking for his mother, after all.

Dylan seemed to have promised Colin so much, all the assistance and protection and useful influence that you might expect from a successful, well-connected older brother. Colin had adored him and looked up to him, that much was clear; and Dylan had won all the affection he might have wanted without having to deliver things he had promised. Dylan had planned to reveal everything to us on this tenth visit, Colin claimed, but up until his death Dylan had been unwilling to bring together his two parallel lives. I tried to imagine Colin's disappointment, the stretches of faith required as the years went by and Dylan still insisted that it wasn't the right time, putting it off again.

Dylan might have deferred forever his promises to help Colin, but he'd given him the potential means to extract the assistance from us that he'd insisted we would provide. It suggested a level of antagonism toward all of us that was still hard for me to fathom. Had Dylan been envious of us, I wondered, when I'd spent so much time being envious of him? His interest in my family – in all of our families – came back to me. He visited his own family back in LA every now and again, but never for Thanksgiving; instead, he loved to accept invitations from the rest of us to join our own family celebrations. He went to New York once with Tallis and cooked a whole turkey. Tallis had complained afterward about being pressed into work in the kitchen making stuffing and pumpkin pie, which he despised, but Dylan had always talked about it in glowing terms and seemed to believe that he'd performed a public service by providing a real Thanksgiving meal for the English people in our midst.

He had gone to Cameron's place one year, and Brian's, and had come with me to New Jersey in senior year. That's when he met Lily and she formed her terrible crush on him. I'd been anxious about having Dylan around my family for such an extended period, perpetually embarrassed by them, and guilty about feeling that way. But he'd seemed to enjoy himself: he'd put on an apron and basted the turkey for my mother, and everyone agreed that it was the best turkey she'd ever made, and he refused to take credit for it. I'd felt his attention on us, his interest in the traditional ways we did things. Was there a toast we usually made, he asked; did we say grace?

'Oh no,' my mother said, charmed, 'but if you'd like to say something about what we're thankful for, that would be wonderful.'

'All I can say is that right now I'm thankful for your delicious turkey,' he'd said, and raised his glass, drank his red wine.

It all looked different when I remembered it now, knowing

what I did. Although there was a gulf, wide and dark, between the bare facts of my new knowledge about his origins and my sense of how he'd actually felt about it, which could only be a poor guess. In any case, I seemed to remember him scrutinizing us – my tactless, pretentious mother, my checked-out father, my angsty sister – as though we represented something foreign, almost exotic.

'Your sister's great,' he'd said that night as we were going to sleep. My mother had set up the inflatable mattress for him in my room, with neatly folded-down sheets and more blankets than he could possibly need. 'And your dad – he's hilarious. He's like Mr Bennet.'

'Not really,' I said.

My father had made some scathing comments at dinner about the new neighbours across the road and their overly large new cars, but that was about the extent of his similarity to Elizabeth Bennet's father as far as I could see.

'You never do Thanksgiving at your house,' I said. 'What's that about?'

We'd turned out the light and the conversation had the aura of childhood sleepovers, staying up past the proper bedtime.

'It's such hard work,' he said, his voice tired and unusually cold. 'Happy families.' He stretched and turned over. 'I'll invite you next year. Want to come?'

'Sure,' I said. 'That would be great.'

I can't remember what he did the following year; I think he was travelling, in London or Europe somewhere, with the writer he was working for as a personal assistant – a prelude to the first major publishing internship. He didn't extend the invitation again. I think I recognized even at the time that it was something he'd said to change the direction of the conversation, to please and placate me, which isn't to say that it had seemed insincere.

'Elliot?' Cameron said, interrupting my thoughts. 'I said what do you want to do?' We were on the Strip, not far from the hotel. 'We're going to the pool.'

The idea of the pool was in some ways appealing; I imagined lying down on a flat sunlounge and closing my eyes, burning and not worrying about it, listening to the little splashes made by people swimming. But it would have involved conversation, and being around the others.

'I really need some time to think,' I said. 'To decompress. It's a lot to take in.'

Cameron nodded. 'OK,' he said. 'We'll talk tonight.'

Tallis glanced in the rear-view mirror. I could sense that he was looking at me even through his sunglasses. He looked back at the road. I knew they'd formed an unbalanced sort of triangle that didn't include me, but I found that I didn't care much. I wanted to let them work it out. I had no money to worry about spending on Colin, after all.

'I'll give you a call this afternoon,' I said. 'After lunch.'

'Sure,' Cameron said.

Brian smiled at me and I smiled back, and then I remembered Cynthia's silver dress and smooth back. He pushed the screenplays toward me. 'Take these, would you? I don't care – I don't want to see them.'

I took them. Tallis pulled up outside the hotel's front entrance and I welcomed the warm, open air as I left the car.

I hadn't given much thought to what I would do with myself for the afternoon, consumed simply by the desire to be alone, to be away from the other three. My room was blissfully quiet, the bed neatly made, all objects carefully straightened and aligned, the remote control sitting there on the desk. I turned to the heavy stack of paper I'd carried up from the car. Colin's screenplays. I lifted the one on top, the thinnest one. *Recession Road*, an original screenplay by Colin Andrews. I leafed through it, enough to gather that the movie started with a car crash: car wrecked in a ditch, a group of friends inside the car, one of them badly injured. I paged forward. One of the survivors pretends to have been the driver, the one who wasn't drinking. He grips the steering wheel to make sure his prints are there. I paged forward again. Injured friend on life support. Later on a scene heading: INT. FUNERAL HOME – DAY. I thought at first it would be the funeral of the protagonist, the pretend driver, but it appeared to be his father's. I suspected that if I read on, I'd find a blackmail plot. My memories of the hours immediately following the crash had always remained sketchy. I wondered whether Colin's script would be able to fill in the gaps, or provide fictional pieces of memory in place of those that had fallen victim to the blackout effect of shock.

I glanced at the next one in the pile. *Farewell, My Lovely*. An adaptation of the Raymond Chandler novel. I knew the book from having read it years earlier; I tried to remember whether there was a film of it already. In my mind it was confused with another book, *The Lady in the Lake*. I looked through it and thought I recognized pieces of Chandler's dialogue, but couldn't tell what time it was set in; it seemed to be contemporary, or possibly futuristic. One of the characters grabbed another character's cell phone and threw it out the window. That wasn't in the book. Pages later, an old-fashioned radio was turned up too loud. I leafed through it, confused, and put it down.

Somehow it made sense that Colin would be obsessed with the movies, with noir plots; that explained the heavy-handed envelope trick, the weird sense that he was following a formula or enacting a familiar piece of a story. But in that case, I guessed, he should be prepared for it all to turn out badly for him. Wasn't it usually the blackmailers themselves – the anonymous voices on the phone, the shady pornography dealers, the sly amateur gangsters – who wound up with a bullet in the first or second act? He must have had some other genre in mind, or maybe he thought it would turn into a different kind of movie. A buddy film; an upward-mobility story; a melodrama? I didn't like the idea that he was drawing inspiration from our experiences, from stories that Dylan must have related to him. I wondered whether there were other outlines or scripts in his drawer, about plagiarism and date rape and illicit affairs between students and teachers.

I turned on the television and made my way through a complicated menu, past the expensive new-release movies and porn to the free stations. Commercials seemed to be on every station except some shopping channels and a children's cartoon – a smiling, inane, computer-animated Winnie the Pooh – which went to a commercial in the two seconds I spent looking at it. A woman's excited voice pronounced the positive educational attributes of a miniature, candy-pink computer. Little fingers hovered over the keyboard. I moved on and came to something that looked like a soap opera, with that yellowish false light and thin-walled sets. A dark-haired woman stared pensively at a point just above and to the left of the camera; a man entered and they argued; he grabbed the phone in her hand and threw it to the ground and she pressed her hands to her face; a commercial began. Startled, I glanced back at the script I'd just read with an unnerving sense of having seen it played out on the screen before me.

Pressing the buttons on the remote control made no difference to the volume; a line of white bars appeared on screen but remained the same whether I pushed up or down. I found the button to turn the sound off completely and it worked. I kept scanning and wound up with the hotel's guide to Vegas. The camera panned over the pool in silence – blue water, palm trees, sky, bikinis, white tiles – and I thought about the others down there in the expensive cabana. The image on the screen switched to a lion opening its mouth in a wide, exaggerated yawn, a lazy roar. I turned it off.

I hadn't wanted to think about the funeral when Brian mentioned it in the car, but now it was all I *could* think about. My mind swung back in what was becoming a sickeningly familiar movement, the reassessment of memory in light of new discoveries. I thought about Colin, his slim, dark figure at the back of the room gathering mass and shadows to itself in my remembered image of the event.

Leo had invited all four of us to speak if we wanted to as part of the service. Cameron and Tallis had declined. I had talked briefly, found a quote from Robert Burton about friendship and what a powerful medicine it was against the evils of melancholy. It was a clumsy speech. I hadn't reckoned sufficiently with my own nerves and hadn't written it down in enough detail; I found myself staring at two small crumpled pieces of notepaper covered with dot points and a page from Burton's *The Anatomy of Melancholy* with a star in the margin next to the relevant lines. I muddled through, forgave myself; everyone else was stumbling, too.

Brian stood up immediately afterward and surprised all of us with a calm, tender statement: eloquent, understated, touching. Now I found myself wondering about the powerful ambivalence he must have been struggling to control, remembering his reported words in Cynthia's voice, *I'm glad he's dead*, and the doubleness it gave to everything he'd said that day, a harsh cast of irony. For every expression of affection, the intimation of its opposite.

He had concluded with a passage from *In Memoriam*. My attention had drifted by that point and was brought back with a snap by the two words of the title. They were unmistakable, but still I wondered helplessly for a second whether I might have misheard, and then I recognized the cadence of the poem as he began reading.

It wasn't so strange that he read from that poem; it was a logical one to choose. The poem had been in my own mind in the days leading up to the funeral, flitting in and out mainly in the form of inarticulate, half-remembered images that I tried to steer away as soon as they appeared. The spreading, menacing branches of the graveyard yew tree; the ghastly ship sailing home with its tragic burden. Most troubling, hardest to eradicate, was the picture of the bleak dawn city street, empty of people, a lonely, foreign landscape of slick cobblestones and gray pearlescent sky. I'd pushed it away when it snuck up on me; cast resentful thoughts at the morning fog and faint rain on campus that called it to mind.

'Behold me, for I cannot sleep, / And like a guilty thing I creep / At earliest morning to the door . . .' Brian's hand passed unconsciously over his tired eyes as he spoke.

I'd wondered anxiously whether he knew, whether there was a message for me in there somewhere, and, if so, what exactly it might be. By the time he finished and took his seat next to me, I had recovered. It wasn't a choice with any special significance. I was overtired and stressed. And if I was showing any outward signs of stress they could all be put down to symptoms of grief.

Snatches of birdsong and squabbling, chirping noises reached us through the funeral home windows from the trees outside. The day was absurdly full of sun and life, the opposite of Tennyson's mournful, drizzly London street. And yet the very harshness of the California sunlight had its own blankness, its own incandescent emptiness, and every doorway I looked at for the rest of the day filled me with a little shiver of dread, reminding me of those silent doors the coffin had passed through, with such inhuman, pneumatic smoothness, on its way to the cremation machine.

In my hotel room now, I thought of Colin in his seat towards the back of the chapel and wondered whether he had made the connection between the poem and me, whether he'd even known about the paper by then, whether his attention had been brought more sharply to me for those moments.

I'd been driven to reread the Tennyson in the week before the visit to Vegas for the first time since college, and had pulled the book out from its place on a bottom shelf in my office but so far hadn't gotten around to actually opening it. It was there in my suitcase now, a thick paperback collection of his poetry, the elegy in there among the other poems, the monologues and odes and sonnets. I reached for it through folded clothes and took it back with me to the bed, placed the screenplays on the floor, and opened to a page at random. It was an early poem, 'Ode to Memory', and I quickly turned the page and leafed through until I came across the distinctive four-line stanzas of the elegy.

I'd been reading for a while when the phone began to ring, a muted bleeping sound. I considered it mistrustfully, letting it go on for five or six rings; I started to wonder how long it would go before it rang out and went to voice mail. For a brief second, my heart rose up dizzyingly at the thought that it might be Natasha, and sank just as quickly when I remembered that she didn't know where I was staying, and had my cell number, and would have no reason to call me in any case. Nevertheless, it was her face I had in mind, her distinctively modulated voice I imagined meeting mine when I picked up the receiver.

'Hello?'

'Elliot? It's Cynthia.'

I still had the strange sense of unreality I'd felt when the phone started to ring, part of my mind still dwelling in the page, not transitioning out into the present.

'Hello,' she said. 'Did I wake you?'

'Wake me? No.'

'How are you?'

'I'm OK, I'm good. I wasn't asleep.' I felt slightly insulted by the idea, unsure why. 'How are you?'

'Excellent. What are you doing?'

'Uh, reading.'

'What are you reading?'

I didn't want to tell her. I stared at the page – the tight, vicious, symmetrical stanzas – felt again the odd softness of the paper, unable to think of something else to say.

'Tennyson,' I said eventually. I was an English professor, I reminded myself. It wasn't that weird to be reading Tennyson.

'Tennyson? What Tennyson?'

'*In Memoriam.*'

'Oh,' she said, a drawn-out sound of pity. 'Of course, I'm sorry.'

'That's OK,' I replied, not sure what exactly she was apologizing for.

'I love that poem so much. I remember reading it in college.'

'It's great, isn't it?'

A brief silence passed, during which I felt sure she was conjuring an image of me very far from reality: grieving man finding consolation in the words of the great poet, in the town where he had shared so much with his lost friend. There was a poignancy in this idea that appealed to me, and yet also shaded into a kind of sentimentality. I wasn't sure whether to leave

Cynthia with the idea intact, or to correct it – but then, how to correct it without exposing my guilty, complicated relationship to the poem?

'So, I'm heading over to the Paris soon for lunch,' she said.

'OK.'

She sounded as though there was a good reason for telling me about her plans, but I couldn't think why. With some irritation I remembered Brian's promises about how independent she was and how willing to stay out of our way.

'Is Brian going with you?' I asked.

'Oh no. I just saw him at the pool. It seems like it's really important for him to get some guy time, or some alone time, I don't know. Maybe they're going to a strip joint. He's with Tallis. They claim to be staying at the pool.'

She laughed, a brief, relaxed sound that made me think about how little she knew him, really, and how little she knew about what was happening.

'Elliot,' she said firmly, 'we talked about getting lunch today – last night – you said to give you a call when I was heading out. That's all.'

It came back to me. We'd been standing at a bar towards the end of the evening, talking about her plans for the day ahead. I had indeed expressed interest in accompanying her to lunch at Paris, and – this was fuzzier – had managed to pull out some statistics about the hotel: how tall the fake Eiffel Tower stood compared with the actual one in Paris, how good the buffet was supposed to be, the beauty of the ceiling with its painted sky . . . We had stayed there once several years before – on our third or fourth visit, perhaps – and I had spent most of the time with a terrible hangover from drinking too many kinds of liquor. The combination of whisky with anything else was disastrous for me, and there had been several different cocktails, all experimental, fashionable recipes with too many ingredients. Many hours had been spent staring at the beige walls of my room and the ornately carved, faux-walnut wardrobe that took up about one-quarter of the available space.

'The food there is supposed to be really good,' I said, aware that I was repeating myself from the previous evening.

'I know. I'm starving. Are you hungry?'

'Yeah, I think so,' I said.

'I'll meet you in the shop. The one near the elevators. I'll be down there in, oh, ten minutes.'

'OK.'

Her technique impressed me. Somehow I had agreed to meet her for lunch without ever actually agreeing, as such. It wasn't an unpleasant sensation, and I found it oddly relaxing to have decision-making power lifted from me for a moment.

I returned to the idea I imagined Cynthia had about me reading *In Memoriam*, and decided that while this image was totally wrong, it was also somehow true. The poem had always bound me to Dylan, although in ways that had nothing to do with the content or meaning of the verse. Since he died I had been aware of a nasty sort of irony or poetic justice in that being the poem in question – it would have to be an elegy for a dead friend, wouldn't it, and worse, one I'd never mastered, just as I imagined in my more maudlin moments that I'd probably never mastered the art of friendship, of emotional connection, to Dylan or anyone else.

Would it be possible, I wondered, now that he was gone, now that the image of our friendship I'd carried for years was wrecked and was being reconstructed moment by moment, in more and more unlikely, distressing, implausible ways – would it be possible now to read the poem with fresh eyes, to understand it?

I could picture so clearly how that story would go: I would

sit on my bed and read the poem from start to finish, glancing up every now and again to take consolation from the ancient, indifferent mountains, and at last understand something about Tennyson's grief. If I was going to really fulfil that particular fantasy, that version of the narrative, I would stay up all night, tumbler of whisky by my side, and type out in one single, brilliant, heartfelt, typographical-error-ridden draft the essay I should have written eleven years ago. I briefly pictured myself walking into an aged Professor Stanton's office and handing it to him with a humble, understated flourish, to his bewilderment and surprise – and then walking out of the building for the last time, newly unburdened . . . The Hollywood treatment.

The book sat on the bed, stubbornly staying open to the page I had been reading earlier. I would reread the poem, I knew then with a clear-headed sense of purpose, and the words would lose some of their opacity, but it would not deliver the epiphany that took place in the little story I had just imagined for myself. If I came to an understanding of whatever Tennyson had to say it would not be through any fellowship of feeling with him, but through a knowledge of how bluntly my own confused, stupid grief was estranged from his. The lack of coincidence between my experience and the feelings encoded in the poem was the frame through which each began slowly to come into focus. My sense of this difference was like a dark blot of inky substance that both obscured and revealed the words on the page, each dissolving into all its separate characters and coalescing back into syntax, something that made no sense at all, and then some. I looked at the page again blindly and didn't need to reread the words to experience a sense of understanding that felt at once fresh and familiar, as though it had been under the surface for a while, steeping and percolating mysteriously, and was now ready to appear, though not by any means complete.

I envied Tennyson the way he was able to preserve the ideal image of his friend. A particular form of mourning attended this second, other loss that I was experiencing now – the loss of an idea of Dylan as I thought I had known him, our friendship as I thought I had understood it. I remembered the awful coffee he had brought me with that paper, the way he had presented it so sweetly, and his easy, comforting embrace. I wished for the return of all that innocence I'd lost, and despised myself for it. The sad finality of it all settled upon me and I felt a deep longing for him to arrive at my door at that moment, for him to walk in with that familiarity with my space he always took for granted, and half-sit on the desk with his arms folded, and reassure me of something. Even now, it was too hard to allow myself to be angry with him, although I knew it would have made sense to feel that way. The logical place for it seemed to open inside me and stay empty, numbly waiting, another kind of hole alongside the others that were part of my grief.

I stared at the book for a while longer, waiting for it to close itself – it was staying open at a precarious angle, the front cover lifted up as though about to fall shut. Eventually I picked it up and closed it, left it next to the broken clock on the stand beside the bed.

II

Cynthia was in the shop when I arrived, browsing a shelf of tourist paraphernalia, mostly in the form of dice: candy-coloured plastic dice, key rings with plastic dice attached, packs of cards with dated photographs of casinos on the back, all the colours too yellow and red. Large sunglasses hid her eyes. She stood there with her head bowed, examining a set of yellow dice as though waiting for them to reveal a secret code. She turned, as though responding to something I'd said, and the big dark frames gave a vulnerable, childlike look to her face. Her mouth was lipsticked in a pinkish-orange shade that reminded me of tropical fruit. She smiled and the pensive look was gone, and I stopped wondering whether she had been crying and was hiding it with the sunglasses.

'Hey,' she said and set the dice back on their stand.

I bought a packet of cigarettes. 'Marlboros,' I requested, unthinkingly choosing Dylan's usual brand, and changed it to Marlboro Lights a second later. The pack sat hard and squarish in the pocket of my denim jacket. The cashier handed me a book of matches.

Cynthia bought a packet of gum, and chewed rhythmically as we began our walk through the building to the monorail station. It was a long journey through brightly lit, windowless caverns. Every once in a while she consulted a folding map of the hotel and gave the general impression of knowing where she was going. We passed by a sign that pointed to the pool, and I caught a whiff of chlorine, a glint of sunlight reflected off blue water, and wondered whether Brian was there, hanging out with Tallis in the shelter of the coveted cabana, drinking too much and going over what to do about Colin. We made it through the gaming rooms, past the expensive, showy restaurants and the cafeterias, the Starbucks and the Dunkin' Donuts, through halls of shops filled with ever-cheaper merchandise and pawnshops.

It was the first time I had ever caught the monorail. At other times in Vegas if we ventured beyond our hotel it had always been in a taxi, or occasionally a rental car or the Deuce bus. I liked the Deuce; it drove reliably straight up and down the Strip, was air-conditioned and cheap. Tallis had some kind of aversion to any train-style public transport. It seemed to stem from a traumatic experience of getting stuck on the London Underground, something to do with an escalator breaking down at one of those deep stations. I'd tried to explain to him once that the monorail was above ground, but he wasn't interested and I let it go. Now, walking through the bowels of the hotel with Cynthia, I wasn't so sure that the monorail experience would be a good one for him.

Eventually some doors took us into a parking lot, and then via an escalator to the station. We waited for a few minutes on the platform. The place had a strange hush, as though something terrible and violent had happened just before our arrival and the others waiting there had been stunned into silence. There was a family of six, all overweight and identically dressed in shorts and polo shirts of various colours; an overly affectionate young couple (just married, I thought, noticing a sparkling ring on the girl's finger); a young woman, out of place in a business suit complete with pearls and briefcase, sweating visibly. The young couple whispered and giggled, a hand in each other's back pocket. The smallest of the polo-shirt family, a young boy, broke ranks and stepped to the edge of the platform, where he spat hugely and aggressively onto the track. There was a second or two delay before his big sister strode over and whacked him on the side of the head, then pulled him back over to the group. His mother and father looked on impassively.

I shrugged further into my jacket despite the heat, hating the place. The dry air around us smelled of old plastic and traces of concrete dust from the construction site across the way. The train arrived with its sleek, robotic whir seconds after I'd lit a cigarette.

The monorail shuttled along a path parallel to the Strip, around the back of the big hotels, from the MGM all the way up to the Sahara at the very end, miles away. From windows on one side of the carriage we watched the backs of the hotels go past, the neglected side of the buildings: crumbling brickwork; fading paintwork; multistorey parking lots made of rotting concrete.

The windows on the other side of the carriage looked towards the distant desert, showing us endless blocks of construction sites populated with enormous earthmoving machinery. Everywhere, something was being knocked down, something was being built. We looked down onto flat rooftops of one- and two-storey buildings below – bars, restaurants, souvenir shops – pale lunar landscapes of concrete and air-conditioning units, crisscrossed with pipes and bristling with aerials.

WE HAVE 21 YEARS LEFT ON OUR LEASE announced one place, in those movable plastic letters you see on old cinema signs, although these letters looked as though they hadn't been moved for a while. It was a surreal protest of permanence in a zone of chaos and what seemed to be cyclical, ongoing destruction and renewal. WE ARE HERE TO SERVE YOU the sign finished, in smaller, insistent capitals.

There was something arresting, almost shocking, about the sudden falling away of glitz and substance in that small distance between the front of the massive hotels, the face they showed to the Strip, and the back. We weren't miles or even blocks away, we were simply behind the buildings, and yet the drop from prosperity to desperation and emptiness was dizzying. It wasn't the same as going backstage and seeing the actors without their make-up, or discovering how the magical trapdoor works, although it felt something like that. It wasn't exactly disenchantment, although it did make the illusions of the Strip seem more garish and daring than ever. *Stage Door Casino* read the rotating sign on top of the 21-year-lease building, reinforcing the theatre metaphor that was flickering in my mind.

I think what unsettled me most was what felt like a lack of decorum about these things – the lack of a proper division of front and back, decorated and undecorated, glitz and trash, all the cool, glossy interiors and the brutal exterior machinery that made them and kept them cool. Backstage should be hidden with a curtain or a door from the audience, surely; it shouldn't be so – well, just so easy to see all the crap and falling-apart stuff out the back. It was there to be seen as the view from the tourist monorail, and there was no expectation that seeing it all from the back would diminish the front-of-house glamour, or qualify it in any way.

Across from us a young father and mother were sitting with a toddler who squealed with delight at the machinery in the back lots as we passed. One whole long block seemed to be a parking lot for all kinds of equipment: bulldozers, excavators, dump trucks, steamrollers, all in rows, in shades of orange and yellow, showing signs of wear and tear and rust.

'Diggers!' the little boy shouted ecstatically. 'Diggers! I want to ride on them!'

His father smiled indulgently; his mother stared out the window, her gaze wandering past the rows of digging machines and further out, past more empty blocks to the strip malls and parking lots and townhouses in the streets beyond.

We arrived at the stop for Paris, which was also the stop for Bally's, the casino I hated most. It was hard to say exactly why: it wasn't the most garish or spectacular, or even the most tasteless. We had never stayed there, but I'd spent hours in it with Tallis one night at the blackjack table, a few years previously when he had decided to make that his game. I had only recently accepted the fact that I don't much enjoy card games in general – I had never really embraced gambling, but at least I'd always thought that card games had some style. My experience that night only confirmed my sense that they were boring. I didn't lose or win much, and, to my surprise, ended up slightly ahead at two or three in the morning, when Tallis was down by hundreds of dollars, or maybe more. I stopped keeping track and drank too much rum.

I wandered with Cynthia through stretches of underground corridors lined with shops almost identical to those at the MGM, although slightly more low-rent. There were one or two sad signs for lawyers' offices that assisted with borrowing more money on your mortgage and getting instant cash for assets. My sense of time had skewed all over again, and as soon as we were out of the reach of sunlight I felt unhinged, jet-lagged, with no bodily sense of whether it was morning or afternoon.

Cynthia grinned at me cheerfully. The gum had disappeared somewhere between the monorail platform and where we were now. 'How's your hangover?' she asked brightly.

'I think it's jet lag right now,' I said. 'How's yours?'

She gave a little grimace. 'Not too bad. Not too great either. I need another one of those greasy breakfasts. Or a huge plate of crepes. Will they have those at the buffet? Or are the crepes just at the crepe place?'

'I have no idea. Sorry. There'll be a lot of things to eat.'

We stepped onto an escalator that took us up through a mirrored, sparkling cavern. Strands of heavy crystal beads hung in pendulous, thickly clustered loops from the metal rings of chandeliers above, illuminated by hundreds of bright little bulbs, reproduced in infinitely receding reflections and fragments by squares of bevelled glass on all sides. The light broke into rainbow shards and patterns, like artificial constellations or the showers of explosive sparks from a fireworks display. We both stared upward as the mirrors fractured us into oddly reversed versions of ourselves – a pair of hands here, an endlessly reflected set of eyes there, two backs, two faces, against the metallic shine and depthless black of the background. In some panels the images rippled and curved as though glancing off water, the not entirely smooth surface of a river or a bath. Off to one side, in a corner, or a reflection of a corner, our opposing profiles merged and kissed before disappearing.

I stumbled off the escalator, almost losing my footing, dazed as an animal caught in headlights. That's how they do it, I thought, that's how they prepare you to spend all day in here and lose all your money: dazzle.

'Are you OK?' Cynthia asked. Her sunglasses were back on. I felt an urge to replace mine as well.

I shook my head. 'I fucking hate Bally's,' I said.

'The chandeliers . . .' she said admiringly, sounding as dazzled as I was.

Variations on the same elaborate light fixtures that hung over the escalator were suspended from the low ceilings inside the building: smaller-scale ones, and a few enormous versions that made me think inescapably of the tinkling, murderous crash they would make if they fell to the ground.

The journey to our destination was a long one, again, and I found myself thinking that it would have been as fast to walk the whole way from the MGM. But then we were in the underground caverns of Paris, and I could think only of sitting down and eating something sweet and drinking several cups of coffee.

'It really is Disneyland,' Cynthia murmured as we passed through corridors of shops designed to look Parisian: quaint little shutters on all the windows, some real, some just painted on the surrounding walls; bronzed lamp-posts; a bluish-violet sky brushed onto the ceiling. Any illusion of depth in the painted sky was tempered by criss-crossed shadows of roofs and columns and hanging signs, cast upward by recessed lights. Accumulated tobacco smoke had yellowed the scattered, pale clouds. The contours of everything were all blunted in the same way, as though they had been cast from a mould that had been used too many times and had lost all its proper detail; there were blobs and fat swirls on the architraves and lamp-post bases that looked like a distant echo of the sharp curlicues you might see on a Parisian street.

'I've never been to Disneyland,' I said.

'But you know what I mean, right?'

'Sure.'

It made sense that Disneyland would be the authentic location corresponding to this copied one, rather than the actual city of Paris, the supposed reference point.

The buffet had a humourless atmosphere, crowded with visitors examining the various offerings – supposedly authentic dishes from each region of France, plus the usual salad bar and a kiosk in the middle just for cake and other forms of dessert. People lined up patiently at the salad bar in front of the enormous dishes of peeled shrimp, loading up plates with pink mountains of the things, faces set with the same joyless dedication you saw at the slot machines. Even the children at the ice-cream machines looked serious as they pulled the lever and built the highest possible tower on their cones.

We found crepes for Cynthia, and I left her to choose from a list of possibilities – chocolate, cheese, banana, berries, a bewildering array of combinations – and went about filling my tray with a dozen kinds of pastries and cakes and little cups of chocolate mousse, adding a bowl of salad as a gesture toward the idea of lunch.

'Are you working on Disneyland?' I asked Cynthia when she joined me. She had two plates of crepes that seemed identical, smothered in chocolate sauce, each with half a strawberry perched on top.

A silent waitress in white placed cups on the table and filled them with coffee from a silver jug.

'I have a chapter on the castle,' Cynthia said. 'You know. The one in the Disney logo.'

I could picture it clearly, fireworks exploding over the elaborate pointed turrets against a velvety night sky.

'It's a replica,' she explained. 'Or, you know, "inspired by . . ."'

I was aware of this, somehow; the original castle was Swiss, or German, or somewhere in Europe.

'Have you been there?' I asked. 'To the original one?'

'Do you mean in LA?'

'No – never mind.'

She seemed lost in thought. 'Is there a Disneyland Las Vegas?'

'I don't know.'

'Damn. I should know that.' She brought a guidebook out of her bag and started leafing through it.

'How's your crepe?'

'Oh, it's so good.'

I'd eaten a miniature apple tart, and stared for a while at the rest of the things I'd chosen: a chocolate eclair; a tiny lemon meringue pie; a fruit tart piled with a glistening pyramid of strawberries, lush and red under a golden glaze.

When I looked up, Cynthia's face was preoccupied and almost sad. I thought about how it had looked in the mirrors around the escalator – thinner somehow, waiflike, the spots of pink on her cheeks heightened. I assumed that she was thinking about Brian, and I wondered how he was handling all of this around her. Perhaps she was putting everything down to the unexpected, swamping effects of grief. Maybe the less-than-loving things he had said about Dylan to her made that less plausible; maybe they didn't make any difference at all. That was the thing about grief: it had no precisely predictable processes from moment to moment, day to day, week to week, however much people liked to take refuge in the idea of universally shared stages or steps.

My mother had ordered some books about those stages for me from Amazon and had them shipped to my office. Stupidly, I'd opened the package in the mailroom and had to fend off the curious stare of a student, a girl I'd taught the previous semester who was there to drop a paper into someone else's box. Both books featured images of water on the covers – one, a silvery lake bordered by forests and mountains; the other, a reflective, rippling ocean. I hadn't wanted to take them home; hadn't wanted to leave them in my office, where they would have attracted more curious stares; hadn't imagined for a moment that they would have anything to offer.

My mother had called the next day to check they had arrived, and sounded injured when I'd said that they had. She'd been expecting my phone call to thank her.

'I thought the one about friends would, you know, really help you with this process.'

I couldn't remember whether that was the one with the lake or the ocean. 'Thanks,' I said. 'I'm sure it will.'

'OK, then.' A pause, expectant.

'Mom, I don't know if I'm at the right stage of the process . . . for reading . . .'

'Oh,' she'd said, sympathetically. 'Of course. When you're ready.'

'Thanks,' I'd said again, and found a reason to end the call.

After hanging up I'd found myself captured somehow by the language I had reached for only as an excuse: was it true that I wasn't at the right stage? And would some stage arrive at which I would actually find help and solace in books like those? I didn't like to think so.

In any case, I could imagine Brian explaining away his distance, his state of emotional freak-out, to Cynthia by pleading something to do with grief, a change of heart brought on by being here in this place, with these friends. He'd just discovered how much Dylan had meant to him after all, what an impossible gap he would leave in Brian's life, something like that. It was hard to take someone to task for any kind of offensive behaviour when they were grieving.

'If he didn't want me to come he should have just said so,' Cynthia pronounced, as though the statement were part of a conversation we had been having, or an argument, even though we had been sitting in silence for a while.

I thought about saying something about him grieving, but couldn't do it.

She straightened. 'I'm really fine doing this on my own. I'd always planned to do it that way. So don't feel as though you have to keep me company or anything.'

'No – no, I don't feel like that.'

'I thought you'd all be hanging out together and drinking all day and, you know, talking about old times.'

I wanted to come up with something in response that put a positive spin on what was happening among us all, a frame that could plausibly explain why I couldn't stand the thought of Brian's company right now and was equally reluctant to be on my own with my battered copy of Tennyson.

'It's harder than you thought, isn't it, being here all together without Dylan,' she offered.

I nodded gratefully and allowed her to think she was having some kind of insight into the four of us. Maybe she was. It kept happening, this sense that even the things that were wrong, or were faked, were actually in some sense also true – my grief excuse, our incapacity for relating to one another in a group without him.

'If you don't mind me hanging around I'm happy to tag along,' I told her. 'I wouldn't mind the company.'

Maybe something came across in my voice about how I was really feeling. For whatever reason, she met my eyes with a hint of suspicion before nodding in agreement.

'I can be your research assistant,' I joked, trying to shift the mood.

'Oh, I like that,' she said, smiling. 'Do you get to have research assistants? To do your copying and fetch your books from the library?'

'Not yet,' I said. 'Maybe I'll have one next year.'

'I did that job last year for someone in the English department,' she continued. 'Hours in the library, copying articles from obscure journals, a whole lot of Victorian periodicals . . .'

She started on the second crepe. The chocolate sauce on it looked as though it had gone cold. I looked down at my plate and found that the eclair had vanished; a faint taste of custard in my mouth told me that I'd managed to eat it without noticing.

'Actually,' she said, chewing, 'he was a Victorianist, this professor. The ancient one I worked for. Maybe you know him. He works on Tennyson.'

'It's not really my field,' I said. 'Do you want more coffee?' I collected both our cups without waiting for an answer and went to find us a refill.

The next couple of hours passed in a pleasant, dazed sort of blur, the kind of calming sensation that comes with giving yourself up to someone else's plans when those plans are benign and easily executed. We wandered around the casino floors just like tourists and I watched Cynthia take photographs and write notes in a small spiral-bound notebook. We rode the elevator up to the top of the Eiffel Tower and surveyed the whole sprawling, dusty town with a hundred other spectators, then caught the Deuce bus up to the Venetian and watched people riding in gondolas around the canals.

Cynthia had seemed morose at the buffet, but she snapped out of her mood once we left and assumed a busy, professional manner, checking things off in her guidebook and on various lists in her notes. We didn't talk much; half the time when Cynthia exclaimed 'Look!' or 'Interesting!' I wasn't sure exactly what she was pointing at, and wasn't interested much in figuring it out. I'd smile and shake my head or nod gently – both those gestures seemed to express exactly the same kind of amused, baffled, slightly fascinated reaction that was called for. It was a companionable sort of quiet, and I was interested in her fascination with the place even if the place itself bored me. It wasn't exactly like seeing it through new eyes – it still looked tacky and grotesque to me, and felt hot and uncomfortable – but I attached myself to her pleasure in it, trying to get outside my own thoughts.

Looking back at that afternoon it strikes me how deeply I'd gone into denial about the strange situation we had all found ourselves in. I probably should have been stressing out like Tallis and Cameron no doubt were at that moment, or drinking myself into oblivion like Brian, but I discovered in myself a capacity for aimless passivity that acted like a wonderful anaesthetic. Every once in a while I would observe myself as though from a distance, and watch myself following Cynthia around, and get as far as thinking that there was something else I maybe should be thinking about, this other pressing issue. But if I started putting a name to it – Dylan; Colin; Brian; Tennyson – my attention would flow back to Cynthia again, like a river being mindlessly diverted from its course. It was a bit like being drunk and watching myself keep drinking even when I knew that having another vodka on top of the wine I'd already drunk would make me immediately sick and even sicker the next day, only it felt less self-destructive. It was something like being enchanted, I imagined, feeling as though I'd let the dazzle of all the blinking, reflected lights pass right through my eyes and into some receptive part of my overstressed brain. If I'd been into gambling I probably would have sat myself down in front of a slot machine and lost a lot of money over the course of a few brain-dead hours.

We made our way to the Bellagio and stood there looking at the big pool of water where the fountains went on at night. The grid of lights and machinery was visible under the surface from certain angles, a massive, sinister array of dark metal.

Cynthia checked her watch. 'It's getting close to six,' she said. 'Shouldn't you be getting ready for your seven o'clock date?'

It took me a moment. 'Oh,' I responded, eventually. 'The Flamingo. Yeah.'

Neither of us moved.

'I'm worried about Brian,' she said.

My heart tightened; I was becoming more and more aware of its status as a muscle, a moving, unpredictable thing that wasn't performing its job as quietly as I would have liked. I felt myself reaching for that enchanted, dazed state of mind that had occupied me until the past second, but knew with unhappy certainty that it wouldn't return, no matter how long I spent staring at the chandeliers and mirrors of Bally's or wherever.

'I really enjoyed this afternoon,' I said.

She looked at me, puzzled. 'Really? I couldn't tell. I thought it was all a little boring for you.'

'No,' I said, 'not at all.'

She smiled, but it didn't last long. 'You're trying to change the subject.'

'I don't know what to say about Brian . . .' I said, hoping that it came across as some kind of guy thing, the man who isn't good at talking about feelings, or doesn't want to talk about his friends behind their back, especially with their girlfriends. Again, it crossed my mind that the thing I thought I was performing might actually be real, although not exactly in the way I was presenting it to her. It was all evasion of one kind or another.

'I know. It's OK.'

She took out her phone, and I realized that she had been checking it regularly all afternoon, brief glances and taps at the keys. Now I saw the sense of expectancy in the gesture, and the disappointment when she put the phone away.

'You were expecting a call from him?'

'We're going to the show later but we hadn't made plans for tonight, exactly. I thought he might call to make some. Not that, you know, I expect him to make them or anything, we just hadn't worked it out.'

'No, no, I get it,' I said, seeing her embarrassment.

One of the fountain jets started up, over in a far corner of the array. It stopped after a few seconds, leaving perfect widening circles around it.

A guy all in white, sneakers, shorts, T-shirt, came up to us, his hands full of little cards. He shoved a few of them at us wordlessly and moved on, doing the same to a group of people farther down the path. The same thing had been happening to us all day; usually I was quicker to hold up my hand and refuse, but Cynthia always accepted them, interested. These were the same as others we'd been offered only an hour earlier: one showing a topless blonde smiling coyly with a finger to her lips and a phone number in pink letters along the bottom; one showing an Asian woman in the same pose; the other showing two women, same phone number as the blonde.

I threw mine onto the path, and felt an instinctive stab of guilt for littering, thought about picking them up, didn't.

Cynthia studied hers. 'I thought prostitution was illegal in Nevada,' she said.

At that moment, a billboard came down the Strip in front of us, pulled along behind a black van, showing an enlarged version of the blonde on our cards with the addition of GIRLS!!! in massive block letters, and the same phone number.

'Technically, I suppose,' I said.

I arrived at the Flamingo half an hour late, after endless rounds of getting dressed and realizing that each item – shirt, trousers, another shirt, another – had some mysterious stain on it, including one that looked a lot like a smudge of either my chocolate eclair or Cynthia's chocolate crepe, but it wasn't the shirt I'd been wearing earlier. I sat on the bed trying to figure out how the stain had migrated, gave up, undressed, found myself about to get in the shower before remembering that I'd just had one, and chose the pair of trousers with a coffee stain (I guessed) on the pocket rather than the jeans with what looked like axle-grease marks near the knees. There was something unsettling about all these marks whose origins were unclear to me, indications of gaps in my memory like small, enigmatic black holes.

The digital clock glared steadily, telling me that it was five o'clock. I forgot that it was wrong and felt momentarily confused, checked my watch, tried again to reset it with no success. When the door clicked shut behind me I knew there was something vital I'd forgotten and I checked my pockets in a routine sort of way. I had everything I needed but the feeling persisted.

The Flamingo was busy, and I looked around the bar for a while before finding Tallis and Cameron perched on stools at a small, high table, each staring into his drink. Tallis blinked unsteadily at me when I greeted them.

'You must be really jet-lagged,' I said to him, seeing his shadowed, bloodshot eyes.

'No, no,' he said, smiling and frowning at the same time. 'It's all the sun. Poolside. Bloody exhausting.'

Cameron made a noise of agreement.

Tallis's face had turned faintly pink around the nose and cheeks, and there was a line of violent red across his collarbones just visible through the opening in his shirt where he must have missed with the sunscreen. He drained his glass. 'Get me another vodka,' he said, and for a second I thought he was going to hand me his empty glass as though I were a waiter. He set the glass down on the table and my resentment wavered, looking for somewhere else to land, and then softened. We could have waited for the waitress to come around but I wanted an excuse to leave them. Already, I thought, and it had only been a matter of seconds.

'I'll come,' Cameron said, and slipped off his stool before I could protest.

He rested his hand stiffly on the bar while we waited for our drinks.

'You seemed surprised earlier,' I said. 'In the car. Like you thought there was going to be something else in my envelope.'

He shrugged. 'No. I don't know.' He met my eyes for a second, and looked away. 'Yes. All right. I thought there might be something else, something to do with Dylan. I'm sorry.'

'Like what? What else would it be?'

He looked at me as though he hated having to state something so obvious. 'I thought — maybe — that you were involved with Dylan,' he said in a low voice.

'Involved?' I asked, incredulous. 'Do you mean, an affair?' He shrugged. 'Why would you think that? Wait, were you involved with him?'

'No. No. There was one time . . . he wasn't interested. That's what he said. And then . . . look, he never said anything specific. I don't know why, I started being suspicious.'

'When was this?' I asked.

'In college,' he said quickly. 'Not recently. No. I was jealous, I guess. Back then. I asked him about it, about you. A couple of times. He'd never admit it, but the way he talked — I never believed him.'

'He let you think something happened with me?'

I thought back, trying to piece this idea together with my memories of times I'd spent with Cameron. It made so little sense. I'd always chalked Cameron's irritability, his occasional distance from me, up to some other cause. I remembered how quiet he'd been in the car that day he'd helped me return the stacks of Tennyson books to the library; I'd been so preoccupied that I hadn't thought much of it.

He sighed and put his hand to his collar, as though loosening a tie, although he wasn't wearing one; it was a gesture that went with a suit worn every day. 'I don't even know if I'd put it that strongly. It was in my head. I haven't thought about it for so long; this business with the envelopes brought it up again. You know what it's been like.'

'I'm not sure I do.'

But I did, in a way, remembering how the past had come alive again over the last twenty-four hours. He seemed to be still waiting for me to respond.

'What, are you asking me to reassure you now? OK. I was never involved with Dylan. There was nothing like that.'

'All right, Elliot. I believe you. It doesn't matter, anyway. But, you know. You really worshipped him.'

'Now you're exaggerating.'

'Am I?'

I'd pitied Cameron for a moment, with his little tale of jealousy. But an obscure resentment started to take hold of me. Part of me had expected Cameron's story to take a different direction, I realized, thinking that maybe his mistaken impression had been formed because of how close I was to Dylan. Had I been waiting for him to say, 'Dylan loved you; we all knew it'?

Our drinks arrived and Cameron paid, waving away my attempts to contribute. He stared at the three glasses lined up, martinis with olives perfectly aligned at matching angles.

'I used to be angry with him about it,' he said. 'Even when I thought – you know, that there was something between you – the way he was so careful to just show that side to you, only the nice guy. It was as if, as long as you were around, he could think to himself that he was just that person.'

'He *was* that person to me.'

'To you, yeah. He liked it that way.'

'You make it sound as though it was all some kind of game to him.'

'It was, kind of. I thought you'd seen that by now.'

'It wasn't all a game. Not all of it.' Some of it was real, I told myself, and I knew it was true.

'No, not all of it. Not everything.' He sighed. 'It was hard to stay mad at him.'

I smiled. 'It was impossible.'

He smiled back, and I had the feeling that while I'd convinced him that Dylan and I had never been lovers, he believed as much as ever that I'd been in love with him.

Back at the table I handed Tallis his glass and he lifted it as if toasting us. The glass was overfull and some of the liquid spilled over the side. He swore softly, steadied his elbow on the table and brought his mouth to the edge of the glass, slurped it. I did the same.

'Where's Brian?' I asked.

The two of them exchanged glances. 'He was spending some time with Cynthia,' Cameron explained, his voice dry and neutral. 'He'll be here.'

I nodded. 'How's he doing?'

'I'd say OK, considering,' Tallis said.

I wondered whether they knew about my afternoon with Cynthia, and decided they probably didn't.

'Why did he have to bring her?' Tallis said.

'He didn't know,' I began, ready to defend Brian without thinking about it, as usual.

'It doesn't matter what he knew or didn't know. It was a stupid idea,' Tallis retorted, seeming glad of an opportunity to argue. I didn't feel like rising to it.

'He's going to meet us later,' Cameron told me.

'So tell me what you guys talked about,' I said. 'Tell me what grand plans you came up with in my absence.'

Cameron bristled. 'Don't complain now that we left you out. That was your decision.'

'It's OK, I know, I know,' I said, thinking about how I hadn't decided to leave myself out of the conversation the previous night, and how I hadn't minded anyway, and didn't really care now. 'I didn't want to talk about it, you're right. I want to talk about it now. So tell me.'

Brian was worried, Cameron told me; it seemed to him as though he was the one with the most at stake personally. They had talked over various options, started to go over the cost of what they thought Colin was asking for.

'You're not serious,' I said. 'There's no way I could afford anything like what he wants. And there's no way I could pull the kinds of strings he thinks I can pull.'

'I know,' Cameron said. 'Look, for a start, we're in this together. Some of us — all of us three, actually — are in a better position than you are to contribute financially, if that's what it takes, but we're OK with that, we're OK with putting in more money than you, especially if it turns out to be the case that you can contribute ... well, like you said, if you can pull the necessary strings. That would be your contribution, if you like. We think that this whole college idea is important to Colin. But, again, we're thinking through possible scenarios here. We're not necessarily planning to accede to all of his demands. It's hypothetical.'

'His demands still seem fairly unclear,' I said. 'And fairly deluded. I can't get him into the place I teach at, or fucking Bennington, if that's what he wants.'

'Perhaps he'd be satisfied if he felt as though you'd just done your best to help him achieve that,' Tallis said. 'Even if it doesn't work out in the end.'

'How could I write a recommendation for him? Or make a round of calls or whatever it is he thinks I can do?'

'We didn't say it would be a small thing for you,' Cameron said. 'That's why we'd be willing to recognize it as a substantial contribution. If it came down to that. Which it may not.'

The future took on a new kind of bleakness. Doing anything for Colin, entering into any kind of relationship with him, entailed possibly endless rounds of continuing favours and obligations. And whatever Cameron said about recognizing my potential contribution, if the other three ended up putting actual money into a scheme that benefited all of us, I would remain indebted to them in ways I could likely never repay. If they were talking about paying Colin's tuition and living expenses at a decent college, that was in the realm of hundreds of thousands of dollars. I realized that part of what repelled me most about what Cameron described was the prospect not only of being tied to Colin for life, but of being tied to all of them, in ways I couldn't freely choose.

Only a few days earlier I'd imagined that we'd always be friends, however unenthusiastic I felt about the idea, although I also expected that we would drift apart, as other people seemed to do. This had for a long time seemed like a more or less welcome prospect, and one I had felt guilty about wanting at all. But now I understood that whatever desire I'd had to finally outgrow these seemingly exhausted friendships had always been ambivalent, that it had sat side by side with a longing and a deep belief that was much harder to admit: that as time went on we would keep knowing one another and still perform the same boring but also comforting rituals of belonging.

I recognized that feeling now because I felt its passing, as surely as if I'd watched a familiar person leave the room. I could imagine a future where we stayed connected – it seemed impossible now to think that we could avoid it – but only by this thread, this web of knowledge and deceit, and I felt mainly aversion at the thought of it. The physical distances between our lives in different cities, states, countries felt more than ever like welcome, cushioning barriers.

'Isn't there any way we can get out of this?' I asked. 'Isn't there any pressure we can bring to bear on Colin? Isn't it illegal, what he's doing?'

'Of course it's illegal,' Cameron said patiently. 'In a strict sense. But I don't know. I haven't thought of a way yet of . . .' He sighed, annoyed, not used to being stuck for words, for ideas. 'A way of dissuading him. I'm working on it.' He was bewildered by the surreality of it, just like the rest of us. 'Elliot, we are all obviously worried about the information Colin has. However, we can't be sure that he would resort to extreme extortion. I think not. We talked it over. If he can be placated with, let's say, some help with his college admissions and his college fees, and an introduction to some producers or something like that, that might be the easiest way forward. He seems to want our friendship. As we said.'

I shook my head.

'Perhaps the best-case scenario is that we offer him some help,' Cameron said, 'a real gesture – and in exchange he gives us the information he has.'

'But he could keep copies of everything,' I said.

Tallis nodded exaggeratedly, as if to say that he'd already raised this objection.

'Yes,' Cameron responded. 'But these things he wants – college, Hollywood, respect, whatever – they mean a lot to him. He's not going to want to run the risk of losing those things either. Once we help him, this whole thing becomes somehow . . .'

'Mutual.' Tallis finished the sentence for him, uttering the word like a curse. I could see the unpleasant logic of the idea. Tallis tilted his head back, scrutinizing us both. 'Why don't you tell him Brian's idea?'

Cameron's face remained impassive. 'You know he wasn't serious.'

Tallis turned his bloodshot gaze to me. 'Take Colin out to the Grand Canyon. He might slip on a loose rock or something.'

'Like you'd go to the Grand Canyon,' Cameron muttered.

'No, all right then, not the Grand Canyon. Anywhere he could become, let's say, accident-prone.'

'Push him, you mean?' I said. 'Over the side of the Grand Canyon?'

'Brian is in what you might call a murderous rage,' Tallis said, and I could see that he wasn't drunk at all, however much he might have been drinking. I wondered whether he'd been doing cocaine. I thought of Cynthia, and wished for some myself, for the clear, high, empty focus that would dissolve all this confusion.

'He wasn't serious,' Cameron repeated.

'I know,' Tallis said. 'He just wants the whole thing to go away.'

'It wouldn't simplify anything,' Cameron said, and I was shocked by how much it sounded as though they were rehearsing a conversation that had already taken place, a familiar argument of some kind.

'That is not the problem with that idea,' I said. 'Its lack of simplifying potential is not the problem.'

'It's true,' Tallis mused, as though I hadn't spoken at all. 'It wouldn't necessarily solve anything. It could complicate things.'

'Look,' I said, and tried to meet their eyes. 'Stop talking about pushing Colin into the Grand Canyon. It's ridiculous to even think about that, it's just Brian being histrionic. Look,' I repeated. 'Why can't we just say no? Could we – you know – weather it? Call his bluff or whatever?'

Even as I articulated the thought I wasn't sure my heart was in it. It wasn't the tenure meeting I thought about, or the disappointment and anger of the department chair when he opened the manila envelope; it wasn't that specific. What I imagined was the passageway in the building leading to my office, and what it felt like to walk down it and open my door and feel as though I belonged there. I didn't want to lose that, or have it be so compromised. But that feeling fought for dominance with another sentiment: of not wanting to feel myself tied to Colin, to all of them, into the future.

They both held my gaze, and I could see Tallis trying hard to school his expression; it was in the way his face fell just slightly, in the way he pulled it back together. He felt betrayed, and it couldn't have been something he'd expected from me. He had been the one, yesterday, when Brian had first received his envelope, who had pushed for all of us to deal with it together. I saw now that he was afraid of having to deal with Colin on his own, afraid of the rest of us leaving him the only one willing to buy Colin off.

'You expect us all to go along with you,' I said to him, talking over Cameron, who had just begun to speak. 'You expect a lot.'

'It's not asking that much, is it?' Tallis replied, and I felt with a rush of something – power, relief, anger – that it was the first time during the whole trip that he'd spoken to me with any real sense of taking me seriously, or with any idea that he couldn't take my support for granted. The wounded feeling in his voice took me by surprise. The familiar rationalization started up – he relies on me, I thought with satisfaction, as a friend. But it quickly soured. He couldn't believe I would really argue with him; couldn't bear that I would maintain a point of difference from him about anything that really mattered to him.

'That's not the point,' I said. 'We'll talk about that in a minute.

But who's to say Colin would go through with it, whatever it is he has planned? What if we made it really clear to him: we're willing to offer him some assistance, normal friendship kind of assistance, but no money. As soon as money comes into it, it looks as though we're scared.'

'We are,' Tallis said. 'Well, no. Not scared. Concerned.'

'He seemed fairly focused on money,' Cameron said. 'And he knows we have it.'

'But I don't.'

'But we do.'

'He wants other things, too,' I said. 'You're the ones focusing on money. And some of those other things I suppose I could provide without really compromising myself. Minimal things. Help with his admission essay, for instance. It's not everything he seems to expect – not everything on his terms. But we could see how it played out.'

It was exactly the kind of conflict that Dylan would have instinctively known how to resolve while making everyone feel as though they had got what they wanted. He would have been able to create a consensus, and it would end up being a resolution that benefited him in some way, directly or indirectly. The lack of that mediating presence between us now was so strong that I expected to look down and see an empty stool next to me where there had been none before.

At the funeral, on the phone since then, the times we'd met in Vegas so far this trip – all the times the four of us had been together since Dylan's death – the dynamic between us had been completely in flux, not sure what form to take without him. Now for the first time it began to settle, to harden into new, determinate shapes that were still nameless, still provisional, but distinct from the old arrangements.

'Are you feeling a twinge of conscience, Elliot?' Tallis asked.

'Feeling as though you're ready to make amends, come clean? Deal with the consequences?'

Cameron turned his glass around, shifted it forwards, back again.

'It's a simple matter for you,' Tallis went on. 'You only have yourself to think about. I could tell all of you to go fuck yourselves as well, because this thing Colin has on me, it's not on me, is it? It's on someone else. But I'm not just thinking about myself. Unlike you.'

For a moment I wanted to argue with Tallis, to say that he ought to let his father take responsibility for his own actions, his own failures. But it was obvious that he wasn't ready to do that.

'I have a family,' Cameron said.

'But it was so long ago,' I said. 'How serious would it be for Marie?'

He cleared his throat. 'The truth is,' he said, 'the truth is . . .' I waited. 'It went on for a while longer than I originally said. We stayed in touch – not regularly – it wasn't like an affair, exactly ...'

'You stayed in touch – you slept together – exactly how wasn't it like an affair?' Tallis asked.

'I don't know,' Cameron said. Tallis frowned. 'I don't know how much Colin knows about it,' Cameron continued. 'I don't want to have to find out.'

'How long?' Tallis asked.

Cameron shook his head. 'Couple of years. Look, it doesn't matter.'

'Jesus, Cameron,' Tallis said. 'After you were married?'

Cameron tapped his foot and looked enviously at my cigarette. He'd married Marie not long after graduating; her parents were even more devout than Cameron's, and it was the only way they would accept them living together.

For someone who didn't seem to take sex very seriously, Tallis could be surprisingly judgemental about other people's infidelities, almost puritanical. To be fair, he was also hard on himself in the same way. I'd seen him racked with guilt when he'd conceived a passion at college for another student who was in a long-term relationship, living with her boyfriend. She was an economics major as well, and I used to see them reading the *Wall Street Journal* together in the coffee shop on campus, sitting close to each other, unmistakably about to do something stupid. When they finally started sleeping together, they carefully avoided each other in public, trying to keep it a secret. Tallis lost weight, stopped reading the *Wall Street Journal*, and studied by himself whenever he wasn't with her. A few weeks later she ended it, and he became obsessed with the idea that her boyfriend was alcoholic and abusive, trapping her into some kind of loveless hell. For some reason he decided to confide in me – he thought it was a secret from the rest of us, and I let him keep thinking that it was. He went on an extended drinking binge, and would call me every couple of days after whatever girl he'd taken home had left, or after he'd come back from someone else's bed, heartsick. He didn't often fall in love, but when he did it was like that, hyperbolic and intense until it ended and he went back to his usual emotionally disengaged self, almost impossible to reconcile with this other side.

I wasn't interested in the details of Cameron's affair, and I'd stopped caring whether he was gay or straight or something else. If Dylan had been there, I knew what he would do – the new Dylan, the real Dylan – he would find out something compromising about Colin and counter with pressure of his own. I had no idea how to go about doing that, and doubted whether the others did either.

'Can we stall for time?' I asked. 'Could we hire a private investigator, find out some information of our own about

Colin? To help, you know, persuade him that this isn't such a good idea?'

Cameron seemed impressed. 'I've been looking into that,' he said. 'And if Colin will give us some time, it might work out. But we can't count on it. Dylan was his brother, remember. If he got into any sort of trouble Dylan would have helped him sort it out fairly efficiently, I think.'

'So we need to offer him something, we need to be ready to at least make some kind of gesture when we see him tomorrow,' Tallis said.

'Have you talked to your father?' I asked. He shook his head.

'OK,' I said. 'I'll come along tomorrow morning, tell him how I think I'll be reasonably able to help him, get a clearer picture of how he feels about that. I'll keep an open mind. And you do the costs.'

Cameron nodded.

Tallis smoked and glared at me. 'Where's Brian?' he asked. 'He's late.'

We waited.

I tried to summon up the best feelings I had for Tallis against a growing tide of resentment, to reconnect with the person I'd hung out with in his apartment on those Thursday mornings in college so long ago.

I'd visited him once in London a few years back when I had a research grant to spend at the British Library, and had stayed for a week on the couch in his small, impeccably neat Kensington flat. The sun shone every day, miraculously, the whole time I was there, and I loved the walk through the neighbourhood to the Underground station along elegantly curved streets with Georgian buildings all of the same pale grey stone, white columns supporting the small front porches. It was a fantasy of prosperous London come to life, one with carefully trimmed roses in the gardens and old-fashioned red phone boxes on every other block and a Tudorish pub at the end of the street with low ceilings, timber beams and a fireplace. There was even a tiny park nearby that you could enter only with a key. It was all very picturesque and anodyne, and then I returned one afternoon and found the front fence of the whole row of buildings that included Tallis's flat covered with black spray-painted slogans and anarchist signs, and the letter slot on the front door covered over with a sticker that read 'Class War' in Helvetica Extra Bold. I smiled and realized then that I'd been feeling on edge in the area even as I'd admired it, as though I were walking each day through a film set or an elaborate, bloodless façade. Everything seemed now to be somehow more in balance. When I left the next morning the man in blue overalls and checked cap who had been clipping the roses the day before was scrubbing the graffiti with a soapy sponge, but slowly, as though he didn't really want to wash it away.

Tallis had been unfazed by the vandalism. 'Every month,' he'd said. 'It's the kids from one of the fucking mansions around the corner, I'm sure of it, that Tory politician. Going through their teen rebellion phase.'

He was frantically busy at work and we hardly saw each other at the flat, only when we met for late drinks at the corner pub with the timber beams. But I enjoyed the few minutes I saw of him in the morning, eating cereal standing up in the kitchen in his pinstriped suit, talking back to the radio with cheerful scorn, tying his tie with swift, practised motions. It had done something to recharge my affection for him, my sense that as his friend I had privileged access to this side of him.

There were few pictures in the flat apart from two framed movie posters, one for *A Clockwork Orange* that hung in the narrow hallway and one for *The Conformist*, a beautiful black-and-white image of two women dancing and a black-suited man, almost a silhouette, aiming a gun away from them, right over the sofa where I slept. Film was Tallis's one area of cultural interest, and he always surprised me with his knowledge of foreign cinema, his passionate feelings about the French New Wave and what happened to Italian film-making in the seventies.

A photograph of his parents, in a heavy silver frame, stood on a low table in the corner of the living room. It showed the two of them when they were young, his mother smiling at the camera, waves of fair hair catching the light, and his father smiling at her in profile, clearly in love. I'd been there for four days when I looked at the photograph again as I was getting ready to leave for the library and saw something I hadn't seen or that just hadn't registered when I'd glanced at it days earlier. Richard was holding a baby, a newborn tightly swaddled, in one arm. It must have been Tallis. His mother's radiance was now visible as maternal happiness, but Richard still had eyes only for her; there didn't seem to be any attention to the small bundle in his arms.

Watching Tallis now, I tried to remember his father's face and find some resemblance there. I'd never met his mother, only seen that photograph of her, but his smile was entirely hers.

'You look like your mother,' I said, thinking out loud.

Tallis looked startled for a moment, and shrugged.

'I've seen a photograph of her. At your place.'

He nodded. 'I know the one you mean. The lovely Diana.' He sighed. 'Elliot. I don't mean to be hard on you about this. But you have no idea. My father's not terribly stable.'

Cameron watched him carefully, like before.

Tallis leaned toward me. 'He had a breakdown last year. I went on to New York after the funeral, do you remember?'

I did. We'd travelled to the airport together and caught separate flights to JFK, where I'd changed to a small plane that took me upstate. I had noticed that Tallis was more distant than usual but thought it was all about Dylan.

'Mum had kicked him out again. The drinking was out of control. He set fire to his hotel room by accident, a lit cigarette. She wouldn't take him back. When I got to New York he'd just been released from hospital. He'd overdosed – sleeping pills and Valium. I think he stole them from Mum in the first place. He denied it, said he just got drunk and didn't know how much he was taking, but it was pretty fucking obvious.'

'I'm sorry,' I said. 'I didn't know.'

'It's OK,' he said, as though I were the one who might be in need of comfort. 'He's cleaned up a bit since then. They're together – not that I can really say why she took him back this time and not the other. It's a mystery. But it's, you know, a fragile situation.'

'How badly was the other guy hurt in that fight?' I asked. 'The one who wanted to press charges.'

Tallis appeared to be weighing up how much he wanted to tell me. 'OK, it was a bit worse than I said. But not much. He broke his wrist.' He paused. 'His jaw was fractured. But that was from the fall. The wrist, too. It was bad luck. But, you know, it looks bad.'

I felt sure that if I asked him again, later on, more details would emerge.

'It's not your fault,' I said. 'It's not your responsibility.'

'Oh, yes,' he said, and actually laughed. 'Adult child of alcoholics,' he said, as though he were quoting a diagnostic manual. 'I've heard it all, thank you very much. But what the fuck. I know, I shouldn't have called Dylan, it was a stupid thing to do but it worked out, there was something I could do and I did it. It worked out up until now. So I don't want to screw it up. Do you understand?'

'I understand,' I said.

'OK,' he said. 'Good.'

Brian arrived and clapped me on the back, hard. I slipped a little on my stool. The bandage was still there around his hand, fresh and white, and he smelled faintly of chlorine. They all did.

'Hi,' he said, and glanced around, tense but more confident than he'd looked that morning. 'How's everything?'

'OK,' Cameron said, and nodded. 'It's all good.' I knew he was talking about me. 'No problem.'

'Great,' Brian said, and gave me his smile, the same one from the car earlier.

'Great,' I said. 'No problem.'

'Brian,' said Tallis with great affection, another clap on the back, moving straight from morose to animated. 'Get me another vodka, will you?'

I heard myself repeating words, heard them saying their own words again, echoes. It was something like the uncanny sense of déjà vu, where it feels as though everything has happened before but you can't remember the first time, only the repetition. Except it had a different sort of clarity and a relentless sense that not only had this happened before, it would happen again. The feeling that I'd forgotten something vital wouldn't go away.

12

Brian left after just one drink to go to the cancan show with Cynthia. I had a meal of patchy tapas with Tallis and Cameron and listened to them talk about trouble brewing in the financial world. It got late; they wanted to stay out playing some sports betting game and I started back in the direction of the hotel. At the end of one long block my phone buzzed.

What's up? C.

How was the show? I typed back.

Feathers, sequins, flesh etc, you should have come. Just got out. Brian gone back to Flamingo. Where are you?

We made an arrangement to meet at the foot of the Eiffel Tower. It felt like an imitation of a romantic assignation. I wondered whether it really was one. It was crowded there, with people waiting in line to take the elevator up to see the view. I felt a hand on my arm and there she was, dressed in black.

'Do you want to go up?' I asked, indicating the line.

'No,' she said. 'Not right now. I don't need to see the view again.'

'So Brian's gone to the Flamingo? I just left Tallis and Cameron there.'

'Yeah, he called them and they said you'd just left. I promised I wouldn't cut into his guy time, you know. And he's really moody, it's crazy. I don't think he even noticed all these semi-naked women we just saw. I might go meet him for a drink later but I don't know.' She sighed. 'He's doing his thing. So. Can I ask you a favour?'

'Sure.'

'I need some assistance with my research.'

'Research. Does it involve dancing girls?'

'I told you, you should have come! And no, not exactly. I might just need a male escort for this one thing. Come and get a cab with me and I'll tell you. It's downtown.'

'So you didn't want to go out bonding with the guys?' she asked once we were in the car and travelling along the expressway off the Strip. 'You don't like gambling?'

'Not really, no.'

'I hope Brian doesn't have some secret gambling addiction he hasn't told me about.' She smiled. She was joking.

'Oh, no,' I said. 'Nothing like that.'

'He's still under the weather or something. I hope it's good for him to hang out with those two.'

We rode the rest of the way in silence, her mouth shining in the dark just as it had the night before. She directed the cab past the horrendous neon tunnel of Fremont Street and I breathed a sigh of relief. That place was guaranteed to spark my new-found claustrophobia with its illuminated artificial ceiling spread over several blocks. We stopped outside one of the old casinos in a neglected-looking street, and walked in through elaborately carved doors. Inside it was fitted out in Victorian style, all fake Tiffany stained glass and overstained oak and bronze.

Cynthia consulted her guidebook. 'OK,' she said. 'Here's the thing. They have an actual piece of the Berlin Wall here.'

'An actual piece?' I asked.

'That's right – the real Berlin Wall. They acquired it just after the Wall came down.'

'Where is it?'

'In the men's restroom. There you go. I told you it was research. Come on.'

We followed signs for the restroom, and wandered through a room of antique slot machines under glass and two player pianos pushed against the wall in a haphazard way as though they were in the process of being moved to somewhere else, wood panelling all around us and darkly patterned carpet underfoot. There was a restroom at one end.

'Do you want me to look inside?' I offered. 'See if the Wall's there?' Cynthia agreed.

There were a couple of guys at the urinals, but nothing that looked like the Berlin Wall. Just Victorian-looking tiles everywhere, geometrical black-and-white patterns.

'No?' she said when I came back out. She looked in her guidebook again; we went back past the room of antiques and through the gaming floor. The only other people in the place under forty-five were behind the bars and the card tables. There was a faint smell of overcooked vegetables underneath the usual smoke and chemical aroma. I thought of my grandmother's house, visiting when I was a small child, the plates of faded, boiled carrots and green peas.

'OK, I think this is it,' Cynthia said outside the restroom door just off the main floor.

'Can we leave after this?' I asked.

'Yes, we can leave after this. I know – this place is horrible. I need a drink.'

There it was when I entered the bathroom: pieces of the famous Wall installed behind the urinals, each separated by a cherry-coloured wood panel. The panels seemed to provide protection against splashes of urine falling on the Wall, as well as some extra privacy. The fragments were all heavily graffitied in bright colours. There was a crudely drawn red hammer and sickle on one piece, heavy layers of varnish over the original paint. A beer bottle lay smashed on the hexagonal black-and-white tiles beneath.

I went to the door. 'Cynthia?' I called. She was checking her phone and glanced up. 'Come on in. There's no one else in here.'

She followed me inside and took a couple of photos. I offered to take one of her, and she stood next to the hammer and sickle, gesturing happily toward it like a magician's assistant, blinking from the flash.

Photographs carefully framed above the urinals showed the Wall in its original state in Berlin, and some of the jubilant scenes at its destruction, providing a documentary context for the pieces of graffitied concrete that felt incongruous in this setting. In one of the pictures a group of young men cheered, arms in the air, two of them with arms slung around each other's shoulders. One of them reminded me of Dylan – his straight dark hair and slim, lanky body – and the other reminded me of someone else. I looked for a while before I realized he reminded me of myself. I quickly glanced away, at the other photos – bulldozers, politicians, children, rubble – and back again. He didn't look like me at all, really; maybe around my height, and with glasses. I wondered if there were any photos of Dylan and me together, just the two of us, and couldn't remember.

'You know,' Cynthia said, gazing at the porcelain urinals, 'I'm kind of disappointed. I thought you'd be able to pee *on* the Wall. But I guess that wouldn't make sense.'

'I guess you could if you really wanted to,' I said.

She nodded, her face serious.

'I'm not going to, if that's what you're thinking,' I told her.

'No. I wouldn't ask you to do that.'

'Thanks.'

'Thank you, escort. Or should that be chaperon.'

'You're welcome.'

We heard the door swing open. 'Let's go,' Cynthia said, and we hurried out past the man coming in, reeking of cigar smoke and whisky.

'Do you smoke cigars?' Cynthia asked.

'No,' I said. 'Once in a while.'

'There's a cigar bar here, in an old railcar . . .'

'Do you mind if we see it another time?'

'Sure,' she said, and smiled at me. 'Let's get out of here.'

We walked for blocks looking for a bar Cynthia had read about, through the Fremont Street mall and out the other side onto streets that looked the same as any other city at the quiet end of downtown. Parking lots, corner stores. In the middle of one block, Cynthia stopped outside an unmarked storefront of dark glass. 'This is it,' she said, and tried the door. It wouldn't budge.

We tried to see inside. There was a dim orange glow through the windows, but it could have been a reflection. She tried the door again. After a second it opened, pulled by someone on the inside, a young woman who said, 'Come on in,' in a quiet voice.

We followed her, pushing aside a heavy velvet curtain. There was a short set of stairs leading down. Cynthia was one step behind me, and I managed to catch her arm when she tripped and almost fell. I held on as she straightened up.

'I'm OK, I'm OK,' she said, and I let go. 'Shit.' She reached down to her feet and raised one hand to show me the heel of her shoe, cleanly broken off, a three-inch spike held in her palm with a couple of tiny nail points jutting out of it. She winced. 'I'm not even drunk! This is so unfair. Fuck.'

The steps had left a graze against the side of one calf.

'Does that hurt?' I asked.

'What?' She looked down and brushed her fingers across it. 'No. Skin's not broken. I'm annoyed about my shoe, though.'

There was a bar against one wall, low seats and tables around the room, and a few candles and lamps here and there that didn't give much light, just the orange glow I'd seen from outside. We found a seat in a quiet corner, Cynthia walking with a lopsided shuffle, and ordered drinks from the woman who had let us in.

'This isn't exactly research,' Cynthia said. 'But I wanted to visit all the same. I like the idea of the unmarked door.'

'What's it called?' I asked.

'Drink, or Bar, or something like that,' she said. She leaned down and tried to fix the heel back onto her shoe. It seemed to work but didn't look very secure.

There was an enclosed fireplace set against one wall, emitting more flickering orange light. Of all the things I'd seen in Vegas this somehow seemed the most extravagant. I wondered how they dealt with the heat it generated, how they got it to stay so cool inside. The thick glass around the fire must have been strongly insulated. I wondered whether it was a real fire or gas or maybe some kind of holographic illusion.

'It's weird to see a fireplace, isn't it?' she said.

'I was just thinking that,' I replied. 'Is it fake or real?'

'Exactly!' she said, and laughed gently.

The couch we were sitting on was dark velour, wide and overstuffed. I could make out other people in the room, some faces lit by the lamps, some voices, but our corner felt secluded from the rest of the place.

'How am I going to explain this?' she said, smiling. 'Breaking my shoe on the way into some unmarked Vegas bar?'

'I'm sure it's happened to Brian before,' I said. 'Or the equivalent. Or worse.'

She raised her glass as though what I'd said had been a kind of toast.

'So, how do you like it at BU?' I asked her.

'It's fine. It's great.'

We went through the normal pathways of conversation about graduate student life at an institution, established who I might know on the faculty or in the numbers of recent graduates of the program. We were drinking vodka again, on our second round, this time with tonic. Cynthia reached into her drink as she talked and squeezed the slender piece of lime floating on the surface between her thumb and forefinger, releasing its juice. I lifted my own glass and drank, searching out the faint sour trace of citrus, unable to concentrate on anything except the idea of her wet fingers, which she had brushed against her upper arm, leaving a small smear of liquid. It was hard to find the lime taste through the pervasive tonic bitter-sweetness; if I could taste her arm, I thought, that's where it would be . . .

Something she said caught my attention and I tried to focus. Was she talking about a syllabus? For a class she had taught, or taken?

'Did you say "lyricism"?' I asked.

'Did I say what?' she said, smiling.

'Lyricism.'

'Lyric and what?'

'Lyricism.'

'Oh, lyricism. No! I love that word, though. You know, I've never said it out loud. Lyricism. Why would I be saying that?'

I shrugged. 'I don't know.'

'I wonder when was the last time anyone ever said that word in Vegas.' Her gaze travelled across the room, slow and restless.

'Don't you think there's lyricism here?'

'I suppose the place is kind of poetic.'

'It is.'

'I thought you hated Vegas.' Her smile now was conspiratorial.

'I hate poetry.'

She laughed. 'You hate poetry.'

I shrugged again.

Cynthia crossed her legs and I watched her ankles, the skin taut around the bones there. Her slim legs, the motion of crossing them, made me think of Jodie, the one time I could remember seeing her. It was the last thing I wanted to think about.

Looking at Cynthia I was suddenly exhausted by the weight of the secrets I carried. I swallowed, and it struck me immediately as a guilty, nervous action. Wouldn't you want to know, in her position? I asked myself. Did I have some kind of moral obligation to tell her what I knew about Brian and what he'd done? I knew that the impulse was fuelled by opportunism, and I let it die; that particular piece of knowledge bled into all the other things I knew, or things I'd done, that I wanted to hide, or had to.

I felt the presence of the secrets in my head, in my body – they were thoughts, they were knowledge, but they felt like physical objects. I tried to reduce them in my mind to their simplest form – information; imagined them as particular patterns and connections of synapses, individual little pathways in my brain. Electrical pathways. From this perspective they were neutral, a collection of on-and-off switches. As if in response, the lights of the city in the distance through the windows glittered and winked like faraway stars, on, off, smog and the haze of heat through the window's dark tint producing an illusion of blinking shimmer.

As much as I tried to imagine the information as an impersonal pattern in my brain, the space it occupied in my body felt visceral, a pressure in my chest. My lungs continued to contract and expand in their unconscious accustomed way. It was at this sort of moment of self-awareness – noticing my own breathing – that I expected to feel my heart pounding, a live nervous pulse, but I felt disturbingly numb, and fought an urge to put my fingers to my wrist to feel the reassuring beat of blood.

Cynthia's eyes rested on her glass, her face almost in profile towards me, the clean, sharp line of her jaw. I found myself watching for the correlative beat of her own pulse in that place in her throat. But her skin was smooth and still – and then it was there, a flicker of movement, quicksilver; she raised her glass to her lips and drank and I lost sight of it as she swallowed, and wondered if what I'd seen was her pulse at all or something else, the prelude to motion.

'What is it?' she said, murmuring, her lips hardly seeming to move.

In another place – another region of my brain, a slice of time already gone, or only ever imagined, never real – there was Jodie White, on a white-covered bed; there was Dylan, leaning in to look at her closely in some intimate environment, a bar, her room, the front seat of her broken-down expensive car; there was Brian, thinking only about himself; there were all of us, doing the things we were ashamed of, or worrying about the people we wanted to protect.

It crossed my mind to say 'nausea' or something like it, but it got lost on the way. The distance between us, a few inches of space, seemed wonderfully empty and open compared with the toxic saturation inside me. I embraced it, leaning in to her, and closed the gap, but it imparted none of its promise of grace and lightness, at least at first. I kissed her mouth, and took her face and neck in my hands, pressing my thumb against that place where her pulse had shown, and thought I sensed it, a quick, fluttering throb. She kissed me back. She gasped, a sharp intake of breath, at what in particular I couldn't tell, and I felt that burden in my chest give way like a crumbling wall, overcome by the urgency of another feeling, of the present.

I drew her closer, and fought the urge to pull her completely onto my lap, to feel the weight of her legs across my own. We unglued ourselves after a while and sat with our foreheads touching, breathing hard. I lifted a finger to touch a freckle on her arm, a dark, tiny, perfect circle just visible in the dim glow; and then reached my thumb to another, smaller one farther down, and it seemed full of significance that it was just that far away, a measure tailored to my handspan, the dimensions of my body. I was fairly drunk. I was still thinking about how her skin would taste with that trace of lime juice on it. Now that I looked there were little freckles scattered here and there, and I moved my fingers and thumb from one to another.

'Are you making constellations out of my freckles?' she asked with a smile. That's what she said, but I misheard her for a moment before the right word settled in.

'I thought for a second you said "consolations",' I said.

'Oh,' she said, and smiled again, more broadly. 'Consolations? But no one's losing here . . .'

Losing, she said, and I was overwhelmed suddenly by the idea, the sensation of loss. Not as it seemed to apply to the way she'd said it, like losing a competition and accepting a consolation prize or whatever had run through her mind (did she think I was competing for her with Brian, I wondered; it didn't feel that way at all) but in some broader, more general and yet also more specific way, about what I was losing and what I had lost.

The first random thing that came to mind was the box of books and files that had mysteriously disappeared in my move from New York to Riverford, with my entire collection of twentieth-century poetry (not much) and notes from several graduate courses inside. I remembered the tree that stood out front of our house, a dogwood, and how Lily had liked to climb it with bare feet when we were small and didn't seem to notice her skinned knees although my own stung so much when I followed her up. The tree had lost several branches in a storm years back, but still flowered white and green in the spring. For some reason I recalled with a sharp pang of longing the one time I'd visited San Francisco and developed a huge crush on the city itself, the sheer beauty of it, the way the ocean would appear in little glimpses as you came to the end of a block and looked down the hill, framed by the steep, straight streets, and then was gone again. It was the Pacific, glittering and full of promise, exhilarating pure blue, not the steely Atlantic I was familiar with.

I thought of Dylan and what it was like to be here without him, how all the bright spaces were quietly haunted by his absence however much I tried to ignore it. I thought about the others, and how things would never be as they were before, and how they had never been like I'd thought they were, anyway. It wasn't just the future of a certain kind of friendship with them that felt lost, but also my whole experience of the past, or pieces of it.

Cynthia's body distracted me again. I reached to touch another little spot that I'd already touched before, and couldn't reach it this time without lifting my hand, breaking contact.

'Constellations,' she repeated softly.

I wondered what shape could be made out of lines connecting the dots of her freckles, and pictured the night sky over Vegas, stars all but obliterated by the bright casino displays and the emerald shaft of light beamed up into space by the Luxor pyramid, a piece of pure extravagance that could supposedly be seen from space. The stars had never seemed so melancholy, with their light so old that it came from the unimaginably distant past, so far away that the star could be dead by now. To imagine the dead person as a star was the traditional consolation trope of the elegy, I knew, and wondered whether I'd learned that from the essay Dylan had arranged for someone else to write for me.

I thought about Natasha and what felt like all the lost opportunities with her so far: not having kissed her when I stayed in her bed; not having reached out to her quickly enough when she was sitting on my couch.

Cynthia's hand was on my shoulder and she seemed to become very still. She chewed the inside of her lip. When she raised her eyes to mine it was as though the sun had shifted from the surface of water, a river or the sea, and what had been ripples and reflection was suddenly clear all the way down. What I saw for a second – the sun moved again, her expression changed – wasn't a feeling I could interpret exactly; it looked something like curiosity, and something like desire and reluctance all at once.

Something shifted. Neither of us said 'this is a bad idea' or anything like that, but we both knew it.

My phone rang. She moved her hand from where it was, ready to take it away. I touched her collarbone again, palm against her chest where I could feel the slight swell of her breast, before I reached for the phone in my pocket. I felt sure that it would be Brian, but it was Tallis. It stopped ringing as I held it and read his name on the display.

Cynthia's eyebrows lifted in a question.

'Tallis,' I said.

She nodded. The phone came to life in my hand again, shuddering and bleeping. Tallis again. I opened it.

'Tallis?'

'Elliot. It's Cameron,' he said, and I was confused because it was Tallis talking. 'It's Cameron.' There was panic in his voice.

'Tallis? Where are you?' I asked. Cynthia stirred beside me, pulling farther away.

'They got into a fight – Brian and Cameron. He's not moving – he's not moving, Elliot . . .'

'He's what? He's unconscious?'

'Oh, God . . .'

It's strange how immediately I believed what Tallis seemed to be telling me: that Cameron was not just unconscious but possibly dead. Part of me detached from my body, almost, it seemed, from time itself. I felt all of us become part of a dreadful story, as though our lives had slid in a single second into yet another surreal world of fiction. We had just been friends, drunk and fighting and at one another's throats. Now I wondered whether we had landed in a murder plot, flattened out into killers, accomplices, corpse.

'Where are you?' I asked again, my voice slow.

'In the room. My room. Wait.' I could hear another voice in the background, close by: Brian, speaking in an urgent tone. 'No – yes,' Tallis said. 'He's breathing. He's not dead. Thank fucking God. Brian!' he started shouting.

I took the phone from my ear and held it against my chest. My rib cage thumped – there it was, alive and beating. Time came back and moved sinuously fast and slick, carrying me forward like a wave. The murder story slid away with a sly glance back before it disappeared; that wasn't us after all.

I raised the phone. 'Hang up. Call an ambulance or the hotel doctor, whatever you're supposed to do.'

'There's a doctor?'

How could he not know that, I wondered, with his hypochondria? 'Just call 911.'

'Right. That's the thing to do. Brian's doing it.' A pause. 'Get over here. Room 841.'

I closed the phone. A mutinous feeling rose within me, an impulse whose movement was exaggerated again by the shock, and I wanted only to leave. I saw myself in a taxi, and striding by the slot machines in the airport corridors, and on the plane with my face turned away from the windows, grateful to be travelling so fast. The thing that brought me back down to earth wasn't my injured friend, I'm ashamed to say; I didn't think I could do much to help, and wondered what Tallis had been thinking when he'd called me. It was Colin and our meeting with him tomorrow morning, and the fact that I couldn't leave that unresolved.

'Is Brian OK?' Cynthia asked.

'Yes,' I said. 'I think so. He got into some kind of a fight with Cameron.'

She narrowed her eyes. 'Like a fistfight? You mean, actual fighting?'

'Actual fighting.'

We rose to leave. Cynthia's heel snapped off again as soon as she took her first step. She cursed and slipped off both shoes, carrying them by the straps as we left and flagged down a cab.

Tallis looked Cynthia over critically when he opened his door and greeted us both with a curt hello. 'What happened to you?' he asked her, but looked to me for an answer.

I glanced at her and saw her as she might appear to him: diminutive without her high heels, barefoot, shoes in hand, grazed leg, mouth clean of the shiny lipstick she had worn before I kissed her. There were faint lines of pigment where it hadn't rubbed off completely and a smudge on her top lip. I rubbed my hand across my mouth quickly, hoping there was no trace of it there.

Tallis focused on me. 'And what took you so long?'

'We were downtown,' I said. 'I wasn't even sure if you'd still be here. I tried calling you again but the reception on my phone screwed up.'

I'd spent the whole ride dialling him and Cameron and Brian alternately, watching the bars on the side of the screen waver and slide down.

'Downtown?'

'I thought you might be at the emergency room by now.'

Cynthia went straight to Brian, who was sitting on one of the two double beds. She sat down next to him and talked to him in a low voice, reaching out to touch his face. He flinched. She sat there patiently and took his hand, and then smoothed his hair, and placed her hand gently on his back. He nodded, head lowered, still leaning slightly away from her. There was something deeply intimate about the way they responded to each other, something unmistakably devoted in her attitude. I turned away.

Cameron sat on the other bed with his back against the wall, looking as though he was about to tip over to one side or the other any second.

'Cameron,' I said. 'Are you OK?'

He nodded. A dark bruise had started to form on his left cheek, and his lower lip and the flesh around it was swollen. He held a washcloth to his face that had bloodstains on it. There was a graze and a cut near his temple.

'Why are you still here?' I asked him. 'You need stitches.'

'I don't need stitches,' he said. It sounded as though it was painful to talk.

Cynthia led Brian into the bathroom. I caught a glimpse of his face on his way past, one eye swollen and bruised, a trickle of blood from one nostril. The door clicked shut behind them and the sound of running water came through, and then voices, raised in argument almost immediately, although no words were audible.

'I've been telling him to go,' Tallis said, his back to the bathroom door. 'Go on, Cameron.'

'It won't hurt to get it looked at,' I said. He gave me a weary glance. 'And you could be concussed.'

I knew that concussion was serious, but wasn't sure what the treatment for it was, or whether it even needed any special treatment, or monitoring.

'Maybe he'll listen to you,' Tallis said, folding his arms. There were spots of red on his pale grey suit. Drops of Cameron's blood, or Brian's; his own face was unmarked. 'Sit down.'

I sat at the small desk and regarded Cameron, still slumped against the wall. The blood on the washcloth was dark red against the white fabric. I wondered how it would look to the housekeeping staff when they cleared the room, whether they saw bloodstains all the time. Cameron pressed the cloth against his mouth and I noticed that his lip was also bleeding.

Tallis sat down on the edge of the bed, facing me, elbows on knees, hands hanging loosely.

'So what happened?' I asked. 'Brian looks bad, too.'

'Brian had this idea after you left,' Tallis said. 'He wanted to talk to Colin again. This afternoon, when we were at the pool, he called around and found out that Colin works at New York, New York. Croupier at one of the blackjack tables there. You know,' he looked up, frowning, 'I expected him to be exaggerating. I thought we'd show up and find that he was a waiter at the fucking delicatessen or something. But no. He's a croupier, wearing the tux, the whole thing.'

'You went there?' I asked.

Brian and Cynthia had lowered their voices; I heard only brief exchanges, low tones, long silences between speech.

Tallis rolled his eyes. 'I know, it was a fucking stupid idea. Brian was obsessed. He insisted on going, we couldn't talk him out of it. So we went. Well, of course Colin's working, he's behind the table, he can't talk to us. But he gave us a smile, didn't blink an eye, totally cool.'

I pictured Colin, calm and expressionless as he dealt the cards, flipped them over, called the bets, pushed the chips back and forth.

'Brian lost it, totally. Predictable. I think it was that cool look that Colin had on.'

'He hit him?'

'No, no. He tried to get his attention, started yelling at him. The security guards move pretty quickly in these places. Brian calmed down soon enough. Colin was really unfazed. Or seemed that way. He left me a message just after I called you – just finished his shift, hopes everything is OK for tomorrow.'

'Maybe we should talk on the way to the hospital,' I said. 'We need to get someone to look at Cameron's face.'

'OK, I'll go,' Cameron said, lifting his head from where it had been resting against the wall. 'But don't come with me. I'll take a cab. Tallis,' he said over Tallis's protests, 'I'll go. Don't come. Get some sleep. You too, Elliot. Thanks for coming by.'

'I don't mind coming with you,' I said. 'Let one of us come.'

I thought about all of us in the hospital all those years ago after the crash, the way Cameron had wound up there the longest, and Dylan had stayed with him.

He gazed at me wearily. 'I could do with the time alone. I've had enough company for one day. I'm serious.'

He rested his hand on Tallis's shoulder for a moment, and I saw again the memory I'd surely invented of his hand just like that on Brian's shoulder, the day of the World Cup game. The constricting chill of loss struck me all over again.

Tallis walked him to the door and placed his own hand on Cameron's shoulder as he said goodbye. Then he cracked open two miniature bottles of whisky and poured one for each of us into the thick hotel water glasses. The dry, smoky burn of the drink felt satisfying and rough against my throat. Tallis downed half of his in one swallow and lit a cigarette, smoothing out the covers on the bed before he sat down.

'So,' he said, tilting his glass back and forth. 'Downtown with Cynthia?'

'We were having a drink,' I said, trying not to sound defensive. 'She was down there for her research.'

He nodded and drank.

'So you came back here with Brian,' I prompted him.

'Oh, right. You can tell me about Cynthia's research another time. She's very pretty. Too thin, but pretty. Yes, we came back here to talk it through. Cameron and Brian. It's the same old, same old.' He rubbed the spot between his eyebrows. 'To tell the truth I can't remember what set them off.'

'They're never going to work it out,' I said.

Tallis snorted. 'Not now they're fucking not.' Then he shrugged. 'Although, who knows. Bit of a black eye might clear the air.'

I couldn't imagine what it felt like for Brian and Cameron – being punched in the face, the bruised mouth. I'd gotten a black eye once from a stray baseball in seventh grade, which I was grateful for in the end since it gave me the excuse I'd been looking for to give up even trying to participate in the hated activity. It was dramatic and painful, a deep indigo circle that had faded to Technicolor purple and green as it healed. But this was different. This was raw aggression, an actual fistfight. There was something both primal and pathetic about it; Brian and Cameron seemed diminished, weakened, downcast.

'No one's ever hit me,' I said.

Tallis regarded me with scepticism for a moment, then shrugged again as though he could easily believe it.

'Cameron got that one good punch in,' he said. 'You saw Brian's eye, right? And then Brian hit back and Cameron hit the wall. That's when he blacked out, when I called you.'

I shook my head. I remembered my conversation with Natasha that night in the bar, when she'd asked about Brian and Cameron fighting all the time, and I'd imagined a comical, slapstick version of them punching and wrestling. Now it seemed like a gruesome premonition.

'I panicked,' Tallis said. 'I don't know why. Stress. Sorry. I needn't have.'

Brian and Cynthia emerged.

'What happened to your shoe?' Tallis asked. She had set them down outside the bathroom door and they lay there, small and fragile-looking, the broken one sole up, scuffed along the bottom. Cynthia's face was studiously blank. She bent down to pick up the shoes without answering him. Tallis glanced at Brian with disdain.

I checked my watch, found that I couldn't remember whether I was supposed to add four hours or five. Or three.

'What time is it?' I asked Tallis.

'Late,' he said, exhaling smoke, and put his cigarette out neatly in an ashtray. 'I'm ready for bed. Goodnight all.'

Brian kept looking at him but Tallis wouldn't meet his eye.

'So we're on for tomorrow?' I asked.

He nodded. 'See you at breakfast. Nine sharp.'

The three of us made our way slowly to the elevators. Cynthia pressed the up arrow, and I reached across and pressed the one for going down.

'I'm going to have one last drink with Elliot,' Brian said.

I turned to him in surprise. 'OK.'

'You go on up,' he said to Cynthia.

Her eyes were clear and calm when she looked at me, and I didn't want her to go. The elevator doors opened; it was empty.

'Take your time,' she said. She squeezed Brian's hand quickly before she stepped in and the doors shut.

13

'I don't know what Tallis told you,' Brian said when we were seated at the bar downstairs, the same one we'd drunk at with Tallis the evening before. It was half-empty, no one at the piano, the same piano music in the background. 'The security guards completely overreacted.'

'You have a black eye,' I commented, unable to look away from it. The bruise was both horrible and fascinating, seeming to darken visibly as the seconds went by. Somehow it completed the look that Brian had been edging toward since he had first opened the envelope, the victimized expression. The bartender had given him a second glance, but not much of one, when we sat at the bar. 'It's going to be even worse tomorrow.'

'I know,' he said, not sounding too concerned. 'Can you give me a cigarette?'

I passed him one and lit it for him. He held it in his bandaged hand.

'Is that the hand you hit him with?' I asked. He stared at it confusedly. 'Shouldn't you put some ice on it or something? Or on your eye?'

He shrugged. 'I don't know. I took some codeine Tallis had, some prescription stuff, and some Advil. It's not hurting so much now. And drinking helps.'

It occurred to me that I ought to lecture him for what he'd done at the casino, for getting into a fight with Cameron, or at least try to talk to him about it, but I didn't have the heart. He looked so pathetic with his bruised face and his hair still slightly wet around his forehead from where he'd just washed his face, slicked down in a childish way.

'What happened with Cynthia just now?' I asked instead.

'Just now? Nothing. We weren't fighting. Something happened to her shoe, she said. That's bad luck.' He shook his head. 'It was such a bad idea for her to come along.'

'No,' I said. 'We had no idea it would be like this. Anyway. How was the show?'

'The show? Oh, the Paris show. I thought it would be longer. It was kind of boring – every number was the same as the one before. She said she was going to call you, to go visit that casino downtown . . .'

'She did,' I said. 'We went down there.'

'What was it, some kind of exhibition about the Berlin Wall? I couldn't quite get it straight.'

'Yeah, something to do with the Wall.'

'I hate downtown. Oh, man,' he said. 'You know, I think she's seeing someone else.' I reached for a cigarette for something to do with my hands. 'Some academic in her department, some big-shot asshole.'

'What makes you think that?'

'I don't know. I think they talk on the phone. There's an unlisted number that comes up on her phone all the time.'

'You're looking at her phone?' I remembered the constant subtle checks of her phone that afternoon and felt an irrational stab of jealousy when I imagined that she'd been checking for messages from some other lover, not from Brian. 'What's his name?'

'I don't want to be possessive, you know?' he continued, ignoring me. 'But at the same time . . .'

'You sound paranoid,' I said. 'You always start to think your girlfriends are sleeping with someone else.' This was true. Brian commonly fell into suspicion and jealousy in his relationships. I often thought it was because he was routinely unfaithful himself. 'That always happens after a few months, remember?'

Brian frowned. 'Does it? Well, it was true in that one case, with Bianca.'

'In that one case. Aren't you and Cynthia moving in together?'

'That's the plan. I just . . . Fuck. I really don't want her to find out about this shit.' He rubbed his forehead with his good hand. 'Do you mind if we take a walk? I could really use some fresh air.'

'Sure.'

As we made our way out through the gaming floor Brian stopped and looked down.

'What is it?' I asked, and then I noticed it: a few feet away from us on the floor, a small dark-coloured bird with a sharp-pointed beak. It cocked its head and looked at us. I don't know anything about birds; it was ordinary-looking, no bright plumage or extravagant tail feathers, faintly speckled on the wings. I had some idea that it might be a starling, but couldn't say with confidence what a starling looked like. It hopped toward us by a few inches and its plumage flashed dark watery green, iridescent for a moment and then flat bluish-black again. I stepped back automatically but Brian stayed where he was, transfixed.

It occurred to me that I'd never seen any birdlife in Vegas, or any animals not on display. The bird hopped and then flew past us into the heart of the casino floor. We turned to see where it went but it quickly disappeared from view around a corner.

'What is a bird doing inside this place?' Brian asked, staring after it, dazzled.

'It's bizarre,' I agreed. 'It must be lost.'

He looked at me. 'Let's play.'

'I thought you wanted to walk.'

'No. I hate the Strip at night in any case. So do you. Let's just stay here.'

'It's late. I need to get some sleep. So do you.'

'Fuck it. I want to play.'

I wanted to sleep. But part of me felt as though I had to say yes to Brian. I was still disturbed by the Jodie White story, and angry that he'd fought with Cameron, but I suppose I was also feeling guilty about Cynthia. Mostly I was thinking pretty much what Tallis and Cameron had probably been thinking when they'd followed him to New York, New York: that he was in a volatile mood and shouldn't be left alone. It felt like babysitting a fretful, domineering child.

'What do you want to play?' I asked.

'Roulette.'

Dylan's game. He'd spent an hour or so at a roulette table on the first night of every visit, one of his own private rituals. There was something about the glamour of the game that he'd liked, the dance of the ball, the colourful spin of the wheel, the European flavour of it. I'd played with him sometimes, and had usually lost fairly quickly whatever I was prepared to risk. He was a conservative bettor and had some system of his own, a series of bets that he made one after the other, always starting with money on black. I preferred the riskiest and most basic – money on a single number. It paid off for me just once, the first year we spent there, and I won a couple of hundred dollars.

It started out unremarkably. Brian took a few hundred dollars out of the nearest cash machine on the floor, bought some chips, and we made our way to one of the tables.

'Let's go to a classy one,' Brian said, and looked me over. 'You're wearing your good suit.'

He had on his old, beautifully cut Armani jacket, which he'd always claimed he'd found secondhand but which I strongly suspected had been bought for him at immense cost by his mother. At college he was always receiving packages – clothes and shoes from expensive mail-order services and designers that his mother ordered on his behalf. Most of the time he refused to wear them. We wore the same size and he sometimes gave the clothes to me, including a cashmere overcoat he'd just unpacked from an enormous cardboard box from Barneys when I arrived back at our dorm one afternoon. It was soft and deeply, wonderfully black and warm and probably cost about as much as my tuition for that semester.

We found a table. The three women already there didn't pay us much attention. Brian sat next to one of them, her fur coat slung over the back of the seat, and put his money on red. The woman operating the wheel gave his black eye a long stare and then didn't look at us again.

After a boring half-hour he was down to only fifty dollars worth of chips, and went back to the cash machine while I waited at the table, hypnotized by the spinning wheel, the woman's expressionless voice calling out the numbers. I was conscious of him taking quite a long time to get back, when he appeared by my side and sat down again. The pile of chips he had with him now was considerably larger and of higher value.

I stared at him. 'Brian, how much money is that?'

A waitress came by and placed two drinks in front of us, pinkish-orange things in martini glasses. 'These aren't ours,' I said to her, and she nodded at the woman with the fur coat, who hadn't seemed to look in our direction the whole time.

Brian took a large gulp from his glass and smiled at her. 'Thanks. Is this a cosmopolitan? I've always wanted to try one of these.'

She smiled back at him. The two women next to her were deep in conversation, chain-smoking, one of them laughing softly and the other one sounding drunk and teary. I was horribly reminded of the one episode I'd seen of *Sex and the City*. The woman with the fur coat had symmetrical, perfect blonde ringlets just like the Sarah Jessica Parker character.

Brian put half his chips on the board. 'Did you know,' he said, 'the cash machines here let you take out anything you want. There's no limit. I mean, I'd seen that before on the screen but I'd never actually tested it out.'

'How much money is that?' I repeated.

'Try it, it's great,' he said, sipping at his pinkish drink.

The ball rattled and fell. One of his numbers came up. The croupier pushed some more chips toward him, stern and officious in her fitted white shirt and black vest, hair pulled tightly back.

Was this what I was babysitting him for, I wondered. To stop him making reckless bets? He had money, his family had money enough for an evening of excessive betting in Vegas; there seemed little point in trying to stop him. It was more benign than fighting. I tasted my drink and it was sweet, like alcoholic liquid Jell-O.

Another of his numbers came up. His pile of chips grew. He had one small loss and then kept winning, and risking more, and winning.

Brian had spent his whole life consciously rejecting his wealthy background, deflecting questions about where he'd grown up and gone to school, hiding his roots from people in the progressive circles in which he moved, dressing the part of the politically concerned bohemian hipster, complaining about privilege. But as he sat next to me at the table, risking untold sums of money with casual pleasure, he acted like someone you would recognize immediately as being both rich and comfortable with it. He wore it, even with his black eye and messy hair; in fact, they seemed to add to this aura he suddenly possessed of a rakish playboy aristocrat living hard for a few days on vacation. He rested an elbow in one hand, the other hand lightly holding his chin in a thoughtful pose.

It wasn't just the ease with which he handled the chips, the lack of concern he showed when he lost (although his winning streak was basically continuing); his whole demeanour seemed to shift into a poise I'd never really seen extended so far before in public. It was a lazy, unthinking arrogance that reminded me a little of Dylan. I'd seen something like it at college from time to time; he could switch it on when it was useful – occasionally when dealing with professors, administrators, librarians – and then the Brahmin in his accent would come out more clearly, the long English-sounding vowels I'd heard in his mother's and father's voices when they called for him on the phone. I couldn't help thinking that this was some kind of real self I was witnessing, the preppy scion inside that he worked hard to repress constantly in daily life. It made me uneasy, although it was good to have a break from the pathetic, wounded attitude he'd been wearing.

Before I knew it my glass was empty, and another one appeared in its place. I gathered that Brian had ordered this round. He kept playing; I drank and gave in to my thoughts, circling from what it had felt like to kiss Cynthia on the couch, to the terrible stab of guilt and fear when the phone rang, and back to her, the skin of her arms. Then I noticed Brian was talking with the croupier, and I heard her say 'Full Bet'. The other women stopped talking and focused intently on the ball.

Brian looked at me for a short second before his eyes returned to the wheel. There were only a few chips remaining in front of him; the rest were spread out across the board. His expression was oddly ecstatic and traumatized at once, high with the run of wins he'd just had, and clear with knowing that he was about to lose it all.

I'd seen Dylan make a full bet a few times at roulette after he'd had a couple of losses in a row. He never won the bet and it was always the last one he placed for the night. He'd won a stunning amount of money with it once, a couple of thousand. I hadn't been paying attention, but it looked to me as though Brian had just laid out a lot more than that.

'Brian,' I said. 'How much did you just bet?'

I thought there was no way he was listening, but he answered me right away, as the ball made its final round. 'Forty thousand dollars.'

The ball skipped and settled as the wheel slowed.

'Eighteen,' the croupier said, in a voice unlike her standard cool tone. 'Congratulations, sir.'

'Holy shit,' said the woman with the ringlets. Her friends started cheering and saying, 'Oh my God,' over and over.

Brian nodded and smiled at me. 'All right,' he said. 'We're done.'

I looked around, conscious that we were drawing attention from the other tables. The croupier had returned to her normal remote expression and started counting out chips into a box: Brian's winnings. I'd never been that close to chips of such a high denomination: rows of little plastic circles each worth ten thousand dollars.

Brian pushed a few fifty-dollar chips toward the three women and they thanked him. 'Buy yourselves another round,' he said, and grinned.

More people joined the table: a couple of men in rumpled tuxedos, leftovers from a wedding party, and a lone bride, drink and cigarette in hand, veil showing a couple of burn holes. I thought of all the Vegas movies I'd ever seen and wondered if someone in a concealed room nearby was watching it all happen on a little monitor, alerting the proper authorities that some guy with a black eye had just won hundreds of thousands of dollars at roulette table number twelve or whatever it was. I think I expected a security guard to come and keep an eye on us.

'What just happened?' I asked Brian when he had his box in hand, filled with candy-striped little chips, and signalled that he wanted to leave.

'I made a full bet,' he said. 'And the number came up, so I won. Highest odds are thirty-five to one, so . . . What did she say? There's four hundred and thirty thousand in here. Roughly speaking. I told you that bird was a good omen.'

His eyes were bright. I wondered whether this was the nervous breakdown I'd been watching out for, right here in front of me.

'You didn't tell me that,' I said. 'Jesus. Well, congratulations.'

It made my head hurt just thinking about that much money in plastic-chip form. I thought of student loans immediately, of course, my own huge debt that I planned to carry until I retired; Brian's winnings would wipe it out and still leave too much over to contemplate properly. I thought about a house, a brand-new car, the grand piano my mother fantasized about. The bourgeois turn of my predictable mind depressed me. I guessed at what the money would mean for Brian: a pathway to financing the career he wanted without having to rely on the family money he detested, the hated trust fund. I wondered whether he would do something showily philanthropic with it.

'I think we should find somewhere to sit down,' I said. 'Do you want a drink? And please, not another one of those fucking pink things.'

He laughed and clasped my arm with his good hand, the other holding on to the box of chips. It was a squarish, stiff cardboard box with a lid, black with a dull gold MGM lion on top.

We sat at one of the sports bars with the flashing game screens embedded in the tabletops and Brian ordered us French champagne with his Brahmin voice on, and then I watched that version of him recede and the more familiar Brian resurface, preoccupied and obscurely conflicted. He ran his hand through his hair – the bandaged hand – and winced, and his hair looked untidy again in a way that wasn't exactly rakish any more.

When the drinks arrived he clinked his glass against mine. 'Cheers.' The champagne tasted dry and smooth at the same time, all expensive effervescence.

'I've never seen anything like that,' I said. 'You never see anyone actually winning in Vegas, right? It's so bizarre.'

I was about to ask him how he'd picked number eighteen and then I remembered it was the date of Dylan's death: January 18. Or maybe it was nothing to do with that. Brian was staring at the screen closest to us: a football game, someone being tackled, someone falling over.

'So, are you going to make a movie?' I asked him.

He blinked and refocused. 'What? Do you mean the film I'm working on right now? What are you asking?'

'I meant with the money. What are you going to do with it?'

'It would be useful for making a movie, that's true.' He nodded. 'I'm not going to do that. Although that would be awesome. We could really do with those funds.'

He lifted his glass, and in that motion, the practised way he drank, there was a shadow of that wealthy, entitled self he'd just snapped out of. I started to think that it was probably there in some way or another all the time and I just wasn't used to looking for it.

'Ever since we saw that bird, I've been thinking about it.' He looked at me. 'Didn't you think about it? I thought, what if it all went right and I could win enough, you know, for all of us?'

'I don't know what you mean.'

'I'm going to give it to Colin. If he'll agree to fuck off out of our lives.'

'All of it?'

He nodded and patted the box on the table next to him. I ran through figures in my head as best I could.

'Look, I owe it to Tallis,' he said. 'He played a role back then – he stuck by me even though he was pretty angry about the whole thing, the thing with Jodie.'

I nodded. I didn't want to dissuade him; at the same time it was hard to believe that he would be willing to give it all up.

'Elliot, I know I screwed up badly with Jodie. I was drunk, I was confused, whatever. It should never have happened and I know it. And then Dylan really fucked her over. I've been carrying it around for a long time. I don't know what I can do now to make it better or anything like that. But I can do this. It feels like a sign.'

He was all purpose and sincerity. It was going to be a gesture that bought him some kind of absolution: a favour to all of us, a sacrifice that would make amends for his past transgressions. It seemed hardly fair to begrudge him that, but I did all the same. I didn't want to argue with him about the idea of an omen; Brian's desire to read his good fortune as a sign to assist his friends was in my interests, after all. And everything about this place was designed to encourage superstition, to forge belief in significance, in the very idea of luck, good and bad.

I wasn't a gambler. To me, it only pressed home the absolute randomness of the universe. But I probably was a romantic. I remembered my fingers moving between the freckles on

Cynthia's shoulders, arm, chest, and thought about the faraway stars. Constellations, patterns in the sky: what were they if not invented consolations in place of randomness that would otherwise be terrifying? My fingers tingled. I tried to push the memory away.

'Thanks,' I said. 'But will it be enough?'

Brian's voice was cold. 'I think it will do for now. Maybe Tallis can kick in and make it an even five hundred. If he complains.'

'We should call Tallis.'

Brian paused. 'You should call Cameron. See how he's doing. Here.' He pushed the box toward me. 'You take it. I don't want Cynthia to see it, I don't want her to know about this.'

'Aren't you going to cash them?'

'No. I want to give him the chips. It's . . . I don't know. It's neater that way.'

I agreed. A slow, fierce sense of elation began to rise at the idea that we might really have found a solution. It was a lot of money. And maybe Cameron had been right: it probably all came down to that. Or could be converted into that.

I called Cameron's phone but it rang out, and again when I tried a second time.

'I'm ready for a walk now,' Brian said. 'Or some fresh air at least.' I followed him toward the front doors. 'Hey,' he said. 'Let's take a walk over the Brooklyn Bridge. I've always wanted to do that.' He grinned.

'Should I put this away somewhere?' I asked. The box felt as though it had been constructed of particularly heavy materials to give it extra weight, to make more sense of the value of the light objects it held.

Brian shook his head. 'Nah. Just hold on to it. We won't go far. Just around the block.'

'OK.'

I carried it before me awkwardly, and then held it close with one arm. As we crossed to the New York, New York hotel the sky was dark with night on one side of the Strip and just breaking dawn on the other, the sun rising from behind the sleeping mountains. The sidewalk in front of us was bright with streetlamps and the casino lights. The poem came back to me again.

'Did you say something?' Brian asked.

'Nothing,' I said. 'This just made me remember something.'

'What did?'

What could I say – blankness, emptiness, dawn on the street, the idea of guilt and absolution? 'I don't know.'

He stifled a long yawn. We passed under the cathedral-like arches of the bridge, and walked by the compressed skyline, the collection of skyscrapers around the fountain, the miniaturized Statue of Liberty.

'Did they take the Towers down?' Brian asked. Their absence was conspicuous among all the other significant architectural icons.

'I don't think so,' I said. 'I don't think they were here in the first place.'

The dawn took its time to arrive as we made our way back, still just a faint brightening of the air under the artificial lights along the Strip. When we stood in front of the hotel elevators, waiting for one to open, Brian said, 'You go up and talk to Tallis. I'm going to bed.' He looked at me sleepily.

One set of gilt doors opened and let us in, enclosed us in the mirrored space.

I nodded. 'OK. So I'll see you at breakfast?'

'Yep. I'll see you then.' He clasped my arm lightly and stepped out at his floor without looking back.

I held the box tightly, feeling the effects of drinking all night, and so tired that I was worried I didn't have the right level of control over my hands. I imagined the box falling and spilling the chips over the floor of the elevator or the long portrait-lined hall as I walked to my room followed by the eyes of all the black-and-white stars. I made it there without accident and set the box down on the desk. It looked as though it belonged in a safe, but only because I knew what was in there. If I hadn't known, it wouldn't have been a remarkable object. The black was too shiny; the gold was matte but still tacky somehow. And it contained hundreds of thousands of dollars.

The curtains were open, showing the wide pink sky, the glowing mountains and their lavender shadows, the hushed-looking panorama of Hooters and the other buildings across the way. My room was strewn with clothes and books, the bed creased and inviting, the view partially obscured by the white reflection of sheets and pillows in the glass. I fought the urge to lie down and picked up the phone.

'Tallis? Yes, sorry.'

He complained, his voice thick with sleep.

'No, he's OK,' I said when he asked about Brian. 'I have some good news.'

I told him about the money, the box of chips, Brian's plan, aware that my voice was so worn and exhausted that it was incongruous with anything like good news. He expressed disbelief and wanted to make sure that I'd witnessed it, that I was correct about the amount of money involved.

'I have it,' I said. 'It's with me. We didn't cash the chips.' The collective plural. Brian's actions became my own. 'It's all in a box.' I almost started to laugh. 'It's a small box. It's ...' I struggled to say something about the square, inelegant box, the light plasticity of the chips inside it. 'Never mind. It's all in there. Tallis, did you reach Cameron?'

'Yeah, he called from the hospital a little while ago. I'm never going to get any sleep. He's fine, it's a quiet night there, apparently. Some kind male nurse is attending to him . . .'

'Good,' I said. 'I'm going to sleep now. My clock's broken. Can you call me when it's time to meet? OK. Thanks. Bye.'

I dragged all the layers of curtains shut and lay down in the darkened room.

I was wakened not by the phone ringing, as I'd expected, but by a knock at the door. The room was still dark; disoriented, I wondered for a moment whether I'd slept through the whole day and into the following night. But then I looked down and noticed a patch of brightness on the floor where the yellow morning sun came through the edge of the heavy drapes, dust swimming in the light.

I opened the door to find Tallis there with Cameron and Brian. They filed in.

'I thought it would be easier to collect you here,' Tallis said, 'rather than going downstairs. Have a shower. I'll order some coffee. Are you hungry? Brian? Cameron? Yes? Where's the menu?'

Brian's eye was, as I had predicted, worse this morning, a dark livid purple. Cameron's face looked a lot less dramatic than I had expected: a faint bruise on the side of his jaw, a couple of pieces of stitching tape along the cut on his forehead, and a swollen lip. I couldn't help thinking about Dylan's face after the car accident, stitches in roughly the same place, although on the opposite side. In some strange way it seemed as though Cameron had adopted Dylan's injuries, the injuries he'd caused, in the accident for which Dylan had taken responsibility. I remembered that superstitious feeling I'd had after the crash, the sense that we'd done something we would pay for later, and wondered if that debt had finally been settled.

'What time is it?' I asked, trying to see where I'd put my watch.

'We're not meeting Colin for another hour or so,' Tallis said, reading the menu as he spoke and lifting the phone to dial. 'Yes,' he said into it. 'That's correct. Can I please have . . .'

'I'm not hungry,' I said, though no one was paying attention. Brian was showing Cameron the box, trying to lift the lid, which stuck for a moment before it came off.

I spent a long time in the shower, running over the events of the previous day, the previous night, which now had the surreal cast of a dream, the vivid, haunting dreams you get sometimes in the last hour of a short sleep. It was all strange, but I knew it was true, although it seemed less real than the dream I'd actually had, or I thought it was a dream, at least. Dylan, calmly sitting in the chair across from my bed, leafing through the hotel literature about the lion enclosure, raising his eyes to stare out through the window, focused on the far horizon, somehow evidently aware of everything we were going through and detached from it all.

I emerged to find a tray of coffee and muffins on the desk. Tallis was eating a fruit salad, leaving all the pieces of melon aside. Brian poured me a coffee. Cameron leafed through my Tennyson, not pausing on any page. I had nothing to say to any of them, I realized, and knew with an unfurling certainty that the feeling would stick with me through the whole morning and would essentially never leave.

I found some clothes without stains – where had they been the night before, I wondered, confused – and changed in the bathroom. My face in the mirror when I brushed my teeth looked deflated and tired, deep circles under the eyes, and my freshly washed hair managed to dry in a way that looked as though it had been slept on. I was faintly surprised to see the sadness in my expression, a new seriousness.

I dreaded the meeting with Colin, unsure how it was going

to work out. But the thought of the day just simply proceeding filled me with a kind of contentment: the morning would become afternoon, the situation would be resolved somehow, and then I would be able to leave, finally, and go back to upstate New York, alone.

When I looked back at the mirror the seriousness was still there but the downcast aspect was less pronounced; I wouldn't call it optimistic but it wasn't despair.

We rode together in a taxi, and the others continued to confer while I sat in the front, holding the box on my lap on top of Colin's scripts with their slippery plastic covers. He had arranged to meet us at one of the newer hotels at the far end of the Strip, a smooth, glassy chocolate-coloured edifice surrounded by green lawns and monumentally large fountains. On our way in we passed between a pair of oversized Chinese-style statues of lions, each with one paw raised over a small, stylized cub lying on its back, mouth half-open in an imitation of the big lions' roar. Inside was a strangely beautiful artificial garden, with floor mosaics of colourful flowers, strings of lights woven through the branches of realistic trees and filtered sunlight shining through skylights in the roof. The effect of natural light inside a Vegas building was so odd that it took a moment to get used to it and the soft-edged shadows it cast on the floor.

Colin was waiting for us in one of the restaurants, at a table in a quiet corner near windows overlooking the swimming pool, as eager and well groomed as he had been the day before. He rose and greeted us, and shook everyone's hand except Brian's, who gestured silently, indicating the bandage. Colin nodded, staring for a few extra seconds at Brian's black eye. He stared again when he saw Cameron's face, and glanced from one to the other, checking me and Tallis as well.

'Did you have a good night in the end?' he asked.

Brian nodded, not meeting his eye.

Cameron smiled back. 'It was an eventful evening. Those stairs at the Flamingo can be a little hard to negotiate at the end of the night.'

Colin nodded. 'So they can.'

We sat down. Coffee materialized instantly, and a tray of pastries, laid out by silent, white-uniformed waiters. Colin thanked them.

Cameron wanted to keep it simple. He had instructed Brian to say nothing at all, not even to apologize for his actions in the casino the night before, in case he got 'carried away' and hostile all over again. He and Tallis were dressed for business in their suits. Brian kept his sunglasses on, gazing at the pool outside, where no one was swimming. I sat next to him. A girl who looked like Sally – long straight hair, long tanned limbs, and boyish hips in her bikini – walked along the edge and I waited for her to dive in, but she kept going and lay down on a lounge next to an older man who appeared to be sleeping. Father? Husband? Uncle? She took a newspaper from where it rested beside him and opened it out.

'We've discussed the situation,' Cameron said. 'And this is how we'd like to proceed.' He pushed the box toward Colin.

Colin opened the lid enough to get a glimpse of what was inside. He worked at the tables; he knew how to calculate the value of what was there, at a glance, in around two seconds. He looked up at Cameron and shut the lid – freshly serious, questioning.

'Think of this as a friendly gesture of support for your future plans,' Cameron said. 'I think you'll find enough there to sustain the projects you're interested in.'

Brian reached for a glistening yellow Danish – peaches, or

apples, and custard sunk into pastry – and bit into it, still staring at the water, refusing to engage in the conversation. The rest of us sipped our coffee and avoided looking at the food.

'That's very generous of you,' Colin said, carefully.

Tallis leaned forward. 'Brian's simply not in a position to get you the kind of attention you probably want for your screenwriting plans,' he said. 'He's squandered his talents in the service of political documentaries.' Colin smiled, and then saw that he wasn't really joking. 'Seriously,' Tallis continued, 'he can give you some contacts but I don't think he'll be able to help you out much in that direction, the whole Hollywood direction. Colin, Leo is the person to get in touch with if you're interested in that. I think you know that. That's up to you.'

Colin looked to me, and so did Cameron and Tallis.

'I know someone who can help you with your admissions essays,' I said. Colin's face brightened. 'You have his name already. He was very helpful with a paper I needed to finish. He was a good friend of Dylan's.' Colin held my gaze. 'He's excellent,' I said. 'And I'm sure he'll be well disposed toward you. But that's the only advice I have for you, really. I'm not all that well connected myself. I'm like Brian. I've wasted my talents. I don't know anyone on any admissions committees.'

Colin started to protest.

Cameron spoke up. 'Elliot's advice is very good, I think, Colin. Why don't you think it over?'

I went back to staring at the pool along with Brian, not wanting to look at Colin's face, which today showed me only unbearably familiar contours.

'I think we might have had a communication problem,' Colin said, and his smile was tense. It slackened as he sat there. He turned to me. 'Elliot,' he said. 'Are you behind this, too? Dylan always talked about you, as though, I don't know . . . as though he really trusted you.'

I flinched and caught myself. Dylan would have been a lot smoother than that. 'It's nice of you to say that, Colin. I appreciate it. But I think we've come up with a good solution.'

'A solution?' Colin said. 'Right.'

I looked away again, trying to emulate Brian's air of disengagement, trying to ignore Colin's injured expression.

'We'd like to think we can trust you to be discreet about the information you've shared with us,' Cameron said.

'You think that money can buy anything.' He was stating a fact, not asking a question. There was outrage in his voice at the idea, and a combination of fascination and repulsion at the privileged position of people with enough wealth to actually test it out.

Tallis folded his arms. 'I don't know about that.'

For a moment Colin seemed poised for some theatrical gesture of refusal, a showdown. He could have upturned the box, tossed it to the floor, let the plastic pieces clink and tumble together in a colorful mess – whatever the equivalent would be of tearing up the check, or tossing it into the fire. The chips made a bad prop, with their crazy disparity between substance and value: too light, too small, so little dramatic potential. Cameron and the others had been wrong in thinking that money was what Colin was after. It wasn't what he wanted, or not exactly. But Brian had calculated well: this was more money than he could afford to turn down.

Colin leaned back in his seat with a heavy slump and nodded, and I knew he'd accepted the idea and would agree to whatever terms Cameron laid out. The suit he'd seemed to wear so easily a moment ago now appeared ill-fitting, too big around the shoulders, as if he might have borrowed it for the occasion. His face looked raw around the cheeks, as though he'd shaved too closely. He pulled the box a little closer towards him and rested his hands on the sides of it, lightly. The smile was gone. When he next glanced up, looking in Brian's direction, there was bitterness and resentment in his face. He squared his shoulders, pulling together a more neutral expression.

I let myself imagine for a moment an alternative universe, right here where we sat, in which Dylan wasn't dead. It was what I'd expected, when I'd prepared for the trip, to be doing the whole time, before I understood what Dylan was really like in his relationships with the others. I'd thought that many moments of this visit to Vegas would be coloured with a sense of imagining Dylan there with us, conjuring his presence into every interaction, every activity.

The scene I imagined made me sadder than ever about the lost, undivided sense of Dylan as my generous friend. What would it have been like, I wondered, if Dylan had confessed to me, or to Cameron, or any one of us, instead of Lily? He must have known on some level that she would find it impossible to keep the secret. Had it been a roundabout way of passing the information along?

I tried to picture Dylan at the table with us, including Colin, admitting him as part of his life. But it was a version of Dylan that was becoming increasingly difficult to resurrect; a version of him as I remembered him, growing fainter by the second: generous, inclusive, charming, productive of harmony. I worked hard. I came up with a brief vision of him sitting next to Colin, arm on the back of his chair, smiling at something he said in a way that signalled approval and affection. (Was this how I'd longed, always, for him to act towards me, I wondered.) It flickered and disappeared.

Cameron spoke to Colin in a measured tone; Colin nodded.

Was he picturing some similar scene, I wondered, a moment that Dylan had always promised him would be arranged when the time was right, when Dylan was ready to let us into his other life? I'd schooled myself into a neutral attitude towards Colin, unable to deal with the conflicting feelings of anger and resentment and disdain and pity I'd otherwise been caught in, but this thought made me sorry for him all over again, and hopelessly disappointed in Dylan. It can't have been as simple as just feeling ashamed of his family here, I told myself, a matter of not wanting to admit connections with a place like Vegas. I knew it had to be more complicated, more vexed, than that.

I pushed back my chair. 'I'm going outside for a cigarette,' I said.

Brian shifted in his seat, moving stiffly as though every action brought discomfort. 'I'll join you,' he said.

We left together through the wide French doors leading onto a tiled terrace and stepped past oversized potted plants down to the pool area. A uniformed girl tried to offer us towels. We sat on some squarish wicker seats and declined more offers of towels from more passing uniformed girls. I hadn't really intended to smoke. Brian asked me for a cigarette and I lit one for him. Over on the other side of the pool little jets on the ends of white umbrellas sprayed a fine mist of cool water into the air around the tables they shaded. The girl who looked like Sally was still reading her paper and drinking an espresso. The man beside her had turned on his side and was snoring softly, deeply asleep.

I remembered what Brian had said about his friendship with Dylan being filled with love and hate in equal measure, and thought about asking again what it had really been like for him all those years. It seemed like a conversation we were designed to have some other time, much later, when we had moved farther past our grief, if that's what it was, or our loss, if that's what it was. At any other time I would have reached a point of equanimity, knowing that the time would come – next time in Vegas, for instance, after drinks at the Flamingo. But now it was harder to feel confident that it would happen that way.

People often mistook Brian and me for brothers when we were friends at college. It had always surprised both of us, but the others, Dylan and Cameron and Tallis, just nodded and shrugged, unfazed, if we mentioned it. Sitting with him now, I could understand it. Not just the physical resemblance of height and build, the unremarkable shade of brown hair, the family-like gradation of brown to hazel-green eyes. Here we both sat, apart from the responsible adults inside, avoiding all the important questions.

More than anything, I just wished he hadn't done it. Not only because it was wrong and I hated to think about Jodie being hurt, and the injury she might still carry around. But because it had wrecked something between us, and the exposure of it had been the first crack in my sense of what Dylan was like, and on one irrational, stubborn level within me it still seemed to be the fundamental source of all that had gone wrong.

'Thinking about your paper?' he asked, with a wry smile.

'Oh, that? Yeah. I was thinking about that.'

'Regrets, right?'

'Absolutely. Regrets.'

I wondered whether I looked as worn out and broken down as he did, except for the black eye.

'Elliot? Brian?' Cameron called out to us from the restaurant doors.

I followed Brian slowly inside. Colin was saying his farewells, black box tucked under one arm. He waved to Brian, and leaned over to shake my hand.

'Elliot,' he said, 'I'd still like to touch base with you, you know, when I'm in the process of applying. If you don't mind.'

I shook his hand – he held on too long. I wondered if he sensed the layer of sympathy I had for him alongside all the other feelings of wanting to get him out of my life, and whether on some level he related to what he knew to be true about me, my fraudulent self.

I let myself look him in the eye, Dylan's eyes cast in blue and a slightly different shaped brow. He had settled back into his pose of confidence and once again wore the suit as though it had been tailored to fit him. I could see Dylan again in the way he carried himself, although Dylan would have more effectively hidden the effort it took to produce the effect.

'You know, Colin,' I said, 'you should think about getting in touch with Greta. I think she might like you. Let Sally introduce you.'

I could picture it somehow, now that I thought about it. It was possible that Greta would appreciate the effort, the attempt to perfect himself on her behalf. It seemed possible even that after a few months of sitting by the pool admiring her and Sally and Leo, he would start to fit right in.

'Thanks,' he said. 'I'll think about doing that.'

'Bye, Colin,' I said, and brought my hand to his shoulder briefly in a gesture I never seemed able to get right but this time worked OK, or was at least absorbed into the awkwardness of the whole situation.

He left, walking with purpose, shifting the box from one arm to the other. I started to think about what it would be like to get an email from him, and stopped. I couldn't believe it would actually happen.

He was disappearing into the mass of people wandering through the halls when I remembered the scripts, and retrieved them from the table. 'I'll just be a second,' I said to Tallis, who seemed about to stop me, then relented and turned back towards Cameron.

I caught up with Colin at the far end of the lobby, close to the doors, in the sparse miniature forest of artificial trees. 'Colin,' I called out, and he turned, surprised, and didn't smile. 'I forgot to give you these,' I said, offering the documents.

He glanced down at them, and back at me. 'Keep them, Elliot,' he said, and seemed ready to keep walking.

'No, really,' I said, eager to hand them over. 'Won't you need them?'

He smiled then. 'I have other copies. Hey, did you read them?' He turned to face me more directly. A few feet away from us the sliding doors opened and shut over and over again as people entered and left. 'What did you think?'

I started shaking my head. 'I had a look, yeah, but you know, it's not my thing . . .'

'Everyone likes the movies.'

'Right, of course.'

'You must read a lot of scripts.'

'Scripts?'

'Plays. That's what you do, right? Do you think movies are like what plays were in those days?'

'In the Renaissance, you mean?' I asked, realizing that he was talking about my research. 'I don't know. Similar, I suppose.'

I wondered whether he'd talked about my work with Dylan, and how Dylan would have described it, or whether most of what he knew was gleaned from Google and my faculty web profile.

'Which one did you like the best?' he asked.

'Really, I didn't read all the way through them . . . The Chandler one is interesting,' I said compulsively, never wanting to admit I hadn't read something I was supposed to. 'I didn't finish the car accident story. How does it end?'

'Keep it,' he said, ready to go, all his disappointment starting to show again. 'See for yourself.'

I extended the scripts to him again. 'I'll see the movie.'

He shook his head with a wry smile. 'See you,' he said, and walked away, through the sliding doors, past the giant lions on guard.

The other three were still hovering around the table when I returned, Tallis with a half-eaten croissant in hand. 'No luck,' I said to them. 'He doesn't want them back.'

Tallis sighed, as though I'd failed. I suppose I had. 'Did he say anything?' he asked.

'Not really,' I said.

Cameron leaned his arms on the back of his chair and stared out at the pool for a while. He didn't seem to notice I was back. He looked over at Brian, resting his eyes for long moments on Brian's features, his bruised eye, his serious mouth, as though committing them to memory, his face pained and tired. Brian adjusted the strap of his messenger bag and tucked his thumbs into his pockets, a gesture that accommodated his injured hand, and looked away.

I took a step toward Brian and handed him the scripts. 'Just take them,' I said. He scowled and stowed them in his bag.

'All set?' Cameron asked, glancing around.

Tallis left the last corner of the croissant on his plate and brushed some crumbs from his sleeve. 'Ready,' he said, and we left together.

Cameron's flight was the earliest. He'd checked out before we left, and we said our goodbyes in the hotel lobby while he waited for his bag to be brought around. Brian and I stood together, making small talk about the immediate responsibilities and tasks we had waiting for us when we arrived home, while Cameron and Tallis talked quietly, ending with a fierce, quick embrace.

I decided I'd had enough of trying to negotiate the difficulties of whether to hug or shake hands or try the awkward half-hug backslap; I stood back.

'I'm sorry it all worked out like this,' Cameron said to me.

'What do you mean? It's a good outcome. It could have been so much worse.'

But I knew what he meant. I was still angry with him, with all of them. Cameron and I had probably been the weakest link in the group, the least likely to seek out each other's company, but saying goodbye to him now brought home a sense of sadness and disappointment in how it had all worked out, as he put it.

'Say hi to Marie and the girls,' I said.

He nodded and turned to Brian. 'Thanks again,' he said.

'Yep,' Brian replied, and 'Bye,' and that was it. Cameron lifted his small case off the trolley the bellhop had wheeled over, and walked to the doors.

The three of us made our way to the elevators. Tallis and I made plans to get a cab together to the airport a little later on that I didn't entirely trust. We reached a place where the passageways forked, and Brian headed off to meet Cynthia at a buffet, or the lion habitat – he indicated the general direction with a halfhearted wave. He rubbed his forehead above the black eye with his bandaged hand and squinted at me. 'Be in touch,' he said, putting his good hand on my arm, and I realized that it was goodbye. My misgivings about the difficult politics of bodily interaction disappeared; I gave in to the desire to put my arms around him and laid my palm on his back, feeling affection and regret in a rush. We parted; he said a flat goodbye to Tallis, and we watched him go.

As I wheeled my bag from the elevators to the lobby I ran into Cynthia on her way back from the pool, wrapped in a print sarong, hair still wet and spiky. I wondered whether Brian had caught up with her after all, or whether that had been a story. We greeted each other warily in front of an oversized portrait of some MGM star of the forties: sultry eyes, hair in lacquered waves, gloved fingers holding a cigarette like a weapon. Cynthia's face was sunstruck and flushed, her shoulders bare and elegant.

'You're in love with someone else, I guess, aren't you?' she asked. She raised one hand to cover her eyes, as though shielding them from a bright light.

'I don't know,' I said truthfully. 'Maybe.'

Perhaps I sounded definite and concise, but I felt only lost for words. We had left adolescence behind so long ago, and yet here we were, stranded at the beginning of our thirties with no better or more sophisticated vocabulary for the chaotic mess of our desires than we'd had at fifteen. At fifteen I might have actually been more articulate about these things even though I now made a living by crafting and interpreting words, by being an expert at language.

I thought about Natasha. Was I in love with her? Was I in love with Cynthia? Did that happen – was it possible? – falling in love with someone in a matter of days, hours, when the amount of time you had spent together could be calculated in minutes?

I recalled with sudden certainty the moment it had hit me: when I'd wanted to push Natasha's hair away from her eyes and held back. Her very physical mass from that moment on seemed altogether different from that of all the other bodies around us, made of some denser, magnetic stuff, while I was newly emptied out. Some mysterious process had taken place in which particles of myself seemed to have become unmoored so that I was drawn to her with all the force of gravity on a falling body.

I'd been struck by something that night with Cynthia, when we rode together in the taxi and I responded to her tense silence and became obsessed with the markings on her back, but it had passed. Whatever gravitational push or pull I had felt at that moment wasn't towards her exactly, but simply away from Las Vegas. And I couldn't quite believe that she'd been struck by love for me, thinking of the way she'd seemed to push me back gently the night before.

'But you love Brian,' I said. A short cut, a way around the questions about how I felt or didn't feel.

'I do,' she replied. 'It's complicated.'

It felt excruciating, being drawn so inexorably toward cliché and redundancy in how we talked to each other; we both seemed to recognize it, and shared a look: exasperated, resigned.

'It's always complicated,' I told her. 'Brian is a complicated guy.' That was the most I would ever say to her about Brian's flaws and mistakes and crimes, I decided.

She looked remotely disbelieving, but at the same time as though it didn't really matter much to her whether I thought Brian was complicated or not.

'Did you get enough research done?' I asked.

She rolled her eyes and smiled, showing her white teeth. 'Oh, I don't know. I'm coming again in the summer for a longer visit. If my grant comes through.'

'Let me know if you need an assistant.'

She shook her head a little reproachfully, still smiling, and glanced around at the portraits, the burbling slot machines a few feet away from where we stood, all the incandescent brightness of the signs for restaurants and games. There was less fascination in the way she looked at the place than there had been the previous day, less affection. 'I still can't believe you guys come back here every year.'

'I know.'

There were pieces of me, traces of all of us, scattered all over the city: places we'd visited, blocks we had walked, rooms we had slept in that had been slept in by countless other people before and since. I felt those lines of connection to the place become fainter by the second, evaporated somehow by the events of the past couple of days.

'See you,' she said, after a pause, and reached up to kiss my cheek.

At that moment, when her face was close to mine, her ear inches from my mouth, I wanted to find something more to say, something reassuring. The kiss was awkward, as those kisses usually are, short and soft, but her arms reached easily around me in a close embrace. I breathed out in a long sigh and felt the tiredness gather and descend before she let me go.

The lines of people waiting to check in or out were all long. I sat down in an armchair in a sunken lounge area close by, shades of brown in velour and caramel-coloured carpet, and thought about finding coffee while I waited for the lines to get shorter. The spot where Cynthia had kissed my cheek still tingled. I tried to remember what it had felt like to kiss her mouth, but it didn't come easily to mind, blurred by the static stress of the hours since then. I pulled my phone out of my pocket and stared at it for a while, taking a long time to decide that the walk to get coffee wasn't worth it, and scrolled through the numbers on the screen, my fingers slow and clumsy, until

Natasha's came up. It rang only once before going to voice mail. There was her voice, lazy and curt and faraway sounding, as though she'd been speaking into the phone from a distance, telling me to leave a message. The beep sounded.

'It's Elliot,' I said, cursing myself for not having prepared something to say. 'I'm in Vegas . . . we're leaving soon.' I struggled, even more tongue-tied than I would have been in her actual presence. 'I'll try you again when I'm back.'

I ended the call and looked up at the surroundings that had all but disappeared in the moments I'd been listening to her words and fumbling over my own. I had forgotten about Brian in those seconds, about Tallis, about Cameron and Dylan. I had stopped noticing the horrible, flawless glitter of the wallpaper. Now I saw it again and noticed a peeling patch down near the floor. The little flaws and worn patches in the lobby's decor caught my eye, shining through the gleaming surface. There was a stain on the cushion next to me, an amoeba-shaped ring in a slightly darker colour than the surrounding wine red. A thin thread was escaping from the fabric farther down the leg of the sofa. I could see the join of the carpet underneath the chair across from me, the place where the four pieces met up and didn't quite sit flat, one pushed up just fractionally higher than the others, showing a frayed edge.

I had felt almost drunk when I dialled Natasha, still feeling the effects of drinking all night long, but now I was aware of being quite sober. This fresh light through which I was seeing the world, all the joins and flaws evident, was oddly exhilarating. I felt pleased with myself, as though I were enjoying a new, more truthful vision of reality. My old, blinkered way of seeing my friends had gone, had been torn away, and I could see the underlying, brutal matrix of connection and disconnection.

It didn't last long. It was true that I had shed a skin of some kind, but it would be wrong to be too happy with myself about this new-found stage of maturity, if that was what it was. A fresh wave of exhaustion passed across my body, a flash of vertigo. The stain next to me seemed more ominous – it wasn't blood, I told myself, that was just the colour of the fabric; it was a glass of wine or water that had spilled there. Hopefully no kind of bodily fluid. I fought an urge to look more closely.

'Elliot.' Tallis threw himself into the chair opposite, blocking my view of the poorly matched fragments of carpet. He had changed into a different jacket and shirt and his clothes were incredibly wrinkled, as though they had been wet and scrunched up and left to dry in a lump. I said hello.

'Lovely day for it,' he said with a weak smile.

He was clear and sharp around the edges in my vision, like everything else, although he appeared wobbly and tired. Still, he relaxed into his chair with an unmistakable aura of relief, and I realized how tense he'd been all the way through the meeting with Colin, all the past couple of days.

'Said your farewells to Cynthia?' His eyes on me were cold blue, and a small flicker of a smile crossed his face.

I flinched, wondering whether he'd seen us a few moments earlier.

He shrugged at my silence and turned away. 'Brian won't ever tell her, will he,' he said, with a touch of contempt. His eyes wandered, fixing on a pair of girls in miniskirts and high heels, each dragging a huge wheeled suitcase across the lobby.

I'm not sure what prompted it, the sudden suspicion that enveloped me. Something about that cool, appraising glance of his, maybe, and his disapproval of Cynthia. 'How did they come to choose your room?' I asked, barely thinking the words through before I spoke them.

'What?' He frowned, then showed comprehension after a

moment. 'Oh, the party. You know those places. There were dozens of rooms.'

'So, how did they choose yours?'

He shrugged, and started tapping the fingers of one hand on his knee in a nervous gesture, then calmed it within seconds.

'Glen,' I said.

He glanced up with surprise. 'What about him?'

'You watched soccer with him. Football. He's one of those guys you watched it with, when we wouldn't watch it with you.'

The memory surfaced from some distant recess: Glen's muscled shoulders, the arrogant slouch that belonged to all the lacrosse players, his lopsided smile as he laughed with Tallis at some sporting joke I couldn't understand, plastic cup of beer in hand.

Tallis shrugged again, a twitch of his shoulder, and shook his head.

The things we'd been hiding, the secrets Dylan held over us, I reflected, had all been things we'd done, crimes of our own, apart from Tallis. He was the selfless one, protecting his father, hiding his failings. There was no mistake of his own that Dylan had helped him conceal, apart from asking Dylan to help with hiring a lawyer for his father after the fight, and it was difficult to classify that alongside the things the rest of us had done.

It's not as if this idea hadn't crossed my mind before over the past few days; it hadn't really surprised me that Tallis was the one who hadn't screwed up or done something wrong. He was so careful, always, with his neatly ordered apartment and well-planned career. But a chill started to come over me, thinking back on that carefully arranged place of his, the spotless surfaces and perfectly made bed – except for that one day, when I'd seen it in disarray through the open door. He cleaned up after himself so well.

I looked back at him. He was watching the girls again, his face blank. They had stopped near the end of a check-in line and seemed to be arguing with each other, both talking at once.

'Tallis?'

'I've no idea what you're on about,' he said. 'It's absurd.'

'What is?'

He didn't reply.

'Go on,' I said. 'Tell me.'

'There's nothing to tell.'

'Why were you the only one with nothing to hide?'

'What the fuck? What about my father?'

'But it's different,' I said. 'Where was your mistake? The rest of us made them. I can't believe you never made one yourself.'

'My mistake was getting Dylan to help me with that situation. With my father. That was my mistake.' He showed the same shocked hostility he had the day before when I'd complained about offering money to Colin, an angry, almost wounded disbelief that I would ever seriously challenge him.

'Brian doesn't know, does he?'

'Know what?' he asked, but the aggressive edge was gone from his voice.

'Right.'

One of the girls opened her phone and started talking, fast and serious. The other waited with her arms folded, sighing.

Tallis blinked and pulled himself together, squaring his shoulders and straightening his wrinkled jacket. 'Elliot, come on,' he said, and fixed a smile on me, his eyes creasing. 'It's all over. Colin's out of our lives. Relax.'

A pulse of mutinous anger rose; I held on to it, carefully watched it settle somewhere inside, and committed its contours to memory. I wondered what else had been in his almost-weightless envelope, or was hidden in a file somewhere, and whether he'd been holding his breath for days, waiting to find out how much, exactly, Colin knew. It mattered to me, I was almost surprised to discover, in a way that the details of Cameron's and even Brian's transgressions hadn't. I shook my head, seeing his wall of brashness settling back into place, knowing there was no way through just now, and wondering cautiously how far I should trust my own paranoid imagination at this point.

He accepted my response and sank into his seat, the tension in his body dissipating. Something like our usual dynamic settled back into place, or it looked like that from the outside. The vertigo rose again, just enough to make the room tilt a little. I pulled at a thread coming loose from my armchair's upholstery.

Tallis scanned the lobby as if seeing it for the first time. 'Flash place, this. Nice enough. What do you think about staying here next year?'

I looked at him in disbelief. I'd just been playing out in my imagination several versions of the future, possible conversations, confrontations with him in Kensington or New York, but it hadn't occurred to me that we would find ourselves here again. I followed his glance around the space, the matte and shiny surfaces, the worn spots on all the glossy fittings. 'This cushion is stained.' It was all I could think of to say.

'What are you talking about?'

I wanted to show him the patch of peeling wallpaper, the loose threads, the bad carpet job under his seat. I let it go, not sure what it was I wanted to reveal to him.

'Nothing,' I said. 'Do you think we'll come next year?'

A few moments ago it had seemed an impossibility, but a strange sense of inevitability began to overtake me. Those other possible contexts for our future conversations blurred and diminished. It felt as though our friendship would be forever constituted within this setting, the artificial city, and was newly impossible to imagine outside of it.

As he considered my question Tallis seemed strangely vulnerable, the veneer of brashness thinner than a moment ago. There was a small cut on the side of his face, a thin line of dried blood, but it didn't look as though he had shaved. He rubbed his hand absently against the bristle. The peculiar mix of resentment and concern I felt was as deeply familiar as ever: that desire to condemn him warring, exhaustedly, with an instinct to protect him.

He hesitated for only a second. 'Oh, yeah. Why not, you know. Why not.'

'I can think of some reasons,' I said. 'But sure, why not.'

ACKNOWLEDGEMENTS

I'm incredibly lucky to have parents who have always supported my writing in so many ways, and a mother who is both a great reader and a great agent. Both Lyn and John Tranter provided time for me to write by spending time with my son, Henry, and for that I am especially grateful. John saved my hard drive and lent me a computer when mine fell victim to a stray glass of milk, and I couldn't have finished this book without it.

Many thanks to Karen Colston for accompanying me to Las Vegas in 2009 and assisting with my research activities there: I owe you many drinks. Thanks to my editors: Jon Riley at Quercus, Sarah Branham at Atria, Jo Butler and Nicola O'Shea at HarperCollins; and to all the people at those presses involved with bringing this book to fruition. Thanks to my agent in New York, Claudia Ballard, for her insightful reading and hard work.

Writing is a solitary enterprise that depends on the support of friends, and there are more than can be named here. I thank Tanya Agathocleous for her hospitality and sustaining friendship; Debra Adelaide; Hilary Emmett; Jenny Mann; Tina Lupton; Trisha Pender; and all the wonderful UTS women writers. Special thanks to Guy Ortolano for sharing some of his Vegas stories. And finally, thanks to Danny Fisher for everything, his unfailing love most of all.